THE RETURN

THE
RETURN
JOE DE MERS

A DUTTON BOOK

DUTTON
Published by the Penguin Group
Penguin Books USA Inc., 375 Hudson Street,
New York, New York 10014, U.S.A.
Penguin Books Ltd, 27 Wrights Lane,
London W8 5TZ, England
Penguin Books Australia Ltd, Ringwood,
Victoria, Australia
Penguin Books Canada Ltd, 10 Alcorn Avenue,
Toronto, Ontario, Canada M4V 3B2
Penguin Books (N.Z.) Ltd, 182–190 Wairau Road,
Auckland 10, New Zealand

Penguin Books Ltd, Registered Offices:
Harmondsworth, Middlesex, England

First published by Dutton, an imprint of Dutton Signet,
a division of Penguin Books USA Inc.
Distributed in Canada by McClelland & Stewart Inc.

First Printing, March, 1996
10 9 8 7 6 5 4 3 2 1

REGISTERED TRADEMARK—MARCA REGISTRADA

LIBRARY OF CONGRESS CATALOGING-IN-PUBLICATION DATA
De Mers, Joe.
    The return / Joe de Mers.
      p. cm.
    ISBN 0-525-94097-9 (acid-free paper)
    1. Jesus Christ—Fiction. I. Title.
PS3554.E11432R48 1996
813'.54—dc20   95-35206
                                                          CIP

Printed in the United States of America
Set in Sabon
Designed by Leonard Telesca

PUBLISHER'S NOTE

For Bunny

ACKNOWLEDGMENTS

My thanks to Sean O'Brien, S.J., Fr. Nikolas Metropoulis, Dr. Adrian Menzies, F.A.C.S., and Professor Akir Malouba. And to the real brains of the outfit, Joan Kay. And Elaine Koster, publisher and editor extraordinaire, and Jean Naggar, the best agent a boy ever had.

Ignorance is preferable to error. He is less remote from truth who believes nothing than he who believes what is wrong.

—Thomas Jefferson

Man can believe the impossible but never the improbable.

—Oscar Wilde

All through history, from the assassination of Cyrus the Great right up to the Michele Sindona affair, the mark of a major conspiracy is when bodies start turning up.

—Professor Robert Prior, Criminologist

THE
RETURN

PROLOGUE

The men were all asleep.

Unprepared. Vulnerable to whatever.

The night swelled above them like a rich, dark sea, placid stars faintly bobbing in the black astral depths. There was nothing to disturb the sleeping group. No low thunder rumblings. No quick, bright, faraway sky flashes. Not the slightest hint of an event that, like a tidal wave of absurd proportions, was about to engulf them.

Fifteen minutes passed. A sigh. A gentle snore. The cry of a night bird wafting on the wind.

Then a different sound.

Huge. Gigantic. A megadecibel roar as sudden as a dreadful explosion. A single volcanic clap so loud it popped eardrums. So powerful the concussive forces squashed the men into the ground, hammered at their heads and ears and necks. Held them prisoner like winter surf drowning a foolhardy swimmer.

Then the light.

Searing, piercingly intense. The kind that could turn eyes into sightless hollows. The light turned off the night like a quick-thrown switch, illuminating the sky brilliantly for a mile in all directions.

It wasn't lightning. There was no brief, jagged, electric flash. The night-into-day effect remained constant, expanding for a full five seconds before it slowly began to fade. Nor was it replaced by an inky blackness. The very reverse, in fact. Color flooded the clouds. Great, wild smashes of green, blue, poster yellow, poster pink melding into a glorious, pulsating rainbow that shimmered and rippled to the four corners of the heavens.

And through this rainbow, dropping down the sky as slowly as a sinking coin tossed into a pond, they saw a man. In vivid and remarkable detail. A long, slim body wrapped in a flowing robe. A narrow, ascetic face. A sorrowful slant to the thin mouth. Benign forgiveness in the eyes.

His arms were raised in benediction.

No parachute billowed over his head. There was nothing to be seen above him, around him, or beyond him but acres of neon-colored clouds.

Down, down through the sky. A hundred feet from the ground now. Fifty. Ten. A slow, majestic arrival like a hero in an opera. Spectacular beyond the power of telling.

Swallowing, blinking, mouths agape, the men gazed. One of them, José by name, found a desiccated voice. "Madre de Dios!" He crossed himself twice. His brother, Firmin, older than José, and wiser, stared as the colors began to leach from the clouds. Stared as the light fled and the night rolled in, and the air-floating figure could no longer be seen.

"Madre . . . no." Firmin's body was shaking, his teeth clicking uncontrollably. He licked his lips. Blinked salt from an eye. "Hijo," he said as he corrected his kid brother. "Hijo de Dios."

PART
ONE

CHAPTER
1

He knew he'd have to go and fetch Doc Hatherley.

He'd have to connect up the battery on the Ford, pray that it would start, then make it into town. He wasn't sure he could do it, and didn't want to try; his eyesight was worse than ever, and his reactions slow as molasses. But it was either that or watch old Sox fade away from whatever was ailing him. And he'd lost enough of his old pals as it was.

He came out of the dark of the barn into the light of the new day. A curtain of misty sunshine hung from the green and distant Smokies, but it would be a while before the ground fog burned away. Rounding the corner of a feed trough, he almost ran into the man who was standing there, standing there as if he'd been de-livered off the back of a truck and left by the barn like a piece of machinery.

"Whoa, now," the farmer said. "You scared me, son."

The stranger looked back at him. The farmer's first impression was of utter calm, as if this fella had no debts, no nagging wife, no crops getting et up by invincible pests, and a line of bank credit as long as your arm. A funny-looking coot, all the same, the old man thought, eyeing the mustache and the scraggly beard. He could've had Cherokee blood with that deep-colored skin, 'cept he didn't have the cheekbones, and was too tall and skinny to be from any of the Nations. Greek or maybe a Turk, he reckoned.

But did they wear a long flowing robe like a Buddhist monk? He'd read about Buddhist monks in the *Digest*. The ones in America were called Krishna something. They beat drums and hoped for a handout, although he seemed to recall they all had shaved heads like they'd got a wad of Spearmint stuck in their hair and had to have it all off. But this fella had a woman's tresses all the way to his shoulders. Different cult, maybe.

"Where you-all headed?" the old man asked.

"To the sea."

Spoke from the roof of his mouth like a foreigner, shaping his words the way an American wouldn't. Said 'em different, too.

"Well, you got a ways to go." No backpack. No water bottle. No change of clothes. These people sure did like to rough it. "I could maybe give you a ride to town if'n I can get the pickup started. Got me a sick horse."

The stranger, unbidden, moved forward. The old man went with him, noticing the way the foreigner favored his left leg like he had a stone in his shoe. Although that couldn't be, because his footwear was a pair of leather-thonged sandals.

Coming into the shadows of the barn, the farmer at first thought old Sox had quit on him, lying there on the hay with no more movement than a sack of cement. But then the horse rolled an eye in recognition of his owner, and a soft whinny fluted from his nostrils.

The stranger knelt. Ran his hand along the horse's flank. Not, the farmer noted, like Doc Hatherley would've done, checking for a busted rib, but almost as if he were spreading on a little rub-down oil. The movement was slow enough for the old man to get a look at the stranger's hand. There seemed to be something wrong with it, although the light in the barn was too murky to see very well.

"You any good with animals?" The doubt in the farmer's voice was quite plain, and his slight confidence was further sapped by what the stranger did next. He cleared a patch of hay, exposing the dirt floor, spat neatly and fastidiously into the dirt, rubbed his finger into the moistened earth, then ran that finger over the horse's flank a second time.

"Old Injun trick?" the old man asked. A skeptic contempt made him want to spit, too. He'd lived seventy-nine years and had yet to see any farm animal cured by anything other than hot poultices and antibiotics.

He watched the medicine man rise. Thought he heard him say, in his soft, mellifluous tone, something about sickness, but couldn't swear to it. Some mumbo jumbo anyway. He told the stranger he'd get the truck, and left to do just that. Hobbled with one hand pressed to his lumbar region around to the little lean-to. Lifted the hood of the ancient Ford, and reconnected the battery terminals, which were rusty from a lack of grease and stiff from old age. Kind of like himself, the old man thought. He coaxed the engine into several halfhearted coughs. Waited a full two minutes, then tried again. The motor moodily refused to catch. He left the lean-to and walked slowly back toward the barn.

He didn't make it.

Had a brick wall suddenly shot up in front of him, he couldn't have stopped any faster. Old Sox, as bright-eyed and bushy-tailed as a colt, came trotting around the barn. A horse he'd thought had about ten breaths left in his antique body was prancing around like a derby winner.

The stranger limped into view. The old man peered hard at him. There was no change to the fella's expression, no proud grin of accomplishment or boastful tilt to his mouth. His face was as peaceful as a Sunday afternoon. He took another disbelieving look at his frisking horse. Not just up and around again, but bursting with a rude equine health the animal hadn't enjoyed in years. The farmer realized his lower jaw was drooping like a teenager's. He snapped it closed and tried to temper the wonder he felt with a stern flash of accusation.

"How did you do that, mister? That horse was dead and gone. Who taught you that?"

The answer, "The power comes through my Father," was one the old man took to mean an inherited skill.

"What does your daddy do?"

"There is nothing He cannot do." The stranger put no special emphasis on the nouns and pronouns he'd used in this and the previous statement so, to the old man, nothing special was implied.

"He must be a right smart fella," he said, his casual comment betraying none of the awe he felt at what the foreigner had done. He checked his recovered horse. It was skittering around like a state fair show-off. "I owe you, mister. Doc Hatherley woulda charged me twenty bucks. Why don't—" He cut himself off. Some folk you could offer money to and some you couldn't. "If you could use a change of clothes, my boy's son left a set here. Said he'd be back for 'em, but he ain't. I reckon they'd fit."

He moved off toward the two-story farmhouse he'd built when he could do things like that. With his gait hobbled by a herniated disk, and the stranger's walk moderated by a left-side limp, they made slow progress. The farmer used the time to reach a conclusion: he couldn't keep something like this to himself. This was mighty peculiar stuff. Tomorrow, or the day after, he'd get the Ford started somehow, drive slowly and carefully into town, and tell everybody what had happened.

Only trouble was, they'd never believe him in a million years.

As he told his cronies over at Johnnie's, there were only three things you needed to be a successful cop: a tin star, a healthy respect for the law, and a mean streak a mile wide.

"Hey, Henry! You might better gemme a dose a coffee, okay?" After a beat Sheriff Rawls looked up from his magazine and raised his volume a tad. "Henry? You there, or what?"

There was no answer from the outer office, no sound at all except for the occasional car angle-parking outside the adjacent general store. The hot noon hour was always quiet. Most any other time was pretty quiet, too, in this rural part of the South. Which was both good and bad for the sheriff—you didn't make the six o'clock news for arresting a speeding Yankee. On the other hand, you could grab a rod, slip away, hook three or four smallmouth, and be back before anybody even knew you'd gone.

Sheriff Rawls returned to the ads in *Guns and Ammo* and wondered whether the county would spring for one of those sexy German semiautos. He'd have it nickel chrome-plated with a beveled well and take the pull down to around two and a half pounds. Be a real honey.

When boots scrunched on the cement step outside, and the

screen door squealed, he tossed the magazine aside. "Henry? That my coffee?"

His deputy walked in pushing a man in front of him, a man who favored his left foot as he was propelled across the floor. The deputy gave his prisoner a rough little shove to enforce the fact that this was police territory now, and that all absconders, defaulters, drifters, and similar trash should be properly respectful.

"Found him wanderin' around. No money. No ID. No nothin'." The deputy, an endomorph with hips like a woman, scowled at his prisoner. Gave him another little shove. "One of them drugged-out hippies, you ask me. Furren, too," he added as if being from another country was particularly heinous.

"Coffee," the sheriff said.

His deputy glared at the man he'd brought in, left the room reluctantly. His boss kicked back in his chair. Propped his tubular legs up on his scarred metal desk, laced his fingers over his death's-head belt buckle, and examined this interruption to his day.

He wasn't crazy about what he saw. In his book, long hair was the uniform of crime. Another tip-off was the swarthy skin. The guy looked like some camel jockey terrorist with that olive skin and that beaky nose. The clothes were new, he noted—jeans and a blue work shirt—probably hooked off a wash line somewhere.

Sheriff Rawls took his handmade boots—there were three-inch lifts built into the heels—off his desk. Knowing he'd have to handle the paperwork—Henry, the dumbbum, couldn't spell to save himself—he slid open a drawer and reached for a charge sheet.

"Speak English?"

"English, Aramaic, Greek, Hebrew. We can converse in whichever language you choose."

Something lassoed the sheriff's mouth, jerked it into a tight little ball. This spic drifter was actually trying to put him down. Which just went to show how dumb some people can be. "Hebrew, huh? You a Jew, Sonny Jim?"

"As I was born," the prisoner said.

"Niggers, Jews, and Catholics," the sheriff said, like a man looking around for a place to throw up. "You know anyone round here?"

"Many have been expecting me." The reply was soft yet, curiously, the voice carried. And, even with the dago accent, Sheriff Rawls noted, it had a not unpleasant timbre, a little like the mayor's who'd been a pol up in Chattanooga several years back.

Rawls picked up a ballpoint and smoothed the charge sheet. "Let's get a little info here. Name?"

"I have many names."

"Just gimme one of 'em. I mean besides asshole and shitbird . . ."

The stranger told him. But whether it was the accent that gave a liquid sound to the vowels, or whether it was because Rawls didn't give diddly-squat what the Yid called himself, the sheriff didn't catch the name properly. He made a clumsy stab at writing it down: Liam Ovgod. An Irish first name and a Russian last name. The guy was a goddamn Red into the bargain.

"Date of birth?"

"It is celebrated on December twenty-fifth."

"It is, huh? Year?"

"Year one, it is popularly supposed."

Rawls tried to cap his anger. Put it on hold for later when, after supper, he'd stroll over to the jail and make this rat turd dance on the end of a cattle prod. He looked at the guy's clear brown eyes. The long stringy hair with the center parting. And the beard also with a center parting. Anybody who wore a beard was hiding something.

"Place of birth?"

"Bethlehem."

"P.A.?"

"Bethlehem," the man repeated.

What a giveaway! The guy couldn't even name a state.

"Height?" The sheriff glanced at the man's lean frame. Answered his own question. "Five ten. Weight?" Again he checked out the lean body. Not much meat on those long bones. He guessed 140 and wrote it down.

"Profession?"

"Rabbi."

"How's that?"

"Teacher."

"Yeah?" Rawls didn't believe him. "What d'you teach?"

"The Word."

"You a preacher?"

"Yes."

The cop sighed. If he had a dollar for every nut evangelist who came south to feed off the Jesus-crazed farm folk . . . and this one a Jew, would you believe. They'd be slim pickings 'round these parts.

"Distinguishing marks or scars?" he asked, making a note about the barbed-wire damage in the forehead.

The prisoner slowly raised his hands. The sheriff leaned forward to take a look and almost winced. He'd seen a lot of wounds in his time, quite a few of which he'd inflicted himself, but this was something else. The skin had healed in shirred layers over a hole in each palm like a Winchester Super Express might make.

"What the hell happened to you?"

With no change in his placid expression the man said, "I was unkindly treated once."

Rawls wasn't surprised; an irritating smart-ass like this invited punishment. Deserved it, too, the smart-ass, bastard wetback. He hovered his pen over the last question. "Ever been in trouble with the law?"

"I was accused of speaking against the Law."

"Agitator, huh?"

"So it was claimed."

The sheriff shifted his truncated body in his chair. He was used to prisoners peeing their pants when they were facing a night in his jail, what with his reputation and all. But this bozo was like a block of ice standing there. The slightly sunken eyes looked levelly back at him. The gaunt features were innocent of fear. It was a little unnerving. Insulting, too.

"Well, I tell you, bub," Rawls said, chewing his words like a piece of tough steak, "I figure the immigration boys are gonna want to talk to you. I figure you're short one little ol' green card. So I'm gonna have to hold you over for a spell."

"I cannot stay," the stranger said. "I have much to do."

A pink flush mounted the short column of the sheriff's neck. His chair banged as he jumped to his feet, rounded his desk, and grabbed the man's arm. "You dumb fuck. You're comin' with me."

He snatched a large key off a wall hook. Hustled the prisoner toward the cells. The sheriff was the town's champion arm wrestler, possessing exceptional strength in his muscular forearms. He bit his fingers into the man's scrawny elbow, but it didn't produce the slightest whimper. He increased the pressure, clamping into the bone. The prisoner didn't even catch his breath. In contrast, Rawls was breathing hard; not through physical effort but in angry frustration.

"Hope I ain't painin' you none."

The foreigner turned his calm eyes on the policeman. His voice came out without a tremor. "There is greater hurt than pain."

Sheriff Rawls rammed the key into a lock. Swung open a cell door. Slung his prisoner inside. Swung the heavy door. It shook the floor when it crashed closed. He wrenched the key around, driving the six-inch dead bolt into its receiver.

"Ain't nothin' greater than pain," Rawls said through his teeth. "You're gonna find that out a little later."

But the sheriff was wrong in that prediction.

When he came back to his office after supper, he found that his postprandial pleasure was to be denied him. There were only two cells in the jailhouse. The cell next to the one he'd thrown the nut preacher into was more or less permanently occupied, at evenings and weekends, by a local citizen named Ron Henshaw. It had a bed and a toilet and washbasin, and was cheaper than a motel, so it suited Henshaw, an unmarried auto mechanic, who took his dinner at Sal's Fried Chicken every night. And the arrangement certainly suited Sheriff Rawls, who was happy to accept the rent money for his own pocket.

Henshaw was lying on his bunk leafing through a book on butterflies, his passion, when Rawls came in.

"Evenin', Ron," Rawls began. "You wanna get lost for a—" He cut himself off.

The cell next to Henshaw's was empty, the door wide open.

Sheriff Rawls was bewildered, a state he seldom found himself in. He looked at Henshaw, looked back at the vacant cell. "Where'd he go? Where the hell did he go?"

"The A-rab?"

Rawls regarded the key he held in his hand. It was the only one.

Nobody got in or out of that jail cell without that key. And he'd had it on him ever since he'd slammed the door on the Jew son of a bitch.

"He left a coupla hours back."

"Left?" Rawls's voice was rising. "What d'you mean, left?"

Henshaw sat up. He'd never seen the sheriff so riled. "Walked out. You rented him the space for the night, right? And bless your heart for doin' that, Sheriff. I had the toothache like to bust my skull, and he just puts one finger on my jaw and says, 'Sickness begone.' His very words, 'Sickness begone,' and I swear to God, that toothache just up and scat. That A-rab, or whatever he is, is one genu-ine, ninety-nine and one-tenth pure, gold-plated healer."

Rawls, a mixture of anger and incomprehension, yelled at his boarder. "What the fuck you talkin' about? How the fuck did he get outta here?"

"Just pushed open the door. It weren't locked."

Sheriff Rawls had become very still. His voice struggled from his throat. "It was so locked. Tighter'n a nun's twat. I locked it myself." He stared at the empty cell, the open door. Looked at the blank walls, the blank ceiling, then said, in flabbergasted repetition, "What's goin' on? Will somebody please tell me what the fuck's goin' on?"

CHAPTER
2

Usually, a blonde as tall and magnificent as this was accompanied by a man, Brian thought, watching her walk into the store—a walk that demonstrated an unconscious grace, a flowing coordination too pretty to be called athletic—but she appeared to be unattached. And he was certainly in a good position to see, being perched on a shelf ladder up near the molded ceiling.

"Pardon me," she said. "I'm looking for something on Reflexology. Can you help me?"

A voice pitched at the deeper end of the female scale, the melody of the South in there somewhere. He climbed down the ladder and got a look at her from a more normal angle. She wore a simple sheath, clingy without being slinky, tastefully outlining contour and dip. No jewelry on display other than several bright plastic bangles embracing her slim left wrist. He decided that this lack of decoration was not in submission to the dangers of the sidewalks of New York—she struck him as a woman who'd wear whatever she wanted to.

"Reflexology? Would that be medical?"

"Partly," she admitted. "But not like *Gray's Anatomy* medical. It's more in the area of body healing. Massage. That kind of thing."

"Massage," he repeated, more interested in the customer than the category. She was certainly a change from the usual female browser that wandered in off the street. They tended to be frowningly intense NYU kids, or boisterously vocal NYU kids, both types united by their fashion plan: a pair of knees-out jeans and a sweat several sizes too big.

"You'll have to forgive me," Brian appealed. "I'm on my own today, and massage is a little out of my field."

"What is your field?" It was an honest enough question, but the way she elevated a corner of her mouth indicated that she was also indulging in a gentle tease.

"History and classics," he told her, listening to how bland and dull that sounded. "Plus languages," he tacked on, as if this last would paint speed lines on such a learned pursuit.

"Greek and Latin?"

"And the Semitics. Hebrew, Aramaic," he replied, aware he was showing off. He didn't have to examine his motive, although it surprised him. It had been quite a while since he'd wanted to star in a woman's eyes.

"Aramaic . . . isn't that the language Jesus spoke?"

"Right. Try aisle five."

"Pardon?"

He started up the ladder, eyes on the ascent ahead. "For books on massage."

"Oh," she said, sounding rebuffed. "Thanks." And walked away.

He knew he'd been rude and was sorry. They'd been no need to be so brusque; a guy could parry a woman's advance without resorting to a broadsword. If, indeed, it had been an advance. He wondered if he were flattering himself, a woman who looked that good. Maybe she was just an extroverted New Yorker who treated everybody to the same quick, semiprovocative smile, and who liked a little mustard in an ordinary, everyday exchange. He felt a nick of guilt at his overreaction. A customer's lighthearted inquiry and here he was building it up to a reckless, thudding pocket of desire.

He stretched an arm toward the top shelf, toward the Graves translation of *De vita Caesarum*. He'd done one himself once, just to keep busy, disagreeing with Graves here and there, although he felt the poet had got closer to a vivid picture of Roman society than Rolfe had.

Still on his lofty aerie, involved in a scandalous anecdote con-
cerning the emperor Domitian, Brian didn't see the blonde leave
and, caught up shortly afterward in a sudden wave of business, he
thought no more about her. Later that evening, in the kitchen of
his spartan Bank Street sublet, her cool, leggy looks and fresh,
amused smile wandered back to him. Of course she'd been interested. She'd handled it with an easy grace, but that had been a
definite come-on. So what? he wondered as he prodded a panful of
omelette into an albumenic mess. It was hardly the first time a
good-looking woman had expressed an interest in him in the last
seven years. A number of past experiences fizzed up in his memory, inducing a moment of embarrassment. Trying to pretend you
weren't getting the message made you look like a colossal boob
when your only defense was a display of naïveté and a tolerant
fixed grin.

Reflexology.

He sat at the tiny table, ate the folded eggs straight from the
steel pan, and worried the meeting in his mind. She'd come on to
him and he'd turned her down. So what was wrong with that?
Why did it nag at him? Easy answer: because it wasn't what he'd
wanted to do. He'd wanted to say something like, "Would you believe me if I told you I've never heard of Reflexology? Why don't
we discuss it over a drink?" Or something equally puerile.

Well, he hadn't said that and wasn't going to.

Hell, he'd probably never see her again, anyway.

But Brian Sheridan, the possessor of an outstanding education,
and an attendant ability to forecast events if the preparation was
based on readily checkable facts, got it completely wrong. She arrived back at the bookstore the following day, an overheated day
finally cooled by a monsoon of summer rain that turned the Village's busted curbs and sidewalks into white-water rivers.

Brian was preparing to close up, locking the day's receipts in the
creaky safe, when a lightning flash shocked its electric blue against
the store window. He looked up as a laggardly thunderclap jolted
the ceiling lights. At that same moment, as if riding the wild elements like a blond and benevolent witch, she blew in through the
door stamping water away. Her hair, matted and flattened, had
been transmuted from shiny gold, and her beige London Fog was

now the color of soggy cardboard. She looked like a survivor of some dreadful marine calamity who'd managed to wade ashore. He was surprised at how glad he was to see her, aware of a vitalizing current like a corollary of the electrical storm outside.

"I came back for the book I was looking at yesterday. On Reflexology," she added, in case he'd forgotten her.

She could have come in a year later, Brian felt, and he wouldn't have forgotten her. He scrambled some words together while he watched the droplets on her face slightly magnify her skin, skin so smooth and pale it put him in mind of the scooped hollow of a fine china teacup. He indicated her swamped condition. "Are you sure something on lap swimming wouldn't be a better bet?"

She laughed prettily, embellishing his line by spraying water when she shook her hair. Brian watched her drip her way into the stacks. Return a minute later holding a large volume. "Yesterday, I thought I could live without it," she said. "Today, I find I can't."

He took the book from her, riffled through it to an illustrated page, and got his first look at the science of Reflexology.

"It looks like astrology for the feet."

"It is, kind of," she agreed. "Only without the advice on love and finance."

She had the most extraordinary green eyes. When she smiled they passed through a mossy viridescence, deepening from pale lime to a light emerald. Brian found he was looking at her and saying nothing for a moment too stretched to be categorized as the time required to gather a suitable comment. He checked the price of the book, thinking to perhaps apologize for the high cost of reading material these days, or some such other gap filler, but it was she who filled the void.

"Do you always do your reading on top of ladders? I saw you up there yesterday. I thought you were just checking something, but then I realized you were deep into it."

"You're right. I've got to cut that out. It's dangerous if you're the kind of reader who falls asleep over a book."

She gave a snort of amusement. "What were you reading?"

"Suetonius. He was the Danielle Steele of the second century."

"I've read Suetonius," she said. "It's Danielle Steel I haven't got around to."

Brian was impressed, not so much by her reading list but by the smooth way she handled his little faux pas. He rang up her cash purchase. Slipped the book and the receipt into a store bag, fully intending to say something New Yorkish like, Read it in health, but, to his immediate surprise, his unruly tongue blindsided his brain.

"If you're not doing anything, would you like to have dinner tonight?" He felt his mouth shaping the words. Heard them vocalized. Almost looked around to see who'd spoken.

"I have dinner every night," she answered, with that not-quite-a-tease turnup of her mouth.

"This would be different." He was into it now, refusing to review. "This would be with me."

"Who's me?"

"Brian Sheridan." He offered his hand.

"Marie Olivier," she said, accepting his hand and his invitation.

He took her to the Coach House, his conscience clear—all he was doing was breaking bread with a personable and intelligent young woman.

Or so he told himself.

"New Orleans, originally," Marie said, shaking out a napkin as she answered Brian's first question. "A writer," she said, answering his second question.

"Fiction?" he asked.

Marie shrugged. "Sure, but I'll never admit it. If you write freelance articles and expect to get paid for them, you have to make up half the stuff. Make it faster. More of a grabber. If you didn't, even the end of the world would sound dull."

"What do you call that, embroidery?"

"More like major tailoring. I shorten the pants and let out the jacket."

The waiter arrived with their entrées plus a little gift from the chef: two tiny mushroom tarts looking like spun jewelry. Marie ate hers with her fingers, and not in a series of delicate bites. She popped it into her mouth and crunched it whole, a hearty trencherman's gesture she made look politely elegant. She had a talent, Brian noticed, for making the most plebeian action something worth watching. Aware of making this observation, Brian bore down, vowing to get his mind away from the physicality of this woman and concentrate on her words. She was asking about his background, asking him to expand on the little he'd told her.

"Archaeology. I knew it was what I wanted to do from the word go. Other kids went to the movies Saturday afternoons, I headed for the Metropolitan Museum. Anyway, I went to college, majored in ancient history, and studied the old languages."

"So how come you're not an archaeologist?"

Brian tried the wine the waiter poured for him. Nodded his acceptance, although he was no expert on wine. "I got sidetracked," he said vaguely.

"Did you get to the Near East, or wherever?" She gave the question an edge of polite interest so that he wouldn't feel constrained to elaborate on his past if he didn't want to.

"I went there for my thesis."

"Whereabouts?"

"The Holy Land."

"Did you go on a dig?" Marie asked, looking at him over her wineglass.

Brian had grown frugal with evidence of his learning, aware that many people feel inadequate or are just plain bored when confronted by a display of knowledge.

"One or two. The wine cold enough?"

"Perfect. Where did you go?"

He cocked his head at her. "Are you sure this is of complete and abiding interest?"

"Tell me," she demanded.

"Lachish."

"I didn't think I'd know it. Crete, Mycenae, Babylon, that's all the Sunday supplements ever cover."

"It's in Judea. The foothills. The heat would make your eyebrows crawl."

"Tell me about the dig. Did you find a goddess?"

With the dim overhead lighting layering the smooth jut of her cheekbones, Brian could have made a comment about goddesses which would have embarrassed them both.

"We were looking to prove a theory," he told her, seeking to escape his fantasy with a leap into the scientific. "That it was Rehoboam who built the Iron Age defenses at Lachish. A mud brick wall on stone foundations."

"Rehoboam." Marie rolled the euphonic name around her memory. "Old Testament, correct? I always got him confused with Jeroboam."

"They're easy to tell apart. Jeroboam was the one who invented the hangover."

Marie was aware that a jeroboam was a four-quart bottle of champagne, so she knew she was being teased—the amateur joshed by the professional. She took it in good part. She'd done it plenty of times herself; specialized knowledge carried its own privileges. "Classicist, linguist, on-site biblical scholar—I would say," she ventured, "that you're a tad overqualified to work in a bookstore."

"I like books. I like the touch of the covers and the smell of the printed pages. I like to be surrounded by all that knowledge and invention."

The answer seemed to please Marie. "Me, too," she said, the admission importing a generous stretch to her mouth and a sheen to her eyes.

They ate in contented silence for a minute, sipped their chilled wine until he asked her for a bit more of her history. He listened as she told him how she'd come to New York a living cliché, the out-of-towner who makes the big move to the Big Apple to write the Novel, the one that succumbs to the white tyranny of blank paper after two hesitant chapters and lives out its curtailed life in the dark oblivion of a desk drawer.

"So you discovered that magazine writing was your forte, and that you were damn good at it . . ."

"Fair to middling. But they haven't found that out yet."

"Does your work take you traveling a lot?"

"Near and far. I was in Detroit two days ago. On a Thai trawler two weeks before that."

"What were you doing, a piece on the Asian fishing industry?"

"No. A piece on Asian gunrunning."

"How's that?"

Marie made a casual gesture as if there wasn't much more to tell. "They were running guns to the Karens who are fighting that rotten Burmese government. But we ran into a patrol boat and had to get out of there fast, so the whole thing was a frost."

"You're kidding . . ."

"It's a crapshoot doing something on spec. Sometimes you come up empty."

"No, I mean you're kidding about what you did. How the hell do you get onto a Thai gunrunning trawler?"

Marie deadpanned it. "You call Thomas Cook and book a cabin."

Brian took in a breath, then expelled it as a laugh. She'd neatly got back at him for his hangover line. "That's fifteen all," he said.

Marie acknowledged the score, then fielded the question truthfully. "A journalist needs contacts. Shady characters as well as upright citizens. In this case, it was a guy in Hong Kong, an operator who can pull in favors in the trade."

"Detroit and Burma. A tour of the world's trouble spots. What were you doing in Detroit?"

"Wasting my time. George Seegrove was supposed to speak at a rally there, but he canceled out. I'm thinking of doing an article on him."

"The televangelist?" Brian looked as if a bad tooth had suddenly twinged. "How could you stand to be around a guy like that?"

"Don't believe all you hear," Marie advised. "Under that facade of fundamentalist storm trooper is the real fundamentalist storm trooper."

The maître d' appeared at their table and tried hard to sell a chocolate soufflé, but Brian asked for nothing more than the check.

He said good night to Marie on the sidewalk. They stood there for a moment shaking hands and stringing it out and doing a lot of smiling. Then Brian put her into a cab—she lived uptown: Yorkville—waved as it sped off, and walked back to his sublet thinking that he'd perhaps allowed his life to become far too closeted, and that more evenings like this one should be mandatory every now and then. So when he decided to ask Marie out again a few days later he was able to rationalize it along those sturdy and sensible lines.

He went ahead and called her.

"I'd love to, but I can't," she told him. "I have to go to the Seegrove rally at the Garden tonight."

"You planning to write that profile or make a decision for Jesus?"

"Maybe both," Marie said, with a smile in her voice.

"I could come with you. We could have a bite afterwards. That is, if you don't already have some company," Brian added, aware too late that an affirmative reply would make him look like a wallflower.

"It's just me, but are you sure you want to come? It's not going to be pleasant."

"I'll close my eyes in the scary parts," Brian said.

They met on Seventh Avenue an hour later, bought tickets, and entered the famous arena. Walked into an enclave of aural and visual riot. Above a huge, ribbon-bedecked stage, giant American flags rained down in a patriotic deluge, while an all-brass high school band played Sousa marches giving every note the same fat-cheeked value.

There were a couple of warm-up speakers, followed by a minister who invoked God's blessing on this meeting of right-thinking, family-oriented Americans, and then the Reverend George Seegrove was introduced.

The crowd rose to its feet and broke into manic acclamation.

Seegrove, as solid as a stuffed toy, the gold cross in his lapel colluding with the harsh overhead lighting, opened his arms to embrace every person present. Then he delivered his vital message: America had been created by God for one reason only, to fight the Antichrist, and the Antichrist was anybody who doubted the unbending, literal truths of the Good Book or supported abortion, advocated sex education in schools, or wanted to take guns away from intelligent and responsible people.

Brian and Marie suffered through another thirty minutes of this, then left their seats and hurried up the aisle through a gantlet of vulgar bias. Made the exit and the sidewalk. Took some deep breaths, then walked east.

After the poisonous intolerance of the rally they were ready for something pleasant and welcoming, and chose a restaurant solely for its cheerful bonhomie. They sat at the bar and ordered draft beer, luxuriating in that first healing swallow of a cold, fresh-drawn brew.

"The guy's a Christian Stalinist," Marie said. "If you don't agree with his thinking, you're immoral, un-American, and should be put up against a wall and shot."

"What always kills me," Brian replied, "is the gullibility. You can bet that ninety percent of that audience didn't arrive at those weird conclusions by themselves. They watched Seegrove expounding on his show, and they bought his message because TV tells them what products to buy."

Marie picked up her beer. Watched its hoppy effervescence achieve its foamy ceiling, a joyful ascent that was a mismatch for her angry mood. "I've watched his show. It's a con. A transparent cash cow. It's syndicated to around two hundred and seventy-five stations. Fourteen million people watch it every week. That translates as something like thirty million cumulative viewers a month. When he runs a special appeal, which is every other time he goes to air, the mail all but swamps the Virginia postal system. A hundred thousand letters a day and most of them containing a ten-dollar bill. And if you don't keep on contributing, you get a note from him telling you he can't pray for you anymore unless you help him do God's work."

"A real charmer. I didn't know there was that much money in it."

"That's the name of the game in the God biz. Seegrove's worth millions. Have you ever seen his show?"

"Once. He was claiming the premillennium was just around the corner."

"What's that?" Marie asked. "A millennium before the millennium?"

"The fundamentalists pulled it out of Revelation," Brian told her. "The Second Coming is supposed to begin a thousand-year period of Christian righteousness, and they believe that when this happens the last trumpet will sound and all those who've been saved will be caught up instantly into heaven. They call this the Rapture. I've seen bumper stickers in the South that say, Warning! In Case of the Rapture, Driver Will Disappear."

Marie laughed. "I must remember that the next time I fly Delta. I'd like a seat in nonsmoking, please, and an unsaved pilot."

They stayed at the bar to eat, their mood picking up. Persuaded by the honesty of the old-fashioned crab cakes they ordered, and the smooth blandishments of a pinot blanc, they were soon able to move on to a less contentious subject, trading favorite movies and books. Listening to Brian expound on a forgotten Merchant Ivory film Marie found herself watching his lips, noting the vertical channel between nose and upper lip which was as firmly outlined as the cleft in his chin. She knew he'd have to shave that chin twice a day to look his absolute neatest, which wouldn't necessarily be his absolute best. She liked a dark jaw on a man, not only for its masculine message but as a counterbalance to the head of hair which, in Brian's case, was an interestingly uneven head of hair, brown drifting into black, cropped close top and front, but allowed to revert to long natural layers at the back.

". . . Christopher Walken was great, but it was set in present-day New York, and maybe people expected something set in nineteenth-century England or colonial India," Brian concluded. Then, after a beat, "You're miles away, aren't you?"

"Oh . . . sorry. No, not quite that far." Marie leaned toward his smile. "How about some coffee?" Brian looked around for their waiter, but Marie slid off her stool. "Not here. I make the best cup of coffee in Yorkville."

Brian stayed seated for a moment knowing he was now in a position he'd hoped to escape. Or was he kidding himself? He had to admit the invitation, and all that it probably entailed, gave him a secret charge, a sexual frisson that tugged at his genitals and dried up his mouth.

The question was, did he offer some kind of excuse and ask for a rain check, or did he go back with her and explain things and thus burst the glittering bubble of delightful tension that existed between them?

He got up and followed her out.

Compensated in the taxi by chatting with more animation than normal, perhaps as a balance for the moaning entwinement that was supposed to follow. Kept up the ebullience in the elevator and the walk down the corridor.

As he closed her apartment door Marie softly stepped into him and kissed the mouth she'd been admiring—a light kiss but loaded with promises, and long enough to allow him to respond.

Which he didn't.

Marie pulled back. Brian's expression was a snapshot of embarrassment. "If you didn't come equipped," she said, "I have some ribbed—"

When he shook his head she flashed her mind back wondering if there'd been signals she'd missed. "You're gay?"

"No."

"Married?" It was halfway between an accusation and a suggestion.

"No."

"Spoken for?"

"In a way."

"Well, then . . ." Words said with a faint echo of what might have been. "In that case, we'll just drink a little coffee."

"Look," he said. "It's nothing that . . . it's not because of you, Marie." He listened to himself making a clumsy hash of it. "The problem is my job."

She gave a half shake of her head, her yellow hair swaying in happy ignorance of the unfortunate moment. "Your job? At the bookstore?"

"I suppose I should've told you before. The bookstore's not my real job. It's only temporary." He moved his hands in hopeless elevation. "I'm a priest."

After a long beat, Marie recovered from her surprise. She was kind, supportive, and companionable, but none of it loosened the knots of Brian's tangled embarrassment.

He stayed for only a few more minutes, then left.

He was certain he'd never see her again.

What a pity.

CHAPTER
3

Merry, lighthearted killers.

That was a fairly accurate description of Hennie Van Boder, Vittorio Vargas, and Ronny Patch who, by coincidence, all approached their work with a firm conviction not to let the dark nature of their employ defuse their natural good humor. None of them saw any reason why they should assume the traditional tight-lipped profile of the professional hit man–for-hire merely because they killed people for a living. So they carried out their chores rather like a contented mailman making his appointed rounds: with a smile for the world and a happy whistle greeting the fresh new morning.

The contrast between them and the man they worked for—Colonel Ralph M. Buehl, late of the United States Army—could not have been greater. Ralph Buehl was the stodgiest of men, who'd never been known to whistle in his life. Had hardly been known to smile. But the arrangement between dour employer and fun-loving employees was an extremely effective one. Colonel Buehl was a brilliant detail man. An expert planner. And while the trio's cavalier approach to their work grated on the ex-officer's sense of order and discipline, results were what he was guided by, and he couldn't fault the three on that score. They never failed to successfully complete an appointed mission, and with a disregard

for collateral damage that even an experienced military man like
Ralph Buehl found a trifle unsettling.

On this particular morning Vargas was behind the wheel of his
big gray Olds, which was parked in the short little main street of
a pretty village in upper Westchester. He had the rearview mirror
swiveled toward him and was primping into it, combing the small
and exact goatee that finished his face. He took inordinate care
of this last feature, and absolutely none of the rest of his appearance, his black, unwashed hair seldom being introduced to the de-
fining influence of a comb, and his clothes chosen for their low
price tags.

"How about that spot where one-thirty-seven comes in?" he
asked, his English filtering fluently through his native Dominican
accent. "On the bend there."

"Nah," Ronny Patch said.

"What's wrong with it?"

"I don't think Buehl would like that spot."

"Why the hell not?"

"Ain't neat enough. Hasn't been swept."

Vargas, realizing he was being joshed, said, with slow civility,
"Fuck Buehl and fuck you."

In the rear seat Van Boder gave a baritone chuckle. He was just
a passenger on this trip. He'd had nothing on his plate anyway,
and as this job was in the country he'd opted to come along for
the ride. He liked being with the guys, and a spin in the boonies
on a sunny day beat sitting in the Blarney Stone knocking back the
suds and putting on weight, enough of which he already had.

Ronny Patch, by contrast, could eat anything he liked and still
have the waist of a jockey. He liked to brag that he weighed the
same today as he had when he'd been in high school. He didn't
mention that, at just under five feet seven, he hadn't grown any
taller since then, either. Resettling his bedraggled Mets cap on his
crewcut, he scratched at his permanent three-day stubble and
turned to their passenger. "Hey, Vee Bee. You ever hear the one
about Jesus walking into Saint Pat's?"

Vargas swiveled the mirror back and pointedly sighed. Though
devout only in an every-fourth-Sunday kind of way he was, all the
same, a little uncomfortable with Catholic jokes. That didn't stop

Ronny Patch who, having very few sensibilities of his own, was careless of them in anybody else.

Van Boder launched an anticipatory grin. "Jesus at Saint Pat's? Nope, I ain't heard that one."

"Okay. It's like this. It's between masses and Cardinal O'Connor's up there at the altar polishing the candleholders and all that shit when one of his offsiders, a young priest, rushes up to him. Well, the rookie's got a face as white as a sheet and his eyes are like saucers. I mean, this is a guy in shock, okay? So he says to O'Connor, he can barely fucking talk he's so nervous, he says, 'They're here.' O'Connor doesn't know what the fuck he's talking about, so he says, 'Who's here?' The kid coughs and splutters and says, 'They're at the door.' O'Connor's getting a little impatient. He says, 'Who's at the door?' And the kid tells him. 'Jesus and Saint Peter,' he says. O'Connor's horrified. 'Are they armed?' he asks."

Van Boder hooted and repeated the punch line. "Are they armed . . . I love it."

"Not bad, huh?" Ronny Patch assumed the glow of the appreciated raconteur. It was short-lived.

"Okay," Vargas said, sounding a little prickly. "Tell me one thing, all right? How come it's Saint Pat's Jesus walks into? Why couldn't it be a synagogue he walks into? You'd still have the same gag, and you wouldn't risk offending a Christian."

"You would not either have the same gag. You nuts? It don't work at all if he walks into a synagogue."

"Sure it does. Jesus was Jewish, right? And the Jews killed him."

Ronny Patch's reaction to that was a parody of outraged denial. "What? You're full of it. It was that governor killed him, what's-his-face. The guy that washed his hands. Ain't that right, Vee Bee?"

"Absolutely. And you know why he washed his hands? Because he'd just been to the john." Van Boder laughed lavishly at his own poor joke while Ronny Patch did his impression of cosmic disillusionment. "This is the best I can do for business associates?" he asked the roof. "A spic anti-Semite and a Dutch moron?"

"Heads up," Van Boder said, tending to business.

The front-seat occupants turned to look at a man who was coming out of a small white clapboard house.

Vargas leaned across the wheel. "You sure that's the guy?"

Ronny Patch reached into his back pocket and took out the snapshot Colonel Buehl had given him. All three of them checked the photograph, then watched the man cross the sidewalk and let himself into a car, a black Infiniti with MD license plates.

It pulled away from the curb.

"An-a one, an-a two . . . " Ronny Patch prompted. Vargas and Van Boder joined him in a vocalized refrain: "Let's rock and roll . . ."

Vargas turned the ignition key. The Oldsmobile's engine muttered with coiled power.

The Infiniti drove out of the village and made a left. It passed a short row of stately nineteenth-century houses, then the town petered out and there was nothing on either side of the road but summer fields and dry stone walls. Beyond them the topmost branches of oaks and maples, lit with blistering clarity, moved under the lazy persuasion of an amiable breeze.

Two miles farther on, the road cleared of its sparse traffic and was patronized only by the elegant black Infiniti and, at a polite distance behind it, the weighty gray presence of the Oldsmobile.

A sign came up ahead advising of the proximity of Route 137. The Infiniti was less than a hundred yards from the spot Vargas had suggested.

"At this time," Ronny Patch fluted, in a singsong falsetto, "please bring your seats to an upright position, extinguish all cigarettes, and make sure your seat belts are securely fastened."

He clicked his into place, as did Vargas.

In the rear seat, Van Boder braced himself against a surge of acceleration.

For the driver of the Infiniti, the other car seemed to instantly materialize. He got a sudden shocked glimpse of the behemoth, roaring and snarling and swinging in madly at him, and reacted by jerking his car away from whatever fool, punk kids or whoever, was playing idiot games with him.

Vargas, a consummate wheelman, judged it perfectly.

He crunched the Olds into the Infiniti, belting the black car off-line and sending it slithering. Its right front tire caught the dusty shoulder of the road, raised there to accommodate a drainage ditch, and dipped over the edge. It dropped just eight inches, but the car's forward speed and sideways momentum was enough to tip it.

It rose up on its right-side wheels and was almost perpendicular when it crashed into an ancient red beech, turning the tree trunk into an ugly hybrid of crushed metal and chunked-up bark.

Up ahead the Olds shed rubber as Vargas braked hard. It came howling back in reverse, Ronny Patch out of his door the instant the car reached the wreck. Patch could see the groggy driver buried in a white inflation. The man looked like a shot-down fighter pilot who'd fallen into his parachute. Curiously, the car's CD was still playing. Patch didn't recognize the Diabelli Variations. He stared moodily at the lifesaving air bag. "Fucking technology," he groused, but cheered up when he saw that a rocky outcrop had breached the car's gas tank. He swung back to the Olds. "Somebody gimme a light."

None of them smoked. Vargas pushed in the cigarette lighter on the dash.

Ronny Patch pursed his scruffy mouth. "That'll take an hour, for crissakes."

"It's either this or find two Boy Scouts," Vargas told him.

The three men watched the road for thirty seconds, ready to deflect questions, but nobody drove by to ask any. When the lighter popped out, Ronny Patch reached in, pulled it out of its socket, tossed it high, and jumped into the car in one seamless action. The Olds tore away a few beats before the lighter completed its parabola and its glowing red coils plopped down in a pool of Super Shell.

The blast, a crimson roil of swirling energy, whooshed after the fleeing car, a wave of scorched air hammering against the trunk.

The Olds dragged superheated fumes for a heady few moments, then Vargas throttled back and swung the vehicle into a tight U-turn. Came back down the road and cruised slowly past the wreck.

The flames were like a wild animal savaging the car. Most of the black paint had been burnt down to the steel, and anything that had once been plastic was now a bubbling liquid froth. The smell was an acrid compound of smoldering rubber and incinerated leather, and, riding above this pungent mix, an aroma very much like that of charred beef polluted the air. Behind the wheel of the Infiniti, the air bag a blackened memory, a crisped figure jerked spasmodically like a Halloween skeleton on a string.

Vittorio Vargas swung the rearview mirror toward him to see how his goatee had fared. Finding it unblemished, he returned the mirror to its intended function, and took the Olds away.

Ronny Patch reached for the car phone. Punched buttons.

"Yes?"

"We're on our way back, Colonel."

"Any problems?"

"Smooth as silk, Colonel."

"Good," said Buehl, and hung up.

Ronny Patch replaced the phone.

"What'd he say?" Vargas asked.

"He said, 'Good.' "

Vargas nodded sagely. "That's why we do this job. Not for the money, but for the praise, right?"

"Right," the other two said.

CHAPTER
4

It was about an hour after sunup when the driver spotted the lonely figure walking along the connector, walking slowly, limping a little like he had a pebble in his shoe or something.

He pulled the truck over and waited for the man to catch up, although the guy didn't increase his pace one iota. It probably hurt for him to put on a little speed.

"Howdy. Where you headed?" the driver inquired.

"To the sea."

"I'm goin' to Charleston if that'll do you any good."

The man got into the truck. The driver took it away. "I figure you could use a ride. You look you been walkin' all night," the driver said, checking his passenger out and wondering if the guy was Mexican. But the Mexes were usually dumpy and broad across the cheekbones, and this guy was bony and thin-faced like the dude that ran the truck stop the other side of Knoxville, and he was Lebanese from, where was it, Lebia, or whatever the hell it was called. "Where you from, son?"

The driver heard the road walker say God's something, and took that to mean God's Country, which he had an idea was a part of Montana. "That where you been living?"

"I lived in Jerusalem," the stranger said in a language he clearly hadn't learned at his mother's knee. The driver congratulated himself on guessing right: Jerusalem was the Holy Land, which was near enough to Lebia.

"I'm from Pensacola, Florida, originally. They call me Bill down there. What do they call you in Jerusalem?"

"Yehsu."

"Yehsu? That's a newie," the driver said, noticing the ruin in the guy's palms. He put an easy two and two together. "You a trawlerman?" Some of those trawler guys busted up their hands something awful on those wire cables.

"I have come to trawl," came the answer. "But not for fish."

"A shrimper, eh?"

No reply. The trucker didn't push it; weren't none of his business, and these road walkers tended to play their cards pretty close anyway. He decided to let this fella get a little rest. The guy had closed his eyes, although he didn't really look as though he were nodding off. More like he was thinking deeply about something.

Hours later, with no advance in the conversation, the trucker swung off the road and stopped. "Charleston," he announced cheerily. "Or the outskirts of. Most gracious city in the South, so the chamber of commerce says. Maybe they got a claim at that," he said to his passenger, who hadn't seen an inch of the trip, sitting there with his eyes closed and all. "About here do you?"

The man got out, and thanked him quietly. He seemed grateful for the ride, the trucker thought, but he was left with the impression that the guy thought it was his due. Not that he would've called him uppity or anything. Maybe he was just well brought up and expected favors. Funny thing was, the guy didn't start toward the downtown, toward the bay, even though he'd said he was going to the sea. He started walking west toward the Savannah Highway sign. The trucker put the inconsistency down to the eccentric ways of road gypsies. And yet, when quizzed about it later, he told his questioners that the man didn't stroll off aimlessly as if he'd flipped a coin for a direction. He moved away, on that gimpy leg of his, like someone who knew exactly where he wanted to go.

Thirty minutes later, a tile salesman stopped for the road walker and took him as far as Gardens Corner, where the 21 connector dips south and runs through Beaufort, and on to Fripp Island and the Atlantic.

Then he got another ride almost immediately from a marine recruit who offered him a lift because of the guy's long hair. He was feeling nostalgic for his own locks which, not long before, a Corps barber had ruthlessly shorn. He'd thought the traveler might have been a rock musician, but one look at those trashed-up hands and he knew the guy wasn't gonna be in the same league as Jimi Hendrix. The recruit had dropped him before turning into the main gate of the air station. He'd been a silent passenger and poor value, and the recruit hadn't given him another thought until much later when, just for picking up the man and being in his presence, he became a Corps celebrity.

He walked past an old burial ground and down narrow streets sheltered from the hot sun by a dark fan of summer oaks. It was an ancient town, Beaufort, yet it could well have appeared to a fanciful observer that the long-haired, olive-skinned man walking through those venerable lanes predated the settlement. He was mid to late thirties, no more, but he had the look of ages in his quiet eyes, his placid demeanor. A kind of timeless destiny in his calm progress through the leafy alleys, as if the weathered, colonial houses he passed had been built the day before and not yet lived in.

He stopped in front of one of them, a handsome dwelling with a wide, inviting veranda and fretted gingerbread frolicking under the eaves. He went up the path. Reached for the bell, but there was no need to summon anyone; a woman was using an old-fashioned carpet sweeper behind the screen door. She left off her work.

"Help you?" It was a question without much of an offer in it.

"I need to rest," the man who called himself Yehsu said, in his curious accent.

The woman wore a pink and frilly apron, and an equally frivolous bandanna around her graying hair. The bandanna jerked in the direction of the porch swing to the right of the front steps. "You're welcome to use the flyer for a spell." She squinted through the dark screen. Her caller was backlit by the morning

sun, lending the outline of his tall, slim body a kind of aura. She
couldn't see his face that clearly, but she noted the gentleness in his
voice, and was impressed by the simplicity of his admission. Most
of the handout bums who found their way to her door started out
with a hesitant question about yard work. But she got an impression of intelligence from this visitor, and something else she
couldn't quite identify. Something comforting and relieving, like
when Doc McMaster manipulated the crick in her neck.

She went out to the kitchen, and got some ice water from the
fridge. Brought it back out onto the porch. The man was sitting in
the flyer, but not lounging in it, feet stretched and body slumped
back. He was sitting tidily upright as if he were viewing something
of thoughtful interest, when all that could be seen from his point
of view were two lackadaisical college kids painting the Hepplewhite house across the street.

He took the water from her. Drank most of it. She noticed he
couldn't wrap all of his fingers around the glass. And the back of
his hand seemed to have been badly scorched once upon a time.
And then those marks on his forehead like he'd fallen against
some barbed wire. This was a damaged person.

"You got a place to stay?" she asked.

"No."

"You got any money?"

"No."

Then she asked him the same question she asked all the callers
who came to her wide and generously shaded porch. "You any
good at fixing things?" Without waiting for a reply, she told him
to come and take a look at something, and led him into the house
and out back to the laundry. The woman toed the bottom of an
ancient Sears washing machine that was rusted and dinked around
the base. "It quit on me six weeks back, and I'm danged if I'm
gonna go out and buy a whole entire new one. I got some tools,
you wanna take a look at its innards."

As soon as she said it she had misgivings. How were hands like
that gonna hold a wrench? But the man didn't crouch down and
take off the front panel, or even lift the loading lid. As the woman
explained it to her cronies later that day, "He just kind of touched
the thing, then slid those cockeyed fingers of his along the top as

if he were sticking down the Tide decal. And, I swear to God, that old bucket of bolts just up and started where it left off when it quit. Right in the middle of the rinse cycle."

"Well, if that don't just beat the band," the woman said, staring at the stranger with his long, dark hair and his flimsy beard. "Nobody's come within a mile of fixing that thing." The stranger just looked back at her with those dark eyes that seemed used to expecting nothing, least of all praise. Still befuddled, the woman asked him what his name was and, thinking him shy when he didn't answer, said, "What do folks call you?"

He told her.

The woman smiled. "Well, Mr. Lord, I'm surely in your debt. If you'd like to room here for a few days, I'd be happy to put you up. I'm Mrs. Creely."

An hour later she fetched him off the front porch flyer, and led him into the dining room. "This here's Mr. Lord," she announced to the assembled guests. "He fixed the washer. Better than new. Y'all make him welcome, now." Then she bustled out to the kitchen to supervise the serving.

There were eight other diners, six men and two women, all of whom stopped their conversation to observe the new boarder. Watched him limp across the floor and take a chair. They recognized a foreigner when they saw one, and were well used to them. A lot of trawlermen were from somewhere else. It was that kind of trade. Mr. Barnes, at sixty-four the oldest of the regulars, still referred to any foreigner as a Portugee, the way his grandfather had growing up on Cape Cod.

It was Bob Jenks who broke the ice. He was a printer who fancied himself an ace mechanic, and had tried and failed several times to fix the washing machine. When he addressed the newcomer, he sounded a little miffed. "What was wrong with it? The electrics?" Yehsu moved his head as he moved his chair, and the printer took that as an affirmative. "I figured it was," he said, to save some face.

"I guess you've had some experience," one of the women offered to the newcomer. "With boat engines and such."

"I am a teacher," was the reply.

"Me, too," the other woman said, showing sudden interest and some uncorrected front teeth. "What's your subject?"

"The word of God."

"Did he say preacher or teacher?" Mr. Barnes asked a man on his right.

"You ain't from these parts . . ." Bob Jenks, still rattled by being bested in the mechanical department, gave his statement a shade of reprimand.

"Judea," the newcomer told them.

Everybody tried out some silent permutations: Judea, Georgia. Judea, Mississippi. Judea, S.C.

A morose young black woman suspended their pondering when she brought in a big china tureen and began ladling out a cumin-spiced pumpkin soup. A strict protocol was observed in the order of serving. Mr. Barnes, who had the longest tenure as a boarder, was served first. Mr. Corvin, who'd only moved in two weeks back, was traditionally served last, but today that dubious honor was accorded the newcomer. The boarders immediately set to as soon as their portions were allotted, allowing them to observe the newcomer without appearing rude. They noted the clumsy way his splayed fingers forced him to hold his spoon, and the slow, almost reluctant manner in which he fed himself. In their minds, the aggregate of this handicap, plus the infirmity of his pronounced limp, and the poorly healed gouges in his forehead, indicated a severe automobile accident somewhere in his past.

A man named Heinz, a quick eater, was the first to break the sound of polite slurping. "You have a ministry, Mr. Lord?" He was a short, excessively broad man who'd attended a Bible school in West Texas for several months before deciding that the insurance business was a safer bet. He was envious of successful big-time preachers, because he might have been one of them had he stuck, and contemptuous of the street-corner no-names who struggled to outhustle each other.

"The world is my ministry," Mr. Lord answered. The reply went almost unremarked. All the major religions stretched to the ends of the earth. The Baptist Bible, for example, had recently been translated into its zillionth foreign language, and was being read all over the globe.

Mr. Heinz eyed the blue work shirt on the man's lean shoulders. He sure didn't dress like a preacher, he opined to himself. He wondered if this dude, with his half-starved look and funny way of speaking, might be one of them cult preachers, like the ones who took the directive of Mark 16:18, to handle serpents, as a test of spiritual purity. That was another possible explanation for the hand damage and the limp. Plenty of folk had been crippled by an untreated rattler bite. "You Reformed or Traditional?" he asked. Then, getting no response to his inquiry, tagged on an addendum. "You are Baptist, ain't you?"

"I baptized before. I shall again," the stranger said in his placidly direct way.

The table wondered about the use of the future tense. Had the preacher been disbarred from the baptismal rite in the past, perhaps for some moral transgression?

"Damn," Mr. Corvin exclaimed. "Forgot my pills." Mr. Corvin was middle-aged, balding, and moderately overweight. He'd found a job clerking at a hardware store but complained of the long hours on his feet, an understandable beef seeing as how he relied on an assist when he walked. He turned and grasped the rubber-tipped cane he'd hooked over the back of his chair. His face squinched as he levered himself to his feet.

"You are in pain?" the newcomer asked.

"I got the gout in the knee," Mr. Corvin explained, with a dour slant to his mouth. "Damn thing seized up on me two years back. Aches like an ess oh bee."

With a slow, languid movement Yehsu rose. Moved the few feet necessary to bring him next to Mr. Corvin. He said, evenly, "You will not need the stick if you truly believe."

Mr. Corvin looked irritated by this unsought opinion. "I believe, all right," he grumbled. "I believe we were put on this earth to suffer, and I'm living proof of that."

"You are living proof," the stranger replied, "that without faith in God, my Father, and love of Him, your suffering will increase in this world and extend to the next."

The boarders swore later that that's what the stranger had said: not "God, the Father," but "God, *my* Father."

Mr. Corvin grunted moodily as he got his cane into place. "I prayed half the night once. Got up next morning and it weren't one whit better."

"A prayer must come from the heart, not just the tongue."

The derisive look on Mr. Corvin's face said he'd been polite long enough, and that, as a gout sufferer, he could be excused a choleric disposition. "I stopped believin' when I started hurtin', Reverend." He began to clump toward the door. "Besides, I never said I weren't no sinner."

The stranger bent his left elbow. Raised his broken left hand to shoulder height. With his unaligned fingers spread, and two of them drooping, his hand took on a folded look, like an origami bird. It dropped onto Mr. Corvin's meaty shoulder as he hobbled by. "By God's merciful authority, I forgive you your sins," Yehsu said in his gentle, biddable tone.

The boarders were contentious about what happened next. Some said that Mr. Corvin kind of stumbled, then pulled up short. Others said he just stopped walking and swayed for a moment. But there was universal agreement that, after that first ambiguous moment, Mr. Corvin's face went from surprise to bewilderment to out-and-out shock as he started walking again with his bad leg moving as easily as his good one. He stopped for the second time. Clutched at his knee like a man frantically feeling for something he'd lost. Walked all the way to the far wall with his eyes expanding at each regular stride. He fumbled for words. "What . . . what in tarnation . . . ?" He stared at the stranger. Stared at the boarders as if they had the answer. The boarders were all open-mouthed. They knew what they'd seen: a laying on of hands. An actual healing right here in Mrs. Creely's dining room! Mr. Corvin had no more use for that cane now than a twenty-year-old track star.

The moment was broken by Mrs. Creely bustling in. She'd sensed something untoward as faraway as the kitchen. She took in the frozen tableau. The dumb, staring faces. Mr. Lord standing so straight and tall and tranquil. And Mr. Corvin on his feet, too, looking like he'd won first and second prize in the state lottery. "Mr. Corvin?" She turned his name into a question, wondering why he wasn't leaning on his cane.

"The pain's gone. I can walk and it don't hurt." There was a blink in Mr. Corvin's voice. It came out thin and breathy. "I can walk normal without this thing." He dropped the cane as if it were something alive and disgusting, and demonstrated his claim by marching smartly around the table. He stopped behind Mr. Barnes's chair, and shot his finger at the stranger. "He did it. The preacher man." He seemed overawed by a secondary realization of what had happened. "All he did was touch me."

Mrs. Creely didn't speak. What could she say? There was Mr. Corvin striding around her dining room table like a spring chicken, when all he'd ever done before was clomp slowly along cursing under his breath.

Mr. Barnes was the first to comment. He'd shipped out as a young man, had circled the globe several times and seen his share of amazing sights. But even he was shaken by what he'd just witnessed. "Well . . . " he said, extruding the syllable to breaking point. "It looks like our friend here can fix more than just washing machines."

Once the word had got around town, which it did with the speed of a wind-assisted prairie fire, of the remarkable events at Mrs. Creely's boarding house, nothing would do for twenty or so of the town's citizens but that they should come view the perpetrator for themselves. Which was why, later that day, with the sun beginning its downward loop in the western sky, the stranger descended from his room, where he'd been resting, to find a restless and buzzing crowd waiting for him outside the front gate.

The buzz dropped to silence when he came through the screen door. Most people in the gathering were quite surprised by his foreign appearance. Around these parts preacher men tended to be fair-skinned sons of the Confederacy with circular, open faces and sensible haircuts. And they garbed themselves in dark pants, a pair of black lace-up Thom McAns, and a white dress shirt, a plain, no-frills ensemble purposely chosen so as not to compete with the brilliant color and dazzling perspectives of the Good Word. But this man's clothes put you in mind of the gas jockey at the Texaco station. And the hair and beard were like those photographer fellas that came down from New York to take pictures of honest folk doing an honest day's work.

The second impression, which nipped immediately at the heels of the first, was that the jeans and the denim shirt were neat and clean and, they had to admit, eminently serviceable. And when they reexamined the preacher's elongated face, they found it composed and settled under its tight skein of skin which, although dark, wasn't anything like a Negro's, being a deep burnished shade of browny gold. As for the long fall of hair, and the parted beard, they changed their thinking about that, too, concluding that it imposed a wise and professorial look rather than anything artsy-craftsy.

The object of their assessment moved down the front steps and along the path toward them. As he drew closer the limp, and the bad hands, became apparent. But these infirmities only cemented their impression of knowledge. Anyone who'd been severely injured had been forced to reexamine priorities, which generally led to a clearer understanding of the eternal truths.

The stranger stood before the crowd and, clearly under no illusion that they'd come for any reason other than to see him, waited for one of them to speak.

"Reverend," one of them called. "I hear you got the touch. I hear you can heal people."

"It is not I who heals," Yehsu replied, "but the One who sent me."

Many in the crowd were well versed in the Gospels, but because it's impossible to vocalize a capital letter, they missed the godly reference. In fact, some of them mentally altered the line to "someone who sent me," so the answer produced a cloud of confusion.

"Which church you with?" somebody else asked.

"There is only one church. The catholic church of God."

The crowd, defeated once again by the ambiguities of the English language, didn't understand that at all. Nobody had ever heard of a Catholic street preacher, although they knew all about Catholics. Catholics bowed down before graven images, and worshiped a bloody heart the way the pagan Aztecs used to. And if there was ever another war when America and Italy were on opposite sides, like they were in World War II, they had to fight for Italy this time.

They parted for the stranger as he walked through the gate.

Trailed him at a cautious and respectful twenty feet, curbing their natural pace to compensate for his handicap.

At Scott's and Bay Street, near the start of the downtown section, they met the first of the sidewalk evangelists. Everybody knew him. Bert Sales was a fixture, an obnoxious one according to some who objected to his aggressive buttonholing. His technique was to latch on to a person at the start of the block, and harangue them with fierce intensity all the way to the corner of Charles, where, if unsuccessful in his shrill entreaty, he left off, retraced his steps, and waited for another unwary sinner.

Bert Sales spotted the limping man approaching, a sinner if ever he saw one, and concentrated on him to the total exclusion of the following group, which was led by several people whom he knew had made a decision for Jesus long ago. The evangelist, wearing black pants, a white dress shirt with the sleeves rolled up above the elbows, and a bent and slightly grubby Panama hat, leaped out at the stranger.

"Cast this, brother! Cast this if you be without sin!"

Every street preacher had some kind of gimmick. Bert Sales's was to thrust a small stone into the prospect's hand and invite the person, in an out-of-context biblical parallel, to throw it if they were perfect human beings. Most people sheepishly handed the stone back, although there'd been one famous cynic who, claiming absolute purity, had wound up, hurled the stone, and starred the window of a department store.

The foreigner stopped. Looked at the stone he'd been forced to accept, then looked so deeply into the face of the donor he could have checked his reflection in the dime-store sunglasses the evangelist wore. "And you?" the stranger asked in his liquid accent. "Are you fit to cast this stone?"

That stopped Bert Sales. Nobody had ever turned the question back on him before. Nobody had ever had the hide to question his credentials. He found the query impertinent, and his reaction sent a quick red tide surging beneath the ingrained hatch marks on his weathered cheeks. "Don't worry about me, mister," he snapped. "I got Jesus in my heart and God in my soul. The question is, have you been saved?"

"I am not the saved but the Savior." The answer, direct but mellifluent, hung between them for a weighty moment.

"Huh?"

"Do not doubt that I have come to save. For that is my mission. Keep this," Yehsu said, handing the stone back, "and if by the time I return to my Father you are able to list yourself among the ones who overcome, then you shall be able to throw this stone across the widest river with a conscience that is clear and untroubled."

Upon hearing the reply, people in the crowd looked at one another in puzzlement. It was true foreigners spoke English differently from Americans, but what did the stranger mean by his curious promise? Overcome what? And what was that he said about his father?

Bert Sales, frowning down at the stone in his hand, was similarly perplexed. It was the same small piece of rock he'd gotten back, but it seemed changed somehow, as if its structural chemistry had been altered, its atoms and molecules rearranged. His bafflement served to dissipate his earlier anger, and, when the stranger moved away, and his retinue began to follow, the evangelist grabbed one of them by the arm, a man named Mat Jarrett.

"Say, who is that bozo anyway?"

"Beats the hell outta me," Jarrett replied, anxious to join the group. "All I know is his name's Lord, and he's got a healing hand like Paul himself."

"You say he's a healer?"

"Cured a guy not two hours back. Lame as a three-legged dog. This fella touches him and, abracadabra, he's walkin' as good as you or me. Bob Jenks and Sam Barnes saw it with their own two eyes." Jarrett broke away. Hurried after Yehsu, leaving behind him a man with his mind in turmoil.

Like some people long to be a concert pianist or a home-run king, Bert Sales wanted to be able to heal; not by going to medical school and writing out prescriptions, but simply by being the earthly conduit for the infinite mercy of Jesus. However, as he'd once confessed to a pal, he couldn't mend a broken teacup with a giant-size tube of Elmer's glue. So whenever he heard tell of a genuine healer, he'd travel hundreds of miles to be in the presence, to mock and scoff if the person was fraudulent, or to burn with a scalding envy if there were the slightest sign of a gift. So when he heard Mat Jarrett's breathless tale, he temporarily closed his sidewalk mission and scurried to catch up with the retreating throng.

A hundred feet past Carteret Street the stores and services began to fall away, and the smell of salt water and the mew of gulls reminded anyone who might have forgotten that this was tidewater country. A short distance farther the town's river shed its python shape, and stretched into a bay full of needle creeks and rounded inlets.

Bulkhead Waterfront Park got the bay off to a postcard start with a fleet of marine craft of almost infinite variety. The colorfully named trawlers were the tourists' favorites, with their clunky lines, tangled gaffs, and picturesque decks on which men with creased faces and hard hands mended nets in the lemony sunshine. And it was to these last that the stranger made his way, his unacknowledged retinue stringing along behind him burstingly curious as to what had brought the healer to this nautical part of town.

The stranger moved down a row of moored trawlers, examining each one with a quiet and solid intensity. The one he finally stopped in front of looked little different from the rest: rusty white, a rat's nest of cables crisscrossing the superstructure, and men repairing gear on the littered foredeck. In this case, two men whom several of the trailing group knew to be the Carew boys, Jimmy and Jack. Until fairly recently they'd been in the roofing business in Macon, Georgia. But, as the brothers had explained, with housing starts down, and people putting off repairs till better times, they'd looked around for a more lucrative and reliable job and had bought a trawler. And were going broke faster than ever. The locals put it pretty succinctly: as fishermen the Carews were terrific roofers.

The two brothers looked up from their chore, and paid little heed to the foreign-looking guy who was watching them intently, although it was their rugged, square-jawed faces he seemed interested in rather than their darning skills. They'd gotten used to appearing in the lenses of tourists' Instamatics, and even though this man wasn't framing them with a camera, they ignored him. One of the brothers, spotting a familiar face in the group on the wharf, an assembly whose reason for being he didn't question, called a morose salutation.

"Hi, there, Davey."

"How's it goin', Jimmy?" the recipient asked, more in the manner of a greeting than a pertinent inquiry.

"Fabulous. We caught enough this morning to feed a family of four if they're on a diet."

"That right? I heard the shrimp were runnin' like scalded cats out there."

"Yeah, well, if they were, they all ran in the other direction," Jimmy Carew replied.

His brother, Jack, came into the conversation. "You know anyone wants to buy a boat cheap, send 'em over."

The stranger spoke up. But because the townspeople hadn't expected him to contribute to the exchange, they weren't listening for him, and weren't sure what he'd said.

"Say what?" one of the Carews asked.

"Look in your hold." The exhortation, delivered in the same even tone as the first unheard directive, offered no reason to act upon it. Nevertheless, one of the brothers, the one called Jack, stirred himself, at least as far as getting to his feet.

"Mister, there ain't nothin' in that hold except a starfish and a foot of salt water."

"You say you caught enough to feed only four," Yehsu said. "Look again. You have enough to feed a hundred times as many."

"Guy's loco," Jimmy muttered. "You're wastin' our time, champ," he called. And yet, as if to disprove his statement, he got up, too, and moved past the wheelhouse toward the stern. Jack went with him, both men looking like con-artist victims, 99 percent sure they were being made fools of, but unwilling to dismiss the remaining 1 percent chance.

Jack reached the hold. Bent down, peeled back a corner of the stained tarpaulin covering the well, and reacted as if he'd been shot.

At the other corner of the hold Jimmy bent back his corner of the tarp. His reaction was different but, in its own way, just as vi-

olent: a sudden grunted sound like a man might make running
into a ghost.

"Not possible," Jack breathed. "It just ain't possible." He
looked at his brother, who, slack-mouthed, looked right back
at him.

"What is it?" a woman called from the crowd.

"It's full," Jack Carew said in a wavering half voice. "The damn
thing's fulla shrimp."

The crowd caught its breath, swayed collectively, then launched
itself along the wharf and jumped the three feet to the deck of the
trawler. They overran the vessel like pirates boarding a merchant-
man. Pounded aft.

Bert Sales was the first to reach the hold. He pulled up sharply,
his eyes dilating behind his cheap sunshades.

The others arrived a half moment later. Surrounded the hold.

Stared in wonder at the crackling, glistening load.

"Hallelujah," a man said, in a breath that sounded like his last.

"Ten pounds," Jimmy Carew said. His body was starting to
tremble, and he couldn't seem to stop blinking. "We caught ten
pounds tops. Sold 'em an hour back from the bottom of the hold.
We never came in with a catch like that. Not today, not never!"

The crowd turned drained and shaken faces toward the stranger
on the wharf. They'd followed him in the hope of witnessing
something dramatic, some outstanding success with an asthmatic
or a deaf person perhaps. But this! A real live miracle conjured up
from a pale blue ocean! They were flabbergasted. Poleaxed. Aston-
ished beyond belief.

The man on the wharf spoke into the stunned silence. Addressed the two brothers; first one, then the other. "What are you
called?"

The answers came back from choked vocal cords.

"Jimmy . . ."

"Jack . . ."

The stranger delivered an order and an enticement. "Leave your
nets and come. There are more important things to catch than
fish."

The brothers seemed to take forever either to understand what had been offered them, or to weigh and consider it, but then, in what looked like sibling affinity, moved at the same time.

Strode across the deck and hopped up onto the wharf.

Looking wildly perplexed and vaguely distressed, they stopped in front of Yehsu, and followed him as he turned and limped away.

On board the trawler only Bert Sales seemed to see any correlation between what had just transpired and a famous historical event. But that realization came a beat behind the connection of a couple of things that linked up in the evangelist's tumbling thought pattern: the sighting in the Tennessee hills, the Mexican shepherds who'd claimed they'd seen the Lord descending in a blaze of glory . . . it had been yesterday's big story. And then this strange person turns up just a couple of hundred miles from those hills. A man with a Semitic face. Shoulder-length hair. Hands that had been cruelly smashed. Feet that had been severely injured. And scars along the scalp such as barbs might make. Or something as sharp as barbs. A man who can make another man walk properly again. A man who can command half a ton of shrimp to appear in the empty hold of a boat run by a couple of incompetent fishermen.

Fishermen . . .

"Jimmy and Jack," Bert Sales said, out loud and unfocused. "James and John. Two of the first disciples. Luke five-six. The miraculous catch of fish."

Another thought engulfed him, and he quoted in a pale shadow of his normal evangelist's voice: " 'And the Lord said, Follow me and I will make you fishers of men.' "

An inescapable conclusion leapt into his head with a force that caused his eyes to roll and his reason to momentarily swoon. As colossal and mind-wrenching as it was, as earthshaking and stupefying, there could be only one explanation.

"It's Jesus!" he cried. "It's Jesus!"

He slumped to his knees, sweat bubbling on his shocked and bewildered features.

Just three people, a man and two women who'd stayed on the wharf, refuted his statement, calling out in genuine alarm and waving their hands. But everyone else erupted in a long, surging moan as they, too, saw what the evangelist saw. They keened and swayed and joined Bert Sales on their trembling knees on the oily deck of the trawler.

"It's the Lord returned!" Bert Sales wailed. "Jesus Christ has come back!"

CHAPTER
5

Less than twelve hours after he'd left Marie Olivier's apartment, locked in a vise of mortification and regret, Brian Sheridan met her again.

By mistake.

And through Reflexology.

When he arrived at the bookstore the next morning he found that a book she'd ordered on that subject during her second visit to the store had been finally located by a laggardly wholesaler. Brian's first thought was to simply mail the volume to her. That way he'd maintain zero contact, clearly the best policy when a man tells a woman that he's a priest and therefore, by definition, about as much good to her as a eunuch.

And that had been his second thought, too. So he'd put the book on the service counter intending to slip it into a Jiffy pack the following day, but the overzealous NYU kid, who did three half days a week, saw the book lying there, remembered the title being on order, and called the customer to tell her the book had arrived. Which was how and why Marie appeared at the bookstore a third time.

She gave no indication that anything of a conclusive nature had occurred between them, yet Brian knew that her feeling toward him had to be altered by the removal of the delightful pressures and rituals which normally exist between an unattached man and woman.

She stood across from him at the service desk, her deferred purchase bagged and paid for, and try as he might, he could read neither hostility, sympathy, nor pity on her lovely face. Maybe another woman would have acted differently, overcompensatingly vivacious perhaps, a high fixed smile in place, but not Marie Olivier. She had too much class to take a chummy, don't-give-it-a-second-thought approach.

Brian kept his conversation pleasantly neutral, stopping himself, in the nick of time, from asking how she'd been, as if they'd been lovers for two years and had only recently broken up.

The arrival of a customer with a question drove a convenient wedge into their reunion, at which point Marie said good-bye. As she turned on her way to the exit to give him a quick smile and a wave, he was certain he was seeing her for the last time, but she surprised him by swiveling again at the door, obeying what looked to be a quick impulse, and called to him. "Brian . . . excuse me, but, do you play tennis?"

"It's been a while. Why?"

She came back to the desk, waited till the customer had been attended to, then said: "I have a court at six, and my regular partner's had to go out of town. It's just for an hour. What do you say?"

"You obviously haven't heard about my rotten forehand."

Marie smiled. "We'll make a perfect team. I have a rotten backhand."

They played at a one-court club, a midtown rooftop affair on Third Avenue. Brian had been a fair-enough player at college, but had rarely played since. His ground strokes were incurably rusty, but his serve came back after a few games and, being tall, he was able to put a lot of steam into it, so was saved from complete disgrace. Marie played the game as he thought she might: with nonstop verve and boundless energy, running down every shot, delighting in her winners, bopping her blond head with her racket on anything she hit long, and once, when she blooped an over-adventurous volley, imploring the gods to tell her how she'd offended.

He enjoyed being back on a court, although he wondered how his underexercised body would tolerate sixty minutes of concerted application, a question his corpus rudely answered much sooner than he expected.

Showered and changed, and strolling out into the club's tiny reception area, his left calf muscle was transmuted, with a gasping suddenness, into a solid block of wood. He cried out. Fell into a chair. Grabbed his leg. Just a simple cramp, yet the level of pain was like eighteenth-century amputation.

With his face concertinaed in distress he felt somebody whip off his shoe. Opened his eyes to see Marie with both thumbs pressed into the ball of his foot, and her fingers grasping his instep with a fierce, squinching pressure. The block of wood became liquid plastic, moldable and obedient. The dark pain shrank to a pale throb. The limb became his again.

Brian took a recovering breath. "Ouch," he said, belatedly. "That was kind of exquisite." He moved to get up.

"Stay there," Marie commanded. "It could lock up again." She kept the pressure on, relaxed his foot, bent it back once more. Did that several times before allowing him to move around. He could walk, but rather like a man with a badly fitted prosthetic leg.

"It needs a little work," Marie announced.

Twenty minutes later they were in her apartment.

She led him into her bedroom, told him to change back into his tennis shorts, and left him while he did.

It struck him, with forceful irony, that this was the exact situation he'd fled from last night, him getting out of his pants in Marie Olivier's bedroom. There might have been some glamour attached to it then; the excitement of the forbidden; a virile cleric-in-exile romantically casting off his priestly vows for the love of a beautiful woman and the thrill of an unknown sexual future. Not now. Now he was just a last-minute substitute, an out-of-shape bookseller with a disabling charley horse. Instead of the faint, teasing scent of goose-bumped skin, and tingling fingers caressing his thigh, it would be the muscular smell of full-strength liniment, and a firm hand painfully correcting wayward tendons and ligaments.

Marie reentered the room carrying towels and a small bottle of clear liquid. She spread out a towel. Patted it. "On your tummy."

Brian climbed onto her bed, the innerspring mattress welcoming him with comforting support. He felt her join him on the bed. Knew she was kneeling. She lifted his right foot and placed it over her thigh. He could feel the looped nub of a towel on his instep. He heard the twist of plastic on glass. The clink of the bottle placed on a side table. He tensed for the cryonic shock of alcohol on his skin, but the liquid was warm and viscous.

"I have to work just below the edge of pain, so let me know if I hurt you."

"The very thought of it hurts me."

He heard her snort a little laugh at his reply, and was pleased. If he could keep it light, it would help dilute his position, sway him from the tactile awareness of the lacy white cotton bedspread and the trace of her perfume rising from it. He tensed again as he felt her thumbs press firmly into the outside of his calf and stroke a long, solid line upward toward the back of his knee. She repeated the stroke, this time starting an inch nearer the Achilles tendon, her thumbs a mercy elevator of relief.

"Yep," she confirmed, "this is one tight gastrocnemius."

"Wait till you get to the calf muscle." He sensed her smile, tried unsuccessfully to close out a thought as her thumbs began their healing ascent again. It was surprisingly close to sex, this, close to the sweet little woundings, the spearing nails, the nip of teeth sinking not so gently into lip and ear. The oil on his skin like a woman's moist arousal. Her position, kneeling behind him, a reverse of male-female preentry. Yet there was nothing sexual in her touch. It was professionally genderless as it went after denseness and compression, concerned only with the world beneath the flesh. He bore down mentally, bumped his thinking into the mundane.

"You're pretty good at this. Where did you learn?"

"Backstage."

"You were an actress?"

"A dancer."

"You didn't tell me that."

"It was just amateur stuff, but it was fun. We used to give each other a rubdown before we went on. I gave up dance but kept on with the massage."

He reviewed what she'd said. A dancer. That explained the

bounce she got into her straight-backed stride, her easy balance on the court, and the compact moon of her buttocks flitting beneath her pleated tennis skirt.

This last memory seemed to plunge his body into a vibrating sexual tension. He'd given himself up to her squeezing hands, her healing fingers, given himself up to this bed he lay on, letting his pelvis press into it as if the woman whose voice he was hearing was not kneeling behind him but spreadeagled beneath him. He allowed the right side of his face to burrow further into the white bedcover. The spice of her perfume filtered through the open weave of the cotton fabric. Beneath the spread the crisp, paisley-patterned sheets were glossed with the fragrance of her hair and the delicious bouquet of her skin.

Marie lightly tapped his heel. "Okay, turn over."

"Why?"

"So I can finish the treatment."

Brian knew he'd become tumescent and didn't want to embarrass either of them. He'd thought that when she was through, he'd ease off the bed in a sitting position and, under the guise of testing his calf, wait till the red inguinal tide had receded. "My leg feels fine. I think I'm done."

"Okay, stay like that. I want to try out that book I bought today."

Brian tried to twist his head to look at her. "Not the one about the serial killer . . . ?" From his awkward position he caught the corner of her smile.

"Trust me," Marie said. "I'm almost an expert."

"I want to know what I'm in for," Brian said, still a hostage to vascular congestion. "Exactly what is Reflexology, anyway?"

Marie layered his leg with a drop more oil, and began her ministrations again. "Zone therapy. Different parts of the sole of the foot control different parts of the body. Massage the right point, and it sends a healing message to whichever part is ailing."

"Sounds like acupuncture."

"Same idea but without the invasive needles. The skin doesn't get broken. Just manipulated. Now what could be bad about that?"

Brian knew he had to get off his tummy because the pressure of his weight, and the warm indentation he'd made on the bed, was working against him. But as that was impossible it was up to his mind to fool his body. What he needed was a concentrated sixty seconds of distracting thought. "You mean," he began, faking intense interest, "that somebody with, say, a thyroid condition can be treated by pinching their big toe?"

He felt her fingers dig into him in playful reproach. "You're clearly a dog of an unbeliever. But, for your information, the big toe is for the brain, a part of your body I think could also use some work." She grasped his left foot in her right hand, rolled her right thumb into the outer part of his foot an inch beyond the ankle. "The ball of the foot treats the thyroid, and different areas of the arch are the outposts for the lungs, heart, ears, eyes, liver, kidneys, et cetera. You tolerating this okay?"

"You're not hurting me."

"I meant the monologue." Marie continued her minilecture for another minute, giving Brian the break he was after. The litany of organs she recited had brought to mind the squeamish procedures of his high school biology class. When she again told him to turn over he could do so having been blessed with contraction.

She watched him raise a hand to scratch at an imagined itch between his eyes, one of his few habitual gestures, she'd noticed. It unwittingly drew attention to the space just beneath the barely hyphenated eyebrows where his nose had been diverted from its angled descent and persuaded into a steeper one. It gave him the look of a gentleman pugilist who'd been tagged just once in an illustrious career.

Lying back with his hands propping his head, Brian returned her gaze. The glow of the late-evening sky, reflecting in from the windows, was augmented by a table lamp, giving her the kind of single source lighting a portrait photographer might have arranged. It magnified the extraordinary fineness of her eyelashes, her slow blink rate holding them together for a millisecond longer than was usual, an action that seemed to feather and lengthen them.

She released his foot. Backed off the bed. "You want to try putting some weight on that leg?"

Brian pushed himself to a sitting position. Put both feet flat on the floor and stood. Took a hesitant step. Then a normal one. Grunted not in pain, but in happy surprise. "It feels great." He moved his head in mock realization. "So that's how Jesus did it."

"Did what?"

"Made the lame whole again. He wasn't a miracle worker, he was a masseur."

It was the first time he'd touched on anything religious since he'd told her of his previous employ, and she hesitated over a response. He saw her cautiously delay the one that had leapt onto her tongue, and took a guess at its direction. "Have I shocked you? Do you think that's in bad taste?"

She lifted one shoulder. "Not as far as I'm concerned. I don't go to church, so I'm not too close to Jesus."

"You should join my parish. You'd be in good company."

Marie wondered what he meant: that his parishioners weren't close to Jesus, or that he wasn't?

"Where is your parish?"

"Wisconsin. Conomahack. A town of stunning ordinariness." He flexed his leg again. "I thought I'd be hobbling for a week. You did a great job, Marie."

"No charge." Marie tilted her mouth in a smile, then left him to change. Went out into the kitchen thinking over his words. If he still had a parish, why was he working full-time in a bookstore? Had he been suspended?

For what?

Drinking? But she'd had dinner with him twice and there wasn't the slightest hint of a problem.

Had he got involved with a woman, perhaps? A good-looking guy like Brian, some neglected housewife comforting God's minister in his lonely mission . . . it was a definite possibility. Whatever the trouble was, it was his business, she told herself.

But she would have loved to have known.

As Marie, busy in the kitchen, considered Brian's past, he was in the living room considering her taste in decor.

He toured a wall of Japanese advertising posters. Their brash Oriental verve resonated against the cool simplicity of the Scandinavian furniture, setting up an absorbing clash of statements. It made sense, Brian felt, from what he'd learned of Marie so far and her startling inconsistencies. An individualist who sought not just the untrodden road, but the one that was closed because it looked more interesting.

He moved over to inspect her book collection and was a little surprised at the range: space sagas mixed in with fine modern literature and a phalanx of nineteenth-century works. He was flipping through a Hardy novel when Marie called out to him.

He found her immersed in the little dramas of cooking.

She nodded at the refrigerator. "I need a volunteer for the beer squad."

He fetched two cans of Piels. Popped them. Marie wanted a glass for hers, which was another small surprise: he would have thought that anyone who played tennis with such vigorous abandon would drink beer from the can. A tiny thing, but it enforced Brian's impression of her as being outside the chocolate box: no simple little illustration on the paper lining to help you identify the various flavors.

She cracked two eggs into a bowl, took up a third, and paused with the knife in her hand. "You staying for dinner?"

In the time it took to respond naturally, Brian examined the moral parameters of the situation. By saying no thanks, finishing his beer, and leaving, he'd be removing himself from temptation. But if he did that he'd have to shun every woman's company with a similar bold show of rejection.

"You bet. Thank you," he said, realizing, as the words issued forth, exactly what he was worried about: few women had a presence like Marie's. It zinged and quivered like an arrow in a bulls-eye.

"I take it you're a chef of some repute," Brian ventured, shifting to less contentious territory.

Marie looked up briefly to donate a vague smile. "I was a terrible cook forever. Then I went to France to do a piece on some of the great chefs, and when I came back I decided to devote six months working on a dish until I got it right. I quit after a year, but at least now I can cook two things passably instead of ten things terribly."

He watched her take a sip of beer. The glass came away from her mouth without an imprint. She wore the lightest application of lip gloss, and just a smidgen of liner to elongate her fabulous eyes, and even these small embellishments were superfluous, Brian thought. Like the planet Venus she'd reach her apogee early in the morning, first thing on a brand-new day when, fresh from slumber and the shower, she'd stand wet and naked in a fluffy towel, beads of water on her skin like tiny translucent pearls.

He endeavored to detour his mind around thoughts like that, not an easy task with her standing right there in front of him.

"Do you always get so personally affected by your writing projects?" he asked, referring to her anecdote of the French chefs and the two dishes she'd mastered.

"Not always. I did a story on suicide once, but I'm still here."

She had a nice way of delivering these lines, starting with a mild frown as though she were examining the oblique angles of a question, waiting a beat, then permitting her mouth to minutely widen as a substitute for the laugh she was too modest to allow herself.

Brian took a stool at the little counter. Sat on it and drank his beer while he watched Marie assemble a dish which had taken her half a year to perfect. She wore a blue-and-white-striped apron over her slub linen sheath, not a sponge-off plastic one but a real butcher's apron made of coarse cotton. A small, flour-dusted cassette radio, wedged between two large pasta jars, reproduced a Rachmaninoff piece, a sonorous, bell-tolling work for two pianos which perfectly illustrated the alluring symmetry of music and cooking.

"How's the job?" Brian asked. "What are you working on right now?"

Marie left off her mixing. Came over to the counter and pulled a copy of the *New York Times* from a shelf. An item on an inside page bore the yellow splotch of a felt-tipped pen. Brian had read the item himself that morning, a report of a rally for the Reverend George Seegrove the night before in Baltimore. "I'm mulling it over," she told him. "I suppose I should do something on Seegrove but a zillion writers have already torn strips off the guy. I'd just be one more carping voice."

"Then go the other way. Do an article on Don Bagley. The guy seems totally genuine. There's no singing or dancing on his show, no sawdust and sulfur. And I understand that whatever money comes in he gives to charity once he's covered expenses."

"That's the trouble. Don Bagley really is a straight arrow. I researched him once. No far-right political agenda, no cathedral fund, no cash-rich broadcasting company. He simply wants to bring Jesus to everybody."

"So why isn't he worth an article?"

"Because America's only interested in villains. They might admire an honest man of God, but they'd rather read about a greedy, power-hungry evangelist."

"Good old-fashioned family values," Brian said.

"Family," Marie repeated thoughtfully. "Maybe I'll do something on that. How incest brought a troubled New Hampshire family closer together."

They ate in the little dining el on a scrubbed deal table. Marie lit candles, but they were on the table anyway, a permanent fixture, so Brian perceived the gesture as a touch of easy elegance rather than a bid to romanticize. He took a forkful of the quiche she'd cooked, then another, and, teasing her, said nothing. Head down, working his fork into its delicate consistency, he received the silent broadcast of her disappointment.

"So what do you think?" she asked in a tone of mild grievance.

He looked up miming a moment's noncomprehension. ". . . Oh, the quiche? Yeah, great. First-class."

"Bastard," she said, the cuss word sounding like a benediction. "Come on, seriously. I'm looking for compliments."

"Four stars."

"Why not five?"

"So you'll have something to work toward."

She slow-blinked in a sham of exasperation, the hesitant candle glow visiting her face and highlighting the smooth escarpment of her features. She looked different in the uncertain light. She'd looked different in the bedroom, too, Brian thought. One of those women whose looks changed without the intercession of comb or cosmetics.

"Do you realize," he asked, "that if you'd stuck at dance the way you did at cooking, you'd be at Lincoln Center today?"

"But I'd only have two steps."

Brian laughed, and this time she joined him. They looked at each other. A battery clock ticked stridently in the kitchen. An ambulance or a cruiser rushed by down on the street, its siren screaming up at the windows until distance dragged it away.

"Why did you give up dance, anyway?"

"I met a guy, and he found me better things to do."

It was a brash confession and a slightly racy one. And it was also a perfect lead-in for a reply. Marie waited to hear him say something like, "That's funny, the same thing happened to me. I met a woman, and she changed my life, too." But Brian didn't offer anything like that. Instead he smiled at her and got up from the table.

"I'd better get going. We've got a sale on at the store tomorrow, and I have to get in early."

Marie walked him to the door.

"Thanks for dinner. Super cooking," Brian said. "You'll have to forgive me for ducking the washing up."

"I'll mail it to you," Marie offered.

Brian kissed her quickly on the cheek, gave a little wave, and walked toward the elevator.

Out in the street, the summer air fanning the heat in his face, he let the thought of Marie flood through him.

That quick, sexless good-bye peck had brought with it an awareness of her body's proximity. A slight brush against him and he'd felt a tingling charge zap through his bones. He wanted his hands on that body, every soft square inch of it. Wanted to feel it quiver and vibrate beneath his shaping hand. Sing at the touch of his tongue.

Slammed by a sudden realization, he stopped walking.

Well, how about that? he thought.

Damn it.

He was falling in love with her.

CHAPTER
6

When somebody pressed the intercom just before midnight Colonel Buehl, annoyed but hardly surprised, knew that it was his partner come calling. He'd become inured to the man's sense of time, which wasn't so much a disregard for the hours of the day but an incomprehension that others were bound by them.

Buehl admitted him without any greeting, and they crossed into the living room together.

Few partners looked more different than these two. People meeting Ralph Buehl for the first time saw an obvious military legacy in the freshly brushed, freshly pressed suits he wore, the starched white shirts that vanished into a trim belt, the plain and ever-present necktie knotted just so. A precise man with a clipped air of muscularity about him, he was an enemy of extravagance in both dress and decor. His spine was as straight as it had been thirty-five years earlier when he'd been pennant winner at the Citadel, and his stiff air of command seemed to increase his already considerable height.

His partner had good height, too, but it was wasted by poor posture. Like a separated Siamese twin, his body was at war with itself, his lack of coordination turning the simplest movement into wayward clumsiness. A Pentagon major had once conjectured that it was nature compensating for his incredible IQ. Whatever it was, it accentuated the odd-couple aspect of the two partners to an almost risible degree.

In his own mind, Buehl referred to his associate as Professor 4-F. He despised the man's puny physique, which would have broken down in the first two minutes of a recruit's training run. Yes, it was true that his contribution to the partnership required no physical prowess, but did he have to be such a total weakling? Thank God they were never seen together. "How's it look?" his partner asked, collapsing into a chair in ungainly sections. He was referring to the glowing computer screen set up on a desk. He knew that the colonel would have been studying it for hours. The colonel spent a lot of time in front of his PC entering data in his stilted military jargon: success quotients, positive and negative surprise factors, etc. Nobody was better at organizing and implementing a course of action than Ralph Buehl. And nobody was better at covering his tracks, either, which was a big reason why he'd gone into business with him.

"We're on-line," Buehl said, taking a seat himself. "Wassenaer's been terminated. And I briefed the Chinese this afternoon."

"Li? You're assigning him to Hecke?"

Buehl nodded and tried to keep the disapproval off his face. His partner mumbled when he spoke, his lower lip extruding as his tongue picked at something inside his mouth. He was an oral compulsive, one of those people who, if they don't smoke or chew gum, worry their teeth instead. Buehl thought the man did it because he disliked speaking to people, and that the tongue picking was an indictment of forced communication.

"I wondered about Hecke," his visitor said, his eyes searching a corner of the ceiling. He seldom looked at the person he was talking to, which made him appear to be addressing an invisible familiar. "I knew he'd start asking for more money before long."

"I covered that contingency," Buehl said, in his crisp, officious manner. "He arrived in town this evening. I've agreed to pay him what he wants at sixteen hundred hours tomorrow. But he'll be in a body bag by then, of course."

Buehl contemplated the food stain on 4-F's jacket, and his tempestuous hair that always reminded him of used Brillo pads. He'd learned to endure the scarecrow appearance, and the agony of listening to the semiaphasic explanations of his ideas, for good solid business reasons. The man was a marvelous conceptualist; even his ideas for the more mundane assignments, like the assassination of Saddam, had been dazzling and would have easily worked had the Agency not pulled rank and carried out their own ineffectual plans. But, Buehl had come to believe, his hold on reality had to be a tenuous one. Now and then he caught a glimpse of something dark lunging behind those elusive eyes. The man's brilliance, he felt, was hostage to an incipient lunacy which would one day send in its account.

"Hiring personnel is your department," his partner said from behind a tooth-probing finger. "But I have to tell you, Li spooks me. There's something funny about that guy."

"There's something funny about anybody who kills for money."

"Isn't that what we do?"

Buehl thought that a scandalous question. "No, it is not! We provide a service. Clients come to us expecting success. We have a duty to those clients, and if we have to have people killed, it's in the *line* of duty. Do you think Li, or those three scruffy clowns, know or care anything about duty?"

The other man didn't press it. He muttered bland agreement then said, "Just be careful with him. I don't like him."

"It's not necessary to like the men under your command. As long as they obey your orders efficiently and without question, emotion is superfluous."

His partner didn't reply to that. There was no arguing with the colonel when it came to patriotism, duty, honor, or anything remotely to do with the military. Moreover, he knew that to stick around now was to invite a lecture on Americanism or the flag, or the merits of General Douglas MacArthur, the colonel's idol.

"I'd better get going. Talk to you later." He untangled his imperfect frame, shambled over to the door, and let himself out.

Buehl was happy to see him go. So clever, but so irritating.

He crossed to the computer and checked his figures one last time. Then, encouraged by what he saw, logged off for the night, removed the floppy disk, and hid it away.

This last action was an unnecessary precaution. Outside of his gangly confederate, and the people he employed, nobody knew that Colonel Ralph Buehl lived in this building. Officially, he lived in an opulent nine-room apartment on the Upper East Side, an abode he'd been able to purchase courtesy of the discreet gratitude of several defense contractors.

Colonel Buehl was what passed for rich these days, although he had no idea of how to enjoy his money. Foreign cars, yachts, vacations in exotic places did not appeal. And, possessing a libido that barely ticked over, throbbing liaisons with plush mistresses were also absent from his agenda. He was the stuffiest of men and would have led the drabbest of lives had it not been for his postmilitary business, which involved him in projects of considerable profit and commensurate personal risk.

When he'd retired from the army—in actual fact, he'd been privately invited to leave—Buehl had used his kickback money to buy two apartments, the tony one uptown, and the one he now occupied under a pseudonym, a one-bedroom on the sixth floor of an old midtown building devoid of amenities. His plan had been to live in the uptown apartment and use the midtown one as his office. But, used to the prosaic surrounds of an officer's quarters, he'd found the luxury of the uptown accommodation faintly uncomfortable, so he'd moved more or less full time to his anonymous business address, which he found perfectly adequate for his few wants and limited needs. And, being bereft of staff as the building was—save for an alcoholic superintendent—his associates could come and go without fear of being noted or remembered.

His associates . . .

Getting into bed, Buehl thought back to what his partner had said about the Chinese. The funny thing was, he felt uncomfortable around him, too. And not just because he was a Muslim and an Oriental, although, God knows, after what he'd been through in Nam, he wasn't crazy about Orientals.

No, there was something else.

A whiff of treachery?

Deceit?

Whatever it was, Buehl concluded, reaching out to switch off the reading lamp, he'd do well to be on his guard.

*   *   *

Sitting in a banquette in the coffee shop of an unfashionable hotel on Forty-fourth Street, Li Xiayong was an exotic fish dropped into a tank a size too large.

He'd chosen the seat, as capacious as it was, so he could watch the reception desk without appearing to be waiting for anybody. But that's what he was doing, one hand yo-yoing the tea bag in his cup, the other sunk into the left pocket of his suit jacket which, even though the sleeve label had sported an S, still hung tentlike on his junior frame. Li was the slightest of men, a tightly wrapped parcel of bone and sinew with only an adult's knowing air stopping him from resembling a bulimic teenager. His face was unmarked, the skin gripping at his cheekbones, the eyes so profoundly recessed in their angled folds they seemed attached to his skeleton.

Beneath the slackness of his oversized jacket, mussing his cheap cotton shirt, was a .22 revolver with standard grips, standard sights, and a standard three-inch barrel. The gun was new and, apart from a factory test firing, unused. It was also unloaded. There'd be plenty of time to slip a round into the cylinder after he'd spotted the target.

He juggled the round he intended to use in the palm of his pocketed hand, admiring its cool and deceptive weightlessness. Or, at ninety-five grams, near weightlessness. A good measure of cyanide wouldn't weigh that much less, he reflected, but he preferred a bullet's indiscriminate, bone-crunching power. And a .22 could crunch bone with ease despite its namby-pamby reputation. A reliable round, too, which was a must in his business; a bad round could mean a botched job.

He adjusted his sitting position, dunked his tea bag again, then left it to drown as a man arrived at the reception desk.

False alarm.

The man was too old. His target was in his late twenties and had yellow highlights running through his hair. Li had a snapshot of him in his shirt pocket given him by the colonel. He didn't need to check it again.

He reset himself to a waiting mode, hoping the target would present himself soon, then he'd have plenty of time to do the job, ditch the gun he'd bought from his regular fence, and get back

downtown to Doyer Street and visit Jenny Choy. He always became aroused after a job. Why, he didn't know.

He checked the street outside the window. Observed a woman
up near a cab rank tolerantly allowing her dog to foul the sidewalk. He didn't like dogs but didn't have the wit to idly dream of
drilling the beast in the middle of its muscle-hunched evacuation.
Li had no time for frivolities. Laughter was the mark of a loafer,
a distraction for clowns and infidels. Not one word of the Koran
was couched in anything but a serious reference; therefore, humor
was unimportant and should be disregarded.

Li belonged to the Ithna Ashariyah sect. They were called the
Twelvers because they believed there had been twelve imams,
twelve manifestations of God, all divinely appointed and preserved
from sin. The last of these had been the Mahdi, the qa'im, He
Who Arises. He'd disappeared over one thousand years ago but
was alive and in hiding, and would appear again—some said any
day now—at the Last Judgment.

"More tea over here?"

It was the waitress standing before him, young and red-haired
and deep-bosomed with, he was sure, a luscious, pink-lipped secret hiding out in a jungle of strawberry thatch. He would have
loved to have found out, but he was hesitant; a small golden cross
dangled above those ripe melons and, apart from Jenny Choy, he
was uneasy with women who worshiped the Nazarene. They had
chosen the wrong prophet. Jesus had been great, as had Noah,
Moses, and Abraham, but in Muhammad all the messages of these
earlier prophets were consummated. Jesus had walked on water,
turned water into wine, but Muhammad had split the very moon
with his finger. There was but one God, not three in one as the
Christians claimed, one God, and Allah was his name.

Li glanced at his watch.

Noon.

When he looked up again the target was walking toward the
registration desk.

Li rose, walked out into the thinly populated lobby, moved to
the entrance, and stepped outside. The lunchtime traffic was a
wild storm after the quiet pond of the coffee shop, repetitive
waves of pedestrians surging by him on the sidewalk. The target

came through the doors and halted as Li knew he would; a stranger to a city never plunges off into the unknown but stops and tries to shuffle the unfamiliar streets into some kind of manageable order.

Li turned and politely offered assistance. "Can I help you? You look a bit lost."

The man was relieved and grateful. "I'm looking for Bloomingdale's? The department store?" He had the Southerner's way of turning a statement into a question.

"I'm going right by it."

"You're funning me . . ."

"Come on. I'll show you."

Li started walking. The target went with him, a shiny smile expanding his mouth. "You sure I'm not taking you out of your way?" he asked, clichés being roughly the same no matter where you were from.

"Not at all. My pleasure."

They moved through the noontime crowds saying the things new acquaintances say to each other. The man told Li that he was a pilot up here on a little business. Li told him that he was a partner in a Chinese takeout on the West Side.

"Reason I want to go to this store," the man volunteered, "is they got these cute little underpants for women? With the days of the week on their backsides? I promised my lady friend I'd get her a set."

Li wondered what this fool had done to upset Buehl. He was never told in what way a target had offended.

"We cross here," Li said, heading into Lexington Avenue.

Li was quite happy to be going to the store. He had an excellent knowledge of his adopted city. Knew the good killing spots, places that he'd reconnoitered and marked for future use. He knew exactly where he'd take Streaky Hair.

"You know what'd really hit the spot right now?" the Southerner asked, dodging a daring bicycle messenger who was riding against the traffic. "A cool brew."

Li's insides curled at the thought but, nevertheless, he followed the target into a bar; at this stage he wanted to keep the bonhomie flowing.

The warm, sweet aroma of malt and hops was sickening. Li hated the place; sneered inwardly at the signed photographs of the millionaire sportsmen on the walls. Looked with loathing at the long oaken bar with its multitudinous bottles. The beer taps, each with its own colorful logo, had their treacherous arms raised in welcome.

Li fought for the privilege of paying. "Cheers," he toasted, and forced himself to take a gulp of the foamy liquid they were served. Managed, with a huge effort, to look as if it were delicious, then excused himself. Found the men's room. Leaned over a toilet bowl, put a finger down his throat, and threw up the foul and hideous alcohol. Savagely flushed the toilet to send the filthy affliction down into the sewers where it belonged.

He took the revolver from his jacket, flipped open the cylinder, slipped the round into the eleven o'clock chamber, and snapped the cylinder back into place. Then he rejoined the man and they left the bar, the visitor prattling on about his lingerie purchase, a transaction he would never get to negotiate.

Ever cautious, Li ran his own personal security check: did this man suspect anything being picked up like that? What if he knew he was being set up? What if he pulled a gun and started firing at point-blank range? Li wasn't afraid to die because the Koran promised resurrection. If he died a martyr, his soul would go straight to heaven where it would remain in the gullets of green birds flitting around the Divine Throne. No, it was failure that scared him. Failure meant a lack of accomplishment, an inability to achieve, and it was an obligated duty, in the quick blink of time spent on this earthly way station, to make the flickering life God had granted you a success that reflected His glory.

"Are we getting close?" the target asked, as they reached Fifty-ninth Street.

Li's grin revealed teeth from which the enamel had escaped. "We're almost there."

They crossed with the light.

Li led the way into the store. Watched the pilot enjoying the glitzy street floor, the glittering counters, the pretty young woman spraying scent at other pretty young women.

They rode the escalators to the fifth floor. Came out into a sea of furniture. On an earlier reconnaissance Li had noticed that relatively few people browsed among big-ticket items like dining room tables and living room suites, so only a light staff was needed up here; and in the lunch hour, that staff was even further reduced.

As they crossed the parquet toward a series of furnished display rooms, Li saw that even the woman who usually manned the order desk was missing. And there was only a handful of customers in this far corner of the store. It was exactly as he'd hoped it would be.

The target was looking around, smiling in puzzlement. "This is furniture. We want, what do they call it, intimate apparel."

"It's in a special section," Li said.

"The naughty section, huh?" The man laughed.

They moved into a kind of corridor that ran behind the main part of the floor. Li checked around him. Three women browsers turned a corner in front of them and vanished. There was nobody coming the other way.

He stopped, then moved into one of the display rooms, this one a luxurious African fantasy: ceremonial wall masks, a reedy kind of plant in an elephant's-foot vase, a chieftain's chair as round as a rising moon, a fake animal skin spread on a cane four-poster bed. He ran his hands over the spread. "Antelope hide. Have you ever felt anything as soft?"

Intrigued by this proprietorial behavior, the man joined him. Felt the nub of the cloth. "Like my lady friend's ass," he said.

Li repeated the phrase silently. If this fool had known that those were to be his last words, surely he would have strived for something a little more pithy.

He picked up a cushion from a zebra-striped sofa, smothered the gun with it, and shot the man in the middle of his forehead.

Dead before he could register either pain or surprise, he fell backward onto the fake spread like a drunkard collapsing.

Li tossed the pillow away, shoved the gun back into his jacket, and left the room, the little corridor still quiet, the rest of the floor unalerted.

He descended to the street level, went deeper still to the basement, and headed for the subway. Caught the downtown express.

The job had gone well, Li thought, which was all the postmortem he allowed himself. The past was unimportant; it was the future that counted.

Buehl had said something about a job coming up down south somewhere. He didn't like to travel, but, like any business, you went where the work took you.

CHAPTER
7

Of the twenty-three people who'd followed the stranger from the boardinghouse, or trailed him down Bay Street, and witnessed the astonishing occurrence at the trawler jetty, all but one had returned to town babbling about what they'd seen.

Five of the returnees were convinced that the man was as Bert Sales had identified him, Jesus Christ, and for the same reasons that had led the evangelist to that staggering conclusion. Fourteen weren't so sure, although they were hard put to explain how anybody but the Son of God could have made a lame man walk and a previously empty fishing boat overflow with a record catch. Especially since Jesus had performed exactly these same two acts in his previous earthly existence—if *previous* was the correct word—a fact attested to in the world's most truthful, most beautiful, and biggest-selling book. And three of the crowd, the man and the two women who'd remained on the wharf, wanted to believe, but couldn't bring their minds to make such an awesome jump. As good Christian folk they'd been taught to expect the Second Coming, and they had, vaguely. But not now. It just couldn't be. Nothing of any import was going to take place in their lifetimes; momentous occurrences happened in the distant past, or the science fiction future, but never in the banality of the rock-and-roll–McDonald's–Budweiser–daytime-soap-opera present. So the retinue totaled only three: the two Carew brothers and Bert Sales.

They'd lagged behind the stranger as he'd walked back toward town, seemingly with no more purpose than he'd exhibited in his walk from the boardinghouse. The foursome had presented an extraordinary contrast: the demeanor of its leader uncomplex, all knowing, serene in its compact certainty, while the other three might have been mistaken for men on the verge of physical and mental breakdown. The brothers' heads were moving in a kind of shocked denial, their walk like a drugged semistagger. Yet, shining through their befuddlement was a sense of stupendous delight.

A step behind them Bert Sales resembled a man at the breaking point of a fever. Thrust with Einsteinian velocity into a situation as appalling as it was glorious, he'd battled to get a handle on it. One minute a street-corner preacher striving to get the Good Word out, the next, an acolyte, so it would seem, in the service of the selfsame One on whose behalf he proselytized. A situation of almost geometrical absurdity; a paradox that couldn't be, yet was.

But why should it be absurd? he asked his flagging reason. For the past twenty years he'd been promising, predicting, assuring all who would listen of the imminent return of the Lord as expressed by the Lord, according to Matthew: "But of that day and hour knowest no man, no, not the angels of heaven, but my Father only. Therefore, keep watch and be ready, because the Son of Man will come at an hour when you do not expect Him."

Well, he sure hadn't expected Him at this hour. And certainly not at this place.

Why Beaufort? Why South Carolina? Why America? Or was Jesus appearing simultaneously to all who believed in him and worked on his behalf, all over the world? But, if so, why had the Return in Glory been witnessed by so few people, a handful of Tennessee sheepherders? Had the Gospels got it all wrong? Was the Good Book nothing but a mess of lies and contradictions like the heathen atheists claimed? The possibility tottered Bert Sales; hammered at his conscious self with a fresh barrage of blows. Had his life's work been based on falsehood?

He had to know.

And there was something else he had to know: was the Final Judgment at hand? Would he have to give an account of himself now before he could break it off with Jesse Edmonds's wife? Was his name in the Book of Life? And, if not, would he be thrown into the Lake of Fire?

He didn't get a chance to ask any of these questions till the following morning.

Around six, with the street empty, and the boardinghouse still quiet, the front door opened. When their Lord Returned stepped out, Bert Sales and the Carew brothers—all three had spent a sleepless night on the porch—scrambled to their feet.

Bert Sales jumped in with the question that had been tormenting him all night. "Lord," he croaked, after a botched first attempt. "Lord . . . why . . . why has thou come again?" It seemed natural to speak in the classical language of the Bible. It seemed right and correct and worshipful. A king could be addressed in everyday English, but not the King of Kings.

The reply came from behind a slow and even look. "To teach the lessons that went unheeded the first time."

"Then this is not the end of the world?"

"This is the start of the world. A second chance."

Bert Sales exhaled in luxurious relief. "I have many questions, Lord. Hundreds of questions."

"I have come to answer questions," Yehsu told him. "Questions beg knowledge, and the spread of knowledge is my purpose."

Yehsu sat down on the porch flyer. There was plenty of room to sit beside him, but it seemed hugely impertinent to Bert Sales to assume such an equality, and standing while the Lord was sitting seemed equally presumptuous; no head shall be higher than the Monarch's. So he sat at his Lord's feet, and was joined there by the silent Carew brothers.

"Why here, Lord?" Bert Sales asked. "Why did you choose America?" The answer was immediate. "Because it is here that my message is most understood but least acted upon."

Of course! Bert Sales had wondered why he hadn't seen something as obvious as this. Hadn't he always thought it a heaven-sent sign that he'd been born in the U.S.A. where the need for deliverance was greatest? It explained a lot of things.

"What's going to happen, Lord? You must know the future . . ."

"No more than any other man."

"Man?" It was Jack Carew who spoke. A tiny muscle spasmed

in his jaw as he swallowed before continuing. "But you are Lord. You are God."

When Yehsu transferred his eyes, his head moved, too, and with the same languid precision. "I am no more God than you. And you are no more man than I. Every minute I am in bodily form, I am but a person. A person subject to the same afflictions and shortcomings that bedevil the lowest among you."

Jimmy, the other brother, also broke his self-imposed muteness, although his words fluttered out at a volume barely above silence itself. "Lord? You sayin' you're the same person now that you was before?"

"If your question asks whether I am a wiser man now than I was before, the answer is no." Yehsu paused, perhaps to give the addendum added emphasis. "Nor am I physically stronger or weaker. I return as I left, but with my wounds healed as your wounds would have healed, and with the same legacy."

For Bert Sales, listening to what he described as divine revelation, understanding was like a stop-motion film of a flower opening, the process reduced to mere seconds. God was giving the world another shot, and had sent His only begotten Son again, not as a babe born in a stable—there was no need for Jesus to come of age among men as he'd done before; his virgin birth, his enlightening ministry, his sacrificial death were known the world over—and not to Palestine, which was no longer an important outpost of the Roman empire as it had been two thousand years ago. But to America, which was now the world's superpower as Rome had been then. God had sent Jesus back in the same form he'd left, leaving the wounds to remind the world of its mean capacity for cruelty, but healing them as a symbol of the spiritual make good that the Almighty extends to all. He'd sent Jesus back unchanged except for an ability to speak the language of the country so he could teach and communicate His message.

Jimmy Carew spoke again. "Lord," he said, bobbing his head on the salutation, "what did you mean about your lessons goin' unheeded the first time?"

"I meant my church is a failure."

The three listeners gasped. Bert Sales couldn't believe he'd heard right. All his adult life he'd had to contend with people trashing the Good Book, sidewalk hecklers assuring him he was preaching an outdated and bankrupt philosophy. Did he have to add to that perfidious list of casuists the movement's founder? "But, Lord," he protested, reverting to his natural speech. "Christianity's a hands-down, flat-out, ravin' success. There's a whole peck of churches, cathedrals, schools, colleges all built in your name. And millions and millions of God-fearing Christians in the world. More than any other creed by a long shot."

Normally, in the process of discussion, a person presented with an easy rebuttal jumps in and strikes while the iron is hot. But Yehsu, sitting there in the porch swing, with all of America yet to be instructed, was content to identify error in his own good time.

"What was my message? What did I teach?"

This was the first question directly put to him by his master, and Bert Sales, desperate not to fail the test, if test it be, cravenly left it for Jack Carew to field.

"Love, Lord. You preached love."

"And was the lesson learned?"

Jack Carew nudged his brother to take a turn. But Jimmy Carew sought refuge in an age-old cop-out by turning the query back on the questioner.

"You sayin' the message didn't take, Lord?"

"I taught the Golden Rule. It has not been acted upon."

Bert Sales leaped in quickly. He was on safe ground with the Golden Rule. Had preached it himself every day of his own personal ministry. "Do unto others as you would have them do unto you."

Yehsu had no gesticulations. When he spoke he kept his ruined hands folded quietly in his lap, yet he came close to nodding at the evangelist's reply. "What are you called?"

The evangelist gulped. "Albert Sales, Lord."

"You seem familiar with my teachings. What did I say about enemies?"

Matthew 5:44 leaped onto Bert Sales's tongue, suffusing him with relief and gratitude that he would not be found wanting. "Love your enemies, and pray for those who persecute you."

"Do you have enemies, Albert?"

Sales felt faint. The Lord Jesus Christ had addressed him by his own personal name. "Enemies," he said, to still his tumbling mind. He thought darkly of Jesse Edmonds, a wife-beating son of a bitch who'd threatened him with emasculation. "Yes, Lord."

"And do you love this enemy or despise him?"

"I hate him, Lord."

"And you two," Yehsu said, addressing the brothers. "Do you also have enemies?"

Both men nodded, then dropped their eyes, unable to boast an attitude any kinder than the evangelist's.

"This is the lesson that must be taught again. Love without condition. For what success can be claimed for any life that is not devoid of malice?" Yehsu rose, a movement whose fluidity was spoiled when the half step he took favored his right foot. "Let us begin."

In the past twenty-four hours Bert Sales had received several shocks of an intensity far greater than most people experience during the span of their entire lives, and this use of the plural pronoun delivered yet another one.

"Us? You want us to help you?"

"John and James will follow me, for it was to harvest them that I came to this place. If you, Albert, follow me as well, you must be prepared to give up everything."

The evangelist blinked hard several times as if to douse the roaring in his head. Jesus had come to Beaufort specifically to gather disciples. That much he had from the Lord's own mouth. And whereas before he'd trolled the waters of Galilee for John and James, this time he'd known he'd find them in Beaufort Bay. Did that mean the Carew brothers actually had been those two fishermen, two of the first disciples? If so, the actual and true meaning of a born-again Christian was revealed: anyone who believed in the Son of Man was reintroduced into the world after death in order to go on spreading His Word. Literally born again.

How about himself? Had he, Albert Sales, invited to follow the Lord on His second ministry, lived in the first century, too? Someone had once told him that Albert was the modern version of Barnabas. And Barnabas of Antioch had taken the word of God to the Cypriots, earning the accolade of no less than John himself for bringing people to the Lord. But wasn't that what he'd been doing for the past twenty years, bringing people to the Lord?

Dazzled, befuddled, and wrapped in the embrace of a great wonder, Bert Sales groggily watched the Carew brothers get to their feet. They were bursting with a surging purpose and flexing their muscular bodies.

"Where to, Lord? Where do we go?" Jack Carew asked.

"A city," Yehsu replied. "Where many can hear."

"Atlanta!" Jimmy Carew said with quick triumph. "A million people there. A lot of 'em good Christian folk. It'd be a start."

His brother nodded enthusiastically. "Atlanta. Sure."

Yehsu's dark eyes contemplated the still-empty street. His gaze circled the area. Stopped on Jimmy Carew's handsome, glowing face. "James," he invited, bestowing something extra without emphasis, "you will lead the way."

It was Bert Sales's impression that his master was prepared to walk to Atlanta, just as he'd walked to Capernaum, Cana, Bethany, Jerusalem. But it was risky to do that in this country. Walking was the province of the poor and the dispossessed. They'd get pulled over by nosy cops before they got half a mile, and the evangelist had a strong idea that, far from embracing the Come Again Lord, and falling on their knees to kiss the ground he walked on, the grim-mouthed, closed-minded authorities would brand him a troublemaker, just as they had in His original ministry.

"I got an auto," Sales said to Jimmy Carew. "I better go get it."

The trip to Atlanta was made in an atmosphere of monastic silence and embarrassed discomfort.

The Carew brothers sat like blown-up photographs of themselves in the rear of Bert Sales's battered Cavalier wagon whose dark exhaust smoke signaled a bottomless petroleum thirst. Every time the car's owner would glance over his shoulder for a lane change, he'd sneak a quick look at the Carews in order to share the burden of the terrible responsibility he'd taken on. But they just stared back at him as if they, too, were struggling to know how to behave with the Son of God sitting in the front seat.

Sales had been torn between doing too little and not enough. With the temperature leveled off in the high eighties, he'd raised and lowered his window several times, worried whether his Lord was being pleasantly cooled or blatantly breeze-burnt. But his Lord gave no sign either way, sitting there with his eyes shut and his face composed in an expression of reconciled peace.

The evangelist twisted in frustration. Questions repeatedly erupted onto his tongue, which he kept a struggling prisoner behind clamped teeth. Sitting not twelve inches away from him were the answers to conundrums men and women had pondered for thousands of years, chief among which surely had to be, What does God look like? But perhaps the reply would be unintelligible to a mere human, Bert Sales conjectured. Maybe God was a microscopic thought being, or a globe of pure and cataclysmic light a hundred thousand miles in diameter. But whatever shape He took, why did He behave the way He did? If God was omnipotent, why did He allow plague and pestilence, drought and famine into His world? And what happened when you died? Were you united with your loved ones?

And how about the lesser questions? the evangelist wondered. How effective were prayers, for instance? Was it worthwhile to pray for rain? For health? For a Friday-night football win? Did God intercede when the Beaufort Gators played Immaculate Conception?

He slid another glance at his passenger, who appeared to be still communing with his Father, so he had no alternative but to go on wondering about the questions which had disturbed his rest for almost two score years. Although, creeping into the equation, as they went by the Decatur exit—just ten miles to Atlanta now— were queries more practical than metaphysical.

Where were they going to stay?

How were they going to eat?

The evangelist knew exactly how much he had in his wallet: a measly twelve dollars. And the Carew brothers, called suddenly away to Atlanta, wouldn't have much more. But surely such a mundane thing as sufficient funds would take care of itself. When people realized, when the citizens of Atlanta got it through their stunned and reeling heads that Jesus had returned, and was on their very doorstep, they'd be showered with money with which to spread the glorious news. Offered the finest accommodations. The costliest viands. All of which they'd turn down, of course. The evangelist was certain that Jesus would want to live as simply as he had during his first ministry. Jesus had abhorred wealth.

No, the problem was going to be one of superabundance; of finding unhurtful words to turn aside the limousines and the luxurious hotel suites that would be pressed on them.

Juggling these thoughts, the evangelist guided his ailing car off the interstate and into the busy downtown streets of the South's finest city.

From a distance Atlanta always put Bert Sales in mind of a bunch of tall poppies leaping up out of a flat plain. But the spot where Bert Sales pulled up had largely escaped the excesses of soaring steel and smoked glass. It was a section full of handsome, older buildings, an area popular with people like charity workers and glad-handing politicians. In fact, if the posters stuck around were any guide, one of the South's favorite sons had been through here recently on the stump. It seemed a good place to kick off the Lord's own reelection, particularly as they were almost right outside a very fine Episcopal church, which would help set the mood.

He got out of the car. Hurried around and opened the door for his passenger. "Lord . . . we're here, Lord."

Yehsu seemed to swim back into the earthly world, open his eyes on an unfamiliar country in an unfamiliar century. With no verbal response he got out and looked around him in a manner that made it impossible for Bert Sales to tell what he thought of these new surroundings. He didn't seem impressed, but then why should he? Sales asked himself. Did he expect the Lord Jesus to gawk like a tourist? Take a snapshot of St. Whatever with those fancy stone gewgaws running around its sun-ripened door?

The Carew brothers, looking nervous and uncomfortable, sidled up to the evangelist. The elder brother spoke out of just a piece of his mouth. "What do we do now?"

Grateful for a question to which he knew the answer, Bert Sales responded like an old pro. The sidewalk was his territory and he could work it better than just about anybody. "We get a crowd together. Warm 'em up. You two shill for me."

Jack Carew creased his heavy brow. "Do what?"

Bert Sales continued through the man's puzzlement: "Then we

let the Lord speak. Catch the fainting bodies, wait for the TV people to get here, and do it all over again for them. The rest will be history."

The brothers chewed that over, checked with each other, then nodded and fanned out. Bert Sales moved to the church steps. Yehsu was standing on the bottom one looking up at the monument to God, his opinion of it inscrutable.

Bert Sales approached him, murmured, "With your permission, Lord," and climbed two more steps, putting himself higher than his Revered One.

Sales turned. Faced the sidewalk which, this being the lunch hour, was beginning to fill up. He sucked in air and spoke from his diaphragm, a way he'd learned of projecting his voice. He'd done it a zillion times, but never in order to deliver the kind of message he had now. He realized how absurdly privileged he'd suddenly become: all those years insisting that Jesus would be back. He'd been dealing with the most elusive side of faith, the intangibles of belief; thin air supported by the flimsy veil of hope and confidence. Well, now he had living, breathing proof that what he'd preached was the absolute, untarnished truth.

This knowledge, and the understanding of his place in history as the first to publicly break the news, fired up the boilers in his chest, and his words came out as if shouted through a bullhorn. "Listen up, good people, and listen up good. Pull out your diaries. Pull out your calendars and mark the day, 'cause you'll never know another one like this one. Today's the day that's gonna change your lives forever. Change the world forever. For just as the world was never the same after Jesus was born in a manger, so shall this day be even more remarkable."

Several people paused. Bible thumpers were nothing new in Atlanta, and this one, a stumpy little guy in a Panama hat with dark patches at the underarms of his creased white shirt, was hardly an exciting visual. But the conviction of the promise he'd just made was unmistakable, and the light in his eyes was not that of the standard hysteric, but of a person who thought he had something different and of genuine magnitude to impart.

From the edge of this small ring of people Jimmy Carew, slipping easily into an unfamiliar role, cupped his hands and called out. "You know somethin' we don't, Reverend?"

"I do indeed, brother. And no man was ever more grateful and thankful for the opportunity to let you in on it."

Jack Carew understood what was required. "You wouldn't be from Beaufort, would you, Reverend?" He pronounced it "Bewfud," the way the natives did.

"I surely am, brother."

"I heard tell there was some kinda miracle took place down there."

Bert Sales was delighted with the Carews. With their big frames and broad, rugged faces, they were unsophisticated, salt-of-the-earth types that people felt comfortable with.

The crowd had begun to grow, the word *miracle* being a guaranteed draw. The evangelist had found that people were fascinated by the superhuman. Anything magic or unexplainable awoke tribal memories of sacred corn gods and profane tree spirits, and the mysterious powers of the witch doctor.

"You heard absolutely right, brother. And I'm here to tell you about that miracle. I'm here to tell you that a man with a gimpy left leg no more use to him than a stuffed owl was made good and whole and perfect in every way. And I know for a fact that that individual had never took a single painless step in all his born days."

"How about the second miracle?" Jimmy Carew called. "I heard tell there was two."

Bert Sales shot a finger at him. "That's a flat-out, indisputable fact, brother. How do I know that? Because the Reverend Bert Sales was a witness to that second miracle. Saw it with my own two eyes, plain as a pig in a palm tree, right there in front of me. A shrimp boat practically sinking under the weight of a record catch. And not five minutes before, that boat had been as empty as an Irish bar on election day."

"One guess who did it," came a different voice. "J.C. himself, right?"

Bert Sales was well used to being mocked; well used to the types that liked to get on his case, in this instance a spotty-faced college showboat in a jock jacket. Traditionally, if he wasn't backed up by at least three of his grinning collegiate buddies, then he had his date with him, as this one had, a giggling, vacuous young woman hanging on his sleeve whom he was trying to impress with his brilliant wit.

"You got it, brother," Sales assured him. "If you're referring to Jesus Christ, you have hit the proverbial nail on the head. Jesus did it, all right. But you know a funny thing? Nobody requested it. Nobody got down on their knees and prayed till their eyes bulged and they lost five pounds of flab. No, sir, Jesus did it all on his ownsome. And not from the boundless spaces of heaven. Uh-uh. If you're thinkin' he sent down a lightning bolt and, bingo, bango, bongo, the deed was done, I have fantastic news for you. I have news incredible but true. News sensational, amazing, and mind-boggling glorious. Are you ready for this, good people? He did it in person. Yes sir, he did it on the spot. That's the incredible, fabulous news I was referrin' to."

From his vantage position on the church steps Bert Sales enjoyed the sight of the crowd beginning to multiply. He was full of exhilaration now. He knew this would be the apogee of his life, his fleeting, mothlike place in the sun, the fifteen minutes of fame which was supposed to be accorded everyone in these hyped-up, media-run modern times.

"How about them miracles, Reverend?" Jack Carew called. "What did you mean about Jesus doing 'em in person?"

"Yeah, how about that, preacher man," the college kid snickered. "Were you standing next to him when he did it?"

It was the perfect lead, and the evangelist grabbed it. "I wasn't but twenty feet away from him, friend. And now I'm even closer. I am standing right next to him. All of you are standing right next to him right this very instant."

The crowd stirred, muttered its incomprehension. Waited for the punch line.

Bert Sales gave it to them in the biggest finish any public speaker ever had. "Better grab ahold of your neighbor, good people. Better hold on tight 'less you want to be set back and floored. You're not gonna believe it for a minute. I didn't. I was in a mind-swampin', leg-tremblin' shock. My blood stopped up and I couldn't feel a thing. But you're gonna feel something. You're gonna feel the rapture of the deep. You're gonna feel fear, love, awe, and, above all, a soul-floodin' ecstasy in about five seconds flat because, dear people, you're about to meet the Lever that lifts the world, the Eternal Emperor, the Elector of Truth, the Archduke of Glory, Lord of All Nations, and the first true gentleman that ever breathed. Ladies and gentlemen, I give you . . . the Lord Jesus Christ Returned."

Bert Sales made an extravagant sweep of his hand. The crowd looked at the man he was indicating. Most of them hadn't even noticed him, and those that had had dismissed him as just another Peachtree character. Now, when he was pointed out as Jesus Christ, the claim was met with scathing derision. This Mexican or Indian or whatever he was, standing there in a work shirt and a pair of Wal-Mart jeans, was supposed to be the Son of God back for a second visit? The crowd laughed. Some of them broke into sarcastic applause. The college kid stuck his fingers in his mouth and whistled. The Carew brothers tried to help by falling to their knees and crying out, "Jesus, Lord God," but it was counterproductive. The crowd had bought them as amiable hayseeds who'd asked the kind of questions that needed to be asked, but when they both went down wailing, they figured they were part of the act.

Bert Sales, and not his audience, was the one who was staggered; enveloped by a suffocating rush of near-palpable horror. They didn't believe him! Jesus Christ was standing there in full view, and they didn't believe it! What kind of dumb pagan morons were these people?

He snatched off his bent straw hat. Strode down the steps. Implored Yehsu from his knees. "Reveal yourself to them, Lord! Show these sacrilegious fools that you are Christ!"

Yehsu just looked at him, as unmoved and expressionless as ever.

Sales had expected the cruel rejection to evoke dismay and hurt and anger, but instead there was only this imperturbable composure on show, this benign serenity with which he viewed a world that, as he'd already explained, had sorely disappointed him. It was fruitless, the evangelist knew. His Lord was beyond an emotion as petty as revenge.

"Show them, Lord," Bert Sales appealed. "If you won't punish them, at least demonstrate your power."

Led by the college kid, the crowd took it up. "You heard him, Jesus, show us. Show us a real miracle."

"Get me two tickets to the Braves game," somebody called, producing some scattered laughter.

The Carew brothers were on their feet. With their mouths clenched, and their hands balled, they looked ready to severely discipline some of the jeering men.

Bert Sales got up from his knees. Swung around on his tormentors, the crow's-feet that tramped across his face etched in radiating anger. "You got eyes, use 'em! Look at his hands. Go ahead, look! You can see where the nails went in. Look at his forehead. The marks from the crown of thorns. I tell you, this is Jesus Christ come again—"

"Come again . . ." The college kid had his hand cupped to his ear in a pantomime of deafness.

Bert Sales rode furiously over him—"and if you can't see that, if you deny the Lord Jesus Our Savior, then you're just as hound-dog low as traitor Judas."

The fuming outburst was rewarded with ragged applause, then Jimmy Carew barged his way roughly through the crowd and appealed to the figure on the steps. "Show them, Lord. Give them a sign."

Yehsu moved for the first time. Slowly climbed two steps to a more elevated position. The grinning crowd shuffled forward a few inches, wanting to hear what this outrageous fake had to say for himself.

"I'm blind in one eye, Jesus," somebody called out, a man whose left eye was discolored and cloudy. "Got it shot out by a BB gun when I was a kid. How about restoring my full sight?" He looked around at the crowd, not only to let them see his handicap, but to enroll them in his smirking challenge.

"Do it, Lord!" Jimmy Carew said, biting down hard on the plea. "Give him his whole sight and show 'em!"

Yehsu turned away from his disciple, layered the dignity of his presence over the assembly. Many of them recognized an undercurrent of strength in his erect carriage, his dispassionate gaze.

They quietened.

Waited.

When he spoke Yehsu's voice had nothing of the elder Carew's beseechment, or Bert Sales's fiery oration, yet it carried a similar amplitude, and was marbled with surprising condemnation. "You ask for a sign. Are your minds so small, your eyes so jaundiced that only the spectacular can impress? I helped many suffering pain. Those having seizures, and the lame and the paralyzed and the demon-possessed did I rid of their afflictions. But these things were done through the miracle of God's boundless compassion. That is the real miracle. I did none of these things merely to demonstrate the power of my Heavenly Father which should be plain to whoever has eyes to view. For whoever is blind to God's omnipotence sees like this man here with only one orb."

The laughter that greeted the reply was of a different variety, either overly loud or subdued and uneasy. Some of the crowd guffawed out of confusion, some from embarrassment. The sincerity of the long-haired foreigner hung in the air like a physical force, and their reaction to it was easy to read: he clearly believed every word he'd said. He really did think he was Christ. He wasn't trying to fool them, he was just plain crazy.

They shifted on their feet. Began to leave, discomforted by the mentally disadvantaged. The raucous siren which suddenly wailed only sped them on their way, and they walked off looking back over their shoulders.

The siren, curtailed in midcry, announced the arrival of a cruiser, its urgent roof lights continuing to signal a dramatic danger. Two patrolmen, one black, one white, got bulkily out of the car. Both had paused for a moment to do the cop belt hitch, a little piece of body language that drew attention to their handcuffs, nightsticks, and sidearms, and the validity of their contract to use all three if need be.

"What's goin' down?" the black one asked. Having specified no particular respondent, he received no reply.

His partner zeroed in on the four swimmers in the reef that didn't belong. The juxtaposition of Bert Sales and the church steps, plus the stubby man's Southern evangelical dress code, tipped him off to the guy's business. There were ordinances against plying that kind of trade in this part of town. "How was the take,

bubba?" the policeman asked, allowing his mouth to host a knowing little curve. "They dig deep for you?"

Bert Sales was fond of telling his few pals that he'd had more
run-ins with the law than they'd had hot bowls of granola. He'd
learned how to handle cops: you had to be strong and indignant
because a servile attitude only expanded their sense of power. "I
never pass the hat," he snapped. "Never have, never will. He who
serves God for money will serve the devil for better wages."

The cop grunted. This was always the downside of rousting the
thumpers, they'd spit chapter and verse at you and turn you into
some kind of heathen Roman soldier. Unable to outmouth the
preacher, he let the law weigh in on his side. "How 'bout a little ID."

Bert Sales dug his wallet from a rear pocket. Whipped out his
Association of Southern Evangelists accreditation. The patrolman
examined it with a distrustful squint that precluded any mitigating
discovery.

"You from outta state, huh?"

"No law against that."

The cop offered the card back, holding it by one corner as if the
rest of it was soiled. "Maybe there oughta be," he said, and took
an inordinate amount of time running his flat eyes over the two
brooding hicks and the long-haired foreign-looking guy. "Okay,"
he said at last. "You on church property. Get your Carolina butts
outta here."

Bert Sales almost burst into flame, his breath catching at the colossal, stupefying indignity. So many words fought for precedence,
so many stinging phrases tumbled into his mouth vying for prior-
ity that, for a long, choking moment, he was incomprehensible.
"Have you . . . do you . . . do you know who you're asking to
leave Christian property? Have you any idea who . . . the one they
built this place for, that's all. The one they built all the churches
for all over the whole damn world. It's *his* property," he yelled, ar-
rowing his finger at Yehsu. "It belongs to *him*!"

The black cop rolled his eyes. "You wanna argue the toss, Reverend, we'll do it down the precinct house."

Jimmy Carew stepped up to the evangelist. Took his arm in a
firm grip. "Forget it. The last thing we want is trouble."

"Now there's a man of wisdom," the black cop declared.

With his neck pulsing, the nostrils of his squat nose flared, Bert Sales surrendered to the pressure on his elbow.

Jack Carew went toward Yehsu. Moved his head in a bob of fear and respect. "Sorry, Lord, but we'd better go now."

Yehsu yielded to the advice with an unchanged solemnity, and the four of them, under the bullying supervision of the two policemen, started walking.

Nobody followed.

Crushed beyond the powers of description, Bert Sales sat on the bed and cradled his face in his hands.

He'd never known such acute mortification, such spiraling depths of dismay. To be given the incredible honor of introducing the Lord to the world, an honor only previously granted the Gospelists themselves, and to have that opportunity founder on the rocks of ignorance and stupidity . . .

And the embarrassment hadn't stopped there. They'd had to get off the street or risk arrest, and without funds a hotel was out, as was any thought of sleeping in the wagon when they found that the car had been towed from its yellow-lined parking spot and impounded. So they'd been forced to accept the only thing left that promised them a meal and a bed.

Slumped in shattered rejection, Bert Sales took his hands from his face and stared at the linoleum between his shoes. It was a heel-marked green and black, popular for its ease of scrubbing. The walls had been painted earth brown but without first stripping away years of wallpaper. The evangelist looked around him, stopped on a window whose louvered shades splayed and drooped, each slat progressively out of sync with its neighbor. It was an apt metaphor for their awful predicament. To have had to come to such a place was loathsome enough, but to be forced to listen to a sermon as the price of admission . . . a well-intentioned man in a buttoned uniform telling them about Jesus stilling the waters. And right in front of him, right there in his reluctant audience of deadbeats, bums, and the just plain homeless, was the man-god who'd tamed those same unruly waves.

Jimmy Carew came over and sat down next to him. The big

man sorrowfully massaged his knees for a moment, his shaggy head moving back and forth in unison with his hands. "I been thinking," he announced. "We hit the streets tomorrow, we can't do what we done today."

Bert Sales knew all too well what they couldn't do; the question was, what was it they could do? "If the Lord would work a miracle in plain sight," he said, "that's all it'd take. But he won't. The same as he refused when he faced the crowd at Bethany. It's all there in the Gospels. He'll conjure up a miracle to heal a sickness or to save a life, but he won't turn it on for a parlor trick." Both men looked mournfully across the room. There'd been a ruckus ten minutes back, two skin-blotched winos brawling over some slight. The Carew brothers had broken it up, and now Yehsu was talking to the combatants, both of whom looked contrite and puzzled.

The other Carew brother wandered over, his hands stuck into the pockets of his jeans, his boots moodily scuffing the linoleum. He stood in front of the evangelist, his wide mouth making a pursed zero while he frowned over something. "I got an idea," he said. "We gotta bring in somebody else. Somebody who'll recognize Lord Jesus and be able to do somethin' about it."

His older brother looked and sounded short on tolerance. "What d'you mean?"

"Like," Jack explained, "we get somebody everybody'll listen to to come right out and swear that this is Jesus."

Bert Sales took another look at Jack Carew, his neutral focus replaced by increasing interest. "You mean an endorsement . . . that's not bad. That could play. But who do we get, and how do we know they'll recognize Jesus?"

Ten seconds into the silence that followed, Jimmy Carew got slowly up off the bed. The name he had in his mouth brought a glow to his skin and a shine to his eyes. "Don Bagley."

Bert Sales's tongue clicked in irritated doubt. "No way we'd get a guy like that. We'd never get in to see him, for a start."

"Yes, we will. We will because we have to."

The prediction was made with such iron confidence Bert Sales didn't try to argue. He reminded himself that Jesus had specifically chosen this man, and his brother, to follow him. Had sought them out on their unproductive trawler, so who was he to say that these slow-talking fishermen didn't have extraordinary hidden talents? But Don Bagley . . . that was asking for the moon.

The evangelist lay down to rest that night plaiting together a cat's cradle of sleep-stealing thoughts. Amid the ripe funk of kitchen odors, unwashed armpits, and booze-induced flatulence, he couldn't get rid of the idea that fate, if not God, had chosen him as Christ's messenger this go-round, and that the feathered wings of his sandals were limp, splayed, soaked, and broken. He tried to lock it out of his consciousness, but the worst-case scenario kept returning to leer at him in the fetid dark.

It was simply this: unless they got somebody with the status of a Don Bagley on their side, the second greatest event since the world began was in danger of being a total and colossal flop.

They found out Don Bagley's address next morning, and spent their remaining funds on a taxi.

The cab drove them out to the patrician suburb of Buckhead, and let them off in front of high wrought-iron gates.

Yehsu, who'd said nothing since before breakfast when he'd preached to a group of uneasy hostel indigents, broke his silence. He stared beyond the bars at the tree-filtered view of a sun-dappled mansion and said, "Someone lies ill in this house."

The Carews swiveled toward him but belayed any comment when a man carrying a cellular phone came out of a gatehouse and lazily offered his assistance. "Help you folks?" He wore a black satin bowling jacket which almost hid the gun on his hip. His manner was pleasant, but his eyes were a lot sharper than his tone, visually frisking the four of them.

"We want to see Reverend Bagley," Jimmy Carew said.

"He expecting you?"

"We gotta see him. We got some fantastic news for him."

The gate man rolled his impressive neck in a slow and negative fashion. "You need an appointment to see the Reverend. The number's listed. Give his secretary a buzz and take it from there, okay?"

Jimmy Carew dipped his head toward Yehsu, said fervently to

the guard, "You won't get into trouble. Not when he sees who we got with us."

The guard remained low-key and polite. "Look, it's not a good time now anyways. There's been an accident."

Bert Sales felt something cold and unnameable judder through him. The Lord had called it.

"Make an appointment. That's the best deal I can offer you." The guard gave them a consolatory lift of his heavy chin, then returned to his post.

"We gotta get in there," Jack Carew said to his brother, as if together they could shoulder their way through the thick iron bars.

Yehsu only had to move a few feet to reach the gates. He placed the unaligned fingers of his left hand near the heavy crosspiece that accommodated the lock and moved them in a gentle wave.

When Bert Sales heard a metallic click, and saw a half-inch gap of space appear between the gates, the tremulous cold feeling speared upward into his chest and harpooned his breath.

The two brothers reacted in tandem, their big bodies jolted, awe and trepidation flattening their faces. Then Jimmy Carew tore his gaze away from Yehsu and pushed at the right-side gate. Held it for Yehsu to go through onto the redbrick drive, his brother and Bert Sales following.

There was no shout from the guard; he had his back to them in the gate house and was fiddling with an electric kettle and jar of Nescafe. They were soon lost to him anyway courtesy of a bunched row of trimmed oleanders. Fifty feet farther on, the drive snaked left and the house, a Californian Tudor, opened up before them.

It was immense. Overpowering. Everything about it was too expansive, the push for grandness succeeding only in making the structure appear more like an exclusive country hotel than a home. The abode had been a bone of contention in the past, some of Don Bagley's detractors claiming that it was sinful for a man of God to surround himself with such conspicuous largesse, but the Reverend's defenders, who outnumbered the other side a thousand to one, had pointed out that it was an understandable reaction to growing up dirt poor on a scruffy Bibb County tomato farm.

This was true, at least the part about Bagley's impecunious

childhood. However, Don Bagley hadn't stayed poor for very long. He turned out to be a consummate salesman, a natural persuader of people, and had put this talent to work selling used cars. He ended up owning a string of GM dealerships and became a millionaire several times over.

Then one momentous evening he'd been talked into going to a tent show, had got up and gone forward and made a Decision for Jesus, and had come to believe that he'd been wasting his life. He'd promptly sold his businesses, attended a Texas Bible college, graduated with honors within a year, and returned to a small Baptist congregation in Atlanta, where he set about selling the comforts of heaven with the same infectious zeal he'd used to sell the comforts of a Cadillac. It wasn't long before his pulpit dynamics got him his own TV show, and he eventually became the darling of the Sunday morning tube, and the doyen of the television evangelists, with a following that numbered in the millions. So when Jimmy Carew had suggested that Don Bagley was the man to put the returned Lord on the map, anybody who knew the Southern religious scene would have agreed with him.

Up ahead the drive tunneled through a massive porte cochere, sun flares rebounding off the roofs of several automobiles parked nearby. The group moved toward the entrance, crossing a stretch of lawn mowed in a perfect checkerboard pattern. Jimmy Carew, who was in the lead, ignored the studded front door and moved under a row of blue-and-white canvas awnings which ballooned out over a cobbled patio. He paused at a stretch of long French windows opened wide to the heat of the morning, and peered in. The room the windows gave on was a shrine to the eighteenth century: dainty Hepplewhite settees, mirror-topped gaming tables, bulging boulle commodes. In the middle of all this resplendent clutter were two men. One of them, in a suit whose light pinstripes lengthened an insubstantial tallness, gazed down at the parquetry, his long face a pattern of distress.

Bert Sales recognized him: Howard Willard. Don Bagley's number two man. Beside him was someone he'd never seen before. Middle-aged, bald, and florid, he was speaking into a minirecorder. His tight voice floated out to the group on the patio . . . "Scalp lacerations and bleeding from the nose, suspected skull fracture.

Vital signs all negative. No pulse, no heartbeat. Fixed dilation of pupils. Time of death, ten-thirty-two."

He switched off the recorder and examined it for a moment as if wondering how something so neat and compact could contain words as tragic as the ones he'd just dictated. He slipped the device into his pocket and was starting toward a liquor cabinet, when Jimmy Carew's tentative entry stopped him.

He swung around. So did Howard Willard, who said, in mild surprise, "Who are you?"

Jimmy Carew moved one foot in front of the other without traveling. "We came to see the Reverend."

"Would you kindly leave, please?"

"If we could just see the Reverend for a minute . . ."

In two long strides Willard was by a phone. He picked it up. Punched two buttons. "Ralph, Reverend Willard. We have some intruders . . . I don't know, either." He replaced the phone and took an angry step toward the strangers. "The Reverend's not seeing anybody. His daughter just died. Please leave."

After a shocked moment Jimmy Carew began a garbled apology which he stifled when a third man appeared.

Bert Sales recognized this person, too, as the Carews did, and as half of America would have. The Reverend Don Bagley had become aptly named after he'd turned fifty, his waist expanding horizontally, his cheeks vertically. He walked into the room like a man suffering from degraded brain signals. He appeared to be struggling with a fact whose terms he understood but whose meaning escaped him. He registered his assistant and the doctor, registered the group by the French windows; seemed vaguely aware that he knew one group but not the other. "Who are they?" he asked, in a superficial replica of his famous basso delivery.

Howard Willard's snowy mane shook the intruders out of existence. "Nobody. Ralph's on his way."

And it was then that Yehsu, moving forward, called out two words: *Talitha koum!*

Bert Sales was rocked to his innermost core. His reaction sent an adrenaline charge racing beneath his skin, stiffening the hairs at the back of his neck. He knew from his years of Bible study that the language Yehsu had used was Aramaic, and that it was exactly the same command that Jesus had invoked in the house of Jairus, an elder of the synagogue, when he'd raised the man's daughter from the dead.

It meant, in English, "Little girl, I say to you, get up."

And, almost two thousand years later, the words seemed just as efficacious. Because, after a zinging, trembling interval of twenty seconds or so, a preteen girl wearing knee boots and riding pants, and with a smudge of blood beneath her nose, tottered unsteadily into the room with a terrible headache and a baffled expression on her flour white face.

CHAPTER

8

"So," Brian said, guiding Marie around a turning van that was trying to bully them out of their pedestrian rights, "do you still think Don Bagley's dull copy?"

Marie held her reply until they'd reached the sanctuary of the opposite sidewalk. "That was a huge surprise. It doesn't sound like his kind of stunt. He's never done anything nutty before."

Brian mock scolded her. "C'mon, be reasonable. Just because he claims that Jesus Christ brought his daughter back from the dead is hardly a reason to question his sanity. Not if you live in the South anyway."

"His doctor says the girl had no pulse. And Bagley's offsider, what's his name, Howard Willard, said he gave her CPR when he found her but she'd slipped away. She'd stopped breathing."

They went through double doors into the bustle of a Gristede's. Marie picked up a basket.

"People go into comas and recover," Brian said, following Marie down an aisle.

"But your vital signs are present in a coma, and the kid didn't have a heartbeat. Bagley's doctor's one of the best medics in Atlanta. He's on the board of the Centers for Disease Control. He's no quack."

"How about the Jesus character?" Brian asked, journeying lightly into mild sarcasm. "You figure he's a quack?"

Marie wagged her head in semiamused bafflement. "Why is it unthinkable that Jesus would appear anywhere else but America?"

"Because this is where the big book contracts are. You watch, he'll get one. *How I Became Christ and Found God*, by Brontislaw Jerkmeister."

"Let's not forget the *National Enquirer*," Marie reminded. " 'Constant Bible Study Turns Man into Jesus.' "

"Or the self-help market. *The Jesus Christ Fourteen-Day Miracle Diet.*"

Marie's mouth assumed the symmetry of a smile, but she curtailed it when she saw that Brian's comments carried something heavier than satire. She reached for a jar of leatherflower honey. Checked its price and placed it in her basket. "I think what bothers me most about the whole thing is not the fact that Jesus has come back, but that he chose Atlanta for his reappearance. Do you think the chamber of commerce bribed him?"

"Whether they did or not, it's working. They're streaming in from all over, according to the news."

They progressed to the end of the aisle, where Marie sank a metal scoop into a fat container of coffee beans. "What did you think of the photograph?"

Brian took a waxed-paper bag from a shelf, coaxed it open, and fixed it to the spout of a grinding machine. "Frankly, that's exactly how I always imagined Jesus to look."

"What did they teach you in the seminary about that? About how he looked?"

Brian delayed his answer in deference to the noise of pulverizing blades. It occurred to him that this was the second time Marie had mentioned his vocation directly, and she'd done it without any studious overstatement, as if his calling were no more special than that of a shoe salesman or a grocery clerk. And maybe it wasn't, he thought. Was being God's agent any more deserving than being the agent for Reebok or Sara Lee? Yes, was the answer to that if, as a priest, you could help people with their private and inimitable demons. No, if you were just a by-the-numbers Bible parrot dressed in basic black.

"A Semitic male in his midthirties. That's all we know. None of the Gospelists thought it was important to describe the man they wrote about, although only two of them ever saw him. It's always been a puzzle. Why didn't Matthew or John tell us what their man looked like?"

"Maybe they thought it best not to," Marie suggested. "Maybe they wanted to maintain some mystery."

"Maybe. Although some commentators think it could've been because Jesus was bald and dumpy with scrofulous skin."

"Hardly the figure you'd want on a crucifix," Marie agreed. "I assume that's who first made an image of Jesus, a wood-carver . . ."

"Undoubtedly. Then the medieval painters endorsed the long, slim, ascetic look, and anybody who painted him otherwise had a vindictive Church to deal with. Michelangelo gave him the body of a linebacker, and Pope Paul the Third read him the riot act."

"According to the reports Bagley's Jesus has the stigmata. Hands, feet, and forehead."

Brian's smile was a thin horizon of ridicule. "That's nothing new. There was a German sect in the fourteenth century that thought it was their duty to suffer as Christ did. So they arranged to be crucified. Some of them survived and walked around for the rest of their lives with their horrendous scars on show." He removed the bag from the grinding machine and carefully closed the top.

Marie was watching his face. "This guy, this fake . . . he upsets you, doesn't he?"

"It always upsets me when people are fooled. I don't like liars and I don't like cheats. I don't like anybody who trades on people's superstitions. Which is a curious thing for a priest to say."

"You can't despise him, Brian. You can't get angry at a crazy man."

"Bagley doesn't think he's crazy. And Willard doesn't think he's crazy. Bagley's church council have all met him, and they don't think he's crazy. They all swear he's Jesus. So I'd say it's Bagley and Willard and the church council who are crazy."

Marie took the coffee from him, tucked its fresh warmth into her basket, and moved toward the deli counter. "It's beyond me. Don Bagley isn't a hysteric. He's got nothing to do with the apocalypse-now brigade. I just can't feature him suddenly going 'round the bend and taking a whole bunch of sober church elders with him."

Brian mimed some heavy musing. "Hmmm . . . maybe this man *is* Jesus." They left the store, plunged once again into the snarl of traffic, and carried the groceries back to Marie's apartment.

"I'll tell you one thing," Brian volunteered, unpacking in the kitchen. "I'd love to get that guy alone for five minutes." He read Marie's surprised look and hurried to correct an assumption. "Oh, I wouldn't hurt him. I have strict standards; I don't hit drunks or biblical characters. But I'd love a private audience. I'd love to hear what Jesus did between the ages of twelve and thirty besides grow in wisdom and stature, as Luke has it. Did he have a normal adolescence? Did he go out with girls? Hang around the well with questionable acquaintances?"

When Marie remained silent Brian knew that his acrimony was making him look foolish. "Sorry. I don't usually get this peeved. But what's happening down south just makes my blood boil."

"Perfectly understandable," Marie allowed. "You've been teaching people about Jesus for a long time. An obvious fraud who's becoming accepted must stick in your craw."

"According to my bishop," Brian said, moodily, "I'm not qualified to teach people about Jesus."

"Is he right?" Marie asked fearlessly.

Brian shrugged. "That all depends which Jesus we're talking about."

Marie didn't pursue it any further. She put supper on the table, and they talked about other things.

They went out later, to a recital at the 92nd Street Y: a string quartet playing works by Chadwick and Amy Beach. Marie enjoyed it. And she knew Brian would have, too, but for the divisions spinning within him. Physically, he was with her in New York. Mentally, he was in Atlanta.

Or so she thought.

However, she was wrong about that.

Brian's mind was not in the sunny South, but the frozen Midwest.

In Conomahack, Wisconsin.

*   *   *

When he woke up, he saw that it had started again.

The snow.

It wasn't the kind that fluttered down prettily in miracle little flakes; the stuff wind-swirled viciously against the pane like a Dickensian ghost hammering to get in.

He got out of bed, slipped into the heavy Indian-knit cardigan that served as a dressing gown, switched on the underpowered space heater, and crossed to the side table where he'd set up a small altar.

He lit the candles. Knelt. Crossed himself. Began.

"Most holy and adorable Trinity, One God in three Persons, I praise you and give you thanks for all the favors you have bestowed on me. I offer you my whole being and, in particular, my thoughts, words, and—"

He stopped. That was a lie. His thoughts were on the icy streets he'd have to face for the afternoon calls. He began again. "My God, I firmly believe that you are one God in three divine Persons, Father, Son, and Holy Spirit; I believe that your divine Son became man and—"

That didn't feel right either, the operative word being *believe*. A touch too hypocritical, that one.

He crossed himself.

"In the name of the Father, and of the Son, and of the Holy Spirit, Amen."

He rose. Snuffed out the candles. Looked out at the tiny, subzero backyard. Some of the local kids had made a snowman out there the day before. It had been a welcome piece of bright fun for a while, but now the increasingly muscular wind was bullying the bulbous figure to its knees, sanding any shred of personality off its once-cheery face.

He took off the heavy cardigan, shucked his pajamas, went into the tiny bathroom, and got under the shower. Let the hot water comfort his neck muscles. Ease some nagging aches and ouches, the perpetual morning legacy of a lousy mattress. He slid a bar of Dial around his ribs, his underarms. Down his flanks. Around his crotch. And thought of Janeen Kruger, one of his parishioners, a pulchritudinous twenty-year-old. Whenever he called on her bedridden mother, Janeen would bring in the coffee wearing a T-shirt that had shrunk in the wash. And as she didn't believe in bras, her breasts led a life of jiggling freedom, swaying under her shirt as if applauding themselves for their splendid dimensions.

He looked down. Saw what his hand was doing and willed his fingers onto the cold shower faucet. The freezing water shocked his blood into retreat. Zeroed in his mind on the twin sensations of chill and discomfort.

He killed the water flow. Grabbed a towel. Vigorously dried off. Oversoaping of the Body. That's what it had been called when, as a confused and gangling youth of fifteen, he'd gone to Confession at Saint Agnes in Hartford, Connecticut, and crusty old Father Haines had threatened him with the ovens of Hell.

He'd come a lot closer to those ovens in later years. He and Nancy Hartog on an end-of-term vacation from Loyola, down there in Florida making love like savages on moonlit beaches.

A year later, nearing the end of his thesis on the political triumvirate of Galilee, Decapolis, and Judea, he'd quite suddenly given up the idea of teaching in favor of a different line of work. He'd become, in succeeding order, seminarian, novitiate, philosophy student, and, finally, a priest forever according to the Order of Melchizedek.

And since long before that day he'd had no intimate contact of any kind. Nine years without the tactile charge of feminine skin; without a woman's warm breath on his neck; without the grainy-silky, mind-wrenching suck and hold of a woman's sex.

Nine years. That certainly felt like forever.

He dressed in his priestly uniform. Fastened the reverse collar. Shrugged into a quilted ski parka. Pulled on overshoes. He left the house and bent into the freezing gusts as he crossed the street to the church. Let himself in. Winced, as he always did, at its drabness, the clerestory windows, swamped by a drab expanse of brown brick, too narrow to admit anything more than a pale, consumptive gloom.

He opened the valves in the clanky wall radiators. Went into the chilly sacristy and donned alb, stole, and chasuble. Prepared the offering, then waited for his tiny flock to straggle in.

By eight o'clock all that were coming that morning had arrived. Exactly nine people, eight women plus Carl Sheppard, who was mildly retarded. One of the women, Vera Bakke, the local parish watchdog, would have braved raging fire and swollen floodwaters to make mass. In the absence of the Holy Roman Curia she'd appointed herself guardian and overseer of Catholic correctness as expressed from the pulpit. Brian knew she loathed him; in her severe and unforgiving opinion he was a clear and dangerous liberal who was verging on being an out-and-out schismatic breakaway.

He ignored her stony stare and began the mass. Carl Sheppard handled the machine which projected the Opening Prayer on a screen rigged to the wall and, as usual, flubbed the change to the second slide.

After they'd struggled through the prayer he got Tina Kresge up to handle the First Reading, which she delivered in a stolid, Wisconsin monotone, and had Jane Smolinsky cover the Second Reading, her ill-fitting dentures lending Hebrews 13 a hissing sibilance.

He took them through the Psalm Response, moved on to the Alleluia and Gospel, then waited for them to settle back and fake attention before beginning the Homily, Vera Bakke watching him with an eye as fixed and terrible as the Ancient Mariner's.

Fifteen minutes later he wrapped up his sermon and, to foot-scraping relief, poured the wine and shredded the wafer for Communion. At the Elevation of the Host, when he touched the toe of his shoe to the foot button, there was no answering bell even though Joe Wilander had said he'd fixed it.

With the Communion Prayer completed the congregation listened to the final Blessing and Dismissal, then moved toward the coatracks at the door. Brian shook each person's hand as they left—except that of Vera Bakke, who vexed her teeth at him as she went by—then he was by himself again.

As always.

He locked up the church, went back to his chilly house, fixed himself a fast bowl of oatmeal, dug out his aged Crown Victoria, and started on his morning rounds, Brian Sheridan, God's missionary in deepest, whitest Wisconsin.

When he arrived back the phone was ringing.

It was Bishop Breen's secretary calling from Milwaukee. Calling to ask a favor: if the good father could interrupt his busy schedule and find some time soon to come and have a little chat with the bishop, his excellency would be most appreciative.

Which, translated, meant, Get your Irish ass over here now!

"Father Sheridan," the bishop said, the words emerging more as an indictment than a greeting. Ensconced behind the hulking statement of a Cedar Rapids partner's desk Bishop Breen who, with his fortresslike chest and massively square head, looked like a marble mason's clumsy attempt at a human bust, pointed to a chair. "Please be seated."

Knowing that this was not the kind of man who respected ceremony, the bishop did not extend his ringed finger as Brian approached. He could have demanded that tradition be followed but, preferring to keep his powder dry for a more telling broadside, he waived the ritual and let the priest get settled. But settled was the last thing Brian could ever be in the bishop's study; its somber confines always made him feel he'd been interred in some early-Christian burial chamber. The fumed oak walls pressed in, their funereal expanse unbroken but for a black framed papal blessing, and a hollow-ribbed Christ with a nerve-screaming face suffering horribly on a thick ebony cross. A paper-strewn refectory table held a jumble of books and church publications plus a row of volumes, the Acta Apolostolichae Sedis, the official documentation that Rome periodically sends out to all the senior toilers in its vast vineyards. But after this brief flurry of busyness, the room resumed its accreted air of gloomy sanctity and severe righteousness.

"I'm in receipt of another complaint, Father," the bishop said, in a voice like barrels rolling on concrete. "I'm told that while celebrating mass last Sunday, you transcended the bounds of good taste."

Brian knew instantly that Vera Bakke, sworn nemesis of scriptural deviation, had struck again. But, unwilling to make it easy for his superior, he opened his face and lifted his eyebrows as if this were extraordinary news. "Last Sunday? I'm surprised, Bishop. I can't think of any incident that could've upset anybody."

Again the barrels rolled. "Then perhaps you'd be good enough to cast your mind back to the Second Reading."

"The Second? It was from Revelation, if memory serves. John's vision of a son of man. Was that, perhaps, a touch too fanciful for some people?"

"The Gospels can never be too anything for a good Catholic," the bishop replied, slathering asperity on his words like a fat man buttering bread.

"I would have thought so, too, Bishop," Brian said, aware now that the thin ice he was skating on was rapidly beginning to thaw.

Breen's knuckly right hand slowly moved over the left sleeve of his cassock in something akin to a saloon fighter's gesture. He inclined forward in his thronelike chair, his simmering anger producing the faint echo of an Irish brogue. "It wasn't what was read out that was offensive. It was who did the readin'."

"I don't understand. It was Stu Thredboro who read. And he read very well."

"I'm not surprised he read well. He's had quite a bit of practice, has Mr. Thredboro. Quite a bit of practice readin' the Gospels, too. And givin' the Homily. You know that, don't you, or have I surprised you a second time?"

"I know that Stu Thredboro was a priest, yes."

"But you don't know," the bishop asked, testing the strain now that this tall slim trout had leapt so trustingly at his lure, "how he came to be an ex-priest, is that it?"

It was in Brian's mind to lie, but he knew if he did he'd salvage nothing from this meeting. "Stu's a friend. I know his story."

"Story?" There was no gap between Brian's last word and this same one from the bishop. "Oh, it's a story, all right. It would make fine lurid readin' in one of those mucky supermarket magazines. You knew his history yet you allowed the scoundrel into the holy sanctuary?" Breen thwacked the flat of his huge hand down onto the desktop. "An insult!" the bishop shouted. "You insulted the Holy Presence! A piece of trash like that, a man who dishonors the cloth, makes a mockery of his vows. A man who betrays our Lord not for silver but for bedsheets."

Brian was in a delicate position; he wanted to defend his friend but had to stay behind the red line of insolence. He kept his voice low and level. "May I point out, Bishop, that Thredboro married her. And is still married to her."

"Sure, he married her. But to do it he divorced God! He's to take no part in the holy celebration other than to pray, respond, and receive communion for the good of his benighted soul. Do I make myself clear?"

Brian made him wait a half beat longer than could be considered polite so that his obedient answer could carry a ghost of censure. Breen immediately picked up on the veiled slight and resented it, resented also the fact that, unlike all his other priests, this one refused to address him as My Lord or Excellency, insisting on the plain but unimpeachable use of his basic title. However, he curbed his desire to hurl another thunderbolt in favor of a light shower of acid rain.

"You're a well-read man, aren't you, Father? A biblical scholar, I believe. An intellectual with some curious opinions. A radical, in other words. Isn't that what some people would call you?"

"That would depend, Bishop, on who was doing the calling."

A derisive grunt from the bishop indicated that the parish priest could add sophistry to his numerous transgressions. "Tell me, Father," he said, in a transparently guileful mood switch, "what's your opinion of the Holy Father's recent encyclical?"

Brian knew from past visits that when Bishop Breen interrogated you it was a little like filling out a form on which the directive was displayed in large block letters: ANSWER ALL QUESTIONS.

"Morally correct, perhaps but—"

"Perhaps?"

"Morally correct, but impractical and inconsistent."

The bishop drove home his reply with three defined desk thumps. "The Holy Father's authority is God-given. If he chooses to be impractical, if he chooses to be inconsistent, he does so to preserve and nourish the Church."

"Bishop, in my humble opinion, the real issue is not to clarify moral teaching but to decide how best to do it. The present pontiff speaks to an authority based on unchallengeable doctrine backed up by the power of disciplinary measures. An alternative approach would stress free communication, the search for mutual understanding, and consensus. If Vatican Two achieved one thing, I'm sure you'll agree it was to legitimize this second approach. And that is the Holy Father's ultimate problem. As the Athenian poet

Agathon noted, 'One thing is denied even to God; to make undone that which has been done.' "

Bishop Breen sniggered his contempt. "And just when did this wonderfully clever Greek gentleman make this weighty pronouncement?"

"Late third century."

"BC?"

"Yes, Bishop."

"Exactly! Before Christ walked the earth. If he'd lived after Jesus, and knew his teachings, he would have known that nothing is denied God." The bishop's anger burst through at volume. "You're full of it, Father! Full of bald rhetoric and blatant self-esteem! You're guilty! Guilty of pride, vanity, and gross stupidity. Forget these lunatic ideas! They're a spiritual sickness. A sin against the Holy Spirit and a rejection of God!" Bishop Breen took a mucousy breath and subsided into pointed analogy. "I had a dog once. Used to chase cars. I beat that dog. Kicked him, thrashed him. But he went right on chasing wheels until, one day, he went under a Chevy and that was the end of him."

Brian remained silent.

"I'll pray for you, Father. I'll include you in my nightly petition on behalf of fools and sinners."

"Thank you, Bishop."

"All right. One more complaint and I'll have you washing bed linen at the hospice. Now get out of here."

"Yes, Bishop," Brian said, getting up. "Good-bye, Bishop."

He'd meant it.

Instead of driving north to Conomahack he'd driven southwest to Chicago. To a solid middle-class neighborhood and a graceful beaux arts red-stone house which some forgotten artisan had decorated with the airy intricacies of a birthday cake. The banistered stoop, a flowing cascade of stone, was now fancifully augmented by foot-long stalactites of ice, lending it a storybook look. The Good Witch of the South would live here, Brian thought, if she were visiting the frozen north; which she's smart enough not to do, he concluded, as a twenty-eight-degree gust tingled his ears.

Ringing the doorbell, he wondered what had prompted such an

inane piece of mind-wandering. A defensive mechanism? A desire to ignore the hurt and disappointment he was about to cause a guy who'd been nothing but kind and helpful and understanding?

The housekeeper let him in, a thin, smiling black woman who seemed to find his mere presence a shining spot in her day. She told him he was expected, took his coat and his overshoes, led him into an office-cum-library, announced him, then withdrew.

"Good afternoon, Monsignor," Brian said. "Have I your permission to approach?"

"As long as it's on your knees, Father," Monsignor Harold Chifley said.

Brian started to grin. "It will have to be. I have blisters on my hands."

They both laughed. Harold Chifley came around from behind his desk. Clasped Brian's palm in a double grip. "It's good to see you, Brian."

"You too, Harry."

"So what have you been doing with yourself?"

"Oh, you know," Brian said, casually, "pursuing chaos and disorder. And you?"

"Same old thing: screaming hysterical psalms of confusion and perdition." They chuckled again, welcoming the levity of their greeting as a quick icebreaker. Not that it was necessary; a difference in age and station had been a barrier to true friendship, but each felt a solid fondness for the other based on shared intellectual interests and a general agreement of what merited loud cheers or derisive pans in modern-day America. Harold Chifley had been Brian's adviser at the seminary, where their affinity had been formed; this came about in part because of a mutual love of the ancient world, and also because they recognized in each other a trusted ally, something of high value in an organization prone to behind-the-scenes maneuvering and up-front politicking. They corresponded from time to time, sending each other articles gleaned from learned publications, and had remained firm, if geographically distant, pals.

"Why don't we sit over here and watch pollution at its source," Chifley suggested, pointing to two Bergere chairs placed near a wood fire. The monsignor, who was wearing casual civilian clothes, hitched at his pants knees and sat down, Brian following his lead. They gave their get-together a moment to settle, that brief pause in a meeting that allows both parties to get a jump on any untoward surprise. At age fifty-eight Harry Chifley had had considerable practice at reading the little signs that people unwittingly give out and, because he knew Brian well, he recognized a man under pressure. He was pretty certain as to the source of the problem but was diplomatic enough not to press.

"You're such a snob," he accused. "It must be a year since you visited."

"Fourteen months," Brian corrected him.

When the older man nodded, an echo of firelight glowed briefly in the circular lenses of his granny glasses, which Monsignor Chifley claimed he wore so that people would think him a strict and brilliant Jesuit. Had that been true the glasses would have failed by half: the intelligence in his face was obvious, but there was no way he could have looked harsh or unforgiving. His features were gentle, molded rather than carved. And even the arrow-straight center parting in his hair, hair that had been the same shade of gray since his late forties, achieved an almost quaint barbershop-quartet effect rather than anything sternly institutional. He was one of those people who change little throughout their adult lives, just the normal loss of collagen giving crease lines a home on his forehead and a perch at the edges of his eyes.

He began a comment on nothing in particular but stopped when the smiling housekeeper came in. She set down a tray, then left accompanied by her employer's "Thank you, Pammy."

The monsignor offered a plate to his visitor, apologizing for the delicate little ham-and-cress sandwiches, which weren't much bigger than a matchbook. "I think she used to work in an English tea room," Chifley said, pouring coffee for Brian. He took some himself, then began to prattle at some length to allow Brian time to arrange an ordered delivery of whatever news he'd brought. "I just sent you a letter. Mailed it yesterday. I clipped an article by Treutcher on the dig at Ras Shamra. I'm not sure if you saw it, but he says that tablet they found is definitely northwest Semitic and could be part of Sanchuniathon's Mythology. If it is that could mean the Canaanites didn't—"

"I'm quitting, Harry."

Monsignor Chifley heard Brian quite clearly but interrupted only his conjecture regarding the people of ancient Palestine and not his reach to the tray. He cut his coffee with a little milk, spooned a few grains of sugar into his pretty blue-and-white Staffordshire cup, and waited for Brian to explain.

"I haven't told anyone else. I just found out about it myself. I wanted to tell you first because you were the one who—" Brian stopped to shuffle the sentence and redeal it. "I was going to say nursed my vocation along, but I'm not sure if that's what I had. Maybe I didn't want to be a priest. Maybe I just wanted the education of a priest."

The monsignor tasted the coffee, then made a repeat trip to the sugar bowl. Stirred the mixture as if great taste could only be gained if the swirl was of the correct speed and flow. "Well," he said, after an extended moment, "let me try one of these miniature offerings and make a few guesses here." He popped one of the infinitesimal sandwiches into his mouth, chewed briefly, and swallowed. Touched his lips with a linen napkin, replaced it on his lap, then spread the fingers of his left hand and began to tick them off. "One, you're lonely."

Brian looked at the flames in the fireplace; incandescent reds and yellows glowing with warmth. "You wouldn't believe how lonely. I know you're supposed to get a household pet, but I don't think I'd find 'woof woof' or 'meow' thought-provoking replies."

The monsignor progressed from his thumb to his index finger. "Two, you miss a woman in your bed."

"Right. If memory serves, they're even better than a life-sized rubber doll."

"Three, you find little stimulation where you're living."

"Oh, I don't know," Brian said, slipping deeper into an uncharacteristic bitterness. He hadn't complained to a single soul in years, and the resentment had built up in stifling layers. "The local library has lots of reference works on sewing and knitting. And for interesting companions there's a swell Friday-night fish fry at the American Legion post. Of course, you can always drive twenty miles to a country club, but they're not too crazy about anybody who isn't a fundamentalist Lutheran."

"Four," the monsignor said, unaffected by Brian's diatribe, "you don't like the weather."

"Ah, that. They should have a saying up there: if you don't like the weather, just wait eleven months. There's a fast spring and a summer so short it hardly comes up to your knees. Which is a shame because summer's when they hold the William Tell Pageant and the Song of Norway Festival, two events not to be missed. Then comes fall, and ten minutes later you're back to a two-toned, white-and-gray Siberia."

"Five, you don't get on with your bishop."

"If Bishop Breen had his way, I'd be burned at the stake as a liberal rationalist fiend."

"And six"—and here the monsignor stopped his countdown and rested his eyes on Brian's troubled face—"your faith is beginning to wobble."

Brian slumped his shoulders. Slowly dismounted from the disgruntled, high-kicking horse he'd been riding. "It was only a little wobble at first, but now it's so big I'm not sure I can correct it."

"Sure, you can. Look, Brian, when a man puts on the collar, sooner or later he starts to wonder whether or not he's made a big mistake. It happens to all of us. You just have to wait it out."

"But what do I do while I'm waiting? Hope for an epiphany? How long can I go on selling a product if I don't wholeheartedly endorse that product?"

"Do you endorse the Church?"

"Parts of it."

"Do you endorse Jesus?"

"The man or the god?" Brian asked, imagining the uproar if he'd given Bishop Breen the same reply.

"The man."

"I endorse his teachings. His message, sure."

"Then what are you worried about? He's the product. You should have no trouble selling him."

"And what do I do about his family? His inconvenient siblings who aren't supposed to have existed. And his mother. A woman the church fathers ignored for three hundred years, then suddenly turned into a goddess." Monsignor Chifley got out of his chair and prompted the fire with a brass poker, knocking the split logs into a more combustible pattern. Then, apparently happy with the rearranged flames, he regained his chair. Brian knew he'd used this bit of business to allow the discussion to shift to another level; a shortcut to get a lot of obvious things out of the way without having to express them. And he was proven right.

"The Church has changed, Brian. Not so long ago it would have been impossible to be a priest without accepting the tenets absolutely and without question. But that's not so anymore. By and large, we're now a social organization as much as a religious one. You no longer have to be a defender of the faith to minister to a flock."

"You do in my diocese."

Harold Chifley nodded in sympathy. "Bishop Breen. Immovable bulwark against creeping ecumenicalism. I know." He raised his hands an inch off the chair rests and let them fall of their own weight. "But he goes with the territory. I can't do anything about the bishop. And it's beyond my power to get you a parish in New York City, where you could hop over to the Forty-second Street library in your lunch hour."

"It's not a change of venue I'm looking for, Harry. I have to find myself a whole new life because I can't hack the old one."

"Because you're bored," the monsignor suggested. "Every day's a dish of pablum for you right now. I think you'd feel differently if you were challenged."

"Isn't boredom a challenge?" The monsignor had no reply. "Harry, everybody wants to be good at what they do. I want a chance to be good at something, too. And it won't happen as long as I'm in the ministry." Brian got to his feet with a movement that reflected his mood: slow, negative, undynamic. "I'll write the bishop, and do whatever other formalities are required."

Monsignor Chifley made no comment. He rose. Walked Brian out into the foyer, where he waved away the housekeeper, and helped his visitor into his overcoat himself. Brian, depressed at having let down a man he admired, sighed a little sigh and put out his hand. "I'm sorry about this, Harry."

Harry Chifley didn't accept the handshake but not, as Brian thought, because he was disgusted with him, but because he wasn't yet entirely out of ammunition. "I don't want you to quit,

Brian. The Church is sailing through some rough seas these days, and we need all hands to the pumps. So why don't you do this. Take some time off. Clear your mind, then have a rethink."

"It wouldn't work. I go to Florida for two weeks, I'll come back tanned and feeling worse than ever."

"Not two weeks," the monsignor said. "And it doesn't have to be Florida. I'm talking about twelve months. You're wading through some pretty deep ordure right now. It'll take a year for you to either think your way out of this and stay in the priesthood, or quit and know for sure that you're doing the right thing."

"A year," Brian said, blinking at the unexpected suddenness of the option.

The monsignor, an expert at timing, gave his friend a moment to consider.

"You could take whatever kind of job you wanted. Go where you like without anyone's permission. You could live in New York, California, or Europe or Asia for that matter. However," he continued, "you'd still be a priest. You couldn't celebrate mass, of course, or conduct any of the sacraments, but you'd still be bound by your vows and expected to keep them."

"A twelve-month furlough," Brian said, playing with it. "You wouldn't regard it as a cop-out?"

"Absolutely not. It's an accepted Church policy that's worked well in the past. It gives a guy time to get a handle on his life, and it can often save him from making a bum decision."

Brian spun the permutations. It was an exciting offer he was being made, a face-saver and a let-off all in one. A way of putting failure on the back burner, which was a very attractive alternative because it was the thought of flunking that rankled the most. What had he told a worried parishioner just last week? If we face up to failure, we grow and become better persons. What hogwash! You either had to escape failure or turn your back on it.

Or defer it for a year.

"Harry," Brian said. "I think you've got yourself a deal."

CHAPTER
9

With his blatantly red hair and skin so fair it looked stolen from a dead man, the last place Ludovisi should have been on a day like this was outdoors. But lately his superior, Father Cresta, preferred to meet in the garden, which might have seemed a curious choice for somebody whose major talent was the behind-the-scenes pulling of cruel and spiteful strings, a pursuit normally associated with dark back rooms and shadowy, ill-lit corridors.

Gaetano Cresta preferred the open air for a simple reason: twenty years ago the Secretariat had been found to be riddled with American and Russian listening devices, and ever since, all the offices and apartments had been scrupulously swept each week. It hadn't been enough, because just ten days previous another batch of bugs—this time of Japanese manufacture—had been discovered; the enclave appeared to have been infiltrated again.

Security swore everything was now good and tight, but, to be on the safe side, they were bringing in an expert from London for a second opinion. It would be a week before the man arrived, so, until then, Cresta wasn't taking any chances. He had a heavy suspicion that, this time, it wasn't foreign powers who were eavesdropping but somebody in the Curia, Cardinal Potolski perhaps, wanting to find out who was in which camp vis-à-vis the nonstop politicking that simmered in expectation of the Holy See becoming vacant.

Father Cresta was being understandably cautious; had even a whisper of his clandestine activities become known to his masters, he would have been defrocked and probably handed over to the Italian correctional authorities. Bearing no rank, a common foot soldier surrounded by a phalanx of generals, Father Cresta's position in the hierarchy was just not high enough for the cardinal secretary of state to look the other way.

Cresta knew this, but the knowledge didn't bother him. He was content as to his status, as well he might have been: an appointment to Rome was the ultimate accolade for any priest, and he'd grabbed his chance and done extremely well. Starting as a simple clerk in the CDW, the Congregation for Divine Worship, his exemplary devoutness and unquestioning obedience had advanced him to his present position of secretary to Cardinal Liegi, who was not only high on his list of papabile candidates but headed up the Congregation for the Doctrine of the Faith, the most powerful dicastery of them all.

That Cresta had, at age thirty-five—twenty-two years ago now—been appointed to this particular department was no surprise to anybody who knew anything about his history. Even as an adolescent he'd exhibited a fervid attraction to the Church and its teachings, an attraction which, later in life, after ordination into the priesthood, had become a slurry of devotion that had gradually hardened into total intolerance of any kind of deviation from the teaching as expounded by His Holiness through Divine Revelation. Anything else was anathema, and was to be put down with all possible speed.

His razor-wire mind, his acerbically brilliant letters to L'Avvenire and Il Sabato defending the Church and its glorious history, its resplendent present, and its sparkling future, had not gone unnoticed by the Curia, which had brought him in behind the high stone walls of the Città del Vaticano where he could use his watchdog talents on a global scale.

However, had they known the truth, these apostolic overseers would have been shocked at some of the methods the cardinal's secretary used, and dismayed that the priest remained morally undisturbed by the consequences of his actions. For Gaetano Cresta, the end—the preservation of Holy Mother Church, and the swift correction of all statements that derided Her—justified the means, no matter how extreme.

"Good morning, Father," Ludovisi said, trying not to squint in the brutal glare that hammered the clipped and ordered lawns. He was from Liguria, where the light rained down from a softer sky.

"I trust you slept well," Cresta replied, a hope not reflected in the economical azimuth of his thin-lipped mouth.

His junior caught the brittle note of censure—he was perhaps two minutes late for this meeting, but, in Father Cresta's book, that was 120 seconds wasted. "I'm sorry, Father. There was a problem with the breakfast staff."

"Breakfast," Cresta repeated, as if eating were a mere frivolity. Indeed, a superstitious person might have suspected that the man's gaunt figure was the result of nightly vampiric visits rather than careless nutrition. At any rate, there was enough silver in his brushed-back hair to frustrate the hungriest vampire.

"What news do you bring me, Father? How goes the Faith today?" Cresta asked, frowning as they passed the Casina, Pius IV's playful little pink-stucco folly. In Cresta's view, the Città's palaces should have presented an aura of strength and permanence to the world, not this chocolate-box flummery. Ludovisi agreed with him about that, but then Ludovisi agreed with Cresta about everything. It was one of the three reasons why Cresta had made him his assistant, confidant, and sounding board. The other two reasons were, one, the Ligurian put the defense of the Faith ahead of any prissy ideas of temporal legal restraint; and, two, having worked for some years at the IOR, the Vatican bank, and smuggled out a list of computer passwords and international account numbers, he had the ability to tap into an anonymous and little-used slush fund the Vatican maintained in Austria, and thus finance Cresta's numerous little schemes and paybacks.

"We have a small problem," Ludovisi answered, "Father Laluma is being obstreperous again."

"Laluma . . ." Cresta crunched the name in his mouth like a bitter pill.

"He's threatening to set up something called the Imani African Catholic Congress."

"Imani?"

"I believe it's Swahili for faith."

"Faith? What would that fool know about faith? Does he have faith in the expressed wishes of the cardinal prefect? Does he have faith in the holy sacraments that have been given us by the Lord Jesus Christ himself?"

The two priests strolled toward the cool greenery of a thick stand of umbrella pines which bordered the quartered grass, a baroque fountain gurgling at the confluence of the lawn's neat rivers of red paving. Strolling was not Father Cresta's style, his regular pace being as swift as his boiling tide of thought, but an outward image of decorum had to be maintained; those tourists standing on the terrace of the Capella Sistina, dazed from viewing walls and ceilings of appalling genius, must only see two religious deep in the appreciation of the Lord's chlorophyll wonders.

"He claims it's a question of symbolism," Ludovisi explained. "That bread and wine are not in common use in equatorial Africa."

"What would he have?" Cresta flung the words from him. "Cold snake and coconut milk?" The priest focused his contempt on the ugly brick pile of the Città's radio station. It looked like a spoof of the baroque splendor of the basilica which owned the immediate skyline. "Is this man in Rome?" he asked after a minute.

"He arrived yesterday. He's staying at a small hotel in the Campo."

"The Campo . . . how appropriate for an insolent churl."

Ludovisi caught the reference: Giordano Bruno, a contemporary of Galileo, and a derider of Christian ethics, had been burnt at the stake in the Campo dei Fiori, his tongue in a symbolic gag.

"Very well," Cresta said, his eyes tight enough to be laced. "He'll no doubt go to see Bishop Oudan first, to cry on his shoulder. After Laluma leaves, slip into Oudan's office. He has a jeweled crucifix on his desk, if I remember rightly. Take it, then get into Laluma's room and put it in his suitcase. The police will act on an anonymous tip and find it there."

"Laluma gets a choice, either conform or we press charges. Excellent, Father."

Cresta shook his head like a man bothered by an insect. "No. We don't give him a choice. He's had his chance. We press charges and see that he's convicted. Eighteen months in a Roman jail should cool his revolutionary ardor, wouldn't you say?"

Ludovisi's smile energized his face; the man he worked for was a genius.

Cresta stopped walking. Turned slowly in the sun to survey these bucolic surrounds, the lazy, lawn-bordered streets empty except for the half-hourly passage of a packed tourist bus or an occasional maintenance vehicle. It all looked so innocent and containable: just over one hundred acres populated by just over one thousand people, most of whom were priests and nuns known by sight to Central Security, and yet the enclave had proven vulnerable again.

"We are under attack, Father," Cresta said to his assistant. "At home and abroad."

Ludovisi knew about the home front—the discovery of the listening devices—but wasn't certain which foreign shore his superior was referring to.

Cresta enlightened him. "America."

"The redemptorist priest in Los Angeles?"

"No. I'm talking about that abomination in Atlanta. That wretch who has the hide to claim he is Christ returned."

Ludovisi was placatory; sometimes his superior saw menace where none existed. "I don't think we need concern ourselves, Father. This man is just a brief candle. You know how it is in America, a headliner today, a has-been tomorrow."

"He is a *blasphemer*!" Cresta hissed. His voice sounded like beach pebbles raked by a violent wave. "His impersonation mocks Christ. And when you mock Christ, you mock Holy Mother Church, the Church which he began."

"I agree, of course, Father. It is a rude and vulgar thing he is doing, but—"

"Rude? It's *scandalous*! This blackguard, this carnival trickster, has satirized two of Christ's greatest miracles, the miraculous catch of fish, and the raising of Jairus's daughter. That's a direct slap in the face. He is jeering at Christianity. And as the Faith is the heart, soul, and backbone of Christianity, his profanity *defames* the Faith."

Ludovisi wondered how best to ease his superior's fears. The fair-haired priest knew America. Had spent quite some time there.

"If I may make a point, Father, I understand your anger, but not your fear. America is a country of fad and fashion. This impostor has probably already been overtaken by the next sensation." Ludovisi allowed his mouth the smallest of smiles. "An extraterrestrial, perhaps. Or a man claiming to be the devil."

"And how do you know *this* man isn't the devil? Doesn't it smack of the Antichrist when a man disguises himself as the Lord, and replicates two of his miracles?"

"A madman or a fool, Father, who will have his time in the sun. But surely nothing deeper than that."

Cresta compressed his narrow jaw. "I do not share your lack of concern, Father. A parishioner in Atlanta, an Italian American member of Catholics United for the Faith, faxed me a report this morning. The child that they claim was revived is the daughter of a Baptist preacher. And this preacher has a television ministry, with a vast audience. If he puts that profane knave on television, his blasphemy will be repeated on millions of picture tubes. It won't be just a case of a mention in a newspaper, with perhaps a small photograph. His loathsome satire of Jesus Christ will be broadcast into millions of homes."

"Oh . . ." A shadow darkened the younger man's face. "In that case, I understand your worry, Father. If Christ is going to be insulted on what would amount to a large scale, we can't stand idly by."

"No, we cannot," Cresta confirmed, through barely parted teeth. "We will monitor this fraud closely, Father. And if he does not vanish from the scene promptly and permanently . . ."— Cresta paused to give the last of his sentence the weight it deserved—"we'll see to it that he does."

CHAPTER
10

Nothing was moving.

Nothing could.

Atlanta was virtually shut down, strangled by the very highways which were supposed to evacuate the populace in times of major disaster. Interstate 285, a loose lasso around the city, flowed easily and efficiently in normal times, diverting traffic away from the metropolitan area and sending it on its way in seven different directions. It was now bulging from shoulder to shoulder, jammed for its entire circumference, its entrance and exit ramps locked up with cars and trucks, pickups and vans and campers that could go neither forward, backward, nor sideways. The major spokes of this wheel, all of which more or less converged on the downtown area, unloaded an intolerable burden on the minor spokes, which weren't designed for an influx of such magnitude, and so broke down into a confused madness of useless traffic lights and blaring horns.

During the nine-hour period in which this stasis was at its most trying, legions of trapped motorists were unable to answer a clawing hunger normally satisfied by the carnivorous joys of a Big Mac, and helpless to quench a thirst usually attentuated by a giant-sized Coke. Stranded between gas stations, they were discomforted by the absence of candy-bar counters and loaned restroom keys. But most galling of all was the forced abbreviation of a journey they'd been convinced would be the most important they'd ever undertaken.

The most maddening thing for the authorities was that the destination of 80 percent of these motorists wasn't Atlanta at all, but a two-thousand-acre farm out near Stone Mountain almost twenty miles east of the Civic Center. Because it was there that the returned Jesus Christ was due to make his first announced public appearance under the aegis of the Reverend Don Bagley.

When the evangelist's daughter, declared dead by a man who could boast thirty years' medical experience, had walked unsteadily into her father's overstuffed living room, Don Bagley had lurched back as though caught by a green Atlantic roller. His limbs shook, and his breathing became a glottal scrape, his every cell invaded by an unnameable terror. Like Bert Sales, he too knew what the Aramaic phrase *Talitha koum* meant. He dragged his saucered eyes away from his daughter and stared at the stranger, his tortured hands, his scarred forehead, the depth and tranquility in his sad, dark eyes. When Jack Carew, as shaken and ashen-faced as his brother, dropped to his knees and cried, "Thank you, Lord Jesus," not to the ceiling but to the stranger, Don Bagley stumbled forward to embrace his child partly, it was Bert Sales's guess, to keep from falling down in a tongue-lolling faint.

During the next several minutes, augmented by enthusiastic verifications from the Carews, Bert Sales took advantage of Bagley's numb stupor to fill him in on the events predating their marvelously timed arrival: how Jesus had come to Beaufort, what he'd done there, why they'd come to Atlanta, their failure there, and why they needed the South's most famous TV evangelist to announce the Second Coming.

The Reverend Bagley lowered his corpulent frame into a delicate Louis Quatorze chair, cradled his whimpering daughter on his lap, and listened to the history, all the while casting fearful glances in the direction of the miracle worker who had left the room to seek the cool shade of a garden elm.

Bagley kept swallowing and breathing noisily as his mind labored with the clash of what he'd witnessed and his faith in the undiminishable correctness of his Bible. He ran a confused hand over his thinning hair and said over and over, "I hear what you're saying. I hear you. But it can't be Jesus. It can't be. That'd mean the Gospels got it all wrong."

"That's what I thought," Bert Sales told him, thrilled to be instructing such a famous celebrity. "But then I had another think. The Synoptics say the Lord will return in glory. Well, and so he did. Some Mexican shepherds up there in the Tennessee hills saw it close up. And a whole raft of people south of Knoxville saw the heavens on fire. It was in all the papers. And every last dang one of those God-fearing folk swore the sky was lit up like a fiery rainbow from end to end, just like it says in the Good Book. The Mexicans said Jesus just kinda floated down and landed soft as a soap bubble. They couldn't tell if he was ten miles away or a hundred yards. They was too scared."

"I read about that," Howard Willard said, looking up at the repeatedly blinking eyes of the doctor. The medic was checking the snuffling little girl's pulse as if expecting her reprieve to be a very short one. "But I figured it was just one more sighting," Willard concluded, as if they were discussing UFOs.

"So did we," Jimmy Carew said. "But when Jesus magicked up a hold full of shrimp, and called for us to follow him, why then, we just knew in our hearts he was the real McCoy." His younger brother, eyes shining with purpose, nodded vigorously.

The Reverend Bagley struggled with the contestable circumstances. "But the Gospels say everybody in the whole world will see the Second Coming. Why just a handful of Mexican shepherds?"

Bert Sales's squared-off shoulders rose a notch and fell again. "God's ways aren't ours, Reverend. But I'm sure I don't have to tell you that it was shepherds that were the first to worship the infant Jesus. Maybe he wanted to pay back the compliment."

Don Bagley shot another look at the calm, still figure beneath the elm tree, battled with a dozen questions, then settled for the one that bothered him most. "But why America? Why not Jerusalem?"

"I asked him that." Bert Sales paused to savor the dizzying feeling that came with being a confidant of Jesus Christ Himself. "You know what he told me? He said he returned to teach his message again because it weren't learned the first time. And he's come to

America because this here country is where his message is most understood but least acted upon. His very words."

An expanding vindication made Bagley's broad face broader still. "That's exactly what I've said all along. What I've preached all along. So many Christians and so few Christian acts."

"You got it, Reverend. We all knew Jesus was gonna return sooner or later, and now that he has, doesn't it make sense that he'd come back to the biggest Christian country in the world?"

Seeing the logic of that, the famous evangelist nodded cautiously. "I guess . . ."

"I just can't credit it," Howard Willard said. His full white hair swayed with his tall extremities, his lengthy head oscillating in a repeated negative. "Little Julie must've just been in a deep faint or something."

"She was dead." It was the doctor who'd spoken, with very little volume. "Not just heart dead, brain dead. And now she's alive. Medically, that's impossible."

"You gotta believe, Reverends," Bert Sales said, addressing both ministers. "Believe and rejoice." He slid easily into his sidewalk persona. "Reverend Bagley, sir, how many times have I sat enthralled in front of the TV set watching your fine program and heard you say that? You gotta take your own advice now. You gotta praise God not only for sending His son again, but for sending him to America. I mean, not that He would've, but what if He'd sent him to Italy? The Catholics would never have stopped crowing."

A look of quick repugnance invaded Bagley's doubtful expression as he imagined the taunts and the imprecations, the unbearable embarrassment.

"And you gotta rejoice, Reverend," Bert Sales said, completing his double-sided point, "because not only did the Deity send Jesus to America, He sent him to the Southern states of America, where the Lord God knew Jesus would get the most fervent reception and be treated to some traditional Southern hospitality, although he sure ain't had much of that yet."

This last statement jogged the house owner into realizing that, whoever that uninvited person was out there on his lawn, and whatever miraculous deed he may or may not have done, he was being ignored.

Don Bagley kissed his recovering daughter, hugged her one more time, then handed her over to his doctor. He rose, tested his legs, and walked with only a minimum amount of unsteadiness across the glowing parquetry and out into the garden. His lieutenant followed him.

Bert Sales and the Carew brothers went as far as the French doors, watched the evangelists move out into the warmth of the morning, cross the clipped grass, and stop a respectful distance away from Yehsu. Watched the miracle worker, gently dappled by the shade tree, open his eyes, and survey this interruption with not the slightest hint of annoyance or discomfort. They saw the gate guard, in his shiny black bowling jacket, strolling tardily around the bend in the drive as if he didn't believe that somebody had got by him.

They were too far away to catch what Bagley said to Yehsu, although it looked to Bert Sales as if the preacher might be stammering his thanks. He wondered what you said to somebody who'd rescued a loved one from the grave; wondered why Bagley wasn't on his knees instead of standing there with a delicate and uncertain look on his face.

He watched Yehsu reply with that placid, all-consuming dignity, a being that even the most hardened skeptic could see was driven by the soft breath of God, yet the TV minister, who'd just been given his daughter back, was almost scowling.

Bert Sales swapped a look with Jimmy Carew, turned all the way around to check with the doctor. The man was torn between watching the meeting on the lawn and observing his young patient squinting into the bright pain of a thumping headache.

Sales looked back at Jimmy Carew, who was riveted to the events in the garden. His eyes had crinkled in baffled disappointment. "He don't believe it," he said of Don Bagley. "He's gonna deny Jesus, like Peter done."

"What more proof does the man want?" his brother asked in anguish.

Out in the hot buzz of the garden a brass lawn sprinkler, designed to quench the thirst of a country-club putting green, plopped a controlled hail of water onto the roots of the elm under which Bagley and Willard stood before Yehsu.

For Don Bagley it was like living the opening lines of an immortal novel: it was the best of times—daring to hope that everlasting glory was his; that he was actually in the presence of the Lord Jesus Christ—and the worst of times—afraid that it would turn out to be an hallucinatory fantasy. Half of him screamed it had to be Jesus. No ordinary human could revive a dead person just by saying a few words in an ancient language. Nobody could do that trick except maybe an expertly trained hospital team working furiously with million-volt electrical gear. His other half said that it couldn't possibly be Jesus because when the Messiah returns, everything in the entire world would be superfluous and would come to an instant stop. But the world had taken no notice. The sun was still on course in a bright blue sky, the birds still chased an insect lunch, and that water sprinkler was still running its lazy, circular route as if the health of a stretch of grass mattered. Nothing had changed one whit, so how could this be Jesus returned?

Bagley glanced at Howard Willard, a monument to frightened uncertainty, then, settling his hesitant gaze on Yehsu, was overwhelmed by the quiet power and stateliness of the man's presence. His composed serenity was like marble come to life. Close up he took in the dark forehead racked by cruel shallow gashes, the deep, wounded eyes, the severely punished hands, their slim fingers curled around an echo of agony. If seeing was believing, this was the risen Christ healed.

Bagley began speaking while he still had voice and nerve. "Forgive me. Forgive me for asking this. But . . . how can I know? How can I know that you are Jesus?"

He listened to the reply spoken in the compelling rhythms of a liquid accent. "There is no knowing. Only believing."

"I want to believe. With all my heart and soul, I want to believe that you are Christ. But how can I be sure?"

"Your daughter lives."

Bagley dropped his chin onto his barrel chest, his eyes weighed down by acute embarrassment. "The doctor said she was dead. It's possible he made a mistake."

"Shall I undo what I have done?"

"No!"

"Examine your response," Yehsu invited. "Immediate, and with alarm in your voice. Would it have been so if you doubted?"

The sun, traveling an apparent half inch, breached a gap in the leafy cover and drilled a flash of UV rays into Don Bagley's exposed scalp. His big body squirmed as if the thin derma of his tonsure had been painfully penetrated. "I have to have proof. I need a sign. Something that'll convince me beyond the slightest doubt."

Yehsu, a stranger to gesticulation, remained within the seal of his indigenous calm. Yet, to the evangelist, he seemed able to change the mood of his answers with fine shades of difference in his eyes, a subtle expansion or contraction deep within those obsidian orbs which was as readable as a flashing smile or a tearful frown.

"Only yesterday a crowd asked me to show them a miracle," Yehsu said. "When I refused, they mocked me. You are more to be pitied than they. You were witness to a miracle, and yet you, too, mock with your doubt."

Bagley gasped at being so labeled, and scrambled to explain his torturous dilemma. "I have to know for sure. I want to be able to tell millions of people to cry hallelujah because Jesus has returned. But I can't do that if it's not true. I have to know it's true."

"You have the power to address the multitude? The means to do this?"

Bagley surged forward in affirmation. "I have a television ministry. I can reach out into eyes and ears and hearts and souls. They say that Jesus didn't preach to more than thirty thousand people in his entire life, total. If you really are him, and you've come back to preach universal love again . . ." Bagley paused for a moment, then continued with a hot splurge of sudden trust. "You could reach a million times that many." He stopped speaking, his mind jamming his tongue. If this was Jesus returned as man, returned to the world the same in body and mind as he'd left it almost two thousand years ago, then he'd be ignorant of twentieth-century inventions. But wouldn't God make him a modern man, with all the knowledge of a modern person? The question answered itself: not if God wanted His son to begin his second ministry in the kind of humble circumstances he'd arranged for him the first time. In that case, He'd send him back to the world as he'd left it so that people would be sure to recognize him. The question was, had He? Was this the Christ standing here sheltering from the hot Georgian sun, or just an ersatz, look-alike fraud?

"You are correct," the object of his anguished speculations said. "To preach God's love is the reason why I have returned."

"Then show me," Bagley implored. "I don't ask for myself. I ask on behalf of millions of Christians."

Howard Willard stepped forward, his long height broadcasting truculent fear. He stooped and picked up two rocks from around the roots of the elm, thrust them at Yehsu, and dramatically borrowed from the Gospels. "If you are the Son of God, tell these stones to become bread."

Yehsu took the rocks but kept his gaze on the evangelists.

A hard voice intruded. "I'm sorry, Reverends." The gate man was walking up, a determined purpose in his stride now. "I don't know where—" The words spilled from his mouth as his jaw looped. "It's the long-haired guy . . . How the hell did he get in? The gate's on automatic."

Bagley straight-armed the air behind him and turned to hush the man's puzzlement. He heard Willard's grunted cry, a sound like that of a man taking a bullet in the gut, and swiveled back.

Yehsu was holding, in his outstretched hands, not two lumpy rocks, but two plain round bread rolls.

There was no way the Reverend Don Bagley would ever completely recover from the events he'd witnessed in his overindulged living room and his trimmed garden. It wasn't like the occasional polarities of life, a personal disaster or an instance of great joy which, as the earth loops through its planetary path, gradually lose their ability to wound or excite. His allotted time frame on the planet was indelibly altered but, catering to his own sanity and relative peace of mind, he found a way to come to terms with what had happened.

The arrangement he made with himself was one of bland and unquestioning acceptance, a self-induced understanding that he'd won some kind of universal, two-thousand-year-old lottery in which the grand prize was of unparalleled worth. He'd been selected not just to be alive during the Second Advent, but to be a principal player. Selected, not "chosen," the way he understood the Carew brothers to be chosen. He refused to regard himself as in any way special. He refused to speculate whether it was fate, chance, or the divine hand of the Almighty that had placed him in this exalted position. It was enough, in his thinking, to serve as the instrument through which the Parousia would be announced to the world without awarding himself an exalted spot in history. Don Bagley, for all his riches, was truly a humble man.

And a practical one.

If it was his job to present Jesus Returned, he reasoned, then he would do it the best way he knew how. So it was toward this end that he liaised with Bert Sales and the Carew brothers to outline what he had in mind.

This happened in the week following what Bert Sales called the Day of the Triple Miracle. He and the Carews had been invited to stay at the house. Yehsu was offered one entire wing, which he turned down in favor of a small guest bungalow that backed onto the garden in which he spent most of his time meditating and praying. Although impatient to begin his ministry, he'd been persuaded that America was too jaded and cynical to accept him on his own say-so, and that, as Jack Carew had rightly surmised, he'd have to be endorsed before Christians would accept that what they'd been brought up to believe would one day happen had indeed happened.

After shutting himself away in his study, where he'd spent intense and solid hours shuffling the options, Don Bagley had emerged a day later and held a meeting with Howard Willard and the three disciples. He'd told them that he'd made some decisions. Firstly, he regretted letting the news get out—his house was now surrounded night and day by hundreds of rapacious media folk and thousands of clammering Christians who constantly overflowed the police barricades—but, seeing the news had become public knowledge, he'd decided that none of them would grant any interviews to anyone—he'd had all the telephones disconnected after the first few hours—and that he'd announce the event officially on his Sunday TV show. And, second—and this was a real surprise—he wasn't going to introduce the Lord Returned at that time. To do that, he felt, while certainly taking advantage of modern technology, would also drain away the maximum impact and natural glory of the Return. Christ would be seen as a one-dimensional figure flickering on a lot of beat-up and badly tuned TV sets, a medium that would have to do for later in His ministry but was inadequate and inappropriate for His first appearance. A Jesus so presented would lack credibility, and credibility had to be the primary objective when you were going to be contending with massive doubt.

Bagley therefore suggested that he simply announce the Second Coming on his show, without presenting the visual truth of the claim, and invite the members of his far-flung audience to come and see the Lord for themselves several days later. To come and see the Lord Jesus Christ in the damaged flesh. To listen to the Lamb of God speak. Then, with two or three hundred thousand witnesses returning to their communities with the astounding news that Jesus really had come back, that it wasn't a con or a hoax but what the world had been leading up to since Roman times, then the way would be open for a TV ministry that would be accepted all across the country.

So that was what they did.

The Reverend Bagley put his unmatchable contacts to work, explaining only that he wanted to organize a gigantic outdoor confab within a week, and that he'd need a venue that could take up to three hundred thousand people, plus all the trimmings and extras and add-ons which would be required for such an event.

That was on a Thursday.

On the following Sunday he went on his regular show at his regular time and, studiously low-key, made the announcement.

Without any preliminary, and offering no explanation as to the origins of his knowledge, he told his audience that he had news of incalculable import. Told them that the Lord had returned, and that it was not the end of the world but a new beginning, and that all those who would like to see, hear, and worship Him could do so on Saturday at an 8:00 P.M. prayer meeting in a field about fifteen miles east of Atlanta, the exact location of which would be signposted on all major roads leading into and surrounding Stone Mountain. He'd had a phone number titled over the screen which, he'd explained, could be called for a repeat of the information he'd just given.

In response, roughly half a million of all the people across the country who regularly watched Don Bagley proselytize on TV, and were convinced that he was a man of God and not just another Sunday-morning huckster, were sufficiently intrigued by his promise to attempt the trip to Stone Mountain. Of that half million souls perhaps 20 percent were wholeheartedly convinced that Jesus had returned simply because the Reverend Bagley had said he had. Many of these people had disregarded what the evangelist had told them about not being alarmed and, certain that judgment was at hand, had given away their possessions and lived the life of cloistered saints for several days in the hope that such behavior would mitigate their past sins.

Another 50 percent were keeping an open mind. While they admired Don Bagley, and didn't subscribe to the theories bruited around that he'd gone over to the hysterics or just plain lost his reason, they really couldn't bring themselves to believe that Jesus Christ was actually going to appear at this meeting, but the possibility that he might was enough to ensure a decision to make the trip.

A third of the remaining 30 percent had taken a firmer position. While they counted themselves fans of Reverend Bagley, they were convinced that he was stunting this time and said so in strident voices. They made the trip to have their commonsense opinions confirmed, and to take the Reverend to task for stooping so low.

The gathering took place on schedule thanks to some dynamic organizational skills displayed by Don Bagley's managers. The field they used, a dry, level two hundred acres of long, summer-brown grass, was donated for the event by a born-again farmer. Hundreds of high school kids were hired to cover the parking chores, and the football teams from several local colleges were enlisted to back up the uniformed security. The stage and the sound equipment were handled by a rock impresario who brought dozens of double Bose horn speakers and miles of wiring to the party. The biggest job was finding one thousand portable toilets, which were trucked in from all around the state.

A volunteer workforce began the preliminary setup on Wednesday and, by the following day, over five thousand people, the early birds, had set up a tent-and-trailer city around the perimeter of the field.

By late Friday this number had swelled to well over a hundred thousand pilgrims bunked down in everything from sleeping bags to three-bedroom, two-bathroom Airstreams.

Around 5:00 P.M. on that Friday night the thin smoke and charred-meat aromas from barbecues and cookout fires spiraled toward a westering sun like a small town bombed into submission. By noon the following day, Saturday, when a solid noose of traffic choked Atlanta senseless, anybody with any chance of making it had arrived. Approximately three hundred thousand men, women, and children milled around that baking field, a king tide of color-ful humanity ebbing and flowing around each other like anemones in a coral sea. Three hundred thousand strangers living separate existences, but sharing a single purpose, patiently got through the day by attending one or several of the prayer meetings which an army of ordained ministers of various creeds and persuasions con-ducted from lunchtime on.

But as patient and low-key as the massed gathering was, with a pleasant civility abroad engendered by a brotherhood or sister-hood in Christ, an unarticulated jittery feeling started to leach through the crowd.

It was the stage that was the problem.

It was wide and deep and it was high, the platform being about fifteen feet above ground level, and it had a nice canopy and a background of reflective stars which would no doubt look pretty when it got dark. But the fact was, that stage was little more than a large, jiffy-rigged bandshell, and the three rows of bleacher seats some workmen were erecting behind the standing mikes only war-ranted the impression of shaky impermanence. It just didn't seem like the kind of place the Lord Jesus would choose to reveal him-self, although there was a rumor circulating, one of a thousand, that the stage would be used only by the Reverend Bagley for his introductory address, and that the Lord would descend from the heavens in a blaze of unearthly glory.

By 6:00 P.M., with dinner over, and a string of plump pink clouds moving like a line of towed dirigibles toward Atlanta, the

assembled masses began to close up, moving toward the stage with
an unsettled hesitancy, vaguely fearful of what was supposed to
happen, but fearful also of missing it.

From the remote position of most of the crowd, the stage
ranged in size from a matchbook to something no bigger than a
dinner plate, and whoever stepped onto that stage would be corre-
spondingly reduced. Some of Bagley's people had wanted large
portable projection screens set up around the field, but their boss
had killed that idea for the same reason he'd killed a TV appearance, arguing that even if Jesus was a mere speck to the far flung
portion of the gathering, he'd still be a live figure, which was in-
finitely preferable to a large electronic representation.

Around 6:45 a Pentecostal nun, who'd managed a position not
far from stage center, saw a vision in the sky, screamed, pointed,
and fainted, causing three hundred thousand necks to hinge upward in an excited false alarm. It was the first time the crowd had
acted collectively, its questioning rumble spreading like an ocean
swell moving across unfathomable depths.

Just before eight, with a soft evening riding the shirttails of the
hot day, a row of lights mounted in the ceiling of the stage sprang
on, producing a moment of focused attention and quickened
pulses. The lights were excitingly bright and full of electric promise which was sustained by the illumination of empty space to be
filled by what?

And by whom?

Those silent questions were partly answered a few minutes later
when a white-robed choir walked out and arranged itself on the
bleacher seats. It was the first indication that the gathering was officially a religious one, and not some kind of Southern Woodstock.

People near the stage recognized the choir as the one which
backed up Reverend Bagley's regular show. People too far away to
see them clearly recalled their harmonious vocals when the familiar opening bars of "Amazing Grace" floated out of the speakers.
The choir, accompanied by a lone keyboard man, ran through a
lengthy songbook of popular hymns and gospels, then demurely
trooped off the stage. There was no question of applause; this was
in no way meant to be entertainment, and the crowd sensed that.
It was simply a mood-setter and, as such, went a certain distance

toward diverting attention away from the mundane and directing it to the untemporal. This mood, however, was intruded upon when a tall cadaver of a man walked out onto the stage and, with a practiced flip of his wrist, adjusted a microphone up to the level of his mouth.

Anybody who'd been a member of the studio audience at Don Bagley's TV show recognized the white hair, the errant eyebrows, and the beanpole figure. The rest of the crowd knew only that this was not Don Bagley and definitely not Jesus Christ.

"My friends . . . " the man said into the mike, and waited to hear the echo of his voice return to him from the farthest speakers. "My friends . . . brothers and sisters in Jesus . . . my name's Howard Willard, and the Reverend Bagley, who'll be out here himself in a minute, has asked me to welcome you all on his behalf, and on behalf of the Prince of Peace."

Howard Willard was a talented crowd manipulator. He paused to watch the effect of his words on the audience, to gauge its texture and feeling. Seated on the grass, fanned out in a colossal, rippling semicircle, it shifted and swayed at the reference to the Messiah, its clotted tension pressing against the stretched skin of Willard's face. Isolated shouts came to him, "Hallelujah" and "Praise Jesus," and other expressions of ecstasy too far away to be heard clearly.

"It's mighty hard for me to describe what I'm feelin' up here," Willard continued, selecting a casual, countrified approach, and making sure he brought in the right buzzwords early. "But I'll tell you this. When I look out at this great congregation it makes me proud to be a Christian American."

The crowd shifted again, heads nodding in self-satisfied agreement.

"Folks have come from all over the country to be with us tonight. From as far west as the dry deserts of California, and as far north as the green forests of Maine. Not to mention from every one of these here great Southern states of America," Willard went on, allowing the suggestion of a comforting cracker accent to slow his delivery.

"Why have they come? Why have you come? Why have you dropped everything to drive the long highways of this great land of ours and be with us here tonight? Well, I reckon we all know the answer to that question. And before the night gets very much older, you'll see for yourself that your trip, your presence here, your decision to respond to the Reverend Bagley's invitation, was not in vain," Howard Willard told them, raising his voice above the susurrant response. "And that what the good Reverend promised will be fulfilled."

Willard paused to observe the reaction he knew that addendum would bring. Many of the crowd were getting up, a burgeoning excitement driving them to their feet. It would have been easy to keep the pulse going, Willard knew, to play those throbbing multitudes like a sailfish, but to do that, to tell them they'd soon be seeing the Lord of Heaven on this very stage, would have been stealing his boss's thunder. So having dangled the bait, and seen it snatched and the hook well and truly gobbled, Willard figured that he'd done his job, and that it was now time to bring on the big guns.

He flicked his glance offstage, nodded, and brought his smile back to three hundred thousand people. "So now I'm gonna bug out and make way"—and here Willard muscled up his voice—"for one of God's special people. A man who's made converts for Jesus"—he pronounced it *geee*-zuss—"clear across the country. A man who's brought hundreds of thousands of Christians back to the fold. A great American, and a credit to the South. Brothers and sisters, the Reverend Don Bagley."

Howard Willard's stilty legs took him swiftly across the stage as the man he'd so verbosely introduced appeared at the edge of the wings. They shook hands and embraced. Then as Willard left, Don Bagley advanced to the microphone, his broad figure bent forward against a white blizzard of flashbulbs.

Like a mammoth tapestry caught by a breeze, the crowd rippled and lumped as a couple of hundred thousand people stood. The applause was polite and controlled, devoid of the usual Southern exuberance, the hoots and whistles and rebel yells; instead, a long, steady surf of acclamation endorsed the fine job this man had done for Jesus these past few years, his solid championing of the role of Christian standards within the community, and his unwavering espousal of the kind of values that made the American family second to none.

The evangelist stopped stage center in his fine blue suit, then, fingers stiff, palms outstretched, suddenly shot both hands into the air in a Stop sign of the utmost urgency.

The applause staggered and died.

After a frozen moment Bagley slowly lowered his arms to show that he was a man of moderate gesture, too, his hands relaxing as they patted the air, directing the crowd to sit down again if they so wished. Nobody took the option; you stood for the important events of life.

As his lieutenant had done before him, Don Bagley opened with the same salutation elevating three hundred thousand strangers to the status of friend and kin, then paused as any experienced public speaker does to confirm attention.

The evangelist used the tiny gap of time to check that the weather was harboring no surprises. It was calm and clear above, the first of the stars beginning to pop hesitantly through the heavy tent of the darkening night. Being moderately nearsighted, the hardened lenses in his middle-aged eyes converted these celestial visitors to undefined dots, and the shining, expectant faces of his earthly visitors, massed and fanned out in front of him, into a vast pointillist painting feebly illuminated by the sparse lighting rigged around the field.

He began to speak, struggling with the knowledge that what he was about to say was more important by a factor of a hundred, a thousand, a million, than anything he'd ever said in his entire life.

"Friends, for the first time since I can remember, I'm finding it hard to express myself. Even if I knew every single word in Mr. Webster's dictionary, I still wouldn't be able to describe the importance of what has happened. The importance to me, the importance to you, the importance to America and the whole world." He paused there to shake his head in effaced bewilderment. It wasn't an act; Don Bagley was a genuine man who'd been capsized by a turbulent sea of events and was still floundering in the shallows of reason and understanding.

"You're here tonight," he said, picking up somewhere in the vicinity of where he'd left off, "because of an announcement and a promise I made on television last Sunday. I told you that the Lord Jesus Christ had returned in body to the earth. And I'm standing here in front of every man, woman, and child in this great assembly to back up that statement one hundred percent. It is absolutely, categorically, no-question-about-it true. As you'll see for yourself in a minute."

The crowd, emanating fear and delight, sucked breath and moaned.

"You don't have to be afraid. This is a time of great rejoicing and humble thanksgiving. The Lord God Almighty has seen fit to give the world a second chance. A second bite of the cherry. So He's sent His son Jesus to walk amongst us again, choosing, for his second ministry, the United States, the most Christian country in the world but, sadly, a country full of people who don't always act the way good Christians should. Maybe this time we'll be smart enough to heed Christ's message."

Vowing change, heads nodded fervently.

"So now that you know why Jesus has returned, you're wondering how he returned, and what happened to him on his return. I'll tell you right now, it's not a story many of us can be proud of, because a lot of people doubted the presence of the Lord. And, to my eternal shame, I was one of them."

The evangelist seemed to be looking every member of his gigantic audience right in the eye when he made that painful admission, and the fact that he'd made it so openly was perceived as more evidence of his honest and manly nature.

"I'm telling you this, good people, because many of you might feel the same when Jesus stands up here before you. Many of you might doubt him."

"No!" the crowd muttered, heads shaking in ardent denial. "No!"

"My friends," Bagley said, his voice a deep wash, swamping the distant loudspeakers, "you need a base for doubt, just as you need a base for belief. And I based my doubt on the fact that Jesus did not return as the Good Book says he will, on the clouds of glory with the whole world watching. But since then I've done a whole heap of thinking, and I realized that none of us foolish sinners deserved to see such an awesomely wondrous sight. Instead, Jesus chose a handful of simple and humble believers to witness his spectacular return, some shepherds tending their flocks in the Tennessee hills who he allowed to see the Second Advent close up. I had those shepherds tracked down. Had my people talk to them. We tracked down just about everybody Jesus has come in contact with since he arrived back on this sinful planet two weeks ago. And you know what? We're all so out of touch with the Lord and his word that almost nobody recognized him. In fact, they threw him into jail."

A gasp like a sudden opening of the earth rolled out of the crowd.

"That's right, good people, they treated Jesus like a common criminal. And even after he'd made a lame man walk again, even after they'd seen the dreadful legacy of the cruel nails the Roman soldiers drove through his hands and feet up there on the cross, they still didn't know who they had in their midst. It wasn't till Jesus found his way to the sea and told two trawlermen to follow him that he was recognized as the Lord Come Again. Their names, good people, were James and John Carew. Two fishermen named James and John. Does that ring a biblical bell?"

The crowd's sharp inhalation was followed by another when Bagley rushed on.

"Jesus filled their empty boat with shrimp. And when he did that, a man named Bert Sales, an evangelist from Beaufort, South Carolina, and a fine Christian gentleman who knows his Bible, recognized a repeat of the miracle of the net, Luke five, four to six, and knew he was in the presence of the Lord."

Seated in the VIP section, a folding-chair section immediately behind the media area, Bert Sales swelled with happiness as the acknowledgment boomed out on the soft Southern night. His body buzzed with pride; his name, previously known only to the downtown locals of Beaufort, was being fed like something warm and nutritious to hundreds of thousands of people.

He checked with the Carews sitting next to him. They were hunched forward like kids caught up in an Old Testament story full of blood and fantasy, their lips pulled back in identical ovals. They reminded Bert Sales of two men, fresh from vacation, fascinated by snapshots of themselves.

Sales turned back to the stage and listened to Don Bagley tell the multitude, in a gripping mix of piety, sadness, and verve, of how the three disciples had brought Jesus to the streets of Atlanta, and how miserably they'd failed there.

"They jeered at Jesus. Laughed at him. Called him names just as they did in his original ministry. And do you know where those philistines forced our Lord to spend the night? In a mission flophouse, among drunks and degenerates."

Out in the crowd women started to weep, and thoughts of fierce vengeance made men ball their hands into fists.

"The next morning . . ." The evangelist, moved by his own sad anecdote, turned away momentarily to cough. Recovered. Turned back again. "The next morning, his faithful disciples brought the Lord to my house hoping that I at least could identify him. Well, I didn't know it then, but I surely know it now, God in heaven guided His son to my door." Bagley turned toward the wings and said something sotto voce that the mike picked up. "Julie? You want to come out here?"

Don Bagley's twelve-year-old daughter, tall in a pretty party dress, stepped shyly onto the stage. Walked toward her father, who put his arm around her small shoulder, hugged her to his robust bulk, then turned back to his audience.

"This is my little girl, Julie. A week ago last Wednesday she fell off her pony and hit her head. I called my doctor, a man who's been in medicine all his life. He pronounced her dead. And she was. I can still see her lying there pale as paper with not a breath left in her little body. And then Jesus and his three disciples walked up my drive."

The majority of the media people present had covered massed events before, all kinds of gatherings, and seen crowds in many moods. But at that point, with Don Bagley standing up there with his daughter telling everybody she'd been dead, and that Jesus had appeared at his door, none of those media folk had ever heard a crowd, even one a hundred times smaller than this one, squashed into silence so fast. Their muteness was a clear result of a vivid understanding; they knew what was coming and were coiled to receive the news.

"The Lord said two words. *'Talitha koum.'* The words he used to command Jairus's daughter to rise from the dead. And my little girl, my little Julie here, was restored to me."

Nervous laughter sprang up somewhere, and there were scattered sounds of cawing ridicule but, a minute later, the scoffing expired, dead from lack of support.

"But still I was not convinced," Don Bagley confessed, transferring his weight in what became a chagrined and awkward shuffle. "My daughter rescued from the dark night of death, and I needed more." Bowed by his staggering presumption, he shook his head, then said, "But the Lord Jesus understands the colossal folly of human beings, their vanity and pigheaded stupidity, and was tolerant and patient with me. And to prove to this doubting sinner that he was indeed Jesus Come Again, he allowed me to witness yet another miracle. Right there in my garden, in the heat and brightness of day, the Lord changed stones into bread."

A great and desperate gasp burst from the crowd, a cry of fear and wonder that throbbed through the night. A multitude of terror-stricken faces bobbed in front of Don Bagley, whatever narrow residue of skepticism they'd nurtured wiped away by the passion of his telling. They knew he believed it had happened—the truth carried its own seal of authenticity—therefore they believed it had happened, and their flesh was made to creep by the thought of something as unknowable as a biblical miracle occurring in a suburban garden not twenty miles west of where they were standing.

The evangelist bent to kiss the top of his daughter's head, then directed her to return to the apron of the stage. In a clamp of hushed fascination the crowd watched the gangling movements of her skinny body, a body which, they were now convinced, would be decomposing in the dark and quilted surrounds of oak and satin had it not been for the miracle genius of Jesus Lord of Heaven.

"So now you know," Don Bagley said, addressing his massive audience again, "how I can be so sure that Jesus has come back. And once I knew that, I also knew that the best way for our Lord to deliver his message in this day and age would not be by roaming the land as he did in Palestine, but to instantaneously reach everybody through the medium of television, but only after people, good Christians like yourselves, had seen him in his tortured flesh, and basked in his magnificent presence. I wanted to bring three hundred thousand people together to see him and to hear him. Three hundred thousand instant disciples who'd go back to their towns and cities and spread the word that the Jesus on the TV sets of America is the real Jesus, the original Jesus, Jesus of Nazareth returned to the world to give it another chance."

Don Bagley stopped speaking and, with the clumsy movements of a big man, knelt down. "On your knees, good people. On your knees for Jesus Christ. Open your hearts, and your ears and your eyes. See and hear the Lord, and take the glorious news back home with you."

The power of a single personality, once confidence is established, was brilliantly demonstrated when the entire gathering, with the exception of the 10 to 15 percent which stubbornly remained unconvinced, got down on its knees. There were even some media people, mesmerized by the evangelist's appeal, who ignored their brief and sank down with the rest of the multitude.

The stage lights blinked and went out, a surprise which produced from the crowd a quavering squeal.

A tiny slot of time passed, a vibrating and impermanent twenty seconds. Then the lights went up on the stage.

Bagley was gone and Yehsu was standing there.

Don Bagley had been reticent to employ this piece of mild theatrics, but, the way he saw it, to have Jesus just walk on as if he were merely the next speaker was out of the question. So he'd decided that a simple blackout-and-reveal would solve the problem of getting the Lord center stage not only with propriety but with a small touch of drama that was necessary and desirable for any presentation.

There'd also been the question of how Jesus should dress. His casual, man-of-the-people clothes were deemed too mundane and workaday for his introduction to the world, and to put him in a suit was to risk the ludicrous. So Bagley decided that a simple robe would be not only fittingly decorous but historically accurate. However—and to his advantage—he'd miscalculated the effect of all this from the audience's point of view. Instead of a dignified presentation, what they saw was a joltingly sudden manifestation as if, a heartbeat ago, the figure up there on the stage had been swirling particles of light that had been instantly transmuted into the shape of a man.

They cried out.

They moaned. Sobbed in an agony of stupefied reverence.

Now, perhaps as many as 90 percent of them were convinced that this was Jesus. Just like the Reverend had said, this was the Lord Returned. Those up front recognized him from the representations in the famous paintings, the illustrated calendars. There was the same tall, ascetic build. The same biblical-length hair and beard. The same godlike bearing in the straight-backed stance, a black anthem of terrible suffering in the sad, dark eyes.

This belief, solid and unchallengeable, spread like an instant and benevolent virus to the farthest reaches of the crowd, and was stunningly cemented when Yehsu slowly raised his arms in benediction, and turned his hands outward.

When people for fifty yards out saw his mutilated palms, and took another look at the thornlike scars imbedded in his brow, the spectacular aggregate of his physical presence and Don Bagley's cathartic testimony caused a long uneven groan to bubble up, and prompted men and women to swoon and topple from their knees.

Camera lights and flashbulbs threw up a demented bombardment. When the stage's glittery backdrop explosively reflected this barrage, the robed figure seemed to catch fire.

However, something happened then that, beyond all question, converted any and all who still doubted.

Fragmented by the tungsten chaos, Yehsu lowered his arms in a stately, preparatory movement and, as the crowd at the top of its adrenaline rush let out another peal of agonized fear, their Lord Returned took a half step forward and looked up at the heavens.

A tremendous roar of thunder came from that black pulsating void, staggeringly loud and long, as if great pieces of the firmament had broken off and were hurtling down.

But, to the ears of the giddy, reeling pilgrims, practically all of whom were extremely familiar with the Bible, there was order to this basso cacophony, a cadenced enunciation within the crashing Niagara that could be identified.

This sound, this vast smash of decibels, was no more distinct than the ragged boundaries of a careering moon, yet it seemed to most of those present to break up into words, individual words that could be distinguished within the sky's mountainous rumble.

And the words were these:

"This is My son, whom I love. Listen to him!"

PART
TWO

CHAPTER
11

Brian spotted him immediately.

Harry Chifley was sitting on a bench in his clericals, which may as well have been a suit of fire for the scruffy park dwellers, who, perhaps suspecting a religious trap, granted him generous space.

He'd called Brian from Chicago the day before. He was coming into town and could they get together? His old friend had called again that morning explaining that, as he would be closeted till noon, and again in the afternoon, he'd welcome a bit of fresh air in the lunch hour, so they'd arranged to meet in Washington Square, a snap for Brian and an easy cab ride from Chifley's downtown meeting.

Brian walked up to him and handed him a deli bag.

Through a stern mask of inflexibility Chifley indicated the bag and said, "What do you bring me, Father?"

Brian bowed his head in supplication. "Egg salad on whole wheat, Monsignor."

"You have done well, my son," Chifley intoned solemnly.

They chuckled. Shook hands. They hadn't seen each other since that frozen day in Chicago, although they'd kept in touch. Seeing him now, Brian realized how much he'd missed Harry Chifley's witty, sane presence. There was nobody he liked more in or out of the Church, and certainly nobody else within the Church with whom he could let down his ecclesiastical hair.

Brian joined him on the bench. "So, Harry, what brings you to New York, New York, a town so nice they named it twice?"

"Fires. There's a couple they want me to put out here. They've made me roving troubleshooter east of the Mississippi. Plus I wanted to talk to you about something. But first, how's life in the Apple?"

"Noisy, abrasive, and exhausting. I like it."

"And the bookstore?"

"Great. I'll be salesperson of the month if the college kid gets the flu."

"Excellent. Now for a really important question: is that a ham-and-Swiss you've got there?"

"You want to trade a half?"

"Done!"

They swapped sandwiches. Sipped at their sodas, Brian allowing his senior to set the pace and shape of the meeting.

"I want you to do something for me," Chifley said, sounding serious. "Can you get away from your job for a while?"

"When?"

"Soon. Like tomorrow."

"That's pretty short notice."

"Can you swing it?"

"If it's really important."

"It's really important," Harold Chifley told him. He said no more about it till they'd finished their lunch. Then, with Brian waiting to hear why he was being so suddenly pressed into service, Chifley guided him out of the park.

A blustering bus, enthusiastically pumping out noxious effluents, made conversation impossible for a moment, then, when it had charged away to pollute another section of the city, Harold Chifley began again.

"You've heard about the recent return of Jesus, I take it? You've seen him on television?"

"Who hasn't? He's all over the box. Magazines and newspapers, the works," Brian replied, assuming this was just polite filler.

"What do you think of him?"

"What else could I think of him? He's an irritating time-waster, although he certainly looks the part he's playing, I'll give him that.

But Jesus speaking English like the corner falafel man, that kind of spoils it for me."

"Me, too. But an amazing amount of people aren't bothered by that. They're convinced he's the real thing."

"Doesn't surprise me. We all love something new and different, and he's the biggest novelty since hot Dr Pepper."

"I'm worried about him, Brian. I'm worried about what's happening."

"Why? It's just America at play. Some poor madman dresses up as Jesus and succeeds beyond his wildest dreams. What's to be worried about?"

"Plenty. If all those stars-and-bars Baptists want to think Christ has returned to give them a second chance, let 'em. But there are Catholics down there, Catholics all across the country, who are buying into it, too."

Surprised by the depth of his friend's concern, Brian framed a less flippant reply. "The Jesus folk don't have a lock on gullibility, Harry. Everybody wants Christ to come back and forgive them. Specially adherents of a faith that's a little heavier on guilt than most."

"But he's talking against the Church. I don't know how closely you've been following it, but he's been firing some very thinly disguised arrows at Rome."

"Harry, I honestly don't see why you're worried. He's just one more tin-pot messiah. We've had them before and we'll have them again. Admittedly, there's never been one that's looked as good or made such a hit, but how long can it be before his Social Security card drops out of his robe and he goes back to being a high school janitor in Dingbat, Ohio?"

"I don't know. But meantime, according to some figures I saw, something like fifteen percent of churchgoers in the South and the Midwest believe implicitly that this is the real Jesus. Sure, we've seen other fakes, but none of them ever had the effect this guy's having. None of them ever appeared in the sky, for a start. And none of them," Chifley added, displaying an astringency new to Brian, "slowly descended to earth, either."

"Hey, come on. A couple of religious crazies claim they saw something, then all the bornagains, whipped up by the Bible thumpers, are suddenly convinced they saw the same thing. Desperate people, Harry, desperate to be proven right. Remember what Francis Bacon said: Man prefers to believe what he prefers to be true."

They were stopped at the corner of Tenth Street waiting for a walk sign, and the holdup produced an uncharacteristic hitch of impatience in Chifley. "They weren't crazies. They were ordinary people, about a hundred of them dispersed over a wide area. It wasn't mass hallucination because there's probably no such thing. They saw something, Brian. And all those people at that outdoor jamboree, when Don Bagley introduced the guy, they heard something."

"Yeah, I saw it on the coverage. The voice of God shouting down from heaven, so those pilgrims claimed. Except when they ran the clip on the news, all you could hear is one exceptionally long thunderclap."

"The media people said they weren't set up to record something like that. But most of them swear they heard God's words from the Transfiguration."

"I'm not surprised. Don Bagley's something of a spellbinder, and it was a very emotional moment, so I read." When Chifley looked doubtful, Brian bore down. "It was contrived suggestion, Harry, and you know how powerful that can be. If somebody says they can see Elvis's face in a potato, all of a sudden everybody else can see it, too."

"I know all that. I've told myself that. But I had a report commissioned, and after reading it I'm certain something's going on. Three weeks back, a man floated down the sky in the Tennessee mountains. I honestly think it happened. So I have three big questions—how did it happen, why did it happen, and who's making it happen?"

The light changed. Swinging his briefcase, Harold Chifley strode vigorously across the street, made the opposite sidewalk, and swung around on his companion. "Something's up, Brian, and I want to find out what."

"Have you tried asking Don Bagley? I thought this guy was his creation."

"Absolutely not. Bagley's the only genuine thing about all this.

I know people who know him well. He's no charlatan. If he says this guy's Jesus, it's because he honestly thinks he is."

"I guess anyone would if he brought your daughter back from the dead," Brian said, with a faint roll of his eyes.

The monsignor started uptown again. "This faker's pulled off a number of so-called miracles. That's one of the reasons why people are flocking to him. After he preached to that huge camp meeting, hundreds of challenged people claimed they could walk again, hear again, see again. That kind of thing guarantees national coverage and a zillion converts."

"But they're not miracles, Harry. And, to his credit, the guy doesn't claim any special powers in that direction. He says what the real Jesus said, that anybody who's healed by him heals themselves through their faith."

"Right. Faith in God. And he says he's the Son of God. So what it comes down to is, believe in me, and you, too, can be made whole. We've had faith healers with us for thousands of years. Got 'em with us now. There are even some Catholic priests who are into it. But none of them claim to be Jesus."

"Forgive me if I'm being astute, Harry, but are you getting pressure from Rome on this?"

"And then some." Chifley's admission seemed to lighten the job he'd been saddled with; the tight squinch between his eyes lessened, and his storming pace slowed. "Officially, the Holy See is regarding this fake as just a passing phenomenon. Unofficially, they've got their fingers hovering over the panic button. They want him exposed before he does any more harm. They've already done some rather indiscreet probing, but they've covered their tracks as usual, so nobody will be any the wiser."

"What did they find out?" Brian asked.

Chifley veered to his left into the recessed front door of an apartment building. He clicked open his briefcase and took out a swollen red folder. "Frankly, they got a shock. It's all in here. Everything we know about him from day one, plus a video of him at that camp meeting, and a cassette tape of an interview he gave afterward. Take it. It could come in handy."

Brian accepted the folder as a man might accept a garish present from a close relative: he didn't want it but was unable to give it back. He asked a third question in a restive aura of unease. "Come in handy for what?"

"I want you to check into him for me. I want you to find out what the hell's going on."

Brian felt a void open up inside him. "Harry . . . look . . . I'm no detective. I'm a bookseller and sometime priest."

"You don't have to go out and buy a trench coat. All you have to do is ask sensible questions. Think of it as an intellectual exercise, if you like. You're good at those."

Brian looked down at the red folder, not a dark red but a bright one, the color of a warning light. He said, with a seriousness that was almost bleak, "I must respectfully refuse, Monsignor."

"Why don't you think about success for a change, Brian?"

"What?"

"Your respectful refusal came with subtitles. You want to know what they said? They said, I'm already taking a time out from one job I'm convinced I can't hack, and I can't use another failure right now."

With a sense of injury and purloined pride, Brian mounted a forceful defense. "That's not true. I don't know if I can be a priest again. I'm in the process of finding out. But I do know I've had zero experience in investigation, so it's not being unconfident to say I'm not qualified to be a snoop."

Chifley nodded his eyes at the folder. "Did you know he speaks Aramaic?"

It was a surprise for Brian. "Middle Aramaic?"

Chifley clicked his tongue, a sound of mild derogation. "And you don't think you're qualified. I didn't know there was such a thing as Middle Aramaic."

Brian was well aware that his quiet refusal added not an ounce to what was, in actual fact, a weightless revolt. Monsignor Harold Chifley enjoyed an exalted position within the Church hierarchy, and any request was an order couched in polite terms. Brian elevated his hands signaling an unhappy but inevitable surrender. "Okay . . . if I have to, I have to. But I'll be doing it under protest."

"Father, I don't care how you do it, just as long as you do it." Chifley paused, relaxed, and let a little warmth seep back into his delivery. "Give it a shot, Brian. Read the folder and think about it. You might want to hire some help for the legwork. We'll pay all your expenses and reimburse you for any lost time."

Brian reluctantly tucked the folder beneath his arm. It was his now, and it appeared to know it, its neon red cover seeming to pulsate as if a capricious imp resided inside. "You want regular reports?"

"Just call when you've got something." Harold Chifley held out his hand and smiled at last, back to his old personality. "Get out there and kick butt, Number Seventeen. Make the coach look good."

Brian inflated a weak grin.

It lasted no longer than the time it took Harold Chifley to step back, give a half wave, and set off uptown again.

His boss wasn't thrilled about him suddenly taking time off, but when Brian talked the part-time college boy into coming in full-time for a while, he was able to leave the bookstore that evening knowing his job would still be there when he got back. Which, he told his boss, should be in about two weeks' time. But when he got home to his apartment, fetched a beer, sat down on the sofa, and read through the red folder, he felt like calling his employer back and telling him to make that a month.

Brian knew he needed help, but it was another twenty minutes before it occurred to him that the help he needed, someone experienced in ferreting out information and running down leads, was due to meet him in a half hour's time.

How could he have overlooked Marie? he wondered. Had it been his subconscious at work? He knew he was in danger of breaking his vows, because if he went on seeing her they were certain to become lovers. On the other hand, she'd be perfect for the job Chifley had handed him, although it would mean being with her on a daily basis, and thus increasing the chance of tumbling into bed with her. But if it was going to happen anyway, did it really matter if it happened sooner rather than later?

They'd scheduled dinner at his apartment that evening and perhaps a movie afterward. Eating in was a habit they'd fallen happily into of late; it saved money on a restaurant, and they could talk without having to shout over the noise of dish clatter.

He waited till they were having coffee before he sprang his idea on her. They were nicely relaxed after the baba ghanoush, the basil-and-tomato salad, the pesto rolls, and a couple of glasses of Beaujolais, and charmed by a lovely Satie sonata which was languorously surrendering its soul to a laser beam. Sitting opposite Marie, watching the gold glimmer of her hair, Brian wondered if he'd ever met anyone who managed to look so perennially cool. Her clothes contributed greatly to this impression—she favored menthol summer colors: lemon and white and apple green. He wondered how long it would take, with the right stimulation, for that coolness to flame up and meltingly generate essence and nectar. The fact that he'd find this out in the near future was something he placed in the back of his mind, but not so distant it couldn't be retrieved in the small hours of the morning and dwelt on at luscious length.

"How's the article going?" he asked, wanting a bland start and a slow build. He wasn't sure how she'd feel about working with him, and was aware that he might have to do some selling.

"I turned it in today. It's just a bill payer." Marie was referring to a feature she'd done, on short notice, for a fashion magazine, a lucrative assignment that was nice to have between projects but came under the heading of donkey work.

"So what'll you do next?"

"Store up strength, I guess."

"Weren't you thinking of doing something on the Jesus fake?" Brian asked, almost ashamed to be leading her this way.

Marie drank her coffee. Placed the cup down in the saucer's perfect receiving circle. "There are too many people working on that one. And besides, I don't have an angle."

Brian almost laughed. "You must have read the script." Marie's shapely underlip, overstated in comparison with its twin, expanded into a puzzled smile. Brian enlightened her. "I've got one for you. An angle. You ready for this?" Off her nod he said, "You do a feature, an article or whatever, with a religious as a partner. A man of the cloth. An Anglican parson or a Baptist minister. Maybe even a Catholic priest."

Perhaps the small scepter of his grin gave it away, for he could see immediately she knew who he was talking about, so he went into detail about his meeting with Harold Chifley, and the job he'd been handed. "I'm going to need some help. Somebody to show me how you go about a thing like this, and I was wondering if you'd be interested in teaming up."

"Insights from the Church's point of view," Marie said, considering the merits of the suggestion. "That's not bad." She thought for a moment more. "Would there be any trouble getting a release from your masters? To sell the article?"

"They'd have to check it out. Make sure you weren't disparaging the Faith."

Something solidified behind Marie's eyes, a compact compression he'd never seen before. "I couldn't slant it, Brian. I don't write to order, and I'd never accept a whitewash job."

"I put that badly. They want me to find out who put this guy together and why. If we found out something along the way that reflects badly on the Church, and if it's true and sustainable, they're not gonna blue-pencil it. The days of hiding their own sins are fast fading. It's innuendo they'd hold the line at, and that wouldn't affect you."

"How do you know?"

"Because I'm getting to know you pretty well. And you're not the type that goes in for insinuation. You might throw a brick, but you'd never write a poison-pen letter."

Pleased by his estimation, Marie's ocular density softened, and a relaxed ease sifted back into her words. "Okay, then. If I get to print what I write, I'm in. But we'd better get started soon. The competition's going to get more and more brutal."

"We've already started. We may even have a bit of a jump on them." Brian reached for the red folder he'd placed on a side table. "This is a kind of on-pack premium that came with the job. Facts and figures on Jesus Two from when he first showed up to a couple of days ago. Interviews with anybody who's had anything to do with him. A chronicle of his life and times back on earth."

Marie opened the folder and spent a minute flicking through it. Impressed with the thoroughness of the research, she asked who'd put it together.

"The Church mafia. Assorted people who do little favors for the Faith."

"Professionals?"

"Nope. Amateur Catholics. Remember when he collapsed from exhaustion the day after that outdoor spectacular? He was rushed to the hospital and kept overnight."

"Sure, we talked about it at some length. I remember that ditsy woman on the news, in the street interviews. If this is the Son of God, she said, how come he'd get sick?"

Brian chuckled. "Aren't people marvelous? They buy the fact that the Son of God suffered horribly on the cross, but they doubt he could catch cold." He dug into the folder. "Take a look at this."

Marie accepted the sheets of paper he handed her but didn't get past the letterhead. "FBI," she said. "I knew they'd be interested in this guy. Any aberration, anyone of any sudden influence, and they're onto it like a shot."

"Read the medical report. They put him through the wringer under the guise of running tests. They printed him first thing, of course, and, naturally, his thumbs aren't on record. Then they checked out his teeth hoping to find a filling. They didn't, although he's had a couple of extractions at some time, and it's possible those teeth contained amalgam, but that's just conjecture. What isn't conjecture is the fact that his molars are all ground down, and one of those molars is supported by wire."

Marie frowned as she read the confirmation of Brian's statement. "If he'd had a mouth full of amalgam, it would've been all over, I can understand that. But what's the significance of the molars being ground down. And the wire support?"

"The wire is ancient restorative dentistry. A strong tooth propping up a weak one. It's a technique that goes back to the Egyptians, and it certainly would have been practiced in Palestine in Jesus' time. The worn condition of the molars is consistent with a person who lived at that time, too. Cereals were their main food source which they ground on a stone. Tiny particles of the stone would get into the mix, and after twenty or thirty years of chewing on an abrasive like that their teeth got worn down."

Marie looked bemused. "As you once said, maybe he is Jesus."

"Medically, it'd be hard to prove he isn't. That doctor who was finking for the Bureau ... look at this here. He really did a number on him. He took a tiny skin shaving from the guy's face, from the bridge of his nose and his temples, and tested them for polypropylene, which I think is what most sunglasses frames are made from. It can tattoo minute particles of polymers into the skin, but there was no trace of this on Jesus Two. So we know the guy never wore sunglasses."

"Which proves nothing."

"That's not the only thing that proves nothing." Brian turned a page of the report. "This doctor ran a neutron analysis for magnesium silicate. Nothing. Ditto for fatty acids like palm oil, lauric acid, et cetera, which points away from any past use of shaving cream. He did find traces of caustic soda and tallow, something that's in modern soaps, but seeing Jesus Two has been with us for at least three weeks, and is presumably washing his face every night, it doesn't do us much good."

The haunting coda of the Satie piece faded as the CD, perhaps out of respect for the beautiful binaries it contained, lapsed into silence. Brian didn't bother to find another selection; he was busy running his finger down a page looking for something.

"Here we go. The wounds. Read what Dr. Feelgood has to say."

Marie perused the sheet before she read it out. "The patient exhibited evidence of blunt trauma in each hand, which would indicate an object, perhaps half an inch in diameter, has been driven through the palm at some time, resulting in metacarpal bone and tendon damage. Similar trauma was observed in the instep of both feet, the second metatarsal bone in the right foot being deformed. A scar was observed on the left-side flank two inches below the costal margin and is consistent with trauma caused by a thin sharp instrument. All wounds appear to have healed by secondary intention." She looked up at Brian. "What's secondary intention?"

"A bandage and time. Nothing artificially closed or sewn up."

Marie considered that for a moment, then dipped her head again. "Shallow multiple trauma was observed on the scalp and forehead in a circular pattern, the wounds being triangular in shape. Skin weals present on right and left scapula areas. No other bodily marks." Marie looked up again. "Whoa!" she said.

"And look at this," Brian invited. "That shy little doctor took—what's it say?—a fifteen-gauge bone needle, sucked out some body fat, and checked it for modern pesticides. Result, negative. Conclusion? And I'll bet he coughed and harrumphed before writing this: 'Without longer and more exhaustive tests, which might produce evidence to the contrary, it is my opinion that this male was born circa 1957, plus or minus five years, as his physical condition would indicate. As to the possibility of his being born hundreds of years earlier than this estimated date, I am unable to refute this on strictly medical grounds, although common sense would indicate the unlikelihood of this being the case.' "

"He sounds like an Irish Catholic from Boston."

"He was certainly Catholic, you can bet on that. And the FBI agent who received this report was probably Catholic. And whoever got a copy from that agent was Catholic. We're worse than the Masons," Brian said with a fluttery grin.

Marie sank back in the sofa. When she folded her hands behind her neck—a rare masculine gesture—the thin silver bracelets she wore tinkled musically in the upper register. Examining the ceiling, she said, "Isn't there a ghoulish part in the Gospels when the risen Christ invites an unbeliever to poke his fingers in his wounds?"

"Sure. Luke mentions it. He says that Thomas, the apostle, didn't believe that Jesus had risen from the dead, so Jesus invited him to reach out and put his hand in his side, which the apostle did, and he was suddenly no longer a doubting Thomas."

"So, according to the Bible, Jesus came back from the dead with his wounds unhealed. And here we have a man who says he's Jesus returned, except, unlike the original Jesus, he can't invite anybody to poke around in his wounds because they're all better now. How does he explain that? Does he say where his body's been parked for the last two thousand years?"

"Nope. Only that he's come back in the same body he left with so that people would recognize him. As for the wounds, he says God healed them and left them on show to remind the world of its cruelty."

"Healed them by secondary intention?"

"Now you're into metaphysics," Brian said. "Age-old questions like how many angels can dance on the head of an Ace bandage."

Marie gave him a look at a smile, then sat forward in the sofa, her face invigorated by the subject. "So what's your take on it? What do you think's happened here?"

Brian opened the folder, tossed the medical report inside, then closed the folder as if it were a book he hadn't particularly enjoyed reading. "I don't think there's any question about it. We're dealing with a sensationally successful and extremely lucky religious hysteric. Besotted by Jesus, who's not only his redeemer but his idol, he starves himself, grows a beard, and lets his hair grow out so he can look like the man he's fascinated with. Determined to emulate his paladin in every way, he puts himself through Christ's agony on the cross, including, apparently, having somebody thrust a large knife into his side and, no doubt, offer him a sponge full of vinegar to complete the tableau. By rights he should have bled to death or died of shock or asphyxiation or whatever, but let's assume he goes into a coma so deep that, when he eventually comes out of it, he's convinced he's risen from the dead. Which leads him to believe, poor crazy soul, that he's Jesus Christ incarnate."

Marie nodded as if this were enlightening news, the contours of thought raising her slow blink rate. But her answer wasn't the one Brian expected. "I don't think so," she said.

"No?"

"No. Look at what this guy's supposed to have done—descended from the sky, gathered disciples, healed people, restored life, filled an empty shrimp boat, not to mention changing stones into bread. Whether he did all of that or not, he's convinced millions that he is who he says he is. And you describe him as sensationally successful and extremely lucky. Well, I don't think anybody could be that successful or that lucky all by themselves. I think he's had some help."

"Religious hysteria's all the help you need. Seventy-five years ago, in a tiny town in the wilds of northern Portugal, three ten-year-old sheepherders claimed a woman who called herself the Lady of the Rosary kept appearing to them on the thirteenth of every month. Finally, seventy thousand people gathered to see if they could spot this lady, too. But they were disappointed. All they saw was the sun plummeting toward the earth."

"It wasn't religious hysteria that got him out of that tank-town jail cell in Tennessee. And it wasn't hysteria that fixed a washing machine and a lame man in a Beaufort boardinghouse, or filled up an empty fishing boat."

"You've been on top of it, huh?" Brian said. He'd hoped for this from her: a quick grasp of new information effortlessly annealed to what she already knew about the subject.

"Everyone's on top of it," Marie replied. "It's turning out to be more divisive than abortion or slavery. In the South, the fundamentalists are expecting heathen New York to be consumed by fire for scoffing at Jesus' return. While in the North, people are laughing at the crackers buying the equivalent of the Brooklyn Bridge. They'll go along with the simple healing, but coming down the sky, conjuring up a ton of shrimp? Get outta here."

Brian got up off the sofa and paced the extremities of his sublet. Although it had been furnished inexpensively, it had been decorated by somebody with a florid eye. The white plaster walls were tyrannized by lurid oil paintings that shrank the dimensions of the room, and as these dimensions were small to begin with, Brian was soon back in front of Marie.

"Let's take it from the top and see what we've got," he suggested. "A chronological recap."

"Go," said Marie. She picked up a pen and a notepad off a side table and began to doodle, one of those people whose thought processes were lubricated by ink, Brian decided. A spotlight beam, designed to illumine some of the paintings, encrusted her hair with an argentine glow, the edge of the light delineating the smooth camber of her neck as she bent over the pad. It seemed to Brian that every time he saw her she'd improved in some infinitesimal way, like a piece of sculpture nearing completion. He wondered whether this was due to an increase in his powers of scrutiny or a slowly ascending level of feeling toward her. He knew the answer, but he still preferred to wonder.

"Okay." He kicked himself back to the subject. "Jesus Two descends from the heavens. I'm prepared to ignore that because that kind of thing is pretty common. You get some freakish weather conditions, somebody says they saw Jesus, and all those of a religious bent are suddenly willing to swear on a stack of Methodist ministers that they saw him, too. Next morning Jay Two turns up at a remote farm in the Tennessee hills and cures a dying horse. Which is interesting because that's how Zoroaster got his start."

"You kidding?"

"Nope. He cured King Vishtaspa's steed and went on from there. But I digress. Back to Jay Two. He cures the horse. Maybe he was just practicing for the real stuff later on but, whatever, it's a bit of a come down after his spectacular aerial performance. But things pick up when he's arrested for vagrancy and he walks out of a locked jail cell emulating Christ who, according to John, could also walk through walls. But let's say this guy isn't quite that talented and did it with the aid of a hairpin which he kept hidden in his long tresses. Any problems so far?"

Marie didn't look up from her pad, so Brian continued his summation, picking it up at the miracles in Beaufort, and ending with the wondrous thunderclap at Don Bagley's gigantic assembly.

She gave it a moment before asking if he wanted her to comment on his résumé. When Brian invited her to go ahead she put down her pad and began.

"A whole bunch of people saw half a ton of fresh-caught shrimp tumbling around the hold of a trawler in broad daylight. Now, I figure that's got to be a whole lot different from an ephemeral vision like the Lady of the Rosary or Jesus descending from the nighttime heavens. I believe those shrimp were real. Therefore, either Jay Two really is Jay One, and performed a miracle, or those fishermen were lying through their teeth about their boat being empty."

"Agreed," Brian said, looking at Marie. "They had to be in on it."

Marie looked back at him with serious intent. "I think it's time we started making a few assumptions," she proposed. "I'm going to assume that somebody is running this number. Why and toward what end, I don't know. But I'm going to assume that they went to an enormous amount of time and trouble to set it all up. So I have to believe that whatever has been reported as happening has happened. And that includes the heavens lighting up, and Jesus Two coming down the sky."

"Marie, I've read every word of the report in that file. Twice. And when people described the way the figure came down, just about all of them said slowly, like a man in a parachute. But there was no parachute because somebody would have seen one. So if you'll pardon the rational thinking, if it's impossible for a man to slide down the sky for a thousand feet with nothing beneath him and nothing above him, then it can't have happened."

Marie chewed on that for a moment, then abruptly got up, asked if she could make a phone call, made it, got no answer, then hung up and explained. "That was to a pal of mine. He's not home right now, but I think I know where to find him. He may be able to help us. Shall we go?"

This was a little too dynamic for Brian, who'd been taught to weigh and consider all actions. "Who is he? How can he help us?"

"He used to be a defense correspondent for a bunch of European newspapers. I met him when I worked out of Washington for a time. He's a pretty cluey guy."

"A defense correspondent," Brian said, letting the phrase hang.

Marie picked up her handbag and responded to his implied question. "He's used to the big picture," she said on her way to the door.

It was hardly an explanatory answer, but it was all Brian was allocated. He didn't press. This was the professional Marie, decisive and emphatic. Good, he thought, he could do with a dose of that. Decision and the resolve to carry it out to its logical end were two things that had been conspicuously absent from his life for a long time now.

"Poppy!" the man cried, a baggy-suited Englishman with a cheery, sun-damaged face. He made a mock attempt at rising off the bar stool, leaned forward, and bussed Marie's cheek. "Dear girl, it's been too long." He hadn't got the name wrong, as Marie explained later; for the sake of expediency he called all women Poppy, and all men Steve. Nevertheless, Marie made the introductions.

"Allan Cromer, Brian Sheridan."

Cromer claimed delight at their meeting, Brian mere happiness. Marie slid onto a stool, Brian remained standing, hemmed in by the after-theater crowd which had begun to swell the numbers. Once the home of sensational platters of hearty *auvergnat* fare, the restaurant had long ago reverted to standard French cooking, *sans flair et surprise*. An old, dark eatery living on its gastronomical memories, it nevertheless managed a pleasantly tired ambience and a staunch Gallic fortitude.

"Where have you been keeping yourself? You're just in time to join me," Cromer said in a convivial rush. He called to the bartender: "Nicolas! Deux plus places ici, si vous plaît." Then to Marie again, "Dadou has cooked a *brandade*. Not as good as his *chipolata*, but quite passable all the same."

"Thanks, Allan," Marie said. "But we've already dined."

Horror spread a suffusion of blood across the Englishman's flabby face. "But it's only ten-thirty. You used to be a journo. What are you now, a farmer?"

Marie laughed. "We'll take a glass of white."

"François! Um demi de Aligoté, si vous plaît." Once again Cromer swiveled back to Marie. "You'll like this one. Perhaps a little tart at first blush, but spreads nice and evenly after that. You a scribe, too, Steve?"

"A bookseller," Brian said.

"Better get on your right side then. I'm halfway through my autobiography. Naming names. Quoting sources. Once it's published I expect to be murdered." The last half of Cromer's sentence was expelled in front of a rheumy cough accompanied by a wave of his hand, a signal of his intention to retain the conversation. He snatched up a cigarette from an ashtray and dragged deeply as if nicotine and tar were the antidote for his poisoned lungs. "Sorry," he apologized, his eyes watery. "Got a bit of a cold."

The sight of the bartender bearing a half bottle of wine worked a swift cure. "Ah!" he said, welcoming the bottle with genuine affection. Then, turning to Marie: "So, Poppy. Been busy, have you?"

"That's why I'm here, to pick your brains," Marie confessed.

"Article for *Gourmet*, is it?" Down the wine road, Dijon to Beaune, that sort of thing?"

"Nope. It's the other half of your brain we're interested in."

"Damn!" Cromer said, somewhat crossly. "Nobody ever takes advantage of my real field of expertise."

"Allan, I want to ask you about helicopters."

"Helicopters . . ." Cromer sighed. "I'd rather talk about the pleasures of the grape, but go ahead, dear girl. Fire away."

"I know in air-sea rescue, for example, they lower a man on a cable to pull somebody out of the water. But that's only, what, forty or fifty feet above the waves. Could you dangle somebody a lot higher than that? I mean, would it be possible to let somebody down from, say, a thousand feet?"

"Absolutely. You're only governed by the thickness of the cable and the size of the drum it's wound around. You can get steel cable not much thicker than a pencil that's strong enough to lift a piano. And you could mount a drum as big as a Toyota on an Iroquois's outrigger. The pilot would have to compensate, of course, but that wouldn't be much trouble for a good man."

Marie thought about that while she traced a figure in the beaded condensation on her glass, the warmth of the crowded bistro swamping the air conditioning. "Okay," she said at last. "Now for something completely different. Did I read somewhere that the Pentagon was playing around with the idea of using weather as a weapon? Do you know anything about that?"

The Englishman's opinion of the Pentagon's ideas was projected by a derisive flap of his hand. "Oh, that was Gold's brainwave. Whipping up a flood and drowning an opposing army like the Red Sea closing over the Egyptians. Great idea, militarily speaking, but we're light-years away from the technology to make it work."

"Would that be Cedric Gold?" Marie asked.

"Who else thinks that big?" Cromer asked rhetorically. "He's a little unstable. I hear he owns a collection of John Martin prints blown up full-size. Anybody would go bonkers surrounded by something like that."

"I don't remember the flood idea," Marie confessed. "I thought it had to do more with thunder and lightning."

Cromer, with his glass to his mouth, confirmed that in midsip. "That was Gold, too. It started life with a French code name, but you know what morons those Pentagon chappies are, they're uncomfortable with foreign languages, so they changed it to the Paris Project. It was originally called Son et Lumière." Cromer looked at Brian. "Know what that means, Steve?"

"Sound and Light," Brian answered.

"Give the man another drink," Cromer said, picking up the bottle and topping up Brian's glass. "And one for the lady, and one for the master." He immediately drank the new wine he'd poured for himself, chewing it in his teeth and closing his eyes on the cusp of ecstasy. "God bless Bacchus," he breathed.

"Tell us about Sound and Light," Marie prompted.

The Englishman returned from his Olympian worship, stuck a new cigarette between his lips, and, zipping a flame from a silver lighter, lit a mouth candle for his other god.

Brian wondered idly who that was, the god of tobacco. Saint Marlboro?

"The sound part was a terror weapon," Cromer told them. "Colossal amplifiers and speakers mounted beneath an Iroquois chopper. The idea was to incapacitate enemy ground troops by bombarding them with thunderclaps, bust their eardrums, drive them crazy, that sort of thing. The light part was a new tactic for night fighting, of course, and another exercise in gigantism. A bank of huge halogen lamps, brighter than the brightest search-light, rigged under an Iroquois again. They were pointed upward at an angle to reflect off a giant mirror-coated dish mounted above them. Turned night into day, as you might imagine. There was some talk of using it in Desert Storm, but they didn't need to. They could have phoned in that victory."

Halfway through the explanation Marie had swung her eyes to Brian, who was looking right back at her. They knew that what they were hearing was an answer to much more than the two questions Marie had posed. Yet both realized it couldn't be as sim-ple as that; the information they were getting would be available to any good journalist who wanted to dig for it, so why hadn't somebody posited this idea in the national media? Where was the snag?

Marie slid off her stool, put a hand on Cromer's rumpled shoul-der, and brushed her lips against his jowly cheek. "Allan, you're a jewel."

"You're leaving? Dear girl, you just got here." Cromer looked like a fat child who'd been told the picnic had been rained out; a man like this lived for company.

Brian delivered a pleasantry and held out his hand which the

Englishman gave a dolorous squeeze. There was a minute more small talk, some repeated thanks, then Brian and Marie took their leave.

Cromer watched them go, sad but philosophical: every cloud had a silver lining, he told himself. He reached for this particular lining, not silver, but a lovely pale straw color: Marie's hardly touched glass of Aligoté.

"So there it is," Brian said. "Not much of a trick when you can see the trapdoor on the stage, is it?"

Drenched by the billion-watt effluents of Broadway, turned alternately red, yellow, and white by exploding billboards and marquees, they headed south, oblivious of the sidewalk crush and the traffic yowl.

"There's still something wrong with it." Marie sounded as if she'd seen the illusion fail in front of her. "All those people who saw the figure in the sky said the heavens lit up for maybe ten seconds. And then they heard the thunder. There was definitely ten seconds of silence before the thunder, right?"

Brian got her point, and laid it out for them both. "So if it was a big helicopter carrying lights, or even a small one, why didn't those people hear it? They're the loudest things in the sky. Even if it was two thousand feet up they still would've heard it whomping around up there."

Wrapped in a thick veil of disappointment, they stopped for a light and said no more for a minute. It had seemed the solution had been handed to them, but when they reached for it there was nothing but thin air.

They got a walk sign and crossed Forty-sixth.

"Who was this guy you were talking about," Brian asked. "Cecil Gold, was it?"

"Cedric Gold. A whiz-kid scientist. Worked for a think tank under contract to the Pentagon. I was certain somebody borrowed his idea, but if they did, they must have used a flying saucer."

"How about a glider?" Brian asked with a minimum amount of hope.

Marie shook her head, and it appeared that the action had changed the hue of her skin the way a Martian might register a negative, but the responsibility lay with the huge Fuji sign they were passing. "A man tethered to a glider would be all over the sky. And a glider can't carry a load like a big chopper can anyway." She clicked her tongue behind her teeth. "Dammit! A helicopter solves everything. But we don't have to ask Allan Cromer if anybody's invented a silent one."

Brian took Marie's arm and guided her around a clamorous group of men, all of whom ogled her, slack grins fronting their boozy breaths. They wore name tags on their suit jackets, and were behaving with the forced bravado of the out-of-towner trying to appear at ease in a city ten times bigger and faster than the one they were from.

Brian halted her at the curb. "You want to go for coffee?"

Marie's forehead was creased in a neuralgic pucker, her teeth pressed into the pink fullness of her lower lip. "I've got something knocking at my head begging to be let in. I better go home and sleep on it."

"What kind of thing? Can you see its shape?"

Marie drew breath to carry an answer, then released it unused. She tried again. "Something's triggered a thought. Something you said, maybe, I don't know. But it won't come and it could be important."

Her bemusement carried an air of vulnerability, something close to a hurt exposure. Brian was hit by a sudden emotion, a protective instinct, and he reacted as if she'd been rudely handled by those drunken conventioneers. He reached for her. Almost put his arms around her but converted the movement at the last moment into a dry peck on the cheek. "I'll get you a cab," he said.

He looked quickly uptown to disguise his fluster, stepped off the sidewalk, and flagged down a piece of the yellow river flowing down the avenue.

He opened the taxi's door. Marie slipped into the rear seat and sat there looking at him, and Brian saw from her expression of permissive expectancy that she'd understood his original intention and was leaving him the option of carrying it out.

As if in a playback of a video projected behind his eyes he saw himself getting into the cab, pulling her to him, quick-kissing her neck and her jaw. Fastening on those fabulous lips. He saw the trip to her apartment, unnoticed by either of them, the transit time lost to the conformance of mouths and tongues. Into her apartment. Clothes flying off with inefficient abandon. The quick, grainy, silken absorption. The smack and collision of bodies sweetly savaging each other.

Brian hit the stop button. The screen blanked. "I'll call you tomorrow," he said, stepping back and closing the cab's door. Marie went on looking at him as the taxi took off.

Brian started in the same direction.

No throbbing questions roiled his mind, nor was he the victim of muddled confusion. He knew exactly why he'd closed that cab door, and it had nothing to do with his vows. The reason was plain and simple: if he was going to have any chance of exposing this Jesus fake, it would be because of Marie's help. She'd just demonstrated that fact, coming up with a weapons expert in nothing flat. And here she was on the edge of some kind of breakthrough, something important for whose retrieval she needed sleep. Which she wouldn't have got very much of if he'd got into that cab.

He hailed one himself and rode downtown, and New York once again became huge and impersonal, and Brian Sheridan perhaps the most single of all its single male residents.

CHAPTER
12

After the meeting at Stone Mountain, at which three hundred thousand people claimed to have heard the voice of God endorse his Son—in exactly the same words as could be found in The Gospel According to Saint Mark—it became impossible for Don Bagley to let the Lord Returned preach on his TV show.

For one thing, a live audience would have been too terrified by the Presence to respond with anything but hysteria. And, for another, the technicians would have been too upset and nervous to do a proper job. So Don Bagley had his huge living room cleared, and a simple set erected in it. He hired a TV crew made up of severe doubters—not an easy thing to find in Atlanta—and, several days after the Stone Mountain event, went ahead and did his show in his own home and without anybody present except the principals.

But his other audience, his broadcast audience, was huge. There wasn't a religious station in the country that didn't want to run every second of his show. The network affiliates and the independents wanted edited versions. And the majors in New York and Los Angeles demanded highlight clips for their six o'clock news programs.

Bagley was delighted by such acceptance, overjoyed by it, but he remained superprotective of his Lord's privacy. When a nationally famous newscaster asked permission to interview Jesus,

Bagley refused, but granted her access to the next best thing: the two disciples the Lord had chosen.

The interviewer, auburn-haired and glamorous, came down on the day of the show, fought her way through the adoring multitudes that were now permanently camped outside Bagley's formidable wrought-iron gates, and arrived at the house flustered and straightening her Dior suit. But, being a seasoned pro, she was soon giving her cameraman an establishing shot out on the patio, plus fifteen seconds of spiel, before going into the living room where her producer had set up a three-chair bookend arrangement: Jimmy Carew, the interviewer, and Jack Carew.

"Jimmy," the woman said, after she'd introduced the two men to the camera, "how does it feel to be chosen by the Lord?"

With his big-boned body wedged into the simplest chair they could find, Jimmy Carew moved his shoulders and feet before he moved his lips. "To tell you the truth, I'm still tryin' to get used to the idea."

"How about, you, Jack?" the woman asked, turning the other way. "Have you got used to it yet?"

Jack Carew fingered the lapel mike clipped to his shirt as if it were an embarrassing floral tribute. "I don't figure I'll ever get used to it. Having the Lord call you into his service . . ." He shook his rugged head. "Lemme tell you, it makes you a mite humble."

The interviewer smiled. Nodded her understanding. "When did you first recognize that it was Jesus on that trawler jetty?"

"When I first laid eyes on him. I just knew in my bones that this was the Lord Jesus standing there."

"That go for you, too, Jimmy?"

"Weren't no mistakin' it. He had the, what d'you call it, the aura. Jack and me, we knew it was the Lord right from the start."

"You mean," the woman said, swiveling again, "that you recognized him before the Reverend Sales cried out that it was Jesus returned?"

Jimmy Carew turned to the camera. When this segment went to air, millions would recognize a robust honesty in that handsome face. "I surely wouldn't want to take anything away from the good Reverend. He recognized Jesus, too."

"But later. After *you'd* recognized him . . . ?"

"As I recall, yeah," said Jimmy Carew.

When it was time to shoot the show itself, Howard Willard got things under way.

With his long figure lengthened even more by the slim cut of his dark suit, he stood in front of the simple pulpit, the set's only prop, and graciously thanked the audience for inviting the *Don Bagley Evangelical Program* into their living room. Then, curbing his love of the spotlight, he wisely limited his words to that short welcome, introduced Bagley, and turned the proceedings over to him.

Bagley, solid and sincere, took up a position behind the pulpit, and stared unblinkingly into the camera as if he were looking every man, woman and child out there directly in the eye.

"My friends . . . Brothers and sisters in Jesus . . . Before God called me to labor on His behalf, I was just a businessman, and I'm afraid I can't boast a fine education. I never finished high school. Never went to Emory or Georgia Tech or any of the other fine schools in the Magnolia State. Frankly, outside of the Good Book, I don't know a heck of a lot. But one thing I do know is that you didn't turn on this program to hear *me* speak. And I'd be some kind of fool if I started preaching the word of God to you when the Son of God is right here in person to do just that. But I did want to steal a moment of the Lord's time to tell you of my immense joy that so many, many people have accepted the fact that Jesus had returned as the Gospels promised he would. And for those that stubbornly remain unconvinced, for those that still disbelieve this glorious fact, I'm going to offer more than just prayer. I'm going to offer living proof. And right this very second."

Bagley had decided to use the blackout-and-reveal again for the same reason he'd used it at Stone Mountain: because he didn't want the Lord to just walk on as if he were the next act. So the set went dark for several moments, and when the lights came up again, the pulpit had been whisked away, and Yehsu was standing there in his white robe, his tortured body ruler-straight, his deep, placid eyes unmoving.

He began to speak in that honeyed voice, his words a condemnation that, at first, were unreflected in his calm demeanor.

"When my Father sent me to walk among you in my first ministry, it was to announce the coming Kingdom of God. But this message was usurped by men who donned costly robes and claimed that they and they alone had a mandate from God to speak in His name. No such mandate was ever issued. These men are guilty of the sin of pride. Of misinterpretation of my words. On this rock I will build my church. The church I was referring to was the Church of God, not the church of His son. Look about you. If there are men who preach love, but also preach duty and compliance to an earthly and Latin authority, accept only the first part of their teaching."

He continued his disparagement for another ten minutes, then seemed to gather himself to finish his extraordinary attack.

"Bold and arrogant, these men blaspheme in scriptures they have altered to suit their purpose. They are blots and blemishes, reveling in their untruths while they feast with you, seducing the naive with their fear-mongering talk of Purgatory. They are springs without water, mists driven by a storm of guilt. They promise freedom while they themselves are slaves to a corrupt philosophy. Turn from such men. Cast them from you, for they are brute beasts, creatures of connivance, born only to be caught and destroyed. For like beasts they too will perish, paid back with harm for the harm that they do."

Subsiding, Yehsu raised his ruined right hand in a gentle blessing and just stood there for a tingling moment. The set went to black, and when the lights came up again, he was gone.

A camera shot a title card, which was superimposed over the empty set, and that was the show—short, extremely simple, and tremendously effective.

Twenty minutes later, with Yehsu returned to his bungalow, and the newscaster and her crew battling to get back through the hordes at the front gates, Howard Willard walked into Don Bagley's study.

"Well, how about them apples . . ." He took a seat and ran his hands through his wiggish white hair. "I'd call that a major surprise."

Don Bagley, leaning back behind his desk, was quietly beaming. "Howard," he said, "I've never thought of myself as an intolerant person. In my book, all roads lead to God. But I have to tell you, when I heard the Lord raking the Catholics over the coals, I could've cheered."

"Me, too. They're prideful people. Elitist. And, funnily enough, I've been wondering if the Lord is happy that that particular brand of Christianity is the biggest on the planet."

"Well, you've got your answer now." Bagley chuckled. "The cardinals are gonna get their long johns in a twist over this one."

"That's what bothers me," Willard said, his bushy eyebrows slanting toward each other. "There's bound to be a backlash. You know how defensive they are. It could get nasty."

"I doubt it. How long can they go on denying that Jesus has come back? A few more weeks and we'll take the Lord to the country in person. They'll come, the Church hierarchy. And when they jam into Yankee Stadium and see Jesus in the flesh, they'll know him. If there is a Catholic backlash, it'll be pretty short-lived."

Howard Willard nodded at that, then, as if canceling the implied agreement, shook his head and said, "Pray God you're right, Reverend."

The rental car, the biggest sedan the agency had, was parked on the shoulder of a dusty road that crossed a lazy loop of the Chattahoochee River.

Hennie Van Boder, who had a much stricter approach to duty than the other two, stood in the sun, perspiring in the extraordinary humidity and looking up the road. Patch had had a message delivered a few hours back. The message designated a meeting place, and here they were.

Waiting.

"Okay," Ronny Patch said to Vittorio Vargas—they were lolling back inside the car playing their favorite game—"it's the top of the eighth, one out, bases loaded, and Alomar's up. Do you walk him or smoke him inside?"

"Walk him."

"With Carter on deck? You're outta your goddamn mind."

Vargas's goatee wagged emphatically. "No, I ain't. Clemens has gone all the way and he's tiring. Alomar hits one out."

"No way. Clemens throws a slider right across the plate."

"Bullshit. That pitch doesn't come any closer to the plate than you do when you're eating spaghetti."

"Whatta you know about the game, you fuckin' immigrant? You could draw a base on balls and still get thrown out at first."

A whistle broke up their little spat. Van Boder was watching an automobile slow its approach.

Patch and Vargas got out of the car and joined him.

"Is it them?" Van Boder thinned his eyes against the glare.

"Gotta be," Ronny Patch said.

The car pulled up, a shiny new Dodge Intruder with an Alamo decal on the windshield. The driver's window zipped down, expelling a cool blast of conditioned air. "You the guy called us?" Jimmy Carew asked.

Patch rasped his fingers over his stubbled chin. "Uh-huh."

"What's up?"

"Beats the hell out of me, Lieutenant. We're just Western Union on this one. You wanna follow us?"

They drove to an industrial park out near the airport, to a section in back of the big national freight carriers. Ronny Patch had never been to this place—a repair yard for airline cargo crates and ship containers—had never been to Atlanta, but he'd been able to make some fast arrangements. With the right connections, and enough money, you could arrange anything in a hurry.

They went past a leaning mesh fence and through a pair of gates that opened onto a sandy yard overwhelmed with metallic junk. When everybody got out of the two cars, a chained Doberman went into a paroxysm of rage at the intrusion.

"What the hell are we doing here?" Jimmy Carew demanded.

"Just following orders, boss," Ronny Patch told him.

The five of them walked toward an aluminum shed that looked like a small airplane hangar.

"Hold up. I'll check it out," Patch offered.

"Check what out?" Jimmy Carew asked.

"We gotta run a safety check," Vargas said with bland assurance. "For banana gas."

Ronny Patch started toward the building. Van Boder went with him. They crossed to a door in the structure. Opened it, and disappeared inside.

Jack Carew looked at his brother, looked at the building glinting dully under the hot sun. Sent an irritated look the Latino's way. "What the hell's banana gas?"

"Believe me, that stuff can kill you," Vargas warned.

A few minutes later the door in the building opened. Ronny Patch called to them. "Okay . . ."

Vargas and the Carews started toward him. Jack went through the door first.

"Hey," Vargas said, halting Jack's brother. "You got a cigarette?"

The door in front of them closed.

Jimmy's face pinched in on itself. "You're worried about gas and you want to light up?"

"Yeah, guess you're right," Vargas admitted.

Jimmy continued walking. Pushed through the door.

On the other side, Van Boder stepped out from behind the door and swung a fist the size of a small melon. It poleaxed Jimmy Carew. He pitched forward and joined his brother stretched out on the floor.

Ronny Patch shook his head in wonder. "Banana gas . . . boy, are they from Missouri."

Chortling at the easy deception, the three men carried the limp forms across a cement floor. In the middle of the floor, a container bearing a shipping line's logo looked as if it were being repaired. In actual fact, it wasn't repairs it had received but a small addition, the result of a phone call from Ronny Patch.

A silent, hard-looking man in stained coveralls appeared and watched as the two brothers were carried into the container. The Carews were laid out against its end wall, one on top of the other in an undignified heap.

When Patch and Vargas and Van Boder came out of the container, the floor man hopped behind the wheel of a forklift. The forklift held a large, inch-thick steel sheet in its grip, held it high and perpendicular. When the man moved the vehicle into the container, the steel sheet cleared the door with just inches to spare all around—it was a little like pushing a square cookie back into its square pack.

He drove the forklift the length of the container, stopping three feet away from the end wall. Here he'd welded flanges to the top, bottom, and sides, and he butted the steel sheet flush against them. Then he fetched some equipment and welded the sheet to the flanges. When that was completed, he took two thin metal strips and his acetylene torch and filled in the small gap between the steel sheet and the top and the right-hand side of the container.

Then he was finished.

What he'd done was create a new end wall; the interior of the container was now thirty-six inches shorter than it had been before.

And inside this invisible thirty-six-inch-wide section, the Carew brothers, who were starting to come around, found themselves sealed up in a suffocating, airtight blackness.

The trio left the building. Got into the cars. Patch and Van Boder drove their rental into Atlanta, Vargas following in the Dodge. Vargas left the Dodge in a poor section of the city with the key in it, then joined the other two.

"Hey," Vargas said from the rear seat as they started back toward the airport, and a plane to New York, "maybe that's what they did with Hoffa. Maybe he ain't buried beneath a building. Maybe he's sailing the seven seas in a container, you figure?"

"Nah," said Ronny Patch. "I heard he's running a restaurant in Brazil with the other two."

Vargas bit. "What other two?"

"Elvis and Jimmy Dean." Then, before Vargas had a chance to disparage him, he said, "Okay, I got one. Somebody walks up to you, they want to know what happened to the two disciples, the brothers. What d'you tell 'em?"

"I dunno. What?" Van Boder asked, already snickering in advance of the punch line.

"You tell 'em they've gone on a car-ews," Ronny Patch said.

Hennie Van Boder guffawed.

Vittorio Vargas groaned.

CHAPTER
13

When the respectful greetings had been received, and the demands of ritual and etiquette satisfied, the Bishop of Rome, Vicar of Jesus Christ, and Successor of the Prince of the Apostles, touched the white zucchetto that covered the back of his scalp—a habit he'd developed of late—gathered his shiny white silk robe and sat his aging body down at the round oak table.

Nine other men followed his lead: four red-gowned princes of the Church, their secretaries—humble priests in their plain black soutanes sitting in back of their masters—and the pope's secretary, a monsignor, who sat behind the master of masters.

Work was being done on the Castel Gandolfo, so the pope had remained all summer in the Papal Residence, and this meeting of his inner circle—it was convened each month, or on occasions in between when events merited it—was taking place in an upstairs room located between two elegant courtyards, the Cortile di Sistus V and del Maggiordomo. The room, Simonetti's bow to his hero, Giuliano da Sangallo, was almost as high as it was long, the ceiling sumptuously decorated, the rest an uneasy accommodation of the plain and practical.

Father Gaetano Cresta, sitting tall in his chair behind the stooped figure of his superior, Cardinal Liegi, watched the assembly settle into an obsequious silence while the pontiff coughed behind a lace handkerchief and signaled for the meeting to begin.

There was some standard business first, the pontiff asking a question of Cardinal Teixeira, Prefect of the Congregation of Bishops, before turning to his secretary of state and moving on to the Church's current situation in Vietnam and Cuba.

Cresta grew increasingly impatient. He was certain the Holy Father was saving the worst till last, and he was itching to get the horrific subject out in the open so it could be attended to. Finally the pope checked with his personal aide for the next order of business.

"Ah, yes," the pope said, his receded brow forming a cloud of concern. "A rather distressing development in America has come to our attention. Cardinal Liegi, this would concern you as much as anybody, seeing that it impacts on the denigration of the Church."

Cresta's superior sat a little straighter, although there were those who might have cruelly claimed that such a thing was impossible. Liegi's body was tight and compact, and as his shoulders were rounded almost to the definition of a hunchback, his head was permanently thrust forward as if he were trying for a better view of something.

"It appears," the pope continued, "that a charlatan has appeared. A man impersonating our Lord. We are informed that this demented personage looks extremely like our perception of how the Lord looked during his earthly ministry. And there are claims that he has performed miracles witnessed by hundreds of thousands of people. Are you aware of this, Cardinal?"

"I am, Holiness," Liegi admitted. "And I am more than a little worried by it. I understand that there are many American Catholics who have been taken in by this charade. It is most unfortunate."

Cresta seethed. Unfortunate? It was calamitous! This blasphemous impostor was denigrating Holy Mother Church and spinning a shockingly sacrilegious web for the naive and unwary. Why were Liegi and the Holy Father being so contained about it?

"It is true that America is a country infamous for its excesses," the pope was saying. "Particularly in the Southern part where Protestant fundamentalism seems to have warped the fabric of much of the society. Nevertheless, we feel that something should be done. We feel the matter should be looked into."

Cardinal Liegi glanced up at one of the richly painted ceiling medallions, an allegorical representation of two aspects of Truth. "I have already taken steps in that direction, Holiness," he answered. "I hope to be able to furnish a report in the very near future."

"Thank you, Cardinal. We shall await it with some trepidation."

The meeting was concluded on that worried note. The pope retired after receiving obeisances similar to those accorded him when he'd entered, then, followed by their secretaries, the cardinals gathered their crimson robes and made a colorful exit.

Cresta arrived back in his office in a driving anger. He'd done what Liegi had instructed him to do long before the meeting: phoned a priest in America, a so-called troubleshooter, and bade him check into the matter. But what was needed was action, not words. This blasphemous rogue in Atlanta, this scoffing wretch, had to be stopped, not just investigated. If a body is bleeding, you don't merely observe and report, you stanch the flow immediately.

Father Cresta sat at his desk and stared at the statue of the Holy Mother, the Blessed Virgin benignly contemplating a silver crucifix that dangled from her porcelain hands. He didn't have to pray to her for her infallibly correct guidance; he knew what had to be done.

And he knew whom he could use to do it.

He jabbed a buzzer on his desk summoning Ludovisi from an outer office. "I want a meeting this afternoon. With Father Santoro. Tell him to tell no one about it. I want utmost secrecy on this, do you understand?"

Ludovisi's blond eyebrows pumped upward at the name. He failed to see how a nobody like Santoro could play any kind of part in a sensitive conference. But he'd learned that, with Gaetana Cresta, all would be revealed in its own good time.

"In the gardens, Father?"

Cresta thought of miniature directional microphones and spying pigeons and leafy tree branches perhaps bristling with disguised electronics. What was needed was some place public but private.

And seeing that they were about to embark on a mission to help the Faith, what better place to plot their course than a church?

After emerging from the subway at Barberini, and wading through a sargasso of revving scooters, smoking buses, and ready-to-kill automobiles, Father Franco Santoro escaped into the relative tranquility of the Quattro Fontane, a pleasant street that sloped up toward Quirinal, once the highest of the seven hills. It had been named for Quirinus, Santoro recalled, who, with Mars and Jupiter, formed the basis of the Romans' religion, a kind of early trinity, before Paul arrived to persuade them differently.

As he labored up the slope's steepening incline, his badly pressed soutane surrounded him like a hot and spiteful shroud. Santoro was porcinely obese, a fact that he acknowledged, although, preferring the kind and understanding terminology of the French language, he thought of himself as a gentleman of dignified embonpoint.

His thoughts spun ahead to this meeting he'd been so suddenly summoned to. Utmost secrecy, Father Cresta's assistant had stressed. What could the secretary of the Prefect for the Promulgation of the Faith want to see him about in secret? And not in his office but in a small oratory in the Quirinal? For the fifth or sixth time Santoro went back over the conversations he'd had in the past week, comments he'd made, opinions he'd expressed. But he'd said nothing that could have upset the cardinal. He never discussed doctrine. Never discussed the Holy Father except to inquire about his health. He talked about his work, which was his hobby and his avocation, and about food, which, alas, was his passion. What could Father Cresta possibly want with him?

With a heavy unease seeming to increase the grade of the hill, he plodded on toward this puzzling rendezvous.

Father Cresta had always liked the little oratory in which he waited, even though his enjoyment was tempered by Pomarancio's ostentatious frescoes that blazed from the walls, pretentious works illustrating the story of the Cross, the figures too theatrical for a strict representationalist like himself.

He was the only person present, a situation which he'd arranged with a fast phone call to the Suore Missionarie di Gesu, the order that looked after the church. He'd simply told the nuns that he and another priest would like to pray surrounded by the finest representation in Rome of Jesus' dreadful and magnificent sacrifice, and did they think they might hold at bay, just for an hour, any tourists who knocked on their door. The sisters had been flattered that a cardinal's secretary—*the* cardinal's secretary—wanted to offer orisons in their little sanctuary and had flutteringly agreed to arrange a private interlude.

So here he was, he told himself, waiting for an overweight nonentity to arrive so he could charge him with an extremely important and sensitive and perhaps dangerous mission.

He heard the sound of the front door opening, then a nun in a long dark habit led in the waddling priest who was using a handkerchief to wick up moisture from his bulbous brow. The nun padded away to a far door. It closed, and they were alone.

"Father Santoro," Cresta said. His greeting of any peer or subordinate was never anything warmer than a brief acknowledgment of the other person's identity. "Sit here, please." Cresta was himself sitting behind the last pew in one of the cane-bottomed chairs that were regularly set up there for the tourists, and he indicated the one next to him.

It gave a soft wheeze of stress as it took Santoro's weight and for a horrible moment Santoro was afraid it might collapse. He would have died of embarrassment; he wanted to look in control of things in front of the cardinal's secretary. Santoro knew himself to be a master of vacillation, a chronic dissembler, and a man who woke up each morning expecting to find disaster's calling card slipped beneath his door. He needed the discipline, the guidance, and the example of someone like Gaetano Cresta. Although he thought him almost an antisaint, the apotheosis of a person full of compassion and love, he still felt that he was the best Roman Catholic he'd ever met.

"I'll come right to the point, Father," Cresta said, fixing Santoro with a gaze that defied rupture. "We are meeting in strictest confidence. This conversation will be known only to ourselves and, officially, will never have taken place. Do I make myself clear?"

Santoro's response tumbled out. "Yes, Father. Absolutely, Father."

The fat man was painfully anxious to please, Cresta saw, and knew he'd chosen wisely. He hadn't selected him for his professional expertise; he had no use for that—the man was a philatelist; the Vatican issued its own stamps and coins, and Santoro worked in a section of that department—but because, being terrified of authority, he'd do as he was told.

And there was another reason: the island where he'd spent most of his youth. An island whose ways and language he'd still be very familiar with.

"I want you to help me, Father. I want you to help me help the Faith. Will you do that?"

Santoro's nod belied his understanding. "Of course. Anything. What do you want me to do?"

Cresta circled around a reply, a shark demoralizing a grouper before the lunge and snap. "For some time now, the Faith has been under attack in America. I refer not to the regular antipapists, the homegrown hate mongers or the competing religionists with their pitiful, unprovable creeds, but of American Catholics, Catholics who feel they can listen to the revealed wisdom of the Holy Father but hear only the parts they're happy with."

"Ah," Santoro said, to indicate agreement.

"Too many of them approach their Faith as if it were a pizza to be ordered according to preference. They feel they can pick and choose. And, whether they realize it or not, whenever they do that they make the acknowledgment of holy truth impossible. However"—Cresta altered his sitting position, disgust twinging his mouth—"recent events have accelerated the drift within the Church. I'm speaking, of course, of that colossal fraud who has the mind-boggling audacity to claim that he is the Lord Jesus Christ."

Santoro knew all about this, of course. It was the talk of the Vatican, one of the main topics at lunch today, in fact. One more sad example of the eccentric and religiously misguided Southern states of America. His shrug was almost one of forgiveness. "It's the fundamentalists down there, Father. Their own faith is so thin and feeble and wrong, they'll jump at anything."

"It's not the fundamentalists that bother me," Cresta told the cool spaces of the painted church. "They can pick up as many rattlesnakes as they want, for all I care. It's the Catholics down there I'm concerned about. They're listening to this madman. Have you read some of the things he's been saying?"

Santoro's fleshy jowls moved in wobbly unison. "I know he's been talking against the Church."

"Talking against it?" When Cresta hit the first word it was like a spring propelling him to his feet. He spoke down at Santoro, firing his delivery at him from an acute angle. "He's not talking against it, he's raving against it. He sounds like John Wycliffe preaching the abolition of the papacy. Can you believe it? A man disguised as Christ, and they're listening to him."

A response was called for, but Santoro was reluctant to comply. He'd never seen the cardinal's secretary so angry before, not like this, his sharp white teeth and his long body compressed as if he were pushing an automobile. "I grant you," Santoro began, trying for a note of placation, "that this madman is guilty of extremely bad taste and insulting behavior. Perhaps even blasphemy. But I can't see him actually doing much damage."

"You can't see him doing much damage . . ." Cresta tilted his upper body forward a notch, and Santoro felt his rancor like heat from an oven. "You evidently haven't been following events, Father. I have. Perhaps I'd better apprise you of the situation. In the Southern states of America, where we need every Catholic we can get, in parts of midwestern and southwestern America, as well as Southern California, the congregations are shrinking. If a church used to get a total of five hundred faithful for three masses on a Sunday, it's now getting at least fifty less. That's a ten-percent drop-off. And the drop in attendance is increasing. They're staying away because they either actually believe this man is Jesus, or they're giving him the benefit of the doubt. These are Catholics I'm talking about. Born and brought up in the shadow of Holy Mother Church. And in spite of all that teaching, in spite of what they know from their Gospels to be God's living truth, thousands of them think Jesus has returned. A few cheap tricks and those fools are awed. Some of them are even converting to the Baptist faith, if you can call total immersion a faith."

"That's terrible," Santoro admitted. "Awful."

"Yes, it is awful, isn't it?" Cresta echoed, on the edge of parody. "And if it's allowed to continue for much longer, we'll have a crisis on our hands. We could be facing a schism."

"Surely not," Santoro said, emboldened enough to present an opinion. "Surely it can only be a matter of time before this fraud is unmasked. The apostates will return, tails between their legs, they'll be welcomed back to the fold, suitably disciplined for their wavering faith, and, like a broken bone that's properly set, the Church will be stronger than ever."

"Stronger than ever . . ." Cresta had a demeaning way of repeating somebody's last sentence and making it sound like the most asinine thing he'd ever heard. "You seem unable to grasp the fact, Father, that the Faith is under attack in America. We're facing a resurgence of the *episcopi vagantes*, insolent and aggressive rebels tunneling at the foundations of the Holy Creed. We have black priests who want spontaneous demonstrations in the aisles. Oriental priests who want to improve the teachings of Jesus Christ by folding in those of Confucius. White priests who want permission to fornicate. Women who think they should be allowed to take Holy Orders in spite of Christ choosing only males for his apostles. The spirit of rebellion is rife in America, Father. Out of control."

"Yes, but—"

"What if just five percent of American Catholics, fascinated by this charlatan's television persona and his self-inflicted stigmata, dazzled by tales of his healing powers, his miracle working, swept along by the momentum of fad and fashion . . . what if they break away and form another faction? We're talking about the possible loss of five million members of the Faith, or do you think that figure's inflated? Perhaps I'm wrong. Perhaps it would be a mere four million we'd lose. Does that make you feel better, Father?"

Santoro stared up from his inferior position, gathered blood showing through the skin of his inflated cheeks. "But surely the cardinal, with his peerless American contacts . . . surely he can bring his influence to bear."

"The cardinal's peerless American contacts," Cresta replied, with a look of pitiless scorn, "comes down to a monsignor in Chicago who will no doubt look into the matter and report back that the situation is exactly as we know it is, which will accomplish nothing."

"Then what is to be done?" Santoro asked in all innocence.

"You cannot guess?"

After a long moment of struggle Santoro had no alternative but to display his stunted sense of projection. "I'm sorry . . . no."

Cresta slashed a glance away, angry at the sluggishness of the mind he was dealing with. Santoro caught the movement, and its message, and retreated further into self-abasement. "You'll have to forgive me, Father, I never was too quick on the uptake."

Father Cresta positioned his thinly ravaged figure several feet away from the glowing priest, giving himself room to move to an even more domineering position when he got to the meat of his bullying pitch. "We have to seriously interfere with this poseur. We have to get rid of him."

"Expose him, you mean. Yes, of course. But I fail to see how I can help in this matter."

"We don't have time for an exposure. He must be stopped immediately," Cresta explained, then added, with a hissing brutality, "We have to kill him."

Santoro's face slipped to one side, then slowly reassembled in its various flabby components. "You can't mean it . . ." His voice was reduced by shock. "We can't do that . . ."

"We must."

"We can't. Not murder somebody. We're priests. We can't take a life. Only God can do that."

Cresta took a small step closer, one of several he'd left himself, and for the first time his delivery was spiked with a note of accommodation. "Naturally, you're startled, Father, and you have every right to be. But consider this . . . there are some people with such a capacity for evil that it can't be a sin to get rid of them. If you'd had the chance to kill Stalin or Luther, or the apostates Calvin and Knox, you wouldn't have hesitated to strike a blow for humanity and the Church. Under certain circumstances, an execution isn't murder, it's a correction of an abnormality. God could only approve of such a step. A firm and righteous defense of the True Faith."

Santoro babbled in continued shock but Cresta interrupted his spluttering.

"Which would you say God would judge more important, Father?" He moved closer to crowd the fat man's space. "The life of a blasphemous fraud or the perdition of millions of Catholic souls?"

When Santoro shook his chin another one repeated beneath it swayed in negative agreement. "Are you sure about all this? Are you certain it wouldn't have the reverse effect? Killing this man could make him a martyr."

"No," Cresta said flatly. "Not if he's killed in the right way. If he dies an undignified death, he'll never become an icon. People aren't going to worship an image of a man lying in a pool of blood on some broken sidewalk. The associations are too strong and too numerous. He'll look like a slain drug dealer or a riddled terrorist."

"You don't know that, Father," Santoro said, in rare contradiction. "It might not make any difference."

The reply was like a stick snapping. "Of course I know that! Do you think the Faith would have been so universally embraced if Pilate had sentenced Christ to instant decapitation? God, in his infinite wisdom, made sure His son died a glorious and memorable death so that Jesus' appalling agony could be a part of our consciousness forever. There is nothing else for it. This monster must be killed. And you have to arrange it."

Santoro felt the oratory's classic configuration undergo a rapid and radical change. The vibrant frescoes seemed to fly off the walls and advance on him in dizzying review, and the scent of the altar flowers became a solid cloying mass in his nostrils. He managed a suffocated gasp. "Me?"

Cresta took the last few steps separating him from the space immediately in front of Santoro's upturned, staring face. He leaned over that face, a narrow tower of rectitude. "It has to be done neatly and cleanly with no possible backlash. A professional must be engaged. You're from Sicily, Father, where such a person can be readily found, I do believe. I want you to go there immediately and do this."

"Go there?" Cresta might have been suggesting a trip to Purgatory. "But I left Sicily thirty-five years ago. I'd be as much a stranger there as you would be, Father. Besides, I don't know anybody in the Mafia. I never did."

"Money buys everything in this material world. Including introductions. You'll be provided with sufficient funds to hire an expert. He must be an impeccable gunman and thoroughly experienced so we can count on his efficiency. A shot rings out, the impostor falls, and the culprit is never found. Death by persons unknown."

Distress and dismay gave Santoro the sagging mouth of a goldfish. He suddenly couldn't remain seated any longer. Had to move or die. He swung his beamy legs, angling them off his sticky chair, and Cresta was forced to grant him space. Breathing as if he'd just climbed stairs, Santoro said, "I don't think I could do it, Father. I just don't have it in me. Please, I beg you, ask somebody else."

"Impossible. Only three people know about this. You, me, and my secretary. To ask somebody else would bring in a fourth person and lessen secrecy."

Santoro knew he was trapped; knew he was part of it now. It was hideously repulsive but it was a fact: he'd been enlisted to arrange a murder. He made one last thin stab at getting off this brutal hook.

"Father Cresta . . . I've seen photographs of this man. And he looks remarkably like, well, the image I have of the Lord. Perhaps the one we all have."

"And?"

"And, well, I've read the accounts of what they're calling his miracles. Witnessed by apparently reliable sources . . ."

"And?"

"So I can well understand how some gullible parishioners could have been overwhelmed by a talented magician. But couldn't this be pointed out to them? If he could be shown up for the faker he is, then there'd be no need to . . . to physically dispose of him."

"Father Santoro, you are giving me a very curious impression." Cresta tried to keep his voice and his anger tamped down. "Is there the slightest doubt in your mind that this dangerous maniac is not who he claims to be?"

"Of course not. He can't be Jesus. It's beyond imagination to think that the Gospels could be mistaken. Even if they were, and the Lord returned not to the whole world but to a single city, it would be to Rome, not America. To his Vicar on Earth, whom he'd embrace, not slander." Then, as a thought rotted the under-pinnings of this, Santoro said, "It's just that he looks so much like Jesus. And the amazing things he's done have been attested to."

Cresta's voice could have belonged to a man brandishing lethal weapons. "For false Christs will appear and perform signs and miracles to deceive the elect. The sun will be darkened, and the moon will not give its light. The stars will fall from the sky, and the heavenly bodies will be shaken. At that time men will see the Son of Man coming in clouds with great power and glory. And he will send his angels and gather his elect from the four winds, from the ends of the earth to the ends of the heavens." The cardinal's secretary paused to set restraints against his temper. "Apart from the false Christ deceiving with miracles, do you think any of that has happened, Father?"

Santoro shook his head with vigor.

Cresta knew he needed this Sicilian clod and that it would be counterproductive to flay him for his scandalous and irreligious musings. He therefore subjugated all other previous roles to that of feared chairman, all-powerful dean, strict and severe com-mander. "I have every confidence in your ability, Father. I know you have the inner fortitude necessary for success in this undertak-ing, a success which, alas, must go unacknowledged by your im-mediate superiors. However, I will know who has helped the Church in her time of need, and you will have my everlasting ad-miration and thanks." Cresta turned slightly so that he faced the doors. "I think you'd best start immediately. May the blessed saints grant you all possible speed and good fortune."

Santoro played host to half a shuddering breath, nodded to Cresta's presence, and, smothered by the enormity of his assign-ment, left the church and walked in a daze down the hill named for the original god of the Holy City of Rome.

CHAPTER
14

Marie woke with it in her frontal lobes: the thought that had spent the deep night in a slow and misty journey across her subconscious.

She reached out and punched buttons, which resulted in a repetitive B-flat undoing a cloak of sleep one hundred blocks to the south.

"Hi. Did I wake you?"

Brian's mouth worked in slight advance of the rest of his faculties. "No, no. I've been up for at least twenty seconds."

"I know how they did it. Come for breakfast. Come now." Unaware that she was talking like a telegram, Marie hung up, slapped her thigh in mild triumph, went into the bathroom, and stepped under the shower, permutations spinning through her head. She dressed quickly, too preoccupied to choose with her normal good eye, then went into the kitchen and prepared breakfast.

She had everything on the table by the time Brian got there. He'd come in the hurry she'd urged: his hand hadn't held a razor since the previous day, and he'd simply finger-combed his hair. In chinos and a crushed shirt under a cotton jacket, only his steady brown eyes and the sagacious line of his forehead kept him from looking like a tough guy in a film noir festival.

Marie waited till they'd both had half a cup of coffee before explaining. "I thought it was something you said when we were walking down Broadway last night, but it turned out to be something I saw. Something that was pretty hard to miss. The Fuji sign."

Brian still didn't get it. The Fuji sign meant only bright lights to him, and while bright lights was the subject under discussion, it still didn't tell him how anybody could get a huge bank of them to stay up in the sky. "Please," he appealed. "I'm just a simple priest. Give me another clue."

"Think of Goodyear." Marie was smiling, though not through any sense of superiority—a journalist was trained to investigate, a religious the very reverse—but because she was charmed by the air of remissiveness that mixed in so appealingly with his unbrushed hair and the masculine shadow on his jaw.

"Film and tires. Tires and film . . ." Brian bought time with another sip of coffee, but a connection refused to present itself. Feeling like an idiot, he shrugged and made a face. "I give up."

"They both fly blimps."

An airship. A behemoth of the skies. A huge undercarriage to which a bank of lights and a barrage of speakers could easily be rigged. A fat, slothful aircraft that could hover like a tethered balloon while it lowered a man on a cable. Now Brian really felt like an idiot.

"They have electric motors," Marie told him. "A thousand feet above you you'd hear little more than a hum, if that."

"I love it," Brian said. "It's perfect. But is it possible for anybody to get their hands on one? I mean, there can't be too many blimps for hire, can there?"

"Not huge ones like the Fuji blimp, no. But I know there are smaller airships that do aerial surveying, film work, that kind of thing." It was a good point Brian had made, and it presented an inherent advantage which Marie picked up on. "It'll make it that much easier to check," she said. "If we were checking small planes or choppers, it'd take forever."

"Where do we start?"

"I don't think we'll have to look any further than Atlanta. This whole thing seems to be centered around there, and they'd want to contain it."

"Makes sense," Brian conceded. "They do a lot of film work in Atlanta."

With a small measure of surprise Marie said, "How do you know about film work in Atlanta?"

"I know somebody who lives there. A fabulous cook. Runs a catering service for the film crews. She used to live in Conomahack. She was about the only person there who read books that didn't have a busty young woman on the cover cowering in front of a Gothic mansion."

"You still in touch with her?"

"We swap letters. Hers are marvelous. When she left Conomahack, the IQ average plummeted."

"What's her name?"

"Bunny Carlson."

Marie turned, leaned back in her chair, and pulled a phone off its wall bracket. Put it down in front of Brian. "Call her. Ask her to find out who has an airship for rent."

Brian reached for the phone as if it were a sleeping pet of uncertain temperament. "What do we do if she locates somebody?"

"Then you get to see Bunny." Marie said it with no particular emphasis, yet Brian detected a serrated shape within her words. Warm and funny and bright, Bunny Carlson had been a pal, an intellectual soul mate, with no desire for an entanglement with a celebate. She'd admitted an attraction once but had told him it would take her too long to get the rust out of his back muscles, and she didn't have that kind of time. However, he thought, if Marie wanted to think he'd had a yen for somebody, that was okay; it saved him from the stigma of asexuality. Although that was one misconception he was planning to explode.

Brian called information, got the number in Atlanta, and punched it in. He spoke to his friend, traded some fast up-to-date news, explained what he wanted—though not why he wanted it—gave her Marie's number, and hung up.

"She's going to call around and get back," he told Marie when she brought in cereal and toast. They ate for a while, the main subject on hold as Marie talked about this and that, the edge gone from her voice. It made Brian wonder if her softening was because she'd heard, in his half of the just concluded phone call, the absence of any triste phrases or stilted pauses which could stud a conversation between two people who'd been more than just good company. It shifted his opinion a little as to how Marie regarded him. It was flattering to think that she saw him through so colorful a prism, and exciting to think that she'd attached a proprietary claim to their relationship.

The buzz of the phone brought him back, and he answered it, certain it was Atlanta returning his call. It was. Marie got up and fetched him a pad and pencil.

"Hi, Bun Bun ... yep, go ahead." Brian wrote down some names and a number. "That's it? Just the one outfit? ... Okay, super. I'll give him a call." Brian listened for a long moment, then shot his eyes at Marie. She stared back at him. His cheeks had etiolated, and he was holding himself very still. He thanked the woman on the other end of the line in a tone quite different from the ebullient one he'd used to greet her, hung up, and dropped his eyes to the pad. "The name of the company's Airship Inc. Owned and flown by Peter Hecke." He looked up at Marie, and said in that same lithic voice, "We won't be talking to him. He came up here to New York, but he never got back to Atlanta. Remember that bizarre slaying in Bloomingdale's a few weeks back?"

Marie had already had a second to absorb the news; she'd guessed the pilot's fate from Brian's reaction. "A blimp pilot is murdered, and the Carew brothers disappear. They're mopping up, Brian. They're getting rid of the evidence."

"But the Carews apparently left a note. Something about not being worthy enough to serve the Lord."

"Do you believe that note?"

Brian got up. Moved his head in a small baffled arc. "Who's doing this? And why? Bagley hasn't asked for one red cent. Televangelists build networks, churches, campuses. If they're not trying to build a glass cathedral or Fundamental U, what are they planning?"

The ability of the brain to absorb a shock, drop down a gear, then come up to speed again was evidenced in the way they regained their places at the table and considered this latest development. With no intention of drinking it, Marie stirred her lukewarm coffee, watching the swirl of the liquid reflect the maelstrom they were on the verge of plunging into. She took a breath and began to organize facts, supposition, and hearsay into some kind of order.

"Let's see if we can get a handle on this. If my old journalism teacher were here, he'd tell us to approach the problem as you do a news story: what, who, when, where, how, why. We know what and we know when and we know where. We've got a pretty good idea how. But we don't know why and we don't know who because I don't see Bagley behind something like this. We need a reason and we need some names, and the only name we've got that even comes close is the guy Cromer told us about, Cedric Gold, who we know invented some sound-and-light weapons for the Pentagon. He also proposed using weather to create a flood and wipe out an opposing army. How did Cromer describe it?" Marie knew what the Englishman had said, but she wanted to get Brian thinking on this.

"Like the Red Sea closing over the Egyptians," he responded.

"Then he said something I didn't understand," Marie confessed. "He said Gold had a collection of full-sized John Martin prints. I've never heard of John Martin."

Brian had; he was dazzled by his work. "He was a nineteenth-century English painter. He was known as Mad John Martin. Painted huge dark apocalyptical canvases usually with biblical themes. Joshua commanding the sun to stand still, that kind of thing. There's one at Yale that's sensational. A painting of the flood with two moons and a lightning bolt slashing right across it, and a tiny Noah's ark hidden on a far mountaintop. Once you see his stuff you never forget it."

The sun, reflecting off a window in a building opposite, sent a shard of nervous light shooting into the apartment. It crashed silently against the glass of a Japanese poster like an arrow from God. Brian didn't believe in omens; he was a fan of rational thought. He applied a little to what he'd just told Marie.

"Is there a connection here or just a coincidence? This man Gold admires John Martin, a man who paints religious scenes on a vast scale. A man who painted *the* modern painting of the Old Testament flood, a painting with two moons in it. Is that the kind of thing that sparks a guy like Gold? Does he imagine the effect on the tides if the earth suddenly attracted another moon, and try to apply it to a military weapon? He fails at that, so instead he invents sound-and-light weapons, pyrotechnics in the sky, aping the Bible again. Gold sounds like some kind of religious freak who draws on the testaments for his ideas. So if you wanted to fake the Second Advent, maybe he's the guy you'd go and see. Or somebody like him."

"There's nobody like him," Marie said. "But I think we could be getting carried away here. We have one name and we're in danger of talking ourselves into believing he's part of this. These so-called secret weapons are never very secret. People in the weapons industry always know about them. There are dozens, perhaps hundreds, of people who could have tailored Gold's invention any way they wanted to."

Brian found that, while Marie had been talking, he'd written the name Gold on the notepad. He'd surrounded it with tiny strokes imbuing the word with the glitter and worth of its precious namesake. He scribbled a series of Xs through it.

"You're right. If it was that easy . . ." He let the thought sink of its own weight and fished up a new one. "What if we try to get to some of the other players? Like the lame man in the boarding-house who was miraculously cured. I'll bet you a hundred bucks he'll turn out to be a retired washing-machine repairman. He's got to be in on it. And Don Bagley's doctor. And his gate man. Performers all in this little production."

Marie thought they were too late for that. "If they were in on it, and they've heard about the pilot being killed, they've probably already run for cover." She raised her hands. "I just don't know where to go from here."

"Shall we try a little fresh air?" Brian asked. "See if that sparks anything?"

A few minutes later they were strolling past the closed nighttime joys of Yorkville, the bars and restaurants yawny and squint-eyed at nine o'clock in the morning. They walked for an hour without saying much, miserly with a conversation devoid of ideas. Having moved aimlessly north, then west, they ended up on Madison Avenue, where they silently window-shopped a couple of blocks of smart little stores.

Finally, Brian shrugged, glanced at his watch, and said, "Well, I guess my brain isn't coming in today."

Marie kept her eyes on the sidewalk. "It's my fault. I'm not giving you anything to hit off. Maybe bringing me in on this was a big fat mistake."

It was a good ten seconds before Brian stopped walking. "A mistake," he said, straining for a thought that danced just beyond retrieval.

Then popped onto a mental screen.

He grabbed Marie's hand and hurried her back to the previous block. Marie fired questions at him, but Brian didn't explain until they'd reached one of the little specialty stores they'd passed, this one specializing in Oriental antiques. In the window was a small world of porcelain dreams and coral fantasies. Pale green Sung figures, a baying camel, a wild-eyed horse of the Ming, a set of glazed-pottery polo players whose game had been undecided for the last six hundred years. But the object of Brian's fixed attention was a portrait of a middle-aged Chinese, a man wearing the layered ceremonial robes and the curious mortarboard-like headgear of the ancient emperors. He had a thin, skimpy chin beard and equally anorexic sideburns, a mustache like a broken eyebrow, and eyes as cruel as a steel trap.

Brian nodded at the painting as if he were personally acquainted with the worthy. "I know where we can start. I should have thought of it way before this."

Marie looked at Brian. Looked at the painting. "You're saying this gentleman can help us?"

Brian gave that a nod. "By a mistake he made. That's Yang Ti, second emperor of the Sui. He set some kind of record for arrogance and personal depravity. Built a new capital for himself full of pleasure palaces, and a two-thousand-mile canal system. All of it with forced labor, half of which died on the job. The people hated him so much he wisely sent a double in his place whenever he appeared in public. The people knew it was a double and were pretty frustrated."

"And his mistake?"

"He got cocky. He went out one day in place of his double, thinking the crowd would never know. But he gave himself away.

He admired a bayonet, a *tz'u tao*, belonging to one of his guards, and when he pronounced the word he gave the *u* in *tz'u* four tones. Everybody knew his double was from Lo-yang on the eastern plains, where they pronounced that word with just two tones. They fell on him like a ton of bricks."

"He was undone by his accent," Marie said, somewhere between amusement and admiration. She knew now what was in Brian's mind. "That's not bad," she said. "We find a Henry Higgins, a grammarian or whatever, and get his take on Jay Two's accent. You know somebody?"

"Sure," Brian said, tilting his unshaven jaw. "But the name isn't Higgins, it's Blas. And it won't be *his* take because he's a her."

Within forty minutes of going back to Marie's apartment, making a phone call, and picking up the Jesus folder, they were getting out of a cab in front of Columbia University.

The woman Brian had arranged to see, a professor in Near Eastern languages and civilizations, knew Brian only through correspondence—they'd traded views on an Akkadian tablet that had come to light—so this would be their first meeting.

They were directed to her office, a cramped and unsociable cubbyhole with just two small chairs allowed on the other side of a scratched metal desk. Like many offices inhabited by scholar-teachers, the place was far heavier on pamphlets, folders, and catalogs than it was on learned tomes. The walls were blank save for a framed photograph of the professor, in grubby work clothes and a sun hat, standing within the meticulously stringed lines of an archaeological dig. The woman who came around from behind a desk looked a lot more chic in the flesh than she did in the snapshot.

"So there really is a Father Brian Sheridan," Evita Blas said, offering a small, hard hand.

"You look just like your letters," Brian responded. He'd meant it as a joke, but he was struck by how close it was to the mark: Professor Blas was neat and concise with no superfluous poundage to her small frame. In her midfifties, she had silver hair pulled back so sharply it seemed to have fixed her eyebrows in an expression of permanent interrogation. The eyes, olive black, and the porous quality of the skin over her stretched cheekbones confirmed an Iberian bloodline, a fact further attested to by the heavy copper torque she wore on her left wrist.

"Evita, this is a friend of mine. Marie Olivier."

"I'm happy to meet you," Marie said, admiring the concise togetherness of the other woman; the beige woolen suit, the half-heel Italian strap sandals. The academic looked at her for a half second too long, a look with a subtext that said that this was an awfully good-looking young woman for a priest to be squiring around. Brian caught the brief inference and overcompensated.

"Marie's a writer," he informed her. "A journalist. I asked her to help me out on a chore. I'm sorry to be so mysterious, Evita, but I can't really tell you much about it."

The woman held up an understanding hand. "Don't give it a second thought. We all have our projects and we all protect them." She pointed to the skimpy chairs. "Tell me how I can help you."

Brian presented the red folder. Took out the cassette tape Harold Chifley had told him was in there and which he hadn't bothered to play. "There's a man's voice on this. I was hoping one of your colleagues could maybe pinpoint his accent for us."

Without commenting Evita Blas lifted a phone, punched three digits, spoke into the phone for a fast twenty seconds, then hung up. "He's got a tutorial, but he'll come as soon as he can. Gamal Makram. Near Eastern languages. He's very bright." She picked up the phone again. "We're going to need a cassette machine." She made another call, then the three of them made small talk for ten minutes, the archaeologist asking Marie polite questions about her work. Marie felt like a dunce talking about the techniques of magazine writing, very much aware that if she hadn't been there, Brian and their hostess would have been sifting through the deep and dusty layers of the fabled cities of the Euphrates.

But her discomfort was short-lived; the door opened before very long and a serious-looking student delivered an elderly cassette player and a third spindly chair, then, on the way out, almost walked into the man Evita Blas had called.

A robust lime aftershave had him trapped in a saccharine clutch, its scent easily defeating that of the rose he held plumply in his hand. After the introductions were over, and Brian had explained what he wanted, the new arrival, Gamal Makram, a nut-brown, floppily dressed man with a spheroid face and a struggling head of hair, chanced the just-delivered chair, then nodded pleasantly at Brian.

"Go ahead," he invited. "Let's hear this mystery man of yours." His accent was eastern Levant, Brian guessed; Lebanese or perhaps Egyptian. The big man lowered his heavy eyes, brought the flower to the bulb of his nose, and concentrated as Brian loaded the tape and hit the play button.

Yehsu's liquid voice floated into the room, a hollow, echoing quality behind it, taped, as it had been, by somebody in a studio audience. It ran for just three minutes; then Brian clicked off the machine and checked with Makram, who was moving his head ponderously, his chuckle sounding like a mild attack of hiccups. He said into the rose, unaware he was holding it like a microphone, "I think I know that voice."

"You're not alone," Brian said. "By now half the country does."

Makram asked Brian to replay the tape and, after Brian had complied, brought the solid concretion of his body forward in his chair. He cleared his throat, then made a slow and weighty pronouncement. "The way he shapes his vowels, the slight gutturals on his aitches, the plosives underpronounced, the retroflex *r*'s . . . at first I thought this man was Turkish. But now I think a little farther west. I'd say he's Syrian. But he had a parent who was from Turkey. His mother, maybe."

"Syrian," Brian repeated. "Where would you say he learned his English?"

"Impossible to say. He has the long *a*'s, but that doesn't mean too much. I learned my English in Lebanon and I've lived in America for thirty-five years and I still have the long *a*'s. I'd like to borrow the tape, if that's okay. I'd like to listen to it a few more times. Maybe I can get a little closer for you."

Brian recovered it from the machine and handed it over, giving him also his phone number. Makram got up, disturbing a fruity gust of lime, shook hands with everybody, and left.

Brian considered what he'd been told. When he looked at Evita Blas, she read his uncertainty.

"There's nobody better in his field than Gamal. If he says Syrian, the guy's Syrian."

Brian wasn't having any real trouble with the opinion, he was just worried that, if it was wrong, any extrapolation from it would be worse than useless.

His hostess pulled out a desk drawer, took out a handbag, and got up. "I have to go, but you don't. If you want to have a think about it, you won't be bothered here. Or I could give you a pass and you could use the library if you like."

They left with her. She invited Brian to keep in touch, then they traded good-byes on the sidewalk.

"Nice lady," Marie said, watching the woman swing away on her crisp Italian heels.

They walked for a minute, Marie remaining silent, waiting for Brian to comment on their progress. She didn't feel they'd made that much, couldn't see how the discovery of the fake's nationality, if indeed the Lebanese linguist was right about that, was going to help them. And, to judge by Brian's face, which had a strained and loaded look, he didn't feel they'd moved too far, either.

"We need some quality thinking time," Brian proposed. "We have to go through this folder again, read through the transcripts of the guy's sermons word for word. Most of them just repeat the testimonial parables, but there's a lot of extemporary stuff, some of it pretty vitriolic, and some of that could maybe hint at something."

"Like what?" Marie asked.

A dispirited breath folded Brian's shoulders inward an inch. "That I can't tell you."

Marie hadn't meant to deflate the brave little balloon Brian was trying so mightily to fly, and she hurried to keep it aloft by urging they do as he'd just suggested, go to the university library and there, in comforting peace and quiet, hammer away until they got somewhere.

"Okay. But not this library. We need to specialize."

He took her a block south of the college to a Kinko's, where he had the entire folder copied. Then they cabbed it downtown to a place Marie had never been before: a Catholic Information Center.

A woman sat at a desk immediately inside the entrance in an area devoted to newspapers and magazines, a little like a neighborhood Christian Science reading room. Through a door, deeper into the building, the library opened up. Its ceiling seemed to be supported by open-shelved books, not an inch of wall space on view. Surprisingly, there was a CD-ROM computer station at one end and, not so surprisingly, a long reading table dividing the room lengthways.

Marie took a seat at the far end, and Brian, who'd taken some sliced-up computer paper and two pencils from the computer station, sat down opposite her. He opened his folder, removed the stapled files, and stacked them neatly.

Marie did the same with her copies and waited for suggestions.

"Okay," Brian said. "You read it and I'll read it. Most people reveal something of themselves when they open their mouth, even a messiah. Look for inconsistencies. Idiosyncracies. Patterns. Mistakes."

"When he's repeating the Gospels?" Marie looked a little blank. "That's your department."

"You'll do okay."

Brian fetched several books which he thought might assist her: a Bible concordance, a New Testament, and a treatise called *The Hard Words of Christ*, and left her to her task. He settled to his own and went carefully through the pile of typed pages.

He reread the verbatim transcripts from when the fake had appeared, courtesy of Don Bagley, on television. The inclining curve of the man's diatribe against the Church was evident. Again Brian asked himself a familiar question: why was he doing it? Was there a purpose or was the guy simply a renegade Catholic, or an antipapist Protestant?

A third of the way through the pages it occurred to Brian that he was starting to get a glimmer of one of the things he'd advised Marie to monitor. Wary of snatching at answers, he went back to page one and began yet again, this time making meticulous notes.

Twenty minutes crept by, then a middle-aged woman, fussy and discomposed, hurried in, looked up something in the Catholic Encyclopedia, gave a pyrrhonic little harrumph, then bustled out again.

There were no more visitors that morning; nothing to intrude apart from the thick clatter of traffic noise seeping in through the high windows. At one point Marie paid a second visit to the computer terminal and, with its help, located a book which she brought back to the table. She read silently from it for a minute, kept the page, and sat back. Brian saw that she'd discovered something but continued with his work till he'd finished the last transcript, and only then did he push the folder away and look up at Marie.

"You find something?"

"A possible inconsistency. But it may be just that and nothing more."

"Let's have it," Brian said, prepared to either cheer or shrug.

"Page three of the fifth transcript. He's not crazy about certain aspects of the religion that sprang up around him. He's talking here about the fixed holy days as an example of how the religion has ballooned out of shape."

Brian knew the sermon she was talking about, although nothing in it had struck him as being out of the ordinary. He turned to the page and invited her to proceed.

"He's talking about Palm Sunday, Pentecost, Epiphany, Ascension, et cetera, names that are pretty familiar. But he used one I'd never heard of, so I looked it up. See, about six lines from the bottom? Hypapante?" She tapped the book she'd taken from the stacks. "According to this, it's Greek for meeting and doesn't seem to belong to the Western church. And, as far as I can see, all his other references are straight out of the King James Bible. You think there's anything in that?"

Brian pointed a finger at his temple and shot himself in the head. "I went right by it. Three, four times. Hypapante. Right there in black and white."

"Then it means something?"

"You bet it means something. It means it's ten to one he belongs to the Orthodox church. Nobody in the Western church would use that word. We call it Candlemas because it basically celibrates Mary's purification. Hypapante celebrates Christ. If this guy's Syrian, and we've got to go with that, then he probably came out of the Syrian church. In fact"—Brian paused a moment to lasso an obvious thought—"we can get closer than that. The West Syrian church." He slapped the flat of his hand onto the table in delayed revelation. "That's why he's got his knife into Rome. He's a Jacobite. A Monophysite."

"A Monophy-what?"

Brian spoke quickly. "The Council of Chalcedon affirmed the dual nature of Christ, both human and divine. The Jacobites rejected that and insisted that Christ had only one nature, a monophysite nature. The Syrians split with the Church and some of them have been sworn enemies of Rome ever since." Brian grabbed up a transcript and waved it exaggeratedly over the table. "Hell, all you have to do is shake it and it falls into place. Makram, the plump Lebanese, said one of the fake's parents was probably from Turkey. That's where a core of the Jacobites, the purists, still live."

Marie attempted an interjection, but Brian wasn't stopping.

"The Jacobites were also known as Syriani because their doctrine was associated with the Syriac language. We know that Jesus Two speaks Aramaic, right? Well, Syriac is based on the East Aramaic dialect of Edessa. And in case we need any more connections, Edessa was occupied by the Turks for five hundred years."

Marie was delighted to have made a contribution, especially one which Brian found so promising. She wanted to look good in his eyes: bright and sapient. On the other hand, she thought a touch wistfully, it would have been nice, after hours of modest intellectual bestowal, to get him into a hot, soapy tub and show him that she wasn't just a thinker. She switched off this brief reverie and got back to specifics.

"Is that enough to track him down? He's out of the West Syrian church? How big is the membership?"

"Large. And scattered. Turkey, Syria, Egypt, Iraq, Canada, the U.S., and a bunch of other countries. We'd never get him unless we knew something more about him. And I think . . ."—Brian strung it out—"fingers crossed, that we do." He referred to his copious notes. "You found inconsistency, I found pattern. Seven words that appear again and again, in various contexts, whenever he stops preaching and starts lecturing. I'll read 'em out . . . Okay, the first word is *discipline*. The next is *study*. Then, *early morning. Hungry. Teaching. Library.*" Brian looked up expectantly. Marie, so recently bemoaning the one-note nature of her contribution, now found even that under review.

Brian was considerate. "I got it because I've lived it. Getting up at the crack of dawn. Studying in the library till all hours. Always hungry because the food's so lousy. The relentless discipline. The constant teaching. I think this guy's been through a seminary. And pretty recently, too. I think the experience has marked him, and it's coming out of his subconscious. And there's something else that supports that possibility; if you wanted somebody who speaks Aramaic and has a knowledge of Greek and Hebrew, and is wholly familiar with the Gospels, a Jacobite seminary would be a good place to start."

"You think he's a priest?"

"Maybe. Or maybe he's a dropout. Like me. But whichever, he's going to be impossible to nail unless we make some assumptions that turn out to be right."

Marie closed the books she'd spread out in front of her, closed them with a decisive and confident snap. "That's the way you handle any kind of investigative work. You reach the best conclusion you can based on what you believe to be the facts, then steam ahead. And if you're wrong, you're wrong. So, until we know that, why don't we assume that Jay Two is or was a student in a seminary belonging to the West Syrian church, and try to locate the seminary."

Brian jumped up, no dynamic purpose behind the move, simply a response to Marie's brisk buoyancy. "Fine. The question then becomes, assuming this is a homegrown thing, did whoever set it up find him in a Middle Eastern seminary, or did they get him from one on their doorstep?"

"Their doorstep," Marie declared.

"Why do you say that?"

"Because English was another requisite. One of the most important. And the chances of finding an English-speaking, Semitic-looking man in this country have to be a lot better than finding one in Syria or Iraq or wherever."

"True. But their choice would've been that much more limited. I know there's a Jacobite seminary in San Francisco, but it may be the only one in America."

Marie flung an extravagant hand at the book stacks. "Let's find out."

"I can do that with a phone call," Brian boasted.

They left the library and went to Brian's apartment, where he called Harold Chifley in Chicago. The monsignor asked him how it was going.

"We're creeping up on something. It's only a guess, but who knows?"

"We? You brought in some help?"

"I needed some. We spent most of the morning in a library."

"Good," Harold Chifley said, and Brian knew that his friend was imagining some studious and bespectacled male student enlisted to sift through weighty volumes.

Tweaked by guilt at this deception, and his decision not to correct it, Brian hurried on. "I have a question. Something for your ecumenical contacts."

"Go ahead."

"I need to know something about Jacobite seminaries in this country. Specifically, how many there are and where they're located."

"Uh-huh," Harold Chifley said. From eight hundred miles away Brian could see him assimilating this piece of arcane information and battling to apply it. He told Brian to leave it with him, and Brian settled back for a long and impatient wait, but the extraordinary depth of Chifley's contacts was illustrated when he returned the call within five minutes.

"There are three in the U.S. San Francisco, Cleveland, and Watertown, New York. And there's one in Canada in Elton, Ontario."

"Got it. Thanks, Harry."

"Brian, I'm busting to ask you questions, but I'm going to demonstrate my God-given willpower by just saying good-bye."

"Good-bye, Harry." They hung up. Brian turned to Marie. "Get ready to hit the road." He showed her the names he'd taken down.

"What do you want to do first?" Marie asked, checking them over. "Cover upstate New York and Ohio, or go to the Coast and get that out of the way?"

"I'm tempted to try the eastern ones first, but I'm pretty sure the Jacobite patriarch lives in San Francisco, so the seminary there would probably be the biggest, which would've given them more choice."

Marie wasn't impressed with this point. "Maybe they found that less is more. Maybe they went to San Francisco, bombed out, and found just what they were looking for in Watertown."

"You want to try Watertown first?"

"It's your call."

"Could you get away this evening?"

"In a pinch."

Brian crossed to a phone. Called an airline, spoke for several minutes, then came back to Marie. "Okay. We're on the five o'clock to San Francisco."

Marie reached for her handbag. "I'd better go and get a few things done." She moved to the door and, on the way out, said, "There's a lot of hype written about San Francisco's eateries, but there's one I know, the Corona, that's as good as they say it is. You'll love it."

After she'd left, Brian considered that restaurant recommendation. Eating out was certainly nothing new for them, and yet he'd caught a note in her voice, like a votive offer, that this time, tête-à-tête in an alluring candlelit room, away from the constraints of New York in the romantic city by the bay . . . He reviewed the thought and immediately refuted it; knew he was guilty of a biased reading. The Corona was probably a steam beer–and–crab joint full of noise and fun. Surely, she'd given up on him by now. He wondered morosely if she didn't see him as an encyclopedic capon, a great partner if you were going on a quiz show, but hardly the guy you'd choose for a weekend in Acapulco.

Or San Francisco.

The trip got off to an unpromising start when technical reasons delayed their flight for two hours.

Then everything went from bad to worse.

When at last the plane got off the ground the ill-tempered passengers were poorly served by a cabin crew understaffed due to the illness of two of their number. Then, because of an air traffic controllers' go-slow in the Bay Area, the plane was forced to stack over the Pacific, flying high, repetitive circles until grudgingly allowed to land.

Brian expected the cab they took into town to fit in with the general run of things by blowing a tire, but it sped them to their destination without mishap, an efficiency that turned out to be useless as the hotel couldn't find any record of their reservation and, being full to bursting, could not accommodate them. Brian was distressed at this news. He'd read about this place, the Clift, and knew that the rooms were handsomely furnished, and that just off the lobby was a wonderful redwood-paneled bar that was a great favorite with couples.

They waited a further twenty minutes while a hotel clerk called around a very tight town, finally locating space for them in a less-than-first-class establishment on Sutter, blocks away from where they wanted to be.

They checked in there hurriedly, had a fast freshen-up, then got a cab to the Corona, the restaurant Marie had mentioned, which turned out to be charming, soft-lit, and full of pleasant and happy diners. But they were fifteen minutes too late to be included among them, the kitchen having closed for the evening. Too exhausted to try anywhere else, they bought some apples and milk at a nearby deli, took them back to their unwelcoming hotel, and said good night, certain that whatever malevolent sprite they'd offended was finished with them and would now leave them in peace.

They were right in one way, wrong in another.

The message light was blinking when Brian let himself into his room.

"You had a call from a Mr. Makram," the operator informed him when he checked with her; before he'd left New York Brian had called the Lebanese academic and told him where he'd be staying in case he came up with something. The Clift had passed on Brian's new number. "He wants you to call back immediately," the operator said. At Brian's request, she went ahead and made the connection for him.

Brian looked at his watch as he listened to Makram's phone ring; it was 2:15 in the morning back east. "Mr. Makram? Brian Sheridan. You sure it's not too late to call?"

"Who sleeps anymore?" Makram asked, with a coagulated chuckle. "How is San Francisco?"

"Crowded."

"Well, I've been listening to the tape you lent me," Makram told him, getting down to business. "That is a very interesting voice."

Brian got a neurasthenic flash: the man was going to revise his opinion. The fake was a Moroccan or a Muslim Cypriot or something. They were back to square one. "Are you having second thoughts, Professor?" Brian clenched his body against the answer.

"No, no. I'm more than ever convinced he's Syrian." Brian stopped strangling the phone. "But you asked me where I thought he'd learned his English," Makram reminded him. "I have a theory on that. Shall I tell you?"

"Please."

"The more I played the tape the more I heard something. When he says, 'Look about you,' the diphthong in the word *about* is accented. It's only faint but it's there," Makram continued, his manner maddeningly cumbrous. "He doesn't pronounce that word to rhyme with *out, shout, doubt,* he shades it so that it almost rhymes with *boot, shoot, hoot.* And that kind of pronunciation has a definite association. I'd say he learned his English in Canada."

Brian wondered why it hadn't occurred to him; he was quite familiar with the Canadian penchant for twisting certain vowel sounds. "Canada," he said.

"I'm certain of it," Makram stated. "I hear nothing of an American speech pattern in his voice, so I would go so far as to say he's had very little exposure to this country in the past, if any. Does that help you at all?"

"Tremendously. Thank you, Gamal. You've saved me a lot of time." Brian got off the line wishing the grammarian had had his insight about twelve hours earlier. Nevertheless, he began to feel the build of excitement. Before, with four seminaries to choose from, they'd been looking at a time-intensive, hit-or-miss proposition. Now they could zero in with a degree of certainty.

A large degree of certainty.

Brian replayed the tape of the fake's voice in his memory; heard all the things Makram said were there: a Syrian accent melded to a Canadian one. Evita Blas was convinced that Gamal Makram was the best in his field, and with what Brian could now hear for himself in his recall of the fake's accent he was sure that a visit to a California seminary would be a waste of time. And they'd already been profligate enough with that particular commodity.

He picked up the phone. Called Marie's room across the corridor. "Hi. You asleep yet?"

"You joking? Everytime I close my eyes I see a seat-belt sign light up."

"I have some news."

"The hotel's on fire," Marie guessed.

"That could only improve it. No, it's something else. I had a call from Gamal Makram and guess what . . . we're gonna make the record books. We're gonna go down as the only couple in history that went to San Francisco just for an apple and a glass of milk."

CHAPTER
15

Even though one meant the beginning of the ordeal—the start of long hours of arctic air, atrocious food, and sudden alarums and excursions—and the other the merciful end of these tribulations, Father Santoro feared the landing as much as he did the takeoff.

He hated the swoop and dip of an aircraft as it locked into its approach, always half convinced that the pilot had suffered a heart attack in the middle of guiding it in. On this particular flight—four days after that most singular meeting with Father Cresta in the little oratory—his hands squashed the armrests and he hunched his body, perhaps unconsciously feeling that by sinking lower in his seat he'd have less distance to fall. But these proved to be needless precautions when the plane touched down in a soft landing, and the buckle and scream of rubber, plastic and aluminum, cartwheeling in a spectacular roiling ball of exploding jet fuel, was postponed yet again.

Thirty-five years away. He felt like a disembodied spirit returning to rattle and clank the rusty chains of memory.

He disembarked and rode an Air Italia bus to the terminal. The entrance was guarded by a suspicious-looking cop controlling a slinking German shepherd whose descent from a wolf might have been only a matter of a few months back. But inside the terminal it was too soon after lunch for officialdom to pay the passengers much more than token interest. Then he was through to a makeshift cab rank and walking in full sunlight. And what sunlight! Like light baked in a porcelain kiln and sliced into fine white pieces. A mile off it changed, becoming gray and shuddery, but close up it shimmered and swayed like a blanket of gauze on the point of combustion.

The taxi driver quoted an outlandish price for the trip down-town, and when Santoro came back with a counteroffer, the driver asked another man whether or not he could accept the fare, which meant, Santoro was certain, that the driver belonged to one of the junior families which had the cab concession. He knew that, sooner or later, he'd have to begin on this extraordinary mandate, so why not now?

As the taxi rushed him by a cerulean sea, and tiny villages of brilliant decay, he assembled some words in his mouth and poured them out before he could change his mind. "I'm interested in sporting goods."

"Eh?"

"I'm interested in buying some sporting goods."

The driver checked the plump face in his rearview mirror. He could tell from the guy's old-fashioned suit—Santoro had shed his priestly garb for obvious reasons—and clunky Sicilian that he was one more mainlander back for a sentimental journey. "What kind?"

"I like to hunt. Where would be a good place to buy a shotgun?"

"Amalgi's. On Settino near Marchese. They got 'em all."

Santoro leaned forward. Spilled money on the passenger seat. "And if I wanted something smaller?" He couldn't believe he was saying it.

The surprised driver switched his eyes again to that cherubic face. You never know, he thought. He took a hand off the wheel to sweep the money closer. "I dunno. Maybe Sacchi's on Albergheria. But I really dunno."

Santoro checked into an old hotel that had been refurbished, a place where the celebrities had always stayed, went straight to his room, flopped into a chair, and tried to decipher the Rosetta stone of his emotions. Five stories beneath the closed windows the Via Roma sent up a muffled din that smothered the whomp and mut-ter of the air conditioner. The Via Roma! Right outside the window. And Mariano and Stabile and Belmonte and a hundred other streets and squares that were embossed forever behind his eyes. He was tempted to rush out into it all, expose himself to it like a film to light and process it instantly, a human Polaroid.

No.

Do what you came to do and leave, he advised himself. Don't sprinkle a poverty-ridden childhood with the shiny gilt of nostalgia.

He called down for a cab, picked up the attaché case he hadn't let out of his sight since he'd begun the trip, then went down to the street where the taxi was waiting. He drew breath to tell the driver to take him to Alberghería, but that wasn't the address his tongue shaped. "Quattro Canti," he said, immediately rationalizing the switch to himself: the Corners weren't far from Alberghería, and the walk could only do him good. Everybody knew you were supposed to exercise after a flight.

He examined his shoe tops for the slow ten-minute ride, paid the driver, got out, and looked at his city for the first time in his new life.

Part of it was the same, part of it wasn't. The Canti hadn't changed; the same baroque ice-cream sundae still stood on each corner of the crossroads, the end of the new city, the start of the old. But the cars! That was the Corso? The avenue he used to dash across without even looking?

And the noise!

There were new Sicilian jokes now, jokes he now fully understood. What's the first thing a Sicilian asks when he buys a used car? How many hours on the horn. They'd never change, these people. Their primitive minds equated noise with life. Shout, yell, beat saucepan lids and you frighten away death; and death was about the only thing a true Sicilian respected.

Santoro walked south on an avenue cut like a firebreak through the blue exhaust smoke, and moved into the Plaza Pretoria with its pink-and-gold church, Santa Caterina, which he'd once thought had been melted by the sun. He'd seen a lot of pale-faced, white-gowned brides come out of those doors, their brand-new husbands sweated by tight suits and nervousness. Opposite the church was the enormous Florentine fountain, La Fontana de Vergogna, as it had been popularly called, the Fountain of Shame, because the statues had been sculptured nude. Santoro saw that the male figures were still missing their penises, knocked off by shocked citizens years ago, perhaps to shelter those innocent young brides from the truth for a little while longer. That male privates docked in female ones had been just an outlandish rumor until he'd reached the age of nineteen and met Filippa Maltese, whose memory still promoted release in the small hours of the morning.

He shook that guilty thought and allowed the piazza to lead him through the smell of roasting coffee into Maqueda and the old shopping lanes. Even blindfolded he could still have found his way around this area: Casa Professa, Porta di Castro. Whatever you needed was here in random and cornucopian abundance, trades funneled together for centuries without prejudice. And the food on display! The wonderful *latterias*! His spirit soared at what he beheld: huge open bowls stiff with yellow clotted cream, cases of fat brown eggs, plump tubs of golden butter, inflated wheels of glistening cheese, their broad blue veins alive with delicious breeding, all of it tumbled together in cholesterol madness.

He dragged himself away from the beckoning windows and checked his bearings. He knew exactly where Albergheria was from here, and he began to worry about his course of action once he got to Sacchi's. He only knew what he remembered hearing thirty-five years ago, the rumored keys and talismans you needed if you wanted to connect. If they'd changed or been forgotten . . . Fear of failure, an old acquaintance, returned to weigh his steps for an uncomfortable few minutes, but this familiar dark nimbus was quickly dispersed when, after cutting through a series of deserted passages, he came out exactly where he knew he would, a few yards from Sacchi's. He still knew the town. He'd be fine.

The bar was interchangeable with any of the other bars in the old section in that its front looked like its back, stacked crates of Horst beer giving the entrance an unearned, monumental look. Santoro moved inside, the fanned gloom hiding the scarred history of scattered tables and chairs. A truncated bar displayed the favored labels of Palermo: Stellata, Tutone, San Silvestro. The man dispensing behind this bar was young, Santoro was unhappy to notice, maybe too young to know anything.

He ordered a grappa and checked the place over again. The pa-
trons, all men, looked ordinary enough: strong, short-statured
men punishing tabletops with dice cups, their betting energy and
concentration total. Even so, he had no doubt that a gun could be
bought in such an establishment. There would be only one sup-
plier, one source, and it was logical to suppose that if you could
buy a gun here, you could hire somebody to pull the trigger.

He coughed and looked at the young bartender who, seeing his
untouched grappa, came over and asked him did he want a beer
to chase it with. Santoro put a fifty-thousand-lira bill onto the bar
and, like a good ten-pin bowler, tried for a smooth delivery and a
quick release but succeeded only in rushing it. "I need to see a
priest," he gabbled.

The young man didn't connect the money with the request; all
he saw was an overweight Italian, loaded with money like they all
were, who'd been with a hooker and wanted to ease his guilt.
"There's a church around the corner," he said. "You wanna beer
or not?"

Santoro shook his head, picked up the money, and headed for
the door, shame and failure twin badges of crimson in his cheeks.
He knew exactly where he was going: straight back to the hotel
for his suitcase, then the airport and the first plane back to Rome.
He should never have let Gaetano Cresta convince him he was
qualified for this. What did he know about the Sicilian Cosa
Nostra? Brimming with bitter discord and a humbling sense of ob-
scurity, he hurried through the crowds.

Then slowed.

What braked his pace was the thought of what Father Cresta
would say: the icy insults, the acid disparagements, the imprecations he'd rain down. He couldn't face that; even though he might
deserve every scathing word, he dreaded the scene. There was
nothing he wanted more than the secretary's admiration, and every
step that took him farther away from that dark little bar back
there took him a step closer to the nomenclature of flop, miserable
washout, pathetic bungler.

Santoro stopped.

Turned.

Went back to Sacchi's.

Halted outside and peered in. The young bartender was gone, replaced by a much older man. For the umpteenth time in his life Santoro knew he'd been a fool. He'd tried to deal with the son when it was the father he should have been speaking to. He moved back inside.

"Hey, Sacch! We're dyin' of thirst over here," one of the dice thumpers called. The bartender, clearly the bar's eponymous owner, delivered some licorice-scented sustenance, then returned to the bar. He found a stranger there, sitting on a stool.

"I'll have a grappa."

"Beer chaser?"

"No." Having had a dress rehearsal, Santoro's performance lost a lot of its clumsiness. He didn't push the bill across the bar but finger-and-thumbed it as if checking for intaglio printing. "But I'd like to buy something else."

The owner took a longer look at his new customer and decided he was a collection of rights and wrongs: the dark eyes were right, the fusty old suit was wrong, the language was right if a little stilted, the clutched attaché case was wrong. "What's your name?"

"Franco Santoro." It was the first time in years that combination of words had passed his lips without a paternal prefix.

"I don't know you."

Santoro ran a cursor down his memory bank. Came up with the name of a man who'd left the island at about the same time he had, somebody who they said ran errands for the Mafiosi out La Cuba way and had gone to New York. "How about a friend of mine, Arnaldo Di Betta?"

The owner's face unclenched. "Now, him I used to know. What the hell happened to him, anyway?"

Santoro rang a change on an old phrase. "He died of death in America."

"That where you been?"

Santoro felt it would be smart not to answer that question; show a little skill for a change. He placed the bill down on the bar and used it for a drink coaster, proud of this little maneuver and happily surprised that things were going so well. As far as he could tell he wasn't even sweating. "I want to talk to somebody," he said. It sounded nonchalant to his ears. Maybe even professional.

"Yeah?" The owner ran a rag over the bar. It passed very close to the novel green drink coaster. "Who?"

Santoro held the reply for the briefest moment. "A priest."

The owner's lack of reaction was too extravagant not to have significance. He was a stumpy type, a man of latitude, with heavy skin and a good thick head of hair. Santoro watched the man's rag include the fifty-thousand-lira bill in its cleanup; watched him turn and go in back somewhere. Heard him pick up a phone and dial, mumble something, heard a long minute of silence, another mumble, then the phone replaced. The owner reappeared.

"San Dominico. Ten o'clock tomorrow."

For a wretched moment Santoro felt he was being laughed at; San Dominico was a church.

"Sit in the back. He'll find you."

There was no tip of the mouth, no guffaw from the dice players in response to some secret signal; the man meant it. The meeting would take place in a church. Why not? Santoro reasoned; Sicilians didn't venerate a church the way most Catholics did. A Sicilian regarded a church in the same way a German or a Swiss did a city railroad station: a convenient meeting place, a center of social activity.

Santoro walked out of the bar buzzing with a sense of personal accomplishment, a feeling he experienced so rarely it was almost equivalent to a morphinic rush.

He'd got over the first hurdle.

He was on his way.

Milk flowed from her severed arteries instead of blood.

It was probably the most popular window in San Dominico, Saint Catherine's beheading portrayed in brilliant stains of red, yellow, blue, and green, and, of course, white for the milk.

Sitting in the second row from the back, in the gloom and mystery and sanctified odor of the tawny brown, twin-towered, Mexican-looking structure, Franco Santoro nervously checked around him. He could count only two males; the rest of the space being peopled by women, about a dozen of them, all in their forties or fifties, kneeling in solo and desperate obeisance in front of

a statue of Mary praying, Santoro guessed, for intercession on behalf of errant sons, daughters, husbands.

He glanced at his watch, which he could barely see, and settled
himself down. Ten minutes late wasn't really late. Someone would
come.

He went back to staring at the story of Saint Catherine. The
previous panel showed a bearded man twisting in fire, representa-
tive of the fifty philosophers she'd defeated in debate, all of whom
the emperor Maxentius had burnt at the stake for their failure. In
the second panel she was lashed to a spiked wheel, an ordeal she
survived, Santoro recalled, unlike some of the spectators who were
killed by flying splinters when the wheel broke apart. Dismissed
from the Church calendar for many years now—probably because
she was rumored to have married Christ in heaven—she nevertheless lived on in her perilous adventures, frozen in Technicolor glass
in this most Sicilian of churches.

Santoro shifted in the hard seat. Became aware of scrutiny on
his left. A man, ordinary-looking, was sitting two rows back, his
expression one of chilly evaluation. He met Santoro's stare
brashly, searched his eyes for signs of treachery, then, after a long
beat, apparently decided that it was just a rookie's nervousness
showing on that plump face. He moved his neck as if he were
heading a soccer ball, got up, and left.

Santoro followed him out of night into baked daylight. Wad-
dled in his wake through a coil of shopping lanes. Saw him enter
a *bottega*, brushing proprietorially through the multicolored plastic fly curtain protecting the doorway. Santoro halted. He knew
that once he went through that doorway he'd be releasing the
brake of a locomotive that would rush unstoppably all the way to
the iron buffers of its terminus in Atlanta.

He took a firmer grip on the attaché case, and on his resolve,
and brushed the plastic strips aside.

A powerful corporation of aromas—ground coffee, hessian, and
dried cod—controlled the little store, with black pepper and or-
ange water junior partners. Behind a counter, and a ceiling-high
sand castle of olive-oil cans, a skinny youth scooped sugar from an
engraved brass balance into squat brown paper bags.

Santoro advanced across the rough board floor to the shop's

only interior door. Entered a storeroom in which bulging rice sacks had been stacked as if to withstand a siege. The man he'd followed was sitting at a card table, its Formica top a Rorschach test of brown cigarette burns. With gray beginning to invade his short black hair, and a puffiness surrounding his abbreviated neck, Santoro thought him to be about his own age, a man with cartilage damage showing in his wandering nose, and a cigar in his mouth, a thin cheroot twisted like a chocolate-colored cheese stick. From his seated position he dragged on the cheroot and expelled a cancerous pointer at the only other chair, and watched the Italian's ungainly moves as Santoro pulled it out and sat in it. The man noted the way he balanced the attaché case on his lap, not willing to risk the floor, and knew there was cash money inside. But then he'd suspected that anyway. He ashed the cigar on the long-suffering Formica, then returned it quickly to his mouth as if his jaw would unhinge unless firmly clamped.

"You got something you want done?" he asked, like an odd-job man looking to split wood.

"Yes," Santoro said, adding nothing further to the abrupt reply. Although poor at dealing with businesspeople, he'd learned enough to know that it was better to take a quiet seat at the rear when you were launching into new territory.

The smoker saw that he was going to have to lead, and did so, speaking in street Sicilian but slowly and with no particular emphasis. "You got a sick pet you want put down?"

"That's right."

"Where?"

"America."

"That's a big place."

"Atlanta." Santoro checked on himself and was amazed: here he was arranging a man's death and the words were coming out without a wobble. Father Cresta would have been proud of him.

Behind a nacreous exhalation the man on the other side of the table said, "I'm gonna need a name and a snapshot."

Santoro worked the combination on the attaché case—the date and month of his ordination—and clicked the lid open. He took out, and placed on the ruined table, a photo clipped from a news-

paper. The smoker picked it up. "This guy?" he asked, with no in-
flection in his voice.

Again Santoro used the simplest affirmative.

That brought forth a deep drag and an inspection of the curly
tube, as if quality control was an area its manufacturers were going to have to seriously address.

"You've read about him?" Santoro asked.

"Sure. Thinks he's Jesus, right?" The man removed a stray piece
of weed from his lip. "It's gonna cost."

"Why?"

"A celeb hit? You're in for a lot of setup time. The target's
gonna have security. Bodyguards, whatever. A guy like this, he's
not gonna stroll by you on his way to the Laundromat. A guy like
this you put down when he's up there on a stage or something.
You gotta find a spot that gives you a bead on that stage. And it's
gotta be a spot that lets you walk away after the job's done. That's
all setup time. It's gonna cost."

"How much?"

The man didn't appear to know the answer to that until he'd
consulted a smoky oracle. "I can get you a good man for twenty
thousand U.S. plus expenses."

Santoro covered some of the table damage with the attaché
case. He leaned into the noxious cloud to make his emphatic
point, silently cheering himself on. He found strong words and an
attitude he didn't know he owned. "I don't want a good man. I
want the best man. How much for the best man?"

"He's real expensive," the smoker said, gauging reactions.

"What's his name?"

"Vizzini. But, like I say, he costs."

"I'll pay thirty thousand. Half in advance. In return, I want
someone who's done this kind of thing many times before. He's
worked in America before. A crack shot. Is that this Vizzini?"

The other man nodded a firm validation. "That's him."

Santoro opened the attaché case. Graced the scarred table with
bundles of hard-packed, paper-bound lira. The other man quick-
counted the money with his squinted eyes but wasn't crass enough
to reach for it, or concerned enough to want it out of sight.

"When do you want it done?"

Santoro had read up on the phenomenon. "He'll be at a big rally on the twenty-sixth. It's indoors, but he'll stop outside to bless the crowd."

"Vizzini's gonna need a local contact. You'll have to take him through this on-site. Tell him exactly when and where the mark's gonna be. Help him get set up."

A note of mild alarm degraded Santoro's newfound confidence. "I can't be any part of this. Not on the American end."

"Then gimme someone who can."

Santoro spun the permutations: for safety's sake he was certain Father Cresta would refuse to widen the group, which only left Father Ludovisi, Cresta's secretary. Santoro felt the sharp scalpel of jealousy probe his innards. This Vizzini would get the job done neatly and cleanly if he was as good as he sounded, and if Ludovisi got the role of contact man, he'd share the credit. Cresta would regard him as a hero, which would be most unfair seeing that he, Franco Santoro, had set the whole thing up. He was damned if he was going to let that snide little toady bask in Cresta's admiration.

"Very well, I'll do it," he told the other man.

"You'll need Vizzini's flight number and arrival date. Where can I reach you?"

"You can't," Santoro said quickly, horrified that this man might recognize a Vatican phone number. "I'll contact you."

The man scribbled some numerals on a piece of paper and handed it over. And that seemed to be that.

Santoro left the little store as if he were walking a foot above the ground. He'd done it! Hired a professional. The thought brought a brocaded thrill of danger and daring. He'd stepped into the lion's den and withstood the meaty breath. He'd been accepted by the underlife as a serious player. A man to be reckoned with.

Trembling with a rampant satisfaction, he gave ten thousand lira to a woman collecting for the repair of the city's cathedral. He smiled at her as he would a co-worker, which he felt she was. After all, they were both out on the streets of Palermo helping the Catholic Church.

She in her way, he in his.

CHAPTER
16

New Hope, Pennsylvania.

Elton, Ontario.

The Canadian town reminded Brian of the American one, except Elton seemed more honest, lacking the broad wink and the nudge in the ribs that its American cousin delivered in its reach for the cute and the Disneyesque. In this pleasant little Ontario town you could believe that artisans had once inhabited those pretty little cottages, and worked the multistoried mill whose waters made a respectable growl, if not a mighty roar, in their abbreviated and rocky plunge.

Marie felt the same way regarding the Pennsylvania comparison; the drive from Toronto had traversed similar topography to that around Bucks County: deep rolling hills backdropped by dark detached clouds foaming up like shaken Coca-Cola. Marie had been across the border a number of times. She liked Canada and had once thought of moving to Toronto, the most livable city in North America, but, in the end, the dynamics of working in the U.S., of being plugged into the creative current whose voltage is greater than any other country's, outweighed her admiration for what she thought a more civilized society.

They checked into an inn on a hill on the outskirts of the village. The building had never been anything but a hostelry, so there'd been no need to remodel. The rooms admitted acres of external light through floor-to-ceiling windows, slept their guests in feathery four-poster beds, and took care of their clothes in mahogany highboys any one of which would have brought thousands of dollars at a New York auction.

After showering off the dust of travel, and resting for a while, they met downstairs at seven for a drink in the unique little bar—a series of adjoining alcoves—then moved into the capacious dining room. The tables were almost all occupied, but each one had its own order of space and privacy. The cooking was bright and inventive, Californian before that singular cuisine lost its way in fad and specious innovation, and the wine a first-class chardonnay from the Niagara Peninsula. The pleasant ambience, the fine vittles, and the greeny blue wash of the evening pressing against the long French windows softened the immediacy of their quest. The day had been a long one containing, as it did, the customs-immigration hassle of an international flight, plus the wait for a rental car, and the challenge of unfamiliar highways, so they were more than ready to allow the cordial hospitality to sustain them while they caught their breath for the morrow. Which was something they discussed while they sipped their coffee.

"There shouldn't be any problem," Brian said. "I had Harry Chifley call the seminary and ask the rector would he mind if he had a couple of visitors. There isn't a churchman in North America who'd turn Chifley down. They all know how powerful he is, and in these days of ecumenical cooperation, nobody wants to be seen as a churl, so we're expected."

Marie squeezed a twist of lemon into her coffee, and sipped the rich brew. "Do I have to disguise myself, like Lady Esther Stanhope?"

"Who's Lady Esther Stanhope?"

Marie faked heart palpitations. "Don't tell me there's something I know that you don't."

Brian looked a little abashed. He hated to fly his flags of knowledge and was constantly reeling them in. "Outside of my field, I'm a stumbling dunce. Who is Stanhope?"

"One of those intrepid nineteenth-century British explorers. She disguised herself as a man and went to Mecca."

"You won't have to do that. A seminary isn't a monastery. Besides, I have an idea that it would've been easier for Lady Esther to pass as a man than it would be for you."

Marie accepted the compliment with a smile that occluded her eyes, an effect that compressed their warmth and heightened their glow. She'd changed into a clingy dress for dinner, sleeveless and plain, its cool citrus color praising her fair complexion, its contours exaggerating her trim height.

The quiet moment was broken politely by the wife of the owner, who offered them a liqueur. They took it in a basement bar, another surprise in this inn of nice surprises: small tables, a tiny dance floor, recessed lighting set low, it had the look and feel of an intimate little boîte, the kind that New York used to do so well when people preferred romance to sensation. The music was live, an uncommon duo of vibraphone and acoustic guitar playing the slow-tempo standards of the great songwriters. Half a dozen couples, pleasantly afloat on the ambient mood, their dance no more than a swaying glide, left just enough room on the floor for the new arrivals. Brian took Marie's hand, held her close without actually hugging her, and began to move her to the music.

Five seconds was all it took for him to know he'd been right when he'd thought about her in all those small-houred, strawberry-colored dawns, wondering if she'd fit seamlessly against him. He already knew the scent of her just-washed hair, but he'd never inhaled the perfumed throb of her neck, or felt the custom match of her hand cupping into his, or the faint muscular movement transmitted to his palm from the delicate small of her back.

He inched his head away. Turned his face, the move becoming the harbinger of an embrace.

He watched her eyes. He wanted a deeper shade from those green irises, a green light, but they'd neutraled to gray, steady on his without comment. He lowered his gaze to her slightly distended lips, the puffed lower one putting him in mind of a slice of wild fruit.

His kiss surprised him more than it did Marie; he hadn't been conscious of making the move he'd been planning for so long. He went in on her underlip, just a quick, momentary visit, but it was a piece of time, like all time, that was irretrievable.

He returned for a second, then a third helping of that exotic produce, staying each time for no more than a nibble. He moved his head, changing the angle, kissed the vanishing point of her mouth, detecting now, in the currents and rhythms picked up by his hand bringing her to him, a message of uncertainty.

Or was it reluctance?

His mind quavered at the thought; it was what he dreaded most, that having once been given a chance, and having opted out, the fires he hoped were banked and invisibly smoldering had been doused by weeks of neglect. However, he found, with a surge of racing excitement, that his fears were baseless.

Marie looked at him deeply, a look that lay somewhere between sensual and cautious, and tallied the situation. "Are you sure?" she murmured. Her tone promised understanding if he chose to back off.

He kissed the pulse beneath her jaw; an emphatic answer.

They went to her room only because it was closer.

Wanting to lock out any possibility of regret, Brian gave her a chance to have second thoughts. He slipped the tip of his tongue just inside the edge of her teeth. Marie's mouth opened like a flower in the sun. She made a sound like a strangled sigh, snaked her tongue around his, and sucked it like a Popsicle. She lunged her body against his groin, her pelvis rising up into him in a quick hip thrust.

They rid themselves of grasping clothing, clashed and clung in hard and soft nakedness. It had been too long delayed, this union, for any employment of finesse: they surged against each other in furious ignition. Wrenched apart. Went at necks and faces, two breathless people sucking air from each other's mouths.

He spun her around, backed her up against him, not yet entering but grasping her to him, hands cupping, fingers nippling, teeth worrying the slim muscle along the smooth white ridge of her shoulder. Twisting, spinning, Marie pulled him with her, and he was inside her a moment after they fell onto the bed in a twined collapse.

They thrashed together, bucking and slamming, needing that first release like a pain-defeating drug. And when it arrived, borne on the sound of their cries, they flopped together in a confusion of limbs, then slithered apart, their banked-up accounts depleted for the moment.

The pale glow of a garden light, accumulating through the windows, covered them like a thin blue sheet. Brian fashioned the azure outline of Marie's arm, her flank and hip, planed the soft grain of her skin beneath his moving fingers, one thumb slowly circling the nubbed rise of a dark areola. His lips followed the trail his hand had blazed, tasting the light sheen of exertion, learning her patterns and textures.

He pushed off his elbow, tenting his body over hers. Marie felt the buzz of his tongue skim her nipples like the wings of a hummingbird. She laced her arms around his back, felt the hard, tectonic shift of muscle; pulled him down to her to let him batten on her breasts, then released his head, encouraging his southerly direction. Her navel, whorled like a pale cream cowrie shell, accommodated his fluttering tongue, the slope of her stomach aiding his descent to her blond thatch. The air seemed to hum with iron and flame, her breath spasming when Brian, with an almost unpardonable delight, accepted her liquid gift.

Marie snatched at breath as her soul began its meteoric rise. Cried out from the top of the high minaret he took her to. For some minutes she floated on the cusp of an altered state, then signaled her readiness and guided him.

For Brian the blue surrounds of the room became a flooded inland sea, each hunching stroke drawing him to greater depths. Over his bobbing head the ceiling was the still, unrippled surface fathoms above his deepening plunge, Marie a mermaid grown long encircling legs. He faintly registered her whispered petition not to wait for her, his staccato battery of grunts demonstrating the impossibility of that.

She held him.

Gentled him back from the dead.

He listed to his left, rolled onto his back. Listened to the hum of the planet and the hydrogen roar of the transiting stars.

Something limitless condensed inside him. He felt a peace and spaciousness expand within him as the letdown he'd expected was supplanted by a boundless distillation of well-being. This lovely woman lying next to him in the furthest projection of nudity, becalmed in the quiet blue light easing in from the garden, could not possibly be the instrument of his moral-spiritual stumble. What stumble? There could be no stumble, not for coalescing with another human being. It was like banning breathing. How could a gasping man be expected to love God more because he was short of breath? It was a fusty and out-of-touch Church that enforced celibacy, not a jealous deity; and if he'd offended the Church by embracing a woman in an act of pleasure, admiration, and intimacy, then maybe that balanced up the number of times the Church had offended him.

Marie stirred. Took his hand. Not to place it anywhere exciting but merely to lead him up off the bed into the bathroom and the shower stall.

They rinsed away the residues of their adhesive endeavor, toweled off hastily, then, still a little damp, got back onto the bed.

"How long have we been in this room?" Marie asked, shifting position so that her left leg jigsawed into his right one.

Brian kissed the shallow scoop beneath her throat. "Twenty minutes, two hours. Somewhere in there."

"Well, however long it's been, I can't remember a nicer time."

"I'd second that thought, but it's hard to remember that far back." He felt her lips stretch against his cheek, and was happy at her reaction. He'd wanted to introduce this subject soon, to get it out of the way and assuage her concerns for him on that score, although she apparently had none. She understood, he saw, that he'd waited for as long as he had to make sure there'd be no remorse on his part, which meant she knew him as well as he knew himself.

He stroked his fingers slowly through the wet slick of her hair. "It's been seven years since my last trip to the well."

"That's a long time," she said, and he knew she was not referring to the slacking of his thirst, but the wait with the bucket in his hand.

Brian sighed. "It had to be easier being a priest in the good old days."

"The rules were different?" Marie asked the blue of his shaved jaw.

"Hugely different. The clergy could marry and have a family. And for twelve hundred years, they did."

"What brought about the change?"

"Insecurity. The Church fathers saw sexual power as a rival to religious power, so they made it taboo." Brian shifted and stirred, the history an old irritation. "They wanted their shamans to remain pure, a throwback to the vestal virgins and the temple cults. They still permitted a priest to marry but with one proviso: he had to keep his hands off his wife."

"Doesn't sound too practical." Marie wasn't really a principal in the conversation, too busy nuzzling his ear and relishing the natural affinity that had matured between them. Discarnately attached before, their coupling had removed the last obstacle to a deeper concord.

Brian replied to her comment. "It wasn't, so their answer was to ban marriage altogether. The priests responded by keeping nubile lovelies in their houses to test and prove their moral strength. Kind of like a hopeless fatty on a diet who keeps a banana cream pie in the fridge."

Cocooned into him as she was, Marie's chuckle was smothered behind his ear. "I assume they made a few visits to the kitchen . . ."

"Couldn't stay out of the place. So then the authorities decreed that all priests would, in future, live without a woman and sleep without a woman because, they said, a priest is supposed to aim for a life of exemplary supernatural perfection. Plus, and I'm quoting dogma here, he must witness by his way of life to the transcendent reality that fills and grips him. Well, I've met a lot of priests, but very, few who I thought were filled and gripped by a transcendent reality. And when was the last time you heard of somebody leading a life of exemplary supernatural perfection?"

"Outside of the president and the secretary of state, I can't think of anybody."

It was a gentle rib, a mild little witticism designed to show him that in no way did she feel like a home wrecker. Brian recognized this, and the consideration behind it, and curled her closer to him.

As stormy as their clash had been the first time, the third time was as calm and unruffled. Beneath him, her blond hair fanned in a golden spill, Marie was a boat carrying him through the rock and dip of the night. Above him, she was the sail of that boat. Driven by billowing winds of delight, she took him on an argosy of the senses, an adventurous voyage of discovery that drifted on and on into the small hours of the morning.

The day proved to be an Indian giver, snatching back the pretty crimson bauble it had offered at its beginning and leaving in its place tense gray clouds that skittered nervously overhead as if transporting banned substances.

Brian switched on the windshield wipers of their rental car, but the sky refused to give generously even of precipitation, and he canceled the lever a minute later. The road, sparsely traveled, wound through featureless fields, grassy expanses denuded of trees that rose every now and then to embrace miniature hills, the summer richness those hills had displayed the day before stolen by an absconding gloom. The personality of the unsettled weather seeped through metal and glass and attached itself to Marie. She'd been silent and edgy since they'd left the inn, and kept fiddling with the scarf she'd knotted over her head. Brian picked up on her agitation and moved to dilute it.

"You'll be fine, Marie, stop worrying. These are not sophisticated people we'll be dealing with. You'll eat 'em with a spoon."

Marie tried to blast herself out of her jittery mood, a mood that, normally, was as much a stranger to her as depression or despair. "It's just that I've never worked this way before," she explained. "I've always told people, look, I'm a journalist, will you talk to me? And they either say yes or they say no. I've never actually tried to fool anybody before."

"I respect that. But we can't be up-front with these people. If Jay Two came out of this seminary, they may know it and be too embarrassed to admit it, or they might try to hide it for a bunch of other reasons. I don't like fibbing to anybody, but we're going to have to do it."

Still uncomfortable, and reflecting that discomfort, Marie said, trying not to sound too petulant, "You said I wouldn't have to wear a disguise."

Brian lifted his eyes from the deserted road to take her in. "You call a head scarf, a plain dress, low-heeled shoes and no makeup a disguise?"

"It just doesn't feel right. I just don't look like a nun. Nuns are either tiny and birdlike or a size eighteen."

Brian switched his attention back to the road and the lone car that passed them in the opposite lane. "I've met nuns who had figures like a movie star. In fact, I met one who *had* been a movie star. Stop worrying."

Despite his argument, she was right in a way, Brian admitted to himself: the scarf purloined the glamour that yellow hair often awards a woman, and the low-heeled shoes took away much of the leggy look, but that still left a lot of unhideable features, like the eyes of a Nilotic queen, and the erect, almost regal carriage of her long and frictionless body. For a woman whose sexiness was as inherent as Marie's, a religious was not a category she fit with ease. With a second glance at her, different from the first, Brian dwelled on that sexiness for a gratifying moment. From the distance of several hours he was able to look back at the previous night, memory gilding their union ever so slightly, and feel a shimmer of flawless and exhilarating warmth. He'd known this would be the test, the fabled morning after, the clichéd, unromantic light of day, and he was delighted, enchanted to find that the black falcons of remorse he'd feared might now be pecking at his insides were safely perched and hooded. Whether they would eventually appear, thundering down the sky of his conscience to claw and tear at his soul, was a matter of conjecture, and he resolved not to dwell on the possibility.

He checked the directions he'd been given at the inn and, a half mile later, turned up a dirt road and followed its uneventful wanderings until a group of buildings slid into view. The main one looked like a tall red ship becalmed on a green Atlantic, the outer buildings a less important part of the convoy. As they got closer the main building changed its nautical reference and became a mansion of confusing styles. Uncertain as to its identity, the building sported armorial escutcheons on Dutch gables and massive chateauesque chimneys before settling down to the plebeian existence of unadorned red brick. High up on this drab red expanse a clock had died at some forgotten 3:52, perhaps frozen to death one subzero morning. On the western side a half-built addition rose, its skeletal innards bone white against the sullen sky. The attendant buildings, severely plain after the excesses of their larger brother, were clearly animal shelters and other appurtenances of a working farm, cow sheds and tumbling corrugated piggeries.

A silent housekeeper wearing a floor-length apron admitted them, and led them down a dark corridor chilled by quarry tiles and sanctified by a dramatic and dolorous air. Some past administration had tried for a Romanesque flavor and failed miserably, the once-rectangular doors and windows now rounded and arched and looking defeated by the architectural fascism.

The office they were shepherded into continued the irascible motif of the corridor, but the man who rose to greet them—swamped by his long black robe, the carved wooden crucifix worn around his neck looking large enough to be a penance—was the antithesis of the decor outside. He looked like a beaming garden elf, a forest sprite who'd decided it would be fun to dress as a cleric. His dark eyes glittered with merriment, his prominent nose seemed party to the joke, a perpetually smiling man who appeared to be responding to some amusing punch line. Hirsute to an extraordinary degree, his hair ballooned above his skinny forehead, and his full-face beard looked dense enough to trap light.

He offered his delicate right hand. "Father Sheridan, I take it?" He didn't say the words as much as peal them, his voice having the timbre of temple bells.

"Father Zaim. Good of you to see us at such short notice. May I introduce Sister Mary Ellen, who is a sister in more than just title."

"Siblings? Delightful," Zaim tinkled. He shooed them into large refectory chairs and regained his own seat, a gas-operated office chair pumped up to its highest extension. "Monsignor Chifley told me you were traveling with a companion. Naturally, I expected another priest."

"A last-minute change," Brian lied smoothly. "Father Wysinski was taken ill. I asked my sister to come because she's involved in education, too."

"Ah," Zaim said, as if education was the most noble calling he could think of. "And tell me, Sister, which order are you with?"

"Maryknoll," Marie said. "Brian and I are both with Maryknoll in White Plains."

Brian had been certain Marie would prove to be a trouper, the kind of actress who leaves her nervousness backstage, so he wasn't surprised to hear her deliver the coached reply without a trace of the unconfidence that had rattled her earlier.

"I do hope we're not putting you out, Father," Brian said to the smiling elf.

"On the contrary, I am flattered by your visit," the little man said, the crotchets and quavers in his voice waltzing through his syrupy Middle Eastern accent. "Flattered that so fine a churchman as Monsignor Chifley would even. know our little seminary existed."

"I can assure you, Father, he has great respect for all branches of the Orthodox Church, and keeps up with its teaching facilities. That's why we're on this trip, Sister Mary Ellen and I. To hopefully gain insight and keep our methods fresh and up-to-date."

"How extraordinary." The bearded priest wagged his head as if he'd just received splendid news. "For nine hundred years the Roman Catholics and the Eastern Orthodox have been schismatic antagonists, but now the ancient anathemas are receding to such a point that your great church is willing to learn from ours." He completed his statement turned toward Marie, a clear call for some kind of response. She handled it wittily enough for Brian to have to suppress a smile.

"Ecumenism, Father. The only hope when you're surrounded by nonbelievers."

"Just so," the little priest agreed, his bearded chin rising and falling like the busy blade of a shovel. "Well"—he sprang up in his role of woodland sprite—"what can I show you first?"

He took them on a tour of the lower floor—the classrooms and dormitories occupied the upper floors, and were off-limits to all visitors—which at first appeared to be nothing but dark halls and short corridors full of the same egregious architecture they'd noticed on their way in. However, standing out like a diamond mounted on cardboard, was the little chapel Father Zaim led them into. It was a breathtaking surprise, a miniature replica of a Byzantine wonder complete with a glowing iconostasis screen and a rainbow of gilt tilework arcing over the shining altar. Next to the chapel, close but separate, was a room of veneration devoted to the history of the religion. Four oil paintings, lavishly surrounded by rococo frames, were positioned in places of honor, and the seminarian invited Brian to guess at the identities of the subjects, perhaps intending a long commercial on behalf of the Eastern Church when the visiting Catholic priest admitted ignorance.

"I'd better warn you, Father," Marie said, wanting to cement her role as immediate relation and nun, "my brother is something of a scholar in church matters. He may just surprise you."

The look that Brian directed toward her contained a cautionary wince. "You're putting me on the spot, Mary Ellen."

When Father Zaim rubbed his hairy hands together, he looked like a small trained bear. "A church scholar. Then he should have no problem," he said, anticipating an easy victory. And Brian, like Marie, saw then that he wasn't quite as genial as his sparkling demeanor indicated. There was an adversarial undercurrent flowing beneath that smile, in all likelihood fostered by the traditional enmity between the two divisions of the faith.

Brian studied the paintings a second time and was reassured. It wasn't going to be that difficult; there were basically four standout figures in the history of the Syrian Church, and the style of ecclesiastic robes the subjects wore tipped him off as to who was who. He was familiar with the likeness of the man in the first painting anyway, a Greek monk-theologian, his head a skimpy container for his outsized brain, whose writings he'd studied.

"Seeing that this portrait has pride of place," Brian said, "I'd say that's Severus."

"You are right," Father Zaim said, delighted at the Catholic Church, in the person of Brian, recognizing their founder. "He was tried for heresy. For teaching Monophysitism," Zaim told them, proceeding with his commercial in spite of the correct answer. "And in response he wrote the Philalethes. I don't suppose you'd know what that is, Father?" Zaim asked the question with a mischievous little grin, as if a Catholic priest's knowledge would be too parochial to extend to esoteric Greek commentaries.

Brian couldn't resist setting up his patronizing host. "I'd only be guessing, Father."

"And what would be your guess, pray?"

"Oh, if I had to say something, I'd suppose I'd say the Philalethes was a commentary on the orthodox Christological doctrine of Saint Cyril, patriarch of Alexandria, four twelve to four forty-four, whose teaching had been quoted against Severus."

Zaim's caterpillar eyebrows scampered up his face. He looked at Marie, who kept her expression emphatically neutral. The cleric, anxious now to score some points, indicated the second picture, a portrait of a stern-looking sexagenarian with the invincible stare of an early church father. "Perhaps you can tell me who this is," Zaim said, certain that the young priest couldn't be so lucky a second time.

"I'd say that's Jacob Baradaeus, bishop of Edessa. But I could be wrong," Brian said, an eventuality that Zaim was finding increasingly remote.

"You're not wrong, Father. It is Jacob Baradaeus," Zaim said, trying to unglue a smile like a fake mustache. "What do you know about him?" he asked, a glutton for punishment.

"Very little, I'm afraid," Brian confessed, with a helpless little opening and closing of his hands. "Baradaeus is his latinized name. I believe it's Burdana in Syriac, which means 'garbed in a patchwork garment,' so I'm told. He's the Jacob after whom you Jacobites are named, of course. As bishop of Edessa he greatly enlarged the church, although I've heard that a large part of the credit belongs to the monastic movement fostered by Rabbula, John bar Qursos, and, without doubt, Philoxenos of Mabbug."

"Without doubt," Zaim confirmed, blinking rapidly. Then, not brave enough to ask Brian to identify the last two portraits, suggested they press on. They returned to the tour, the seminarian scampering beside them like a child, although he'd left a good part of his bubbling spirit back in the portrait room.

Marie, deciding it was time to make some discreet inquiries, edged into it via the long way around. "How many languages are taught here, Father?"

"The lessons are in English, seeing as our students will be preaching in English. But they also study Greek and Hebrew and, of course, Syriac."

"The Edessan dialect, would that be?" Brian asked innocuously. "With the Aramaic variations?"

The black-shovel beard dug into the air. "Just so." Used to enlightening his visitors, the seminarian seemed a touch indisposed to entertain someone as comfortable with the history and esoterica of the Syrian Church as Brian was. The merriment he'd previously displayed had been replaced by something distracted and brittle, a change both visitors didn't miss.

"How many students, Father?" Marie again.

"Twenty-seven at present."

"Is there much of a turnover?"

"Dropouts, you mean? Rarely. We screen our applicants thoroughly."

"And the faculty?" Brian asked, again as if he were just showing polite interest.

Father Zaim preceded his reply with a quick, reactive glance at the Catholic priest, a glance which he canceled too late for it not to mean something. "Except for a novice who's recently joined us, all our instructors have been with us for years. We only accept students every five years, incidentally. At the end of that period they graduate into ordination, and a whole new intake arrives."

Brian stopped. He'd spotted a sign on a door written in the florid consonants of the Syriac alphabet. "Ah, the library," he said.

"We're building a new one," Zaim told them, moving to walk by the door. "When it's finished you must come and see it. This little one is far too small for our needs."

"May I see it anyway?" Brian asked.

When Zaim hesitated Marie said, "Libraries are Brian's hobby. He collects them the way some people collect stamps."

Zaim nodded in compliance, moved to the door, and opened it halfway. Marie, a step ahead of Brian, glimpsed a circular room, small and cramped, with steel stacks jammed with books extending above a normal ceiling height. There were four tables accommodating six chairs apiece, one of those chairs being taken up by an absorbed young man making notes from a large volume. Father Zaim closed the door before Brian could advance. "I'm sorry," he apologized. "I'm afraid we can't disturb the students."

"Perhaps we could come back later," Brian suggested. "I'm sure you have a fine copy of the Antiochian Liturgy. I'd be interested to see that."

"Alas, the library will be occupied. We have our term examinations today," Zaim said, and turned immediately toward the hard sound of footsteps in the tiled corridor. "Father Mouani," he called. "Just the man I need." He made the introductions as the priest he'd corralled walked up. "Father Mouani will show you the more practical aspects of our existence and, afterwards, bring you in to lunch with the faculty. If you'll excuse me, I must return to the pressures of stewardship."

They thanked the little man, and fell into step with their new guide, who, it seemed to Brian, had it not been for his black cassock and carved crucifix, could have stepped off the streets of Damascus yesterday. He was second-generation Canadian, he told them in a delivery devoid of the accent which might have been anticipated from the look of his golden skin and classic Semitic features. He was in his midthirties, Brian judged, but with the eyes of an old man, a watery and sallow yellow floating in them like the residue from an oculist's eyedrops. He held his right hand on his left elbow to comfort an aching joint. Altogether, not a well man.

"How long have you been teaching here, Father?" Marie asked, starting from scratch.

"Three years, Sister. Before that, I was teaching in San Francisco."

"Does that make you a veteran or a neophyte?"

Mouani slid his pained mouth into an angle of polite amusement. "I'm the new arrival but one. Almost the baby."

They left the building and went out into a gray gloom. The ill-tempered tantrum the day had threatened had still not appeared, low clouds full of nothing but impotent menace hovering overhead. The outer buildings the sick priest showed them around were the usual confusion of barns and lofts and farm machinery with the usual disbursements of distinctive odors. The excursion was of zero interest to the visitors except as an opportunity to keep Father Mouani talking about the faculty and the students, but the priest answered all questions with a pinched reticence which led them nowhere.

Wanting to get back into the main building, convinced that this part of the tour was a dead loss, Brian tried to curtail the expedition, but Mouani, zealous in his responsibilities, herded them into one more building. This one featured a partly eviscerated tractor whose oily lifeblood was being transfused by a young priest. Brian recognized a novice when he saw one, as much by the dirty job he'd been stuck with as by the inchoate beard and cheery personality.

Mouani introduced them; the young man's name was Charou, another Canadian by way of Damascus. They chatted with him for a polite few minutes, then took their leave and followed Father Mouani back toward the main building. The priest seemed to have run out of even tour-guide conversation and, to fill a gap of silence which was approaching rudeness, Brian said, "We appreciate you taking the time for all this, Father. I know how hectic it gets when you're running exams."

Mouani crimped his elbow against a rheumatic invasion and said, "Thankfully, our examinations are not for another four weeks yet."

"Oh," Brian said. "I was misinformed."

Once they'd reached the main building, Brian asked the priest if he and Sister Mary Ellen could spend some time in the beautiful little chapel before they took up Father Zaim's kind invitation to lunch. The Canadian escorted them there, told them where the refectory was located, and left. Brian accompanied Marie into the gorgeous little jewel box, where they slid into the rear seat, gave it thirty impatient seconds, then hurried out.

They didn't have to discuss their destination. That had been itchingly obvious for quite a while.

They walked quickly down the echoing corridor to the library. The student who'd been using it before had departed, and all four tables were barren of anything but a deep gloss.

"Why didn't Zaim want us in here?" Brian included himself in the question as his eyes made a circuit of the room. "And why send us on a tour of the barnyard?"

"Because he wanted to get in here and get something," Marie replied, and once again Brian was able to confirm the wisdom of including her on this escapade. It wasn't in his nature to come up with quick conclusions, and it was fast thinking, he knew, that would be needed if success was going to rear its shining head.

"He's not comfortable with us poking around, and to play it safe, he decided to remove . . . whatever," he said, extending Marie's suggestion. "This is a library, so it had to be a book. The next question is, what kind of book?"

Marie was right there with the answer. "One that has names and photographs. Either of a student or a teacher who's no longer here. And that'll be the man we're looking for."

She said it without excitement, a simple factual statement produced by intuition. But it didn't fit comfortably with Brian in spite of his recognition of the need for exactly this kind of help.

"It's too early to say that. What you hope for and what is are usually two entirely different things."

Through the light film of a smile Marie said, "I take a more sanguine view. Let's find what is, and see if it's what we're hoping for."

"Good luck on that one," Brian said. "That's what archaeologists call the Christmas hypothesis." He moved to a bank of catalog files and checked the cards mounted in brass holders on the drawers. "Okay. What we're hoping for is a missing yearbook. Maybe two." He slid open a drawer. "And if they are missing, we can make a pretty good guess why." He riffled expertly through a rank of cards, recognizing an abridged Dewey decimal system augmented with book numbers from the Cutter-Sanborn Tables. He found the yearbooks listed under Records, and read off the entry. "Yearbooks. Seminary. A five-yearly record of staff and students." In the top right-hand corner were the reference letters and numerals, LF 4578 C, which he also read out.

Marie consulted an easel card on top of the files, a diagram of designation and arrangement. The initials LF stood for Large Format. C indicated the shelf, the third one up from the floor. "You said the Christmas hypothesis?" she asked, moving to the stacks. She could plainly see that they'd lucked into some kind of jackpot; the yearbooks, tall, leather-bound volumes produced when each intake was graduated, stopped at the '82–'87 edition.

She ran a finger over the abbreviated shelf, tracing an outline of dust where the latest volume had once resided. She held up her smudged finger, held it up to Brian as a happy piece of evidence. "Merry Christmas," she said.

They got through the luncheon in a coiled tension masked by platitudes as bland as the wretched cooking.

There were six at table besides themselves: fathers Zaim and Mouani, and four other members of the faculty, all bearded Levantines, two of whom kept stealing little looks at the nun as if committing her lucid eyes and contoured mouth to memory. These two, and one of the others, had their hair caught back in a ponytail, a feature silently noted with interest by the luncheon guests.

At the head of the table, Father Zaim exhibited a remarkable talent to eat and talk at the same time. When forced to pause his oral cascade in order to rend a piece of the pitiless beef, he kept the conversational ball in his court by making a grunting-humming noise to signal that he had more to say and would prove it if given but a few seconds. He'd recovered his earlier personality—the impish, genial one—no doubt, Brian thought, because he was boosted by a sense of security. Brian was pretty sure the seminarian didn't overtly suspect them of prying, but was probably just being cautious around two strangers who'd asked questions about staff and students. Brian doubted that yearbook would be returning to the library. Having removed it, Zaim would want to keep it somewhere safe, locked up. Just why and how he was part of all this was something Brian had not yet got around to considering. Nor did he feel it mattered for the moment. The important part, the part that gave him the same kind of charge as when he'd tracked down a misty figure in an ancient culture, was that he was now positive that Jesus Two had come out of this seminary.

So was Marie.

Normally, she might have distrusted such fast luck, but she felt that in this case, luck was not the right word. It was expertise that had guided them here, Brian's and Professor Makram's, and while you could question chance, you could never question genuine knowledge.

Half listening to Zaim discourse on the unfortunate conclusions of the Council of Chalcedon, she checked with Brian, who felt her glance. The same connected thoughts leaped between them: was the book in the loquacious priest's office? How were they going to get a look at it? Marie felt they might have a chance if they could slip away and poke around, but this possible avenue of action was detoured when, the dreadful lunch mercifully completed, Zaim—who spoke in the past tense to let grammar deliver the message that their visit had concluded—told them how sorry he was he hadn't had more time to spend with them. They said their good-byes to the table, then Zaim personally walked them to their car, not so much a gesture of politeness, Brian felt, but more to satisfy himself that they were off the premises.

"Please give my kindest regards to Monsignor Chifley," Zaim said, grinning at them behind his heavy beard.

Brian assured him that he would do that as he opened the car door for Marie. The little priest waved to them like a school-boy saying good-bye to a couple of vacation pals, then they drove away, rounded a hill, and the seminary disappeared.

Brian pulled over. "So now what do we do?"

Marie raised her hands to take off the bothersome head scarf, then thought better of it. "We have to go back. If we leave now, we've got nothing."

"We'll never get by Zaim."

Marie looked through her side window at the tufted hill shield-ing them, then ahead at the pebbled road. She said, "Let's take an-other look at that tractor." It was an enigmatic remark on the surface, but Brian understood what was in her mind.

"The kid?"

"Let's see what he knows."

Brian was sure that Father Zaim would have sworn his staff to silence as to whatever curious events had taken place at the sem-inary, and was doubtful that the young priest would tell them any-thing, but he kept these thoughts to himself. He'd learned by now to trust Marie's instincts and techniques; he'd been much im-pressed by the way she'd handled Zaim, asking what appeared to be innocent questions and yet surreptitiously digging all the time.

He took the car away, heading for the side road he'd seen on the way in, a rutted track that looked like an access road to the farm, which it proved to be. They drove its semicircular loop, bumping over its ridges and hollows for a quarter mile, then parked the car outside the last farm structure. They found the young man where they'd left him, in the tractor shed. He'd put his tools away and was washing grease off his hands with a green gel.

"Father Charou," Brian said. "Hello, again." Slightly surprised to see them a second time, the young priest greeted them with a youthful openness absent in the rest of the staff. "We missed you at lunch," Brian told him.

Charou dried his hands on a towel and lifted his chin at the resuscitated tractor. "I had to finish my chore."

Brian, sure that opinions of seminary cooking would be the same the world over, gave him a conspiratorial wink. "I used to stretch out my chores, too. Anything to escape the cooking."

The young priest laughed. "It's really awful, isn't it?"

Marie slipped effortlessly into the conversation. "It certainly hasn't improved any since the last time we were here."

Father Charou said, "This is your second visit?"

Brian stayed silent, waiting to hear what Marie was working up to.

"I don't believe you were here then," she ventured.

"I've been here about two years," the young man volunteered, pronouncing the word *about* to rhyme with *shoot*.

"I remember another priest who was here before, but I didn't see him today. A tall man with a ponytail," Marie said, as if she were peering into the far recesses of memory.

"Oh, you mean"—Charou caught his words in his mouth, then, unable to overcome their momentum, released them—"Father Heloum."

"Was that his name?" Marie didn't seem sure. "He was from Syria, and had an accent a little like Father Zaim's."

The young man nodded uncomfortably.

"Heloum," Marie said. "Now I remember."

"I remember him, too. Fuad Heloum," Brian said, then mentally crossed his fingers as he applied the acid test. "I think he told me one of his parents was Turkish."

"His mother. She was from Ankara. And it's not Fuad Heloum, it's Camille Heloum."

Brian battled not to look at Marie, and Marie locked her eyes off. They both knew they'd just heard the name of the man who'd

got the biggest promotion in the history of religious education—
from seminary instructor to Jesus Christ.

With dramatic timing a rumble of distant thunder rattled the
corrugated iron of the shed, and some hard, sleety raindrops began to splotch down.

"Looks like we're in for some weather," Charou said, rolling
down the sleeves of his cassock. "I'd better get going."

"Was he transferred?" Brian asked, a question of simple
interest.

"Something like that." The priest nodded at them. "If you'll excuse me . . ."

Marie smiled at him and, with an imperceptible adjustment to
her body—the way she was standing, the tilt of her head, Brian
couldn't quite figure it out—she shrugged off the guise of a nun
and reverted back to a lovely and sexy green-eyed blonde.

"Father Charou . . ." Her voice was an eighth note lower. "Tell
me what really happened."

Flustered by a change he couldn't name but could feel in the
swirl of his blood, Charou half shook his head. "Father Zaim
doesn't want us to talk about it."

"We're not the media," Marie assured him with womanly comfort. "You don't have to worry. Whatever you tell us will stay
within the Church." Marie wouldn't let him look away from her
warm appeal which a young man might have confused with some
kind of promise.

The priest's Adam's apple yo-yoed in an overture to an answer.
"He won a scholarship. To study in Istanbul."

"A scholarship. Some kind of grant, was it?"

"That's right. A benefactor of the Church, a Canadian living in
the States, apparently. A deacon from the southern branch of the
American Syrian Church came here and got Father Zaim's permission to test us on theology and biblical knowledge. Not me, the
older fathers. Father Heloum was the winner. He's studying in Istanbul, but Father Zaim doesn't want it to get out. He didn't want
any local publicity. He likes the seminary to keep a low profile."

"We quite understand," Brian said, offering no reason for such
a consideration.

"Has anybody heard from him? From Father Heloum?" A drumroll of rain fanfared Marie's question.

"Father Mouani got a postcard from New York. A photograph of a beautiful white clapboard church. Father Heloum had forgotten about a library book he'd left in a bottom drawer. He was meticulous about things like that. Excuse me, I have to go."

"Wait." Marie again. "Please . . ." The priest stopped at the door. Behind him a hard downpour slanted into the fields, gusts of wind breaking up its sharp angles.

"A white clapboard church in New York? Are you sure it wasn't Boston?"

"Not New York City, New York State. A small town. I've forgotten the name."

"What happened to the postcard?" Brian asked.

"Father Zaim destroyed it. As I said, he . . ." The priest broke off, his dark eyes flustered and involuntary. "He wouldn't want me talking to you. I have to go."

Marie had moved closer to the door. She stayed him with a hand, removing it immediately. "Father Heloum won a scholarship. My brother and I are both educators, so we're interested in scholarships. If Father Heloum hasn't yet left for Istanbul, we'd like to meet him."

"This was five or six months back. He must be there by now," the priest reckoned.

"This small town with the church . . . was it a long name or a short one?"

Charou watched Marie's fingers illustrate her question by making a long and small gap between thumb and forefinger. His deep olive skin, flawless in its fresh texture, hunched together above his eyes. "Two syllables, like, um, Rockport or Walton, something like that."

Brian felt the pincers of excitement which had gripped him slacken and fall away. Here was a hopeless puzzle: a small town in New York State, two syllables. How many candidates were there? Five thousand? He sighed inaudibly, submitting to a creeping gloom that was a cousin to the one spreading over the rainy farm outside. But when the young priest spoke again, the pincers snapped back into place.

"I remember I checked it out in the library. I found a picture of the church in a book on ecclesiastical architecture."

Marie had to gate her natural tendency to plow ahead; she knew how critical would be the next minute or so. "Father," she began, carefully stepping her way through a multiplicity of choices, "we know you don't want to get into trouble with Father Zaim, and we understand that, so what if you did this . . . what if you went into the library, got the book you found that church in, and left it open at that page?"

"We'll put the book back," Brian said soothingly. "Father Zaim will never know."

When Charou looked pained and negative, Marie said, "It really is a small request. Nobody can get into trouble for opening a library book, now can they?"

"I guess not," Charou said, lost in emerald depths.

"Do it quickly and it's done," Marie advised gently.

The priest nodded in a way that avoided any definite decision, then stepped hesitantly out into the weather.

Brian moved to the door and watched the figure, the skirt of his cassock delicately raised above the sodden grass, hurrying toward the main building. "Think he'll do it?"

Marie's gesture was as vague and indecisive as the young priest's had been. "I'm not sure what good it'll do us anyway. They drive to New York or wherever, and on the way they stop in a small town for a bite, and Father Camille Heloum buys a card in a store and mails it back. The main thing is we've got his name, and that's a huge breakthrough." She joined Brian at the door. The rain had begun to taper off, a clouded sun already pulling condensation up into the misty air.

Brian watched the hills steam and smoke, and tried to reassemble something as ethereal as those vaporous twists curling into the sky. "Who are they, and why? We're going to have to get that printed on a sign and hold it up every ten minutes."

Marie, in an echo of Brian's thinking, expressed the questions he hadn't voiced. "Did they just get lucky or what? Did they check out the seminaries, in San Francisco and Ohio, then come here and find the perfect candidate?"

"Whichever way 'round they did it, they also had to find a rector who'd play ball." Brian indicated the skeleton of the new library climbing the side of the redbrick building. "And they found one in Father Zaim. How would you like a new library, Father? Just let us borrow one of your priests, and we'll write you a check."

"And what did they tell Heloum? Or did they just kidnap him and brainwash him?"

"Probably no need to do that. I've known priests who got completely carried away by the office. A couple of years of celebrating the Mass, dispensing the wine and the wafer at communion, preaching the sermon to a congregation that can't interrupt you, it's a power trip for some. And sooner or later some of those priests feel they'd make a great bishop. Or a cardinal. Or maybe even pope. Some even develop a messianic complex and have to be temporarily or permanently retired. Whoever these people are, maybe they got a real bonus. Maybe they found a priest who not only fit the bill physically, but mentally as well."

Marie examined her watch and the sky in that order. An incipient clearing was inviting them out. "If Charou isn't tipping us in to Zaim, how long will it take him to find that book?"

"About thirty seconds. If he's going to do it, he's done it by now."

They left the shed in a light shower, walked the stony path, picking their way through puddles and rivulets. Zaim's office was at the front of the building, so they were out of his direct line of sight, but they could still be seen by anybody who cared to look out a side window or a rear one.

They hurried through the last of the rain. Chose the side door. Went through it and stopped just inside the corridor. The tiled surrounds, expert at conducting sound, brought them nothing.

They started off again. Made twenty feet and stopped at the bottom of a staircase. From an upstairs room the drone of a lesson slowly descended to them, a sleepy quality to the pedantic voice.

They moved again. Followed the turn of the corridor.

And almost ran down Father Zaim.

All three of them froze.

"Back so soon?" Zaim asked. His smile was a transparent overlay of rigid suspicion.

"I left my breviary in the chapel," Marie said, within the time span of a natural reply. "I'll just slip in and get it, if I may." She smiled at Zaim and moved by him. Zaim, it seemed to Brian, was drawing breath to call her back, and might have if he hadn't had to field a quick comment.

"The more devout they are, the more forgetful they become," Brian cluck-clucked. "Haven't you found that, Father?"

Zaim transferred his tight, beady look to him.

Brian had caught a whiff of misogyny from their earlier encounter, and played to it now. "Frankly," he said, "I've found that even the most devoted nuns are still subject to the less attractive whims of their sex. Wouldn't you agree with that?"

Zaim snapped his tongue behind his mass of facial hair. "Just so," he said, in uneasy irritation.

Around the corner of the corridor, Marie made the library door. Went through it. And found the library as empty as it had been on their second visit; exactly the same, with one major difference: there was a book on one of the tables.

A large-format book.

Open to a photograph of a white, gingerbreaded church.

She noted the name of the town the structure graced, closed up the book, slid it into a stack of similarly sized volumes, then hurried back to rescue Brian.

"Got it." She patted her handbag. "Sorry to be such a nuisance, Father."

Father Zaim forced politeness. "No trouble."

"Well, if we haven't forgotten anything else"—Brian flicked a teasing glance at his companion—"we'll say good-bye again, Father."

When they started back down the corridor, Zaim said, "That way leads to the side door."

"We parked on the access road and walked back," Brian explained. "We do a lot of walking. For the exercise."

With eyes like broken glass the seminarian watched them go.

Brian felt the black glitter of that dark stare on his shoulder blades, felt its lingering stab as they closed the side door behind them and set off down the muddy path.

"He's on his way to the library right now," Marie said. "He doesn't know for sure that's where I went, but he suspects it."

"Is he going to find anything in there?"

"Not unless he knows the collection upside down."

And when Marie said that, Brian knew that the young priest had done them the favor they'd asked. "Where's the church?"

"Hatfield. It's near Pound Ridge. It's horse country," Marie said, taking his arm. "You'll like it."

CHAPTER
17

This time, Gaetano Cresta chose a park for the meeting.

Actually, a small section of one: the Giardino del Largo in the Borghese Gardens. On weekdays it was visited only by tourists, and on weekends it was swamped by extended and noisy Roman families. Nobody from the Città would come to such a place. It was a good, safe spot for a clandestine conference.

He got there early so that his frown could accuse the fat priest of a lack of punctuality. One had to bear down on inferiors so that they never forgot their place.

At two minutes before the appointed time, the philatelist came hurrying down the sandy path. "I'm sorry, Father," Santoro said, puffing from his climb up the *scalla*. "I'm not late, am I?"

Cresta's narrow face squeezed in further still. "Tardiness is a failing, Father. It smacks of dereliction of duty. But, I didn't come all the way here in this roasting heat to discuss your failings, numerous though they may be. It's your successes I want to hear about. I assume your trip to Palermo can be counted in that category?"

Santoro gave thanks to his favorite saint that he could give a positive reply. "It was everything we could have hoped for, Father. I made contact without any trouble. It was surprisingly easy."

"Discreet and anonymous contact, I take it?"

"Absolutely, Father. They know nothing about me and have no way of getting in touch. I think they think I'm a businessman."

They stopped talking as a Japanese couple walked by. Maintained their silence while the Orientals took a photograph of each other with the little water temple in the background. When the tourists had moved away, Cresta asked another question. "What arrangements have you made?"

"I've engaged a first-rate man. I'm to meet him in Atlanta and help him get set up." Santoro enjoyed using this expression. Adopting the language of criminals, he felt, would show that he could move easily in such a racy environment.

Cresta allowed a mist of doubt to rise behind his eyes. "I hadn't realized they'd actually want you there. That you'd be consorting with a professional assassin. Are you sure you're up to it?"

Santoro flashed back to the excellent way he'd handled himself with Sacchi the bartender, and the contact man in the bottega. He moved on his heels and squeezed an extra quarter inch out of his spine. "I'm not afraid of the underworld, Father. I found out in my dealings with them that, as ruthless and immoral as they may be, they are men like any other."

Cresta was surprised by the reply. This assignment seemed to have infused this overweight cipher with a temporary measure of gumption. "When do you leave?"

"This evening. A flight to New York, then a connection."

"In that case, I won't detain you any longer."

Santoro gave a nod that was close to a bow, and turned away.

"Father Santoro . . ."

Santoro stopped. Turned.

"I want you to know that I have complete confidence in you. Not only to see this matter to a satisfactory conclusion, but to do so without any repercussions whatsoever."

Santoro repeated the nod-bow, swiveled once again, and continued down the sandy path.

His head felt full of helium. His chest seemed to be expanding to twice its normal girth. Father Gaetano Cresta, the most powerful secretary in the Vatican, had complete confidence in him. Complete trust.

Franco Santoro made a silent vow to go through hell and high water to make sure that trust was not misplaced.

Hell and high water.

On the same day that Brian Sheridan and Marie Olivier left San Francisco, Franco Santoro arrived in New York.

However, two hours later he was gone again, winging his way to Atlanta.

He'd been to America only once. His Roman masters had sent him to Washington, D.C., for a week in order to study the latest techniques in postage-stamp production. So Atlanta was brand new to him.

His first impression was that, while it may not have been anywhere near as large or as vibrant as Rome, its summer temperatures certainly compared: the sidewalks boiled under his shoes, and the uncomfortable humidity drew a salty fluid from his pores.

After three hours wandering the downtown area, taking advantage of the chilled air in the multitudinous stores, stores which were bursting with religious paraphernalia—even shoe stores, even bookstores and computer stores were selling religious articles—Santoro decided that the metropolis was a brash and artificial place, a meld of the old and the new that combined in uneasy disharmony. He was impressed, however, by the black people who gave vent to their natural exuberance in colorful dress, unabashed noise, and cheeky good humor. Perhaps it was largely for this reason, he speculated, that the city presented so forcefully its strangled air of partition.

His walking tour culminated with a visit to the Civic Center, which was his entire reason for the tour in the first place, for this was the venue, he'd learned, of the prayer meeting the charlatan was due to attend. And it was while he was standing in the ferocious heat regarding this edifice that a sudden realization dilated his heart and choked his breath: a man would be killed here in four days' time, his death effected largely because of the efforts of Father Franco Santoro, Vatican philatelist.

On one hand, it seemed a barbarous fantasy, a detached event happening in another medium, like watching a shark being fed through the glass of an aquarium tank. On the other, it was a distasteful and unfortunate obligation which had to be seen to its right and proper conclusion for the highest and most honorable of reasons.

And that was the version Santoro held on to as he dabbed his fleshy neck and reviewed his decision to come to Atlanta so much in advance of the event. Until Vizzini arrived, which wouldn't be for another few days, he could do nothing outside of making sure that if for any reason the time and place of the prayer meeting were to change, he'd know about it. But, then, how could he have helped his endeavor by staying in Rome until the last minute? No, it was better to be on the spot and get the lay of the land, so to speak, and accustom himself to the prevailing atmosphere. And there was an extraordinary amount of that commodity abroad in this city. It was like Venice during a plague year, only the plague was a bedazzled, wholehearted, unquestioning acceptance, the evidence of which was endemic. Sidewalk booths had sprung up everywhere, each one trumpeting the merits of its particular persuasion. There were dozens of Pentecostal sects that Santoro had never heard of, devotees of glossolalia and divine healing, some with names he could scarcely credit: the Ninth Assembly Church of Jesus Christ Revealed in Heaven. The First Witness Church of Christ On High in Virginia. The Fire-Baptized Holiness Church of God of the Americas. Nowhere could he look without his eye being assailed by posters, banners, and Scotch-taped store signs attesting to the return of Jesus Christ, many of the signs advertising his coming appearance at a football stadium—an engagement he would not be keeping—a few days after his scheduled obligation at the Civic Center, which, so Santoro had read, had been sold out fifteen minutes after its announcement.

Atlanta seemed giddily obsessed with its new resident, thus demonstrating, Santoro surmised, a woeful shallowness on the part of its citizens. Imagine subscribing to this man, an outrageous impostor who'd hoodwinked an entire nation, or at least a large part of it. But, Santoro mused, perhaps therein lay his attraction: America loved a rogue and cheered loudly for the rebel and the scofflaw, applauded them because Americans hated rules and regulations and confused sensible restrictions with an attack on what they perceived to be precious liberties. A curious people, they gave their all to fad and novelty, which, it appeared, were constantly replenished monthly if not weekly.

Arriving back at his hotel, he sat down for a rest and opened the newspaper he'd bought in the lobby. Jesus Returned, as they were calling him, had pushed everything off the front and lead pages, relegating important national and world news to a position not much more in advance of the crossword puzzle. Santoro spoke English only passably well but could read it without difficulty and so learned that tomorrow, at 11:00 A.M., Jesus would be holding an audience, in the privacy of the Reverend Don Bagley's garden, for all Roman Catholic religious. Admittance would require proof of same.

A pang like a wicked thrill skipped through him.

Did he dare?

What risk was there?

How many Catholic religious would be as curious as he was to actually see and hear this mountebank close up? Surely a dozen or so. Perhaps more. Who would remember one priest out of that many?

But could he do it? he wondered. Could he calmly sit there in cold blood in front of a man whom he planned to have shot to death?

Surely the answer to that should be a brave and resounding yes. The impostor clearly wasn't inviting Catholic clergy in order to apologize to them for the thinly veiled remarks he'd already made. No. He probably intended to lecture them on their biblical misinterpretations. Admonish them for being puffed up with conceit. Chastise the Holy Father for wallowing in treasure while half the world went hungry.

Would Gaetano Cresta approve of him attending this audience? Why not? He'd probably say, "Go! Hear for yourself at first hand this man's anti-Roman slurs. See for yourself how seductive he is. What a danger he presents to the Faith."

He'd urge him to go.

So he would.

*   *   *

He gave himself what he thought to be plenty of time next morning, but his mistake was made manifest when the cab driver dropped him off a quarter mile away from his destination.

That was the closest most wheeled traffic could get to the Bagley mansion, for the street which led to it was packed with people who wanted to be as near as they could to what they breathlessly referred to as the Presence. Just about all the residents had complained to city hall, but the police were constantly swamped by Bible-clutching faithful for whom the bullying shove of a riot cop was an acceptable trade-off if it meant another few yards gained.

Santoro would have missed the audience had not a checkpoint been set up especially for it at the most approachable end of the block. Here he found, on the very periphery of the mob, about forty Catholic religious—priests, mostly, plus a scattering of nuns—standing around trying to appear unembarrassed, several of the priests broadcasting smiles that edged toward exaggeration. Since Santoro was wearing a suit and tie, a surly police sergeant wasn't prepared to believe he was a priest, but then the sergeant wasn't taking any of the group at face value and checked everybody's credentials, turning away three enterprising men who'd made their own clericals but couldn't back up their disguise with a complementary ID. The officer looked uncomprehendingly at Santoro's Vatican passport, but, recognizing Italian, called over a minion whose dark hair proclaimed a Tyrrhenian heritage. When this second guardian okayed the latest arrival, they were herded into three police vans which, by dint of siren and sheer weight, carved a slow passage through the sea of pilgrims like an icebreaker in the Davis Strait.

When the high iron gates were opened, a beefy line of Atlanta's finest fought to hold back a crush of moaning men and women who wanted desperately to run down that graveled drive and into the arms of Jesus.

The vans rumbled down the drive, around its bend, and out of sight and hearing of the bedlam at the gates and the massed street beyond them. They pulled up in calm sunlight one hundred feet from the blue awnings of the magnificent house where everybody was invited to get out. To their left, on the green expanses of the lawn, fifty or so seats had been set up in front of a huge elm tree. A soberly dressed man with a beanpole figure moved out of its shade and called to the group, inviting them to advance and find a seat. The seats were set up in a long narrow block, ten rows, five to a row. When the assembly had moved across the clipped grass and seated itself, the man, directly in front of them now, spoke again.

"My name's Howard Willard, and I extend a cordial welcome to you gentlemen and ladies of the Catholic faith. The Reverend Bagley would have liked to have greeted you himself, but he's seeing to other arrangements and asks you to accept his apologies."

Willard paused to let his audience settle. The first five rows were shaded by the giant elm; those seated beyond that had to mask their eyes to get a good look at Bagley's deputy, whose pale skin and snowy hair lent him a flavorless ice-cream look. With his bubba accent banished, and employing a sincere and mannered style to align with the first-class educations of the majority of his audience, Howard Willard continued. "Very shortly you'll meet the one who asked that this gathering be convened. I'm speaking, of course, of the Lord Jesus Christ."

There were a few snorts of derision, but, in the main, the audience was quiet and respectful. Santoro, who'd taken a seat in the third row, guessed that it was their curiosity that had brought them here rather than any desire to mock and scoff. That they would do on the way back to their convents and parishes, shaking their heads at how quickly a confidence trick becomes low-level farce when trusting, simple folk, born outside of the guiding light of the True Faith, are shamelessly taken in.

"It was under this very tree," Howard Willard continued, "that the Lord performed his second miracle on this property, doing what he'd refused to do when tempted by the devil during his first ministry. Before our very eyes he changed stones into bread. It was by that miracle, and the greater one of restoring the Reverend Bagley's daughter to life, that we knew that Jesus had indeed returned to the world as had been foretold."

Santoro was aware of a soft snigger from somewhere behind him. To his right he saw an elderly monsignor shake his head. He turned back to the speaker, who reminded him of an undertaker, and listened to him continue his solemn propaganda.

"Two days ago the Lord came to Reverend Bagley and requested this meeting. Why he didn't say. You will hear his reasons from his own lips. You are indeed privileged to be accorded this incredible honor."

And with that, Willard took a seat that had been reserved for him, crossed his long legs, and waited.

Twenty seconds went by.

There was nothing for the audience to see but the huge elm and its luxurious background: the splendid stretch of Don Bagley's brick-and-timber house. Nor was there anybody in sight; no security people, no sign of guests or servants. Just the hot, quiet morning full of sun and the smell of freshly shorn grass.

Another twenty seconds.

Then Santoro sensed a vivid distillation coming from somewhere in front of him, something trembling and inarticulated like the reflection of a ghost in a mirror.

He heard a slight scrape of movement and caught his breath, as did most of the assembly, when the man who had to have been standing unseen on the other side of the immense tree trunk walked slowly into view.

Santoro was shocked, his large body actually twitching in surprise. The man wore a wide-sleeved gown tied at the waist, a dark brown, shin-length gown made from a rough and heavy cloth, the kind of cloth a bedouin might use to keep out the heat. And sandals whose open straps revealed the ruin in his insteps. Santoro turned an involuntary exclamation into a swallowed cough. Something had been smashed through those feet. And through the palms of the hands. And something had dug chunks out of that serene brow. However he'd received such damage, this was a man who'd known pain beyond that of the rack or the nightmare of the auto-da-fé.

But what stopped Santoro, interfered temporarily with the regular cadence of his lungs, was the extraordinary proximity to the historical vision of Jesus. The face was almond-shaped and tender-boned with the deep-skinned eastern features of the desert Semitic. And the eyes! The boundlessness of space seemed to lie beneath those heavy eyelids, along with an empirical knowledge of the most melancholy of events as well as the most glorious. A slim, almost feminine bone structure barely delineated the shoulders, and yet the long fall of hair looked entirely masculine. The mustache was wispy above the full lips, the parted beard raggedly natural. Santoro had been expecting something akin to what he'd seen reproduced in newspaper photographs. He hadn't been prepared for so close a likeness as this: it was Jesus as imagined by the great painters of the Renaissance, a likeness whose exactitude was shattering in its accuracy. Whatever blasphemous Frankenstein had made this monster, he had a hideous and sensational talent.

Santoro waited for the creature to speak, and when he did, the murmur that had flashed through the shaken audience instantly died.

"Some of you may have heard that I have had harsh words to say about your faith. That I have scolded its practitioners and advised them to reexamine their allegiance to it. What you have heard is true."

Santoro received a second shock; he could have been listening to Jonas Beraq speak. Before he'd learned Italian, Father Beraq, a clerk in the Congregation for Divine Worship, had had to speak English to make himself understood, and the fraud's accent, glistening and syrupy, sounded identical to the clerk's. Father Beraq was from the Catholic community in . . . Jerusalem.

How extraordinary!

Santoro belayed his unease and listened to the impostor continue.

"Your religion had diverged in ways that are callous, cynical, and immoral. Callous because, without regard to truth, certain facts were bent to better fit your church's policies. Cynical because your church fathers knew that the way to compel the faithful to accept these falsehoods was by placing these untruths behind unbreachable walls of dogma. And immoral because those selfsame fathers were contemptuous of established belief given you by the Gospelists."

Most of the audience had recovered sufficiently from the shock of seeing such a clever impersonation to show quiet dissent at these words. The elderly monsignor to Santoro's right twisted angrily in his seat, and there were frowns of annoyance and resentful mutterings from all around, save for one of the nuns—she couldn't have been more than twenty-one, Santoro guessed—whose framed face glowed with infatuation.

"When my Father sent me to walk amongst you the first time, it was to proclaim His heavenly kingdom and His greater glory. He did not send me in order that I might be worshiped and given honor equal to His. The Holy Spirit proceeds from the Father. It does not proceed from the Son, and yet your administrators chose to ignore this in the interests of wider appeal."

Santoro was puzzled; it sounded like the impostor was referring to the Filoque Clause added to the Nicene Creed four hundred years ago. Why would he pick on a thing like that?

"And it was to serve this same interest that my mother was elevated to a similar false plateau. Your fathers claimed that, although she experienced an earthly birth, she did not experience an earthly death. And yet a man one of your own popes declared to be a doctor of the church tells of Timothy, of whom Paul thought well enough to make bishop of Ephesus, witnessing my mother's demise in that city. But your masters chose to ignore that true plebeian fact in favor of a spectacular falsehood."

Now, that was blatant! An attack on the Assumption, one of the tenets of the modern Church. Santoro racked his brains for the identity of the church doctor the fake had referred to. Was it the Syrian, Saint John of Damascus? Not that it mattered. This whole experience was amazing—someone trying to pass himself off as Jesus Christ was holding a private audience for Catholic clerics specifically to lambaste them for getting it all wrong. What hide! But, Santoro conceded, it was an elegant lambasting; controlled and erudite, too. The man had tremendous style. He projected a calm and riveting authority in spite of his obnoxious position. Still, it was degrading to have to sit here and be lectured by a poseur, no matter how brilliant his disguise, and he didn't think some of the clerics present would remain silent much longer.

"The Scriptures were given you," the man went on, still standing there straight and tall with his arms held quietly at his sides, "for your instruction and enlightenment and were not meant to be plundered. For what else is it but theft when you attempt to confiscate the pens of the Gospel scribes who never wrote the words *limbus patrum* or *limbus infantium.* In Latin, Greek, Hebrew, Nabataean, Aramaic, or any other language. Nor did they ever write the word *purgatory.* Nor the word *infallibility* as a quality that could attach to a mortal being."

That was too much; the man had gone too far as was evidenced by the red-faced monsignor who got slowly but angrily to his feet.

"Sir," he said, in a staunch and forceful voice, "I must ask you to stop this invective, which I can assure you we all find most insulting. None of us believes for a moment that you are who you claim to be. We came here hoping that a charismatic but misguided preacher would prove contrite regarding some of the ill-considered remarks he's made about our religion. We did not come to hear our faith further disparaged, nor will we stay if you continue in this vein."

The monsignor sat down to some hearty applause; the assembly had found itself an able spokesman. But so had the fake, Santoro saw. The man who'd greeted them, the tall white-headed man who'd said his name was Willard, leaped to his feet, his previous geniality replaced by a strident rancor.

"It is you who are insulting, Father. To call the Son of God a mere preacher is the height of insolence. I was once told that a Catholic priest is like a candle, communicating the light and warmth of Christ's love and being consumed in the service of God. I fail to see how that could be possible if you can't recognize Christ when he stands before you."

"I will recognize Christ when he comes in clouds with great glory," the monsignor shot back. "Not when he drops from an elm tree."

For a moment Santoro thought that Willard, his eyes enlarged, his pale cheeks puffed by blood, was going to advance on the priest, but instead he swung around on the fake. "Show them your power, Lord. Perhaps if they viewed you on their knees they might better see who you are."

The monsignor's sharp reply brought laughter from the seats. "We can view him on our bottoms and see who he is."

Santoro marveled at the faker's aplomb. He remained locked in a cage of serenity as if he weren't the object of this last remark, or the sour exchange preceding it.

Willard made a second appeal, wrathful and impassioned. "If they won't believe their ears, Lord, let them believe their eyes."

The monsignor jumped in again, pressing his advantage and, Santoro thought, showing off by aping the mountebank's old-fashioned English.

"Belief does not lie in the eyes or the ears, but in the heart. Our ears may deceive us and our eyes play tricks, but our hearts know a false Christ just as they know a true faith." He swept his hand around to include his coreligionists. "This is the True Faith"—his finger pointed contemptuously at the man beneath the tree—"and that is a false Christ."

Once again the white-haired man swung around to the pretender, this time with his arms spread wide in voiceless entreaty. Santoro was riveted; the man's bluff was being called. He was about to be shown up for the sacrilegious trickster that he was. Santoro congratulated himself. He'd been right to come. He could understand now what Gaetano Cresta had been talking about; the man was a dangerous, perfervid, and committed antipapist. He could well see how his saintlike veneer could fool young and unwary Catholics who didn't have someone like this wily monsignor on hand to brilliantly counteract his outlandish claims.

It wouldn't be so hard now, Santoro was convinced of that. He could arrange this man's death in all good conscience.

He watched the monsignor get up from his seat, many of the audience following the elderly priest's lead. This private little meeting was clearly at an end. All that was left to do was to rise with dignity and leave this fraud and his puppet to rue their defeat.

Santoro moved to get up as well, but stopped when he perceived some kind of unnameable overture. Everybody else appeared to feel the same thing, too: the air changing its texture.

Something whipped away its warm summer song and revealed a skittish prelude, a nervous voltage of the kind that precedes an earthquake or a town-wrecking twister.

A moist draft of fear fluttered up Santoro's spine.

And then he saw.

Something was happening to the fraud.

He was beginning to shake and quiver like a man impaled by a lightning bolt, a comparison further strengthened when his gown faded and drained of all color, then burst into a shreiking, dazzling white. Blindingly incandescent, as bright as flaming phosphorus, the brilliance shot into the man's face, transmuting his features into unrecognizable detail then, incredibly, increased its blazing intensity until the light coming from his body matched the astral calamity of an exploding star.

Every single person in that quaking and dumbstruck assembly, well familiar with the Gospels, knew what they were seeing: Christ's anticipation of the Resurrection appearance—the Transfiguration before Peter, James, and John on the mountain.

Howard Willard, with a cry full of wonder, dropped to his knees. "Thank you, Lord," he cried. He interlaced his fingers and rocked his clasped hands in soul-shaking gratitude. "Thank you."

CHAPTER
18

The photograph Marie had seen in the seminary's library hadn't done justice to the little church.

Standing with Brian in a tiny triangular park looking across at the real thing, she saw that it was more than just a noble feat of nineteenth-century carpentry. Freed of the camera's single dimension, the viewer's eye had permission to climb from the porticoed entrance up past the solid-wood rose window all the way to the top of the triumphant spire which, when viewed against a bank of quivering clouds, appeared to be growing skyward. It was far prettier, far more gracious, than the photograph allowed, its windows shaped like angels' wings, its fretwork at once tasteful and humorous. It was certainly the most striking as well as the most dominant building in Hatfield, the public library placing second in those particular categories, a square arrangement of Victorian bricks and windows which had once been the mansion of the village's first family. The rest of Main Street ran for a charmingly concise fifty yards before reverting to the state highway which led into, and out of, town.

Brian looked away from the vertiginous steeple, and surveyed the scene behind him: a slow-rising embankment which led to an untended graveyard full of long grasses, leaning gravestones weathered beyond reading, and several toy-sized American flags inserted beside the graves of veterans of various foreign wars.

"It still doesn't make sense," he said, turning back to Marie.

She nodded her head in agreement. They'd been over the same fruitless ground on the flight back from Toronto, and in the cab to Manhattan, and had each spent the night in their own apartments to see if two separated heads were better than one. This morning, no closer to a solution, they'd rented a car, and made the hour's drive to this village, agreeing to put the discussion on hold until they'd seen what the town of Hatfield might care to reveal. But so far—and they'd walked around the town twice, and driven its environs twice—it appeared to hold no suggestion of midnight secrets in the soft fold of its elderly oaks, or its burgeoning agreement with the beautiful day.

Marie unfolded a road map. Studied it for a minute. "If they drove from Elton to New York, they'd pick up the Thruway at Niagara Falls, and either stay on it all the way, or turn west at Newburgh here and come down six eighty-four. So if they did either of those things, what were they doing in this village?"

"What do we have here?" Brian asked, sweeping a generalizing hand around him. "We've got a church, a library, a town hall, a general store-cum–post office. We've got a liquor store, a sports store, a hairdresser, two realtors, and three antiques stores all selling the same rockers, hex signs, and cedar breakfronts. We've got a service station whose owner dabbles in classic cars. We've got a doctor, a dentist, a lawyer, and two interior decorators. We've got a nursery a little way out of town, and a famous country restaurant halfway between that and Pound Ridge. So out of all those things maybe the big attraction was that service station. They stopped to gas up."

Marie stretched the wings of the map, her right index finger shadowing red lines. "Mount Kisco's much closer to the Thruway. Way bigger, too. Most of these little towns don't have gas stations."

Brian consulted the map, the fourth time he'd done so since they'd bought it in the general store. "Maybe they weren't going to New York. Maybe they were headed for Connecticut."

"If they were, they would've kept going through Danbury here, or taken route seven south." Marie raised her head. The village was quiet and calm in its summer dress: bucolic, innocent, friendly. She'd never thought herself particularly responsive to inert vibes, the good or bad personalities which some people can denote in a house or a collection of them, but the village seemed to be too ordered, too well mannered. "If they were driving south, there's just no reason for them to stop here. Unless they had business here or in Pound Ridge."

"Then I guess we better check out Pound Ridge," Brian suggested.

"We haven't checked out Hatfield yet. We have to start talking to people."

"And ask them what? Do they remember a tall, slim, dark-complexioned man with an accent who bought a postcard and mailed it from here five or six months back?"

"You're right and you're wrong," Marie told him. "I agree that specific questions probably won't do us much good, but a break in the pattern of this quiet little town, something that occurred six months back that somebody remembers causing a ripple . . . I don't know what it was or even if it happened, but I know that's what we've got going for us. A small village where anything out of the ordinary not only gets noticed, but assumes an importance it wouldn't get in a bigger town."

"What kind of ripple is a man going to cause who gets out of a car, buys a postcard and a stamp, scribbles on the card, and puts it in the mail drop? He's just one more tourist passing through a quaint country village and sending a postcard home." When Marie looked away and kept her answer to herself Brian reached down to the grass and picked up a sliced dandelion, the victim of a recent and indiscriminate mower. He twirled the flower in his hand, the bright yellow petals and sturdy stalk not yet aware of the brutal amputation. "I don't like the job I seem to have."

"Which is?"

He offered her the savaged weed. "Bucket of cold water thrower."

Marie accepted the dandelion as if it were a long-stemmed rose. She drifted her body against his and closed against him. "I like the way you throw water."

He quick-kissed her, receiving from her slightly parted lips a memory of recent delights and a promise of future ones. "You want my candid opinion?" he asked.

She moved her head back to view eyes too benign to match the aggressive thrust of the nose. "Let's have it."

"I don't think they stopped here for anything more important than a cup of coffee and a pumpkin scone. In which case, it's probably the end of the line. We have his name but nothing to back it up with."

"You want my candid opinion?"

He pushed her hair an inch away from her ear to watch the light enamel the gold. "Sure."

"Anybody driving from Niagara Falls to New York who wants a cup of coffee is not going to drive to Hatfield for it. It's just too far out of the way. They came here for a specific purpose, and it wasn't to eat a pumpkin scone."

They went back and forth on it some more, standing in that little green segment fronting an eighteenth-century graveyard, but their only point of agreement was to drive the areas around the village and see if anything suggested itself. Which they did.

All day.

Without success.

They checked into a motel outside Mount Kisco, a well-run place that offered them a rate on a self-contained bungalow. With all the traveling they'd done in the last few days they were ready for a hot shower, some wine, and some honest cooking. But when they emerged from the shower which, perhaps influenced by a desire to save the best of the evening's recreations till last, they took separately, Marie still had a muscle throb between her shoulder blades, an unwelcome legacy from too much sitting in automobile and airplane seats. She knocked on Brian's half-closed bedroom door. He opened it wearing a motel robe, the same thing she was wearing.

"You feel up to giving me a massage? I've got a kink I can't get out."

"Sure, if you've got a manual."

"I can show you all you need to know in two minutes."

"They're your bones."

They went into Marie's room, where she produced a small bottle of coconut oil and a stick of incense, each an essential part of her traveling kit. She heated the oil in the kitchen microwave, took Brian into the bedroom, sat him down, and decorously revealed his left thigh. Using this exposed limb as a trial horse, she showed him how to hold and cup his hands, and demonstrated a simple press and swim. She found some suitable music on the radio—Ravel's reflections on the sea at Saint-Jean-de-Luz—stuck the incense stick into a bathroom glass, and lit it. She turned off the overhead light, leaving on a single bedside lamp, then dropped her robe with a natural and confident nonchalance, and laid it down on the stripped bed.

"Give me your robe," she requested.

Brian slipped it off and handed it over. Marie placed it on top of hers, then lay down on them on her tummy. The pale lengths of her body were painted a half shade darker by the low lighting, faint, elongated shadows gathering beneath escarpment and hollow. With her head turned to one side, her trim profile exact against the white sheet, and her xanthine hair gilding her neck, Brian thought of a ship's sculptured figurehead afloat on Ravel's glistening sea.

He poured a little of the coconut effluent into his hands, sat on the bed, and, following Marie's instructions, straddled her, the insides of his thighs grasping her bottom. He leaned forward, bringing his weight carefully onto his hands. Felt the bubble of her spine as it bowed beneath the heel of his hand, the warm oil lubricating a path along the parallel ridges of her sleek back muscles.

Brian learned a different body than the one whose secrets he'd unearthed two nights ago; discovered the architecture, the underpinnings, the elegant weight-bearing stresses of that lovely structure. It was a revelation, this inside-out knowledge. He'd never seen a naked woman outside of sleep and truly relaxed, limbs limp in a way unconsciousness would not have allowed, nor been granted such privileged travel over so smooth a highway.

After a time they reversed positions. Marie dipped her fingers into the still-warm oil, then began to climb the length of his body in a series of quick handholds, kneading and compressing and creating tensionless energy as she snaked and pumped her way to his shoulders.

He could feel the silky cross-hatching on her mound crushing into his buttocks, and when she stretched forward to thumb-stroke the base of his neck the nubbed papillae of her nipples were like satin abrasions on his skin.

A woman of silks and satins, Brian thought, and extended that to include upper-body strength when, with a hold like a half nelson, she slowly hinged him up from the waist, turning and twisting him. She repeated the movement twice, and when she lowered his head and shoulders, and gently disengaged, he felt as if he were visiting another world whose gravity was only half that of the earth's.

They showered—together, this time—dressed quickly, drove into Mount Kisco, and found a cheerful Italian bistro near the railroad station. They ate spinach lasagne, drank the house red, found out more about each other's life, and deferred the mystery of Hatfield.

They were back in their bungalow inside of two hours, in bed fifteen minutes after that and, ten seconds later, locked together.

Even though they were no more nude than they'd been for the reciprocal massage, they were at another level of nakedness now. Puffed and open, extended and hard.

Marie trapped short, hot breaths. Released them all in a strung-out moan as she spread for his jiggling tongue.

When he came up on her, her long legs rose to jacket his waist, her fingers spearing into his flank, pulling him into the rise of her hips, her arms a metronome rhythming his strokes.

They built together, layer upon layer, each layer a dash toward a peak until, up above the world, dizzied by the rarefied heights, they cried out in triumph and lay stunned, oxygen-depleted, cloud-lost, whereabouts unknown.

In and out of sleep for the last several hours, making lazy love on the journey down from the far crests, they lay mortised together watching an early-morning sky mature into day.

Marie could tell that Brian was temporarily absent, his mind pulled back to the same old puzzle. His desire to succeed in this chase was palpable, and the reason obvious, she figured: what he took away from himself with one action—their physical intimacy—he felt he could replace with another. It would be a form of atonement if he could produce a complete dossier on the Jesus fake; not just who he was, but for what reason he'd become what he had, and at whose behest.

"I can always tell when you leave me."

"Pardon?"

"Your eyes kind of congeal," Marie said.

Brian feathered her shoulder, glided the back of his hand over the beat in her neck. "I don't leave you for very long. And you notice I always come back."

"I'm not jealous," she said, describing a ticktacktoe frame on his chest. "It's hard to compete with a national celebrity."

"Why did they bring him to Hatfield, Marie? For something he needed and didn't have? Like the wounds?"

"You saw the doctor's house. It didn't look like a Brazilian plastic surgery clinic to me."

Brian saw it in his mind's eye, a cottage with a garden and a weathered wooden shingle dangling from a crooked post. He remembered the name on that shingle, Dr. H. Wassenaer. You went to a place like that for flu shots or a sore throat; you didn't go to get your body changed.

Holding that thought, Brian wondered why he couldn't dismiss it as he drifted back into sleep.

He found out a couple of hours later, while he was brushing his teeth. A possible answer was right there in the mirror. It wasn't just the wounds the fake had to have; there was another part of his body they'd had to change as well.

He hurried into the bedroom.

Marie, already showered, was slipping into her clothes. She looked up at him standing there wrapped in a towel and brandishing a toothbrush.

"His teeth," Brian said.

"Well, it's not the molar. That's good and healthy." The dentist removed the X ray from the light box, and slipped it into a little envelope. "My guess is it's referred from that impacted wisdom."

"What do you advise?" Brian asked him from his inclined position.

"When you get back to New York, have your regular dentist monitor it. Wisdoms are funny things. They'll go for years without a twinge, then suddenly blow up on you." He released the dental bib from around Brian's neck, the tiny clasp causing his plump fingers not the slightest trouble. Brian had noticed the man's dexterity, his movements almost prissily neat, the pick flitting and darting with a confident precision. A suety man, rotund as an alderman, with thick-veined forearms sprouting from the half sleeves of his dental coat, he didn't look as though his talent would lie in that direction.

Brian swung his legs off the chair. "Thanks for seeing me at such short notice."

"No problem. That's the upside and the downside of a country practice, you never have patients piled up."

"It certainly doesn't look like a country practice," Brian said, taking in what he took to be state-of-the-art equipment. "I expected a pedal-operated drill."

When the dentist smiled he showed teeth that could have used some cleaning. "You gotta keep up. It's just good business."

Brian asked him how much he owed him, then dug for his wallet. "If you have a moment, I have a question for you." He counted out some bills. "A general question."

"Go ahead."

"I'm a writer," Brian told him, borrowing Marie's profession for a few minutes, "and I've been assigned an article on the history of dentistry. I haven't done any research yet, but somebody told me that, apart from yanking teeth, nobody was doing much repair work until about the twelfth century. Is that true?"

The dentist's glasses had large and heavy lenses, which added another ten percent to his fleshy face. Light slashed the lenses when he shook his head. "They were doing repairs long before that. The Romans had enough technique to drill out caries, but they couldn't do any better for a filling than some herbs in a ball of cotton rag."

"Tough to eat roast peacock on."

"Impossible. But it probably saved the tooth."

"I also heard," Brian said, with no change in his delivery, "that they found a first-century skull in Israel, I think it was. A couple of the back teeth were wired together. Does that mean," Brian inquired, watching the other man with a casual intensity, "that someone who lived back then, let's say Jesus, for example, could have had an orthodontist?"

The man removed his glasses for a swift polish. Without them his eyes looked diluted and used up. "I don't know about Jesus but, sure, they knew enough to do restorative work back then. They'd prop up a weak tooth with a strong one. Early bridgework, you might say."

"Got it," Brian said. "Okay, thanks."

Five minutes later, he was walking up the library path. A dog hitched to a rail outside the entrance watched him come, an elderly spaniel that barked at him. In the mood Brian was in, he felt like returning the throaty abuse. He entered the main room, a large space crisscrossed by open stacks with reading tables slotted clumsily around them. At a cousin to one of these tables, a short one parked in front of a microfiche machine, Brian found Marie. He took a chair next to her, slumping into it. When he spoke he didn't have to lower his voice; apart from a woman stamping books behind a circulation desk, and a browsing senior citizen, the library was empty.

"They didn't come here for the dentist. I hit the guy with a sledgehammer, and he didn't even blink. We're not doing too well."

"You're right." Marie gathered several slides she'd run through the machine and pushed them away as if they were a poor hand of cards she'd been dealt. "There's nothing in the local weekly. I went as far back as January, but it's mainly store ads and cooking columns and who was at the golf club dinner."

"That's too bad."

"It gets worse. I called a pal in New York. An investigator. He has all kinds of access, knows a lot of people including, so he told me, a contact at Immigration in Washington. When I explained what I wanted, he got his contact to ask Canadian Immigration to wire a copy of Camille Heloum's prints."

"And they wouldn't play ball?"

"They couldn't play ball. There's no record of any Camille

Heloum ever entering Canada. Which means he either snuck in, or some filing clerk did somebody a favor."

Brian rapped the table, a forlorn, dispirited action. "So at the end of the day, all we have is a bunch of assumptions. We think we know how they did it. We think we know the identity of the fake. And we think we know where they got him from. But we can't back up one damn word of it."

Marie picked up the slides. Slotted them back into their cardboard box with a resigned precision. "Mere products of overstimulated imaginations."

"I'd kind of hoped to do better." Brian appeared more thoughtful than depressed, but Marie knew there was a lot he wasn't showing. She put her hand on his arm.

"If it's any comfort, this is the fate of most investigations, even the professional ones. You get a beginning, maybe a middle, but rarely a satisfactory end. They just fade away."

"Which is, I suppose," Brian said, uncoiling slowly from his chair, "what we should do."

"We got close." Marie was trying for salvage. "And we might've gone all the way if we'd had some luck in this town, so don't feel too bad."

"Who's feeling bad?" Brian knew his behavior was less than impeccable; Marie had been a marvelous confederate, and she was the last person who should feel the edge of his disappointment. He kissed her cheek. "Sorry. I'm showing you my bad side."

She returned the kiss with some earned interest. "It's better than most people's good side." She left him, walked over to the librarian's desk, and returned the slides. Then they headed for the door.

Outside on the sidewalk, the spaniel barked at Brian again. Brian dismissed the defamation with a tired wave. "Have a good day, doggie."

The canine took exception to the familiarity, lunged forward on its leash, and snapped at the waving hand.

Brian cried out as he snatched his fingers away too late. "Ouch! Dammit, will you look at that! The damn thing bit me."

"Let me see." Marie examined the scrape. "It drew blood."

They'd been followed out of the library by the elderly man

they'd seen inside. He came hobbling up to them looking nervously worried. "She didn't get you, did she?"

Brian rubbed his hand. "Is that your dog, sir?"

The man shot a glance of dismay at his pet. "She's got old and ornery. Gets upset over nothing these days. Lemme see that." The man tilted his head back to peer underneath a pair of half glasses, the short-brimmed golf hat he wore slipping to the back of his thin gray hair. "She broke the skin. That means a tetanus shot. I'm awfully sorry, mister. Lemme drive you to the doctor. I'll pay for everything."

"No need. I probably provoked her."

"Come on," the man said. "I got my car parked up the block."

"What's wrong with the town doctor?" Marie asked.

"We don't have one anymore," the old man told her.

Marie experienced a feeling akin to a psychic's premonition; a prickling awareness on the radar of her skin. "He moved away?"

The man's expression was influenced by an unpleasant thought. "Poor guy was killed in an auto accident about three weeks back."

Brian brought several emotional guests to the next few seconds, but surprise arrived without an invitation. That the seminarian had been transported here for the icy attention of a surgeon's scalpel was logical enough, even though the doctor's little cottage had appeared too innocuous for such an undertaking. But, in hindsight, it seemed almost obvious: a country doctor who could work unobserved, a small town where a recovering patient could be hidden in the medic's house . . . it was glaringly apparent now. And the fact that, to ensure secrecy, the surgeon had been killed, like some of the other players in this weird affair, was also par for the course. But what surprised Brian was that the field markings of whatever game was afoot were slowly beginning to show through.

He calmed the elderly man and listened to him scold the spaniel as he led it away.

Marie watched them go. "When I said we needed a little bit of luck in this town, I wasn't thinking of a dog bite."

"Better a dog than an alligator," Brian said, and went back into the library. He cleaned the tiny wound in the washroom, then joined Marie at the table they'd recently vacated. "We've got to get into that doctor's office," he said.

Marie shook a negative. "Forget it. I've never seen a doctor's office yet that wasn't alarmed."

"Then maybe it's time to dip into your peerless collection of contacts again."

"Bring in a pro?" Marie's tone questioned not his words but his judgment.

"That's not such a hot idea, huh?"

"You don't start consorting with the hard guys, good or bad, until things get really heavy. We haven't reached that point yet," Marie said, a serious set to her mouth. She knew Brian had to be feeling the depths beneath his feet, and wondered if she'd sounded a little too schoolmarmish. She relaxed her voice and said to him in a manner that invited comment, "A doctor killed, a blimp pilot killed, the Carew brothers disappeared, it's no mom-and-pop operation, is it?"

"It's all so spotless," Brian said. "Nothing coarse like a dismembered body found in a trunk. It almost sounds like a CIA thing."

Marie changed focus as she examined a thought that hadn't occurred to her, but maybe should have. "You're right, it does. It has their neatly vicious style."

Brian's pensive look was dissolved by reality. "No, come on. Why would the government want Jesus Christ walking the earth again? Why would anybody, for that matter?"

"It always comes back to that, doesn't it? Why." Marie tilted her head, her eye line coinciding with the Tudor flower design repeated in the molding on the ceiling. It looked as complex and painstaking as this murderous knot they were trying to untangle. She pushed back her chair. "Let's see what the librarian knows."

She crossed to the circulation desk, where, retrieving her occupation from Brian, she told the woman she was working on an article about small-town doctors, and was there anybody who could tell her something about the one in this village who, she believed, had recently met a tragic death.

"I wouldn't want to bother any relatives," Marie said. "But if I could talk to somebody who knew him . . . He must have been a real part of Hatfield."

"He was a lovely man. Always had a kind word for everybody," the librarian said, confirmed in her sense of sorrow. A middle-aged woman oversupplied with calories, she appeared happy to take a moment to grieve as if her own allotted time span was also due to be curtailed. "He was a fine doctor, too. Why is it the best ones always go?"

"I assume he was married . . ."

"Divorced. Years ago. She didn't even come back for the funeral. There were no relatives at all. Just the people in the village here, and some of his hospital colleagues."

"Who would you say knew him best in the village? I really would like to talk to somebody who was close to him."

The librarian hardly had to think about it. "Carol Frankel. Speak to Carol. She was his receptionist for years. She works for Tom Hennecky now. The lawyer just up Main aways?"

Marie thanked the woman, collected Brian, and they left the library for the second time.

They'd passed the law office a couple of times during their reconnaissance of the previous day, a small clapboard house shared with a realtor, who occupied the street floor. The short staircase they climbed opened into what had once been a bedroom but was now an outer office with dark carpeting underfoot and framed legal certifications on the pine-paneled walls.

A woman turned from a filing cabinet at their approach. "Mr. and Mrs. Amis?" She assumed an affirmative and rushed on. "You couldn't have got my message. Mr. Hennecky's been held up. He won't be in for another hour."

Marie corrected the mistake and introduced herself and Brian. "You're Ms. Frankel?" The woman nodded. "I believe you were Dr. Wassenaer's receptionist."

"Yes, I was," the woman replied as if she weren't quite certain of that fact.

"We're working on a feature for *Yankee* magazine," Marie claimed, joining the staff of the Vermont publication at very short notice. "An article on vanishing professions in New England, like the country doctor."

"They seem to be few and far between these days," Brian said, chipping in with a friendly comment.

The woman, late forties and in need of a permanent, released a sad little sigh. "I'm afraid so. So many of them have moved into population centers, medical complexes. They can make a lot more money that way."

"We were wondering if you could tell us something about Dr. Wassenaer's work here in the village," Marie said. "Do you have a moment?"

"Well, yes, I suppose so." Carol Frankel indicated chairs, sat down herself, and flicked her eyes over her visitors: the young woman had a figure she'd always yearned for, and the man, handsome and intelligent-looking, made an admirable consort. "What exactly did you want to know?"

"He was the town doctor and also a restorative surgeon, is that correct?"

"He hadn't practiced surgery for the last five or six years. He said he was getting a little too old for it," the woman said in a tone that conveyed an opinion contrary to her ex-boss's. "So he taught instead. At Mount Vernon Hospital. And, of course, he kept up his office here for general practice until . . ." She wobbled the last word, moisture springing into her eyes. The doctor's demise was obviously something she had yet to come to terms with.

"I'm sure he's sorely missed," Brian said, pretty certain that the town had no idea of the clandestine side of the man's skills. He let a moment of silence slide by in remembrance of the departed, wondering if the receptionist had been in love with her employer.

"It's pretty rare for a country doctor to specialize," Marie said, just an interested aside. "We've found quite a few who are surgeons but in the more commonplace fields."

"Dr. Wassenaer did it all originally. General surgery. Then he became fascinated by microsurgery and began to specialize in hand work. He became quite famous. A doctor in Katonah sent him a patient once, this would have been, oh, fifteen years back," the woman told them, pride swelling her anecdote. "The patient had five fingers on his left hand, that is, an extra index finger where his thumb should have been. Dr. Wassenaer turned that extra finger into a workable thumb. He was a wonderful technician."

"He must have been. You have to be pretty good to work on something as intricate as the hand," Marie said, then, as if it were

an afterthought, "or the feet." But all that the addendum produced was a nod of agreement. When Marie saw this zero reaction, it told her the same thing it told Brian: this woman knew
nothing about any midnight surgery on a priest of the Syrian
Church. Yet they were both convinced she was keeping something
back. She was a little too earnest in her praise, as if by harping on
the dead doctor's legitimate success it would preclude the fact of
there being any other kind. If she'd been in love with him—and
that possibility occurred to Marie as well—then a desire to protect
his name would be natural.

To protect it from what?

The answer to that might as well have been a red slash of graf-
fiti splattered across the wall behind the woman's abundant head
of hair: midnight surgery that she did know about.

Marie honed in on that, presenting her next question in the
same innocuous wrapping as the previous ones. "Did Dr.
Wassenaer have surgery facilities in his office?"

The rays filtering into the room from a ceiling skylight faded as
the sun was occluded by a cloud. As if objecting to this celestial re-
arrangement, a neighbor's child began calling to somebody, a high,
plaintive appeal. Carol Frankel's reply was counterpoint to the
sound. "Yes, but he closed that part off after he stopped doing
surgery."

"And that was five years ago?"

"Five or six, yes." The receptionist tried to deliver a seamless reply, but while she was able to keep her voice faithful, her body betrayed her, her right hand fingering the cross around her neck as
if she were testing the milled edge of a suspect coin.

A silence dropped into the office which, in spite of the child's efforts, began to spread in widening circles. Carol Frankel was lying;
Brian knew it and Marie knew it. The receptionist, aware that her
rickety fib had collapsed, firmly asserted herself as if forcefulness
could still shore up her crumpled position.

"Five years last April. I remember now. That was the last time
he touched a scalpel," she said. But her reply was eaten up by the
teeth of another question.

"Ms. Frankel, what happens to the patients' records when a
doctor dies suddenly?"

"They're inherited by whoever buys the practice from the estate. The patients are advised of the changeover, and if they don't want to remain with the new doctor, their records are mailed to them."

"And no one has bought the practice yet?" Marie persisted.

"No." Again the neighbor's child dominated the cessation of interchange, and again the receptionist's reaction was a spirited defense. "I hope you're not going to ask to look at those records . . ."

"It would certainly help us with this article."

"Out of the question. Those records are private and confidential. Besides, the office is locked, so it's impossible anyway."

Before Marie could reply, Brian put a restraining hand on her wrist. "I think we're taking up too much of Ms. Frankel's time," he said.

Marie received the message, was uncertain as to its point but, nevertheless, rose from her chair. "Thank you for talking with us, Ms. Frankel."

Brian got up with Marie, and accompanied her to the door. "Two minutes," he whispered, then let her start down the stairs by herself. He turned back to the receptionist. Returned to her desk. She was standing, wondering what was coming now.

Nothing could have prepared her for what did.

"I think you've been fibbing to us, Carol. However, that only makes us even, because we've been fibbing to you." Brian pulled his wallet from his jacket. "We're not writing a feature for a magazine. I'm not even a writer. I'm a priest."

The woman's face enlarged as she looked at Brian, then down at the ID he proffered. "A priest," she said, partly in surprise, partly in understanding: she'd known priests who'd had the same look of sagacity she'd noted in him earlier; a composed wisdom that set them apart from other men.

"Are you Catholic, Carol?"

"Yes, I am, Father."

It was what Brian had suspected and hoped for, ever since he'd spotted her little gold crucifix. Her subservient admission held out a promise of obedience. If he was lucky, all he had to do now was level with her.

"I'm not going to lie to you anymore, Carol. I'm going to tell you the truth. I hope you'll believe that." Her nod didn't promise anything, but there was an openness in her eyes that Brian found encouraging. "The diocese in Chicago asked me to check out something. A piece of skulduggery that's casting a big shadow on the Church right now. I think Dr. Wassenaer was involved."

The woman was rocked. Emphatically scandalized. "Dr. Wassenaer was a fine practicing Catholic. He would never have done anything to hurt the Church. Never."

"I'm sure he didn't know anything about it. But I think he agreed to operate on somebody illegally. By what means he was induced to do that, I have no idea."

The receptionist's mouth wavered. Whatever was working inside her head rattled her face like a strong wind. Brian increased the velocity of his gentle accusations just enough to effect a collapse. "Perhaps he was blackmailed. Was that the reason? Somebody had something on him, and forced him to do the work?"

The woman inhaled a kind of reverse cough, and made no move to cover the tears that appeared on her cheeks.

"I think you'd better tell me about it, Carol."

A sudden exhaustion claimed her. She sank into her chair, her voice a low keen. "I don't have any details. I was never a part of any of them."

"There were others? In the past?"

"I suspected something was going on. He always found a reason to get me out of the office."

Brian sat down opposite her. Gave her a moment to regroup. She found a tissue and patted her eyes.

"Tell me about the last one. When was it?"

"About five months ago. He asked me to run several errands for him in New York. When I got back I could tell the surgery had been cleaned, so I knew it had been used. But there'd been other signs before that."

"What kind of signs?" Brian asked, with just enough pressure to keep the flow going.

"There'd be phone calls from a Dr. Rayburn. I met him once, he and his wife. I'm pretty sure he was an anesthetist and that she was a scrub nurse."

"Dr. Wassenaer used them for his"—Brian searched for a euphemism—"after-hours surgery?"

Carol Frankel gave the most regretful of nods, her breath stumbling in her throat. "He was such a good man. I know he didn't do it for money. He didn't care about money. He must have been threatened by somebody."

"This last episode. Five months back. Where did the patient recover?"

"In Dr. Wassenaer's house. I knew somebody was living there. Once or twice I saw Mrs. Rayburn leaving late at night when I was out for a walk. I knew she was tending to somebody."

"You took the doctor's calls in the office. Can you remember anyone who called him, before or after the surgery, whose name you didn't know?"

"No. He would have taken any calls about . . . that kind of thing at his house."

Brian got up. Moved over to a wall, read the name Thomas Hennecky, handwritten in German Gothic style, on an accreditation certificate. "Is Mr. Hennecky acting for Dr. Wassenaer's estate?" The question brought a snuffled affirmative. "Then he'll have the keys to the doctor's office . . ." Another whimpered confirmation. Brian came back to the desk. "Do you think Dr. Wassenaer would have kept records of the operation?"

"He was too good a doctor not to."

"I have to get a look at that record, Carol. The report, or whatever you call it."

Trying for a little control, the receptionist arranged her tongue against her palate before saying: "I can't do that. I can't let Dr. Wassenaer down that way."

"And how about yourself?" Brian asked, much practiced in this kind of moral argument. "Are you prepared to go on letting yourself down? You knew that something extremely illegal was going on, yet you said nothing. That was wrong, Carol. But I don't think you need a priest to tell you that."

The receptionist had one hand fanned across her face, tears popping between the fingers. Brian might have felt like a bully if he hadn't been sure that the woman was crying not for her sins but for a love which, if it had never been offered before, would never be offered now.

"You have the option of repairing some of the damage, and that's a chance few of us get when we stray," Brian said, wondering if he was subconsciously delivering this little sermon to himself as well. "I don't think I'll be able to keep the doctor's name out of it, but his life is unfortunately over, Carol, and yours isn't. If you want to feel better about yourself, and help the Church into the bargain, you'll let me into that office tonight."

She wasn't going to look up at him, and there was nothing more to say anyway, so Brian left. Went down the stairs, and out into the quiet sunshine of Hatfield, New York.

Marie was waiting for him on the sidewalk.

"I put on the collar," he told her.

"Did it work?"

Brian lifted his gaze toward the law office, its white facade enjoying the fine weather, its lone inhabitant surely oblivious to it. "We'll find out when it gets dark."

By 11:00 P.M. the little white town was becalmed like a snowed-in village in a glass paperweight. Summer stars replaced the snow, falling through their unimaginable voyages above the town's oaks and maples, whose uppermost branches conspired in whispers in the late-night breeze.

Anybody driving by, like the police patrol car that made regular rounds, would not have spotted the two figures on the south side of Main Street, tucked in as they were in a side passage of the small cape cottage which housed the office of the town's late doctor.

"I don't think she's coming," Brian said, disappointment giving his voice a ragged shape in the dark.

"You can try again tomorrow," Marie said. "And be either a little more threatening or a little more charming."

"And what happens if that doesn't work?"

She moved against him. Kissed the side of his mouth, and left her lips there. "Then we come back here and neck tomorrow night, too."

Brian pulled back but couldn't determine the expression on her face. "Why are you being so cavalier about this?"

"Because my hearing's better than yours."

Brian heard it then, the scuff of footsteps on grass. A movement near the sidewalk formed into a figure which defined itself as it came closer.

The fullness of the night shrouded Carol Frankel's face, but Brian sensed the depth of her nervousness. "It's good of you to come, Carol," he said, letting her read into the ambiguity of that what she would.

The woman mumbled something, acknowledged Marie's presence with a narrow look, then led the way around to the rear of the house. Ambient light skimmed a grassy backyard, a pond breaking up its featureless spread, a frog singing to the night before it plopped into the still water. The sound was echoed by a metallic squeak as Carol Frankel opened a screen door. A thin flashlight beam illuminated her hand and the key it held, and the lock that accepted the key. She pushed the door open. A guardian dragon began flashing its red eye at them, gathering strength for a full-throated roar. The woman slayed the threat with some magic digits, and the feverish red eye turned a benevolent green.

It was a standard waiting room they entered, the flashlight beam sliding over chairs, children's toys, and a central table piled with magazines. At one end of the room, near a notice board festooned with medical posters, was a waist-high counter and, behind it, a filing cabinet and the desk which Carol Frankel had occupied for half her lifetime.

"Did you want to see the surgery?" she asked, her tone thin and jittery.

They followed her along a short corridor and through an internal door. The flashlight beam played briefly over a surprisingly underfurnished room: an operating table with two ninety-degree arm extensions, a large retractable ceiling light hovering over the table like a mantis, two tall oxygen tanks in a corner, an ECG machine and a row of wall cabinets. Everything was neat, uncluttered, and odorless.

They went back into the corridor and into the doctor's office itself, a plain, functional room with a desk, a hand basin, an examining bench, an old IBM Selectric on a typing table, and a long cabinet holding vial trays, a blood-pressure cuff, a stethoscope and some heavy reference works on a lower shelf.

Marie's reaction was identical to Brian's: even in undefined darkness everything looked too standard, too normal to be the kind of place that had produced a religious monster. Perhaps she'd expected an underground laboratory with water dripping down the walls, she thought. Or if the starry night outside had been violated by thunder shocks and lightning bolts, maybe that would have added the necessary touch to make these rooms sing of malevolency.

The receptionist stood by the doctor's desk radiating indecision. Brian could suppose her state of mind: she'd already repudiated her boss's trust bringing strangers into his practice, now she was vacillating about whether or not to allow any further intrusion.

Brian spoke quickly—use her or lose her. "Where did he keep the special records, Carol?"

The reply, a while in coming, wobbled its way unsteadily toward them in the dark. "In the lockbox, probably."

"And where is that kept?"

The flashlight's narrow beam shot out and splattered silently against the last door of the cabinet. Brian crossed to it. Bent to it and opened it. The flashlight beam fled into the cabinet and picked out the green steel of a heavy box secured to the bottom shelf.

"I need the key, Carol."

Instead Brian got an exonerating explanation. "I've never touched that box. Dr. Wassenaer made it clear that it was personal. I never asked him what was inside."

"You're not opening it, Carol, I am. But I need the key."

From behind the flashlight's hooded yellow eye the answer wavered. "It's taped under the telephone."

When the woman made no effort to prove her claim, Marie said, "May I?" Then eased the flashlight from her limp hand, went to the desk, lifted the vintage dial phone, stripped away the fat piece of duct tape she found underneath it, and peeled the tape off an old-fashioned mortise key. She handed the key to Brian, and held the flashlight steady.

The lockbox opened with a rasping complaint.

There were only two items inside, two things that seemed to explain each other's existence: a blue cardboard folder containing about a dozen sheets of paper, and an old leather satchel stuffed with wads of hundred-dollar bills. Brian removed the folder. Placed it open on the desk. Marie trained the beam on the first sheet, which they recognized as a surgeon's postoperative report. Opposite the patient's name was the letter A, and beneath that a referral name, Potenza, and a date entered next to it: December 2, 1982. The next report was about Patient B and showed the same referral name but had a date ten months later. There were eleven reports in all, the name Potenza on seven of them, and a different name, Farnese, on three of them, the dates progressing from the original December 2, 1982, to one just five months back. This last report was for Patient K and carried the referral name Buehl.

They had only to read as far as the seventh line to know that this was what they'd come to Hatfield for.

Marie folded the report and slipped it into a pocket, a move that brought forth a compact gasp from Carol Frankel. "That's private property," she said, but in a tone that offered information rather than reprimand.

Marie gave her an option. "Would you like me to have it copied?"

When the woman made no reply Brian replaced the folder in the box, relocked it, and returned the key to its adhesive home. He led the way back to the front door holding the flashlight on the security pad for the receptionist to reset the alarm. Then they left.

Outside the house, the three of them silvered by the sudden appearance of a wedge of moon, Brian said, "Nobody's going to know how we got this report, Carol. We never met you."

The moon shivered in the woman's extravagant hair when she nodded sad thanks, its light illuminating her way as, sealed in a painful world of disillusionment, she turned and left them.

"I'm sorry she had to see the money," Brian said.

"I doubt it was a surprise," Marie reflected. "More a confirmation she'd been staying away from."

They drove quickly back to the motel bungalow. Spread out the report, and went through it word by word. It was a black-and-white printed form which had been typed up almost certainly,

Marie claimed, recognizing the familiar IBM typeface, on that Selectric they'd seen in the office.

Dr. Henry Wassenaer   Operative Record
                                       Patient: K
                                       Referral: Buehl
                                       Date: May 2, 1994

Preoperative Diagnosis:
Postoperative Diagnosis:
Operative Procedure Performed: Hand and foot intrusion with osteotomy. Flank intrusion. Scalp laceration.
The patient, a 35 year old male, received 10 cc. of atropine/scolapine to dry up throat secretions 1 hour prior to surgery. Then in the supine position and placed on a warming blanket, both hands and feet, the right flank, and the scalp were scrubbed and cleaned with Betadine. An intravenous cannula of 15 cc. Hartman's solution was administered. ECG electrodes were attached to chest and shoulder to monitor heart rate. A pulse oximeter was clipped to his ear for oxygen saturation readout. Oxygen was then given to raise patient's oxygen level. 20 cc. of Thiopentone was administered inducing complete sedation. His throat muscles were paralyzed with an intravenous agent to allow an endotracheal tube to be inserted down the throat, through the vocal cords into the trachea. Patient was connected to a ventilator machine. A tourniquet was applied and tightened on his upper L arm. Blood was allowed to drain by force of gravity and locked out. Fingers of the L hand were placed in a lead hand to defeat any nerve reaction. The palmar skin was knicked and the fascia exposed. Dissection proceeded as far as the digital nerve, which was then partly severed. The flexor digitorum superficialis was damaged with a metal punch. With the other tendons first being pushed out of the way, the punch was driven through the wound opening with an orthopedic mallet. The 3rd metacarpal bone was fractured, the force required to do this being considerable. To give the wound a look of blunt trauma a Mayo scissor blade was introduced through the hand and reefed around the back of the hand,

tearing the fascia and roughing up the skin around the edges of the wound. The tourniquet was released and the wound packed with 1″ ribbon gauze and the edges cauterized to further roughen it and delay healing. The R hand was similarly treated except the digital nerve and the metacarpal bone were left intact and an extensor tendon at the back of the hand damaged. The L hand was checked, revealing persistent ooze from shattered bone ends and arterial bleeding, which was repaired with a dissolving ligature. Both wounds were repacked and dressed.

A similar procedure was followed with the feet, punching between the 2nd and 3rd metatarsals, care being taken to avoid the dorsalis pedis artery. In the L foot the 3rd metatarsal was fractured.

For the scalp procedure patient was treated with a disinfectant shampoo 12 hours previous. Marks were replicated with a 1″ awl. The wounds were then painted with Betadine and wrapped with ½″ gauze to keep the edges open.

For the flank procedure the skin was nicked 2″ below the R costal margin. A urethra dilator was introduced to widen the wound. Using a pair of Metzenbaum scissors, dissection proceeded through the fat to the anterior abdominal wall. The incision was widened manually up to the bottom rib. A Penrose drain was introduced into the wound to hold it open. The wound was then packed with Betadine-soaked gauze and dressed. Patient was moved for recovery and received in satisfactory condition.

"Thorough bunch, aren't they?" Brian said, reading the last half of the report again. His face clenched in empathy. "Can you imagine the pain Heloum went through? Coming out of the anesthetic with that kind of damage?"

Marie, who never lost sight of the farcical tendrils of life, said, "I'm sure he feels it was all worth it, now he's the Son of God."

Brian's eye roved to the name opposite the referral entry. "Buehl. I take it he's the client . . ."

Marie was looking at the name, too. And reaching a conclusion. "Of the eleven records in that folder Buehl's name is only on this one. The other names are both Italian, Potenza and Farnese. And the reports are all about gunshot wounds, so it looks very much like Wassenaer was a mob doctor. A button gets shot by another family, in a turf dispute or whatever, they drive him up to quiet, peaceful Hatfield, where he can get patched up and nursed back to health without showing his Blue Cross card."

Surprise and disbelief collided on Brian's face. "That's who's behind this? The Mafia?"

"Can't be. It's wildly out of character for the Mafia. For one thing, the families are all staunch Catholics. They'd regard something like this as sacrilegious."

"So was Wassenaer freelancing on this one?"

"Let's suppose he was. Let's suppose this person Buehl has connections. He wants a restorative surgeon who'll do work the AMA wouldn't approve of. So he calls a pal in the mob and gets Wassenaer's name. Heloum is delivered, and the doc goes to work for money. Then he's killed in the general process of neatening up."

"So how do we track down Buehl?" Brian wanted to know. "Check the New York phone book? And the Chicago phone book and the L.A. phone book . . ."

"Why don't we start with my phone book?" Marie went into the bedroom and returned a minute later flicking through the pages of the little black address book Brian had seen before. She picked up a phone. Punched buttons. Brian checked his watch, and Marie caught the action and its significance. "This guy's probably just getting up. He works strange—" She broke off to answer a voice. "Jack? Marie Olivier . . ."

Brian listened to the only half of the conversation he could hear: Marie taking a minute to inquire about health and well-being, then asking the man she'd called whether or not the name Buehl was infamous in certain circles. She spelled it out, gave the man the bungalow phone number, then hung up and explained. "Jack's an investigator. An old pal. He can get access to the NCC plus several other sources I wouldn't even want to guess at."

"The Nautical Cap Company? The Neuralgic Caterers' Congress? I give up."

Marie walked to him. Kissed his chin, a kiss with affection and humor in it. "The National Crime Computer. I keep forgetting you've been living in a rarefied atmosphere."

Jealous of the space and light surrounding her, Brian enclosed her as he returned the kiss. He was aware, once again, of a cessation of existence, the same bodiless liberation he'd experienced whenever he'd held her.

The ringing of the phone twenty minutes later returned him to a specific time and place, and he watched Marie make herself presentable, admiring that decorous quality that made her straighten her clothes just to take a call from someone thirty-five miles away.

"Hi there, Jack . . . Sure, go ahead." She picked up a pen and began to scribble on a motel phone pad, giving an okay as she took down each entry. She'd taken four separate sets of notes before she said, "Jack, let me stop you right there. Would you repeat that last one . . . ?" She checked what she'd written, her eyes switching to Brian, insistent with news. "Jack, you're a jewel and I owe you a boozy lunch . . . Talk to you later." She hung up. Raked a hand through her hair. Read out from the pad. "No record of anyone named Buehl connected to the mob. There's a Buehl in L.A. who did time for insider trading. There's a Buehl in New Orleans up on a homicide charge, and one in Cincinnati arrested for grand larceny. But there's one in New York who's of slightly more interest. Ralph N. Buehl, a retired Army colonel. He was attached to the Pentagon, accused of taking kickbacks, and left under a cloud. Set himself up in the think-tank business." Marie looked up from her notes and delivered the last part of the information in a slower, more deliberate voice. "He's a principal in the firm of Buehl and Gold."

It was like a physical thing, the last name hitting Brian as if it had been made solid and shoved into his ribs. "Cedric Gold," he said. "The man we couldn't bring ourselves to suspect. The man who came up with the sound-and-light weapons for the Pentagon. The man who admires John Martin's apocalyptical paintings. Why did we ever go by him?"

"My fault," Marie admitted. "His was the first and only name we had, and it seemed too easy. Too much of a fluke for the first name out of the box to be the one you're looking for. Anyway," she said, sloughing off her poor judgment in favor of the advance they'd made, "I think you can add the second coming of Christ to his list of big ideas. An idea he came up with for someone who hired the services of Buehl and Gold, although to what end is still anyone's guess."

Brian listened to what she was saying, conscious of the buzz of excitement sparking through his innards. Was it beginner's luck, he wondered, or just a logical result of the right questions producing the right answers? "Well," he said, unable to keep the smile off his mouth, "I would say that the firm of Buehl and Gold is about to get themselves a couple of new clients."

CHAPTER
19

While Brian and Marie fell easily and naturally into some languor-
ous lovemaking in Mount Kisco, New York, Father Zaim, rector
of the seminary in Elton, Ontario, was also in bed, albeit on his
lonesome.

His was strictly an intellectual pleasure: reading. However, on
this particular night the reading was not going well. The book
he'd taken to bed, a treatise on the life of Saint Gregory of
Nazianzus, had failed to grip his interest because, like a trapped
rat patiently eating an exit through a cellar door, something was
trying to break out of the gray matter inside Zaim's overly hirsute head.

For the third time that evening he put down the book and tried
to catch the elusive thing scuttling down the corridors of his memory. What was it that gnawed away at him, and why had it appeared now at this, traditionally the most relaxed part of his day?
He wondered about that as he pensively watched the raindrops
hitting his bedroom window, watching the last part of their swift
trip through the ether end in a slow and streaky surrender to gravity. Halfheartedly, he raised his book and returned to the saint and
his contribution to the final defeat of the Arian heresy but read no
more than a paragraph before he jerked his eyes back to the
window.

Rain.

It had been raining when the American priest and his sister had come on their curious visit, a visit that still didn't sit right somehow. Outwardly relaxed, there'd been more than a whisper of the ulterior about them. The man, what was his name . . . Sheridan . . . had wanted very much to get into the library. Natural for a scholar, of course, and yet . . . Zaim wondered if their actions had been really worthy of his suspicion or if he were just being abundantly cautious since the affair with Heloum. He could take some satisfaction in his handling of that, he felt. There'd been no repercussions although he'd had a moment of great trepidation when Mouani had come back from an excursion into Kitchener with a copy of a popular newsmagazine. But, fortunately, it had been the world news in general he'd been interested in and not the extreme fads and fantasies of America, those being mere grotesqueries of little fascination as far as the teaching staff was concerned. Besides, the photograph inside was an extreme close-up and therefore a little distorted, and with a five-month growth of beard and mustache obscuring much of what once had been a clean-shaven face, and his hair released from the ponytail and brushed out and parted in the center, and those gouges running across the forehead, Heloum's looks had been changed considerably and nobody had commented on any resemblance. As for the evangelist Bagley's TV show, all such trash was forbidden.

The seminarian's thoughts spun back again to the visitors. What was it about them that rang false? Forgetting the breviary in the chapel? But anyone could put a book down and forget to pick it up. Hadn't he done the same thing himself once or twice?

Zaim grew tired of the puzzle and began to read again until a quick gust of rain battered the window.

The rain against the window.

Rain.

When the nun had recovered her breviary they'd left by the side door, saying they'd parked on the access road and walked back. For the exercise, Sheridan had said. And yet it had been raining at the time. Off and on but still, nobody walked in the rain without a coat or an umbrella. Nobody walked through muddy fields for exercise. What had they been doing down there? Looking over the barns? But Mouani had shown them those before lunch. Who'd want a second look at a tractor?

Father Zaim slowly came up off the bed as he answered his own question: it wasn't the tractor that interested them, it was the young priest who was working on it, a neophyte who might prove vulnerable to close questioning.

With an unpleasant taste gathering at the back of his throat Zaim threw off the covers. Donned slippers and robe. Left his room and hurried along the shadowy corridor and up two flights of stairs to the smallest bedroom in the building. He opened the unlocked door—a rule in the seminary—hit a wall switch and banished the darkness.

"Father Charou. Wake up!"

The young man, tugged out of sleep, dallied a moment in that brief valley between unconsciousness and sudden comprehension. "Uhhh? . . . Oh . . . Father Zaim . . ."

"The American visitors the other day. They came back to see you, didn't they? Came back without Father Mouani."

The young man blinked unadjusted eyes. "The other day?" he repeated, as if an event that far back was lost in the mists of time.

Zaim put a little more snap into his bearing to counteract the undignified effect of robe and slippers. "When they left here they parked on the access road and went into the tractor barn where you were working. I saw them go in there. What did you talk about? What did they ask you?"

"Nothing," Charou said too quickly. "Just about farming. About our methods."

A practiced liar, Father Zaim recognized the flags of falsehood and knew that he'd stumbled on something extremely serious: the Americans had been spying, he was certain of that now. His voice dropped a few decibels, acquiring the same hard pungency that flared in his eyes. "Lie to me again and I'll expel you. They asked you about the faculty, didn't they? And you told them about Father Heloum, didn't you?"

"They said they'd met him when they'd been here before," Charou gabbled.

"Stupid fool!" The rain added its own insult, thrashing angrily against the room's tiny window. "They've never been here before.

And I gave express orders that Father Heloum's good luck was to be kept strictly within the seminary."

In a hot brew of shame the young priest hung his head, and Zaim saw that it was worse than he thought. His voice got lower still, vowels and consonants, frosted below zero, shooting out from behind that intense black beard. "You told them about the postcard ..." It was a question as well as a fearful realization. "And you told them where it was mailed from."

Charou pounced on something he could at last deny. "I didn't. No. I didn't know where it was mailed from. I couldn't remember."

Zaim might have concluded his interrogation at that point in favor of severe denigration had guilt not weighted the young priest's gaze. He hunched up in the rumpled covers of his narrow bed, huddling against the stormy night and the chill of his superior, and looked away.

"But they found out," Zaim said, putting words in the other's unsteady mouth. Charou's nod was slow and painful. "How did they find out?" Into the drumming silence Zaim renewed his question with tough little hyphens between the words. The young priest was helpless against such a practiced onslaught. In a tone painful in its suppliance he related how he'd been persuaded to go to the library, find the book with the photograph of the distinctive white church, and leave the book open on a desk.

Father Zaim's body, already squatly compact, was attacked by a lancing rigidity. The woman's forgetful return to the chapel had in fact been a spying mission to the library, not to get a look at the graduation photographs, as he'd guarded against, but to read the name of a small town across the border.

"Be in my office at noon tomorrow," he snapped. He ripped the thin blankets off the bed so the boy would freeze all night as the first part of his punishment, then hurried back to his room.

He lay in the dark thinking about it. How in the world had Sheridan traced him here? Zaim struggled with it for a distressed minute, then began to feel a little better about things when it occurred to him that what had happened might not matter anyway. The American had no proof. Mere suppositions. What harm could result from knowing that Heloum had stopped off on his way to who knew where? He'd go to Hatfield, of course, he and his so-called sister, but what would they find? A store that sold post-cards. The trail would end there, in a small town in New York State.

Still, it would have to be reported.

As embarrassing as it was, Colonel Buehl would have to be told.

Cedric Gold left the three rooms he rented in a West Side brown-stone with just a key in his pocket.

No wallet, no money.

He liked to roam the nighttime for hours and hours but seldom carried cash on these jaunts, not because he feared footpads—he was oblivious to the city's moonlit dangers—but because there was nothing he thought he'd want. Food, drink, recreation of any kind.

He ate dates and honey and raisins and dried apricots in his small apartment, so that was food taken care of. He sipped skim milk with it, so that was drink taken care of. And recreation was gained by tending his peerless collection of Hebrew and Yiddish Bibles.

Gold had graduated from the Talmud, cast aside the Palestinian version. Thrown away the Babylonian one. No longer interested in a postbiblical compendium of law, tradition, and commentary, he rocked instead over the fiery words of the tragic figures of the Old Testament, Yahweh's foam-flecked prophets forecasting dread fu-tures, pleading for amendment and thundering their bloodcurdling monotones of doom and destruction.

For Gold the only events of any importance had all occurred at least four hundred years before the birth of Jesus. As for that par-ticular gentleman, Gold was in no doubt as to his correct place in history. The seventy-two Jewish scholars who'd translated the Old Testament into Greek—the Septuagint—had got it wrong when they'd rendered the Hebrew term, *alma*, which meant a young woman, as *parthenos*, which meant a virgin. The Greek-speaking Christians had, of course, preferred the faulty translation of these prophecies to the correct original, and so had seen a miracle in the ordinary birth of a carpenter's son. But the real Jesus was there for all to see in the Dead Sea Scrolls.

The main figure in the Temple Scroll, the Teacher of Righteousness, had a rival who spoke of the New Jerusalem. But this person, referred to as the Wicked Priest, disagreed with the Teacher about ritual law. The Teacher was clearly John the Baptist, and the Wicked Priest, the man who flouted the law, was Jesus, the leader of a radical group of Essenes, the same Essenes who'd been formed to restore the Davidian kings. And Jesus' grandfather, according to no less a recent authority than Matthew and Luke, was Heli, known as Jacob, a direct descendant of David. So Jesus' prayer, Thy Kingdom Come, had not been in reference to a heavenly reign but to an earthly thousand-year empire of the Jews.

Jesus had vied to be restored to a throne surrounded not by a host of winged seraphim and invincible angels, but by ministers, generals, and petitioners.

Confirmed in this knowledge, Gold had not suffered the slightest spiritual twinge in coming up with the idea, for his Southern client, of replicating the Prince of Peace. All he'd been doing, in his estimation, was reinventing a failed Judean monarchist.

He reached the apartment house he'd been heading for, and pressed the intercom.

Upstairs, Buehl knew that, at this late hour, it could only be Professor 4-F calling. He buzzed him in. Gold found him drinking coffee when he arrived at his door. The colonel didn't offer him any.

"How are things going?" Gold asked, sliding clumsily into a chair.

"We're up to speed," Buehl allowed, discarding his coffee cup.

"He's holding up okay?"

"So I'm told. Although I wish he'd get off his soapbox. He's making a lot of people mad."

Gold slid the tip of his tongue into an upper-left molar. It distorted his cheek and his words came out as if being played at the wrong speed. "Nothing to worry about. It's only the Catholics, and that can only help. The Southerners hate the papists."

"It's opened up another flank," Buehl said, sitting, like Abraham Lincoln, both hands grasping the armrests of his chair. "We knew there'd be resistance from some of those sects, jealousies because he didn't reveal himself to their particular minister in Florida or Tennessee or wherever. And so there is, but it's not a concern. They're too splintered and too localized to do much damage. But the Catholic Church is a different matter. It's a formidable organization, and we didn't want them for an enemy."

Gold crossed one leg over the other and grasped his shin, his knees and elbows forming a sharply angled star. When he answered Buehl his eyes searched a corner of the ceiling. "The Catholic Church won't worry about him as long as he stays in the Bible Belt. They ignore all that Confederate nonsense, all those Sunday morning TV preachers . . . They're not a threat to them."

"In any campaign," Buehl said tersely, "you try to minimize the threat of surprise. Eradicate it if possible. But his ax grinding was something that never occurred to us and it should have."

Gold remained silent for a moment as if rounding up dispersed thought. When he changed position and hunched forward, the angular star formed by his legs dissolved into an awkward comma. "Can't you get him to soft-peddle that part? Stick with the Jesus of the Gospels?"

"I've already made that request. But when you're the Son of God, you're not disposed to take advice from a mere human. Even one who raised you to that exalted position."

When the phone rang, Buehl's raw face contracted into a vexed frown. "Damn late," he muttered. He got up and moved to the phone. Picked up. "Yes?"

"Father Zaim, Colonel. I hope it's not too late to call."

"What is it?"

"I'm afraid there's been a development. I don't think it's—"

"What kind of development?"

"Just something I thought I'd better—"

Five hundred miles to the northwest of New York City, the handpiece seemed to stiffen in Father Zaim's fingers, the voice coming through it hammered out of iron. "What kind of development?"

"Somebody came here. I think he knows about Heloum."

Two seconds of heavy silence. Then: "You mean somebody who knew him before has recognized him?"

"No. This man is a Catholic priest. I have no idea of how he traced Heloum to the seminary, but he knows about the postcard."

"What postcard?"

"Heloum sent one of the staff here a card the day he left with Mr. Willard. This priest found out about it and also found out where it was sent from. A place called Hatfield in New York State."

The silence this time might have sagged the telephone wires. "What do you know about this priest?"

The colonel certainly had retained his brusque military manner, Father Zaim thought. "His name's Sheridan. He's traveling with a nun whom he introduced as his sister, but I'm now under the impression she's neither a relation nor a religious."

"Are you certain he's a priest?"

"Oh yes. He's outstandingly well informed on church matters. No question about it."

A brief silence spread between New York and Ontario until Buehl snapped it. "I appreciate your calling me, Father." Zaim heard a note of praise in the statement and accepted it as his due. "And I'd like to show my appreciation," Buehl added.

"Not necessary," Zaim said, wondering about the size of this new and unexpected windfall.

"I'll send a man up with a small token of my gratitude. Tomorrow night, perhaps. He'll call you and make arrangements for a discreet meeting."

"Colonel, you're far too kind."

Buehl slammed the phone down. He shot a venomous look at his partner as if it was all his fault. "Somebody's traced Heloum to Hatfield."

"A priest?" Gold asked, having heard half of the exchange.

"I told you the Catholics were dangerous. They have enormous resources."

"But how did he do it?"

Colonel Buehl steamed; Gold had an infuriating habit of lapsing into the most kindergarten of thought processes. "He traced him to the seminary. And you told me that was impossible."

"It *is* impossible." Gold was upset by it. When his legs squirmed, his battered sneakers squeaked on the polished parquetry. He waved one hand, then the other. "It must have been just blind luck."

Buehl snatched up the phone. Punched in a number. "The fool should never have antagonized the Church. We've got a potential mess on our hands."

When his call was answered, he repeated the information he'd just received, rattled off some crisp orders, and hung up.

His partner, reacting to these orders, squirmed again. "This is getting a little out of hand, isn't it? The pilot and the doctor, okay. If you're a blackmailer, you deserve everything you get. But the Carews, that was reaching. And now you want to hit Zaim?"

"We had to remove the Carews. They were pushing themselves into the limelight. Bit players who saw themselves as headliners. Way too dangerous to keep around. And as for Zaim, it's only a matter of time before he starts wondering about the significance of Hatfield."

"He'd never guess that in a million years."

"He doesn't have to. All he has to do is realize it's important and he'll want more money or else, the slimy little bastard."

Cedric Gold shifted his eyes a foot to the right of the colonel's stiff and intractable figure. "That'll make five, and we've still got one to go. Three to go if you count this priest and the woman."

"You're being overly concerned. There's no findable link between any of them. The Carews were the only ones connected with Jesus, and, as far as anyone knows, the pressure got too much for them and they took off to parts unknown."

Gold mounted a fresh assault on his teeth. "You gonna arrange a note for the priest, too?"

The colonel was irritated. 4-F's biggest failing was that he had no ability to take a setback and retrench. "We won't need a note," he growled. "People disappear all the time."

PART
THREE

CHAPTER
20

Different cities.

Same midnight.

Same wedge of moon, although the one Cedric Gold had walked beneath on his trip to Buehl's apartment was cloudy and obscured compared to the bright slice that silvered the lawn Howard Willard hurried across.

There was very little chance of him being spotted: there was nobody in the house these days except himself, Don Bagley, Bert Sales, and two black servants, both of whom were too terrified by the heavenly Presence to even go into the garden. Don Bagley went across each night before dinner to commune with Jesus, allowing Willard and Bert Sales to accompany him. That single daily visit was, Bagley felt, intrusion enough, as the Lord spent his time in closeted prayer, and Bagley had made it a strict rule that nobody was to approach the bungalow without him. As for the private security guards, they patrolled the inner perimeter of the garden wall and never came within sight of the Lord's modest residence. All the same, for safety's sake, Willard kept his clandestine visits to a minimum, and hadn't had a private audience since the show they'd put on for the Catholic religious.

He let himself into a semiblackness barely relieved by the blue glow emanating from a fish tank against a far wall. Its solid, underwater quality informed the whole room, its liquid element absorbing all sound.

Camille Heloum was sitting in an armchair, apparently just communing with the dark. He was all ready for bed, Willard noticed, and swallowed a little gulp of mirth.

Jesus in pajamas.

He moved closer and lowered his underfed frame onto the wooden edge of a coffee table. "Everything okay?"

When there was no answer to his query, Willard assumed contentment and spun off to another subject. "You really turned it on the other day. You really like to cane 'em, don't you?"

"When something is wrong it should be pointed out," Heloum answered. "Toleration of incorrectness is in itself an incorrectness."

Willard couldn't get over the guy; when he'd done the rounds of the Orthodox seminaries he'd seen one or two candidates he'd marked down as possibilities, but when he'd arrived in Elton, Ontario, and met Father Camille Heloum, and talked with him for ten minutes, he knew he wasn't going to be looking anywhere else. The funny thing was it had been exactly like an amateur actor responding to his first role: once they got into a costume and saw themselves made up, they became the part. Heloum couldn't turn it off; he used the same sad-firm voice now that he used as Jesus, and from what Willard could see of him in the aquatic light, he was the same monument to dignified suffering.

"You're gonna have to take your knife out of the Catholics," Willard said, the fish tank's glowing egress converting his white hair to a neat sweep of blue seaweed. "We don't want to get them too riled. They could be dangerous."

"They have been dangerous for sixteen hundred years," Heloum said. The pronouncement was studded with accented vowels and syllables but devoid of shade and texture.

A smile of ridicule broke up the long verticals in Willard's face, and when he quoted from the Gospels, it was with a thin undertone of irreverence. " 'And I tell you that you are Peter, and on this rock I will build my Church.' Matthew sixteen, eighteen, I do believe. Just a small mouthful of words and the entire Christian church splits down the middle. Your Greek fathers were pretty stubborn people."

The reply was instant. "They were right to be stubborn. Peter's name was Simon but Jesus called him Cephas, Aramaic for rock, because Peter recognized Jesus as the Messiah. 'You are the Christ, he said, the Son of the living God.' Matthew sixteen, verse sixteen. And Jesus confessed to him that it was so, and it was for recognizing him as such that Jesus told him his church would be built on him. Built on people like him who recognized his divinity. It was a commendation, not an ordination."

Willard held up a hand in the dark. "You don't have to sell me. I know all about Catholic hubris."

Heloum didn't appear to hear. "When the Lord arranged Peter's miraculous escape from Herod's prison, Peter went immediately to the house of Mary, the mother of John, and asked them to report his freedom."

"Acts twelve, verse twelve," Willard confirmed.

"Then he went to another place, Acts twelve, verse seventeen. Luke is no more specific than that, another place is all he says. Yet the Catholics claim it was Rome he went to, a claim based on wishful thinking. There is a huge body of literature that proves that the place Peter went to was the Syrian Antioch. Paul himself puts him there. And Origen, the greatest teacher of his age, says that Peter was the first bishop of Antioch. There is not one word of biblical reference that puts Peter in Rome. Not one word to support his upside-down crucifixion and burial there. These were myths fostered by a jealous Church. Fostered by Pope Damasus, who feared the rise of Constantinople and began discovering the tombs of martyrs, one of which he swore was Peter's."

"Camille," Willard said, trying to turn off the sermon, "you're preaching to the converted."

The statement was ignored, and Heloum's sonorous voice continued its dense flow. "Go there today. Dig on Vatican hill. Excavate beneath the high altar as the world's finest archaeologists have done. Will you find the bones of Peter? You will not, as they did not, because they do not lie there."

Willard shifted position; he hadn't come to hear the Orthodox view expounded, especially when that view was as flawed as the rest. Besides, he'd become a little weary of treating the priest with kid gloves, so he presented a mild home truth. "Sure, you wrangled over scriptural interpretation, but it's always seemed to me that the real issue was geographic. Your people simply wanted to keep the religion centered in Constantinople."

"Where it rightfully should be. Which is why the bishop of Rome has no authority over the universal Church as he claims. The patriarch of Constantinople is his superior in every way."

"Well, you're gonna have to cool it on that one," Willard said, thankful to have returned to the original purpose of his visit. "We never set out to upset the Romans. Okay?"

The only response in the room, the only movement, was the graceful loop and glide of a black-and-orange clown loach when it swam the width of its glass prison to watch a Baptist minister talking with the Son of Man.

After an extended moment Willard uncurled from his seat. He didn't like to stay long, partly for security reasons and partly because Heloum's absorption of his masquerade was nearing totality—how could it not? The man had been swamped by hysterical veneration, deluged with outpourings of love and devotion for almost three weeks—and other people's delusions made Willard uneasy.

"You're doing a good job, Camille. It can't be easy being the most famous man who ever lived. But you have to hold it together for another few days. Just get through the Civic Center thing, and then you can relax."

Willard started for the door, but a question stopped him, stopped him not so much because a reply was expected, but because of its surprising nature.

"What is going to happen?"

Willard turned. Heloum, what he could see of him, seemed enclosed in a fog of abstract uncertainty. "At the prayer meeting?"

"I mean afterwards. After everything is over."

"Nothing's changed. Why?" Willard perceived an inchoate doubt radiating from the priest, and larded his answer with patience. "You disappear from under the elm. I'm the only one who witnesses it. You tell me that you're going back to your Father, and will return at some future date to see if the lessons of your second visit have been learned. Bagley will buy it. America will buy it. You're not having second thoughts, are you?"

"Bagley is a good man," Heloum said, more a ruminative comment than a conversational one.

"He's the best." Willard waved in the approximate direction of the TV set. "You've seen some of those smarmy extortionists prancing around. They're not interested in the word of God. That's not a Bible in their hand, that's a deposit book. Except the money's drying up for them these days. They're hurting because Jesus Christ Returned chose Don Bagley as his spokesman. The Reverend Bagley got Heaven's endorsement and they didn't. That's what this is all about, Camille, helping a true man of God kick those moral criminals off the airwaves."

"He should be told. I don't like deceiving him."

"You'd break his heart. And his spirit. He'd fold up his ministry if he knew. Sometimes, you have to protect people from their own honesty." Willard continued to the door. "Hang in there, buddy," he said, made a gesture of fortitude with his fist, then left.

His trip back across the garden was observed only by some high white clouds the moon was marshaling overhead.

Jesus is my buddy, Willard thought. That wouldn't make a bad bumper sticker.

The Carews bothered him.

Sitting as Willard had left him, in the blue midnight of the bungalow, Heloum wondered why the brothers had been taken out of it. Willard's explanation, that a dramatic disappearance brought about by a feeling of inadequacy would get Jesus big headlines, didn't make sense. He was already getting big headlines. Day after day the media reported loudly and at length on the Miracle Man. Bagley hadn't understood it; the brothers hadn't seemed pressured to him. And Sales, the little evangelist, had been baffled by it, too. Sales had asked him why this had happened when, during his first ministry, all of his disciples—barring Judas, of course—had stuck with him. To answer that, he'd fallen back on the classic unknowingness of the Deity's design, but it was a solution that far from satisfied him personally.

Why *had* they left?

Had they really been overwhelmed by being chosen?

Or was it different on this, his second visit? Were the brothers James and John the traitors this time, and Judas the faithful one? Had they told what they knew to the authorities, been filled with remorse, and fled? But who then was the benign Judas? Sales?

Heloum pressed a hand to his eyes. Some sharp-angled thing seemed to be wallowing inside his head.

He squeezed the bridge of his nose and concentrated.

Were they really lying low in California as Willard claimed, or had he arranged a more permanent hiding place? They'd certainly showed signs of being disgruntled with their subservient roles. Had the brothers been removed as a preemptive measure, having served their purpose?

And did a similar fate await him, after this prayer meeting in three days' time?

That would depend on what purpose he was serving.

Which brought up a question whose answer he thought he once knew: what purpose *was* he serving?

And whose purpose was he serving?

The angled thing inside his skull swayed and shifted. Lodged for a second, then began to move again.

He got a fright when he slipped back in through the French windows of the house: Don Bagley, dressed in robe and slippers, was sitting on an overstuffed sofa, one hand absently moving on its silky fabric, oblivious of any tactile message. In the ambient light spilling in from the garden the evangelist recognized the slim shape of his deputy.

"Hello, Howard. Couldn't sleep?" He sounded far away.

Willard eased into a simple explanation. "I find it hard to turn my head off these nights, Reverend. I thought maybe a little walk ..."

"I'm the same way," the stout man admitted with a drawn-out gesture of unconcern. "Funny thing is, when the Lord first came to us, I slept like a baby even though my heart was racing every night. But this last week it's finally come home to me, this stupendous thing that's happened to us." Bagley stopped for a moment to shake away a web of befuddlement. "It's incredible, isn't it?

That the Lord should return in our lifetime is, of course, staggering. Yet the Second Advent was foretold, so the fact itself should
be anything but surprising."

"Good point, Reverend. And yet Mark tells us that Jesus
thought his return would be within a few years. When he failed to
appear, people began to doubt he ever would."

"That's true. But it's not his return that bowls me over. It's the
fact that I should be the instrument of making that return known.
It's something that I just can't come to terms with, Howard. I'm
an ex–car salesman who preaches the Good Book. Nothing more.
So why me?"

Willard came farther into the room and perched on the sculptured headrest of a chaise longue. "Why do you suppose Jesus
chose Peter and Paul? Because he recognized the missionary in
them. The ability to take his message to the people. And few are
better at that than you, Reverend."

Don Bagley smiled in the dark. "You're a good man, Howard."

Howard Willard clamped his mouth around the reply that
leaped to his tongue. He'd been on the edge of saying, "That's
funny. I just said the same thing about you."

Instead he said, "Thank you, Reverend," and went upstairs to
his room.

CHAPTER
21

Little things.

Things he couldn't quite put his finger on.

Neither of the reverends had noticed anything, Bert Sales was certain of that. But he had. A kind of lessening, or downgrading in the Lord's personality. A reduction in his quality might be a better way of putting it. It was baffling and disturbing, yet there was one thing—it made Jesus more approachable. Which was why Bert Sales, moving across the lawn at the beginning of a bright new morning, didn't feel as uncomfortable as he might have, sneaking out to speak to him.

He found his Lord in the shade of the elm, staring up into its branches, his focus seeming to reach way beyond the thick red foliage.

"Lord," Bert Sales began, removing his battered Panama and bobbing his head in respect. "May I speak with you?"

"What is it, Albert?"

"Well, to tell you the truth, Lord, I'm a little disappointed."

The man under the elm flicked his gaze toward him, then looked past him at something. "And what is the cause of this disappointment?"

There it was. Bert Sales saw it again: a casualness, a lassitude that hadn't been present before.

"When the Carews claimed to be the first to recognize you,

Lord, in that interview they gave, well, forgive me, Lord, but you didn't tell anyone any different. Now everybody thinks it was them went and discovered you."

"You feel relegated in my service, is that it, Albert?"

Sales squinted his eyes against a sun flare, his weathered face turning in on itself. "The Carews took off, Lord. Couldn't stand the pressure, so their note said. But I'm still here. And, well, if you'll forgive me, it just seems that faithfulness should count for something."

"What would you have me do, Albert?"

"Correct an erroneous impression, Lord. Refute their claim in public."

"That smacks of vanity, Albert. A trait I have preached against many times."

Bert Sales shifted his fireplug body. Smacks? The Lord he'd known in Beaufort and those first days here in Atlanta would never have used a word like *smacks*. It just wasn't biblical. And another thing: not once had Jesus mentioned God his Father in this conversation, whereas, before, he hardly ever stopped talking about Him.

"Begging your pardon, Lord, but isn't a little vanity okay if you're proud about something you've done? Something great and momentous, like recognizing the Son of God in bodily form?"

There was no reply.

And that was something else the evangelist found disturbing. Previously, the Lord had never failed to answer questions, and in a way that left you satisfied and hungry for more wisdom. Now he was just looking out at the play of early sunlight on the grass, as if he were miles away. The evangelist decided it was time to pose a query that had been nagging at him for a long time. See if he couldn't get an answer to this one.

"Lord, I read somewhere that my name, Albert, is the modern version of Barnabas. And seeing that I was chosen to recognize you, does that mean I was Barnabas of Antioch, the Barnabas who took the Good News to the Cypriots?"

The man who called himself Yehsu came back from his musings and favored Sales with those deep, half-lidded eyes. The evangelist saw him wince as if something painful had got in behind them, like a sudden migraine or something. "You were not Barnabas," he said, his words showing an unfamiliar tightness. "You were somebody else."

Bert Sales's heart thumped heavily. Had he been an evangelist of even greater importance? Had he been . . . ? But that was ridiculous. What was he thinking about? He couldn't have been . . . Paul . . . could he?

"Who, Lord? Who was I?"

"You were Judas Iscariot."

If a branch of the elm had snapped off and fallen on him, Bert Sales could not have been more shocked. He reeled back. Gaped at the man under the tree.

Judas? *Judas?* The most despised man in the history of the world. A sniveling, greedy traitor who'd treacherously kissed the cheek of the one he'd turned in. *That* was who he'd been? No. He couldn't accept that. It was just too appalling.

Sales waved his hands in front of his face as if warding off something vile and suppurating. He backed away. Turned and quickly retraced his steps to the house. Sped upstairs to his room. Went into the bathroom and dashed water on his face. Rinsed a cloth and pressed it against his inflamed skin. Okay, it was the Lord Returned, and who would know better? But even so, he had to be wildly mistaken. No way could he ever have been Judas. There were some things a man just couldn't accept no matter how pure the source.

Bert Sales lowered the cloth. Looked at his dripping face in the mirror, a question increasing his blink rate. Just how pure was that source? Face it. The only way Jesus could be wrong about the man who'd once betrayed him was if he *wasn't* Jesus.

Sales watched the possibility explode through his head and widen his eyes. He'd always been a prescient kind of guy, and hadn't he been thinking, these last few days, that Jesus had been acting different?

Acting.

Right.

It was almost like an overconfident actor letting down once he knew his audience has accepted him in a part.

Oh, God! Bert Sales leaned his moist forehead against the cool glass of the mirror. Oh, God! The whole thing was a scam. Bagley and Willard had hoodwinked everybody. Bagley and Willard—or maybe just Willard, he didn't trust that slick son of a bitch—had hired this guy to play Jesus and send the show's ratings through the roof. Hired those rubes, the Carew brothers, too. The Carews had seen the change in Yehsu or Ali or Mustapha or whatever the hell his real name was, and hightailed it outta there before the walls came tumbling down.

Well, they weren't gonna catch Bert Sales under a mountain of bricks. No way, no how!

He rushed back into the bedroom. Pulled his wallet from a drawer. Grabbed his jacket. Hurried downstairs and out into the garden. Didn't even look to see if the space beneath the elm was still occupied or not. He kept right on going down the graveled drive, down to the gates and the bunched crowds swirling behind them.

As usual, the media people were in the front line hoping for a glimpse of something, anything, desperate for a crumb of information. When they saw him and recognized him, they set up a loud and plaintive baying. They called to him. Shouted questions. Stuck their arms through the gates and pleaded with him like starving people begging for food.

The evangelist checked their straining faces and recognized a reporter from one of the big Atlanta religious papers. He grabbed one of the security guards and pointed. "That woman there. Let her in."

The woman, a wide-bodied redhead, could hardly believe her luck as she was singled out and pulled inside a barely open gate which took a bevy of guards to close again.

Sales hurried her behind the gatehouse for a measure of privacy. The woman was effusively thanking him, blinking and gulping at her sudden success.

"I gotta real scoop for you," Bert Sales said, his voice hard and vindictive.

"God bless you, Reverend, I won't forget this," the woman babbled. She fumbled with her minirecorder.

"The guy's a fake. A fraud."

"I'm sorry . . . ?"

"The whole thing's a goll-dang scam. We've all been faked out of our Florsheim's. Screwed, blued, and tattooed."

The reporter's face was opening in dismay. "You saying that Jesus—"

"Dang right, I am. He's as phony as a fifty-cent caviar sandwich. That ain't Jesus, that's central casting."

From a bottomless trough of disappointment the woman said, "I can't call in something like *that*. My editor wants to know what Jesus had for breakfast this morning. What he thinks of Oprah's show, stuff like that. If I even hint that he might not be the real thing, the owners'll tie me to a tree and stone me to death."

Bert Sales was peering at her, shaking his head. "What are you saying . . . ?"

The reporter groaned. "Reverend, you don't want my paper." She threw a hand in the direction of the gates. "You don't want any of those papers. You want the *New York Times*."

The evangelist suddenly got it. The news he had wasn't sensational news, it was disastrous news. They had the world's greatest celebrity in their midst. They wouldn't want to lose that. They wanted Jesus back for ten, twenty, thirty years of trivia, wisdom, and miracles. They didn't want a clever impressionist who'd be off the front page by the end of the week.

Realizing his mistake, Bert Sales made another decision; a correct one, this time, he was sure. He marched back to the gate. Told the guards to let him out. Plunged into the media throng, shunting aside all questions. Shoved his way through the solid crush of pilgrims, and emerged panting and sweating at the end of the block.

He was clear in his mind now. A course of action.

He was going to get a bus back to Beaufort, sneak out to his sister's fishing shack at the lake, and stay in bed with his hat on till this whole sorry affair blew over.

He was outta here.

At roughly the same time that Bert Sales was struggling through a mob of people in Atlanta, Li Xiayong was enjoying a much easier passage on Manhattan's Second Avenue.

He strolled past criminal-type youths leaping up at a netless basketball hoop, moved past a row of ethnic restaurants, and turned into the entrance of the redbrick apartment house where Colonel Ralph Buehl lived.

He consulted the intercom, found the numeral that meant six, and the letter that looked like football goal posts, hit that button, announced himself to the crisp answering voice, and was buzzed through the door. An old man with a dachshund on a lead surrendered the elevator to him and he rode on up.

The dim corridor on the sixth floor smelled vaguely tropical and fetid, as if somebody had spilled sea water on the carpeting, but the apartment he was admitted to had good daylight and the fresh aroma of polish rising from the shiny floor, as usual. Nothing had changed since his last visit. There were still no throw rugs in front of the heavy, plain furniture, no photographs or gewgaws in the well-stocked bookshelves, and nothing on the walls except several framed maps of what looked to be battle sites judging by the cannons drawn on them.

Buehl hadn't changed either, he saw. Li had met several Americans in the privacy of their homes and all of them had dressed in a relaxed manner, T-shirts and V-necked sweaters, but Colonel Buehl always wore a white long-sleeved shirt and a firmly knotted necktie, and gave the impression that he'd wear a necktie even when he wasn't expecting company.

Li was correct in this assumption; Buehl always wore a tie because, as an officer, he always had. When a man at a beach barbecue had once had the temerity to comment on his self-imposed dress code, Buehl had told him, in no uncertain terms, that a tie was always correct because it closed off the looseness of an open collar, and looseness was why the country was in such a deplorable state. He wouldn't be seen dead without a tie, he'd informed the man. And he'd meant it.

Buehl gruffly invited his visitor to sit down, ignoring the presence of his partner. Li was surprised to see Gold here this early in the day—he'd got the impression that he was a nighttime person—although if this was an important job, it would make sense for both partners to be present.

Buehl took a large manila envelope from a side table, shook things from it, and began to speak as if the meeting were already ten minutes old. In truth Buehl wanted this briefing over ASAP. He hated all Orientals after what he'd been through, and there was always a curiously unpleasant smell emanating from this one, nothing fecal, more a tart-sweet odor that might have been meant to attract but had the exact opposite effect. Buehl was dead against cosmetics for men; deodorant, yes, that was just good personal grooming. But no sissy aftershaves or body lotions.

"Downtown Atlanta," Buehl said, handing over a detail from a city map. He pointed to two circles made with a felt-tipped pen. "This is the Civic Center. This is where the target will be. This is your hotel here, directly opposite. You're in room seven-fifteen. This is your room key. You don't check in, that's all been taken care of. You go straight up to the room, have you got that?"

"Yes," Li said, looking at the key and the name of the hotel on the plastic fob which he couldn't read. No problem; he'd simply show the key to an airport cab driver and give him some story. He glanced at Gold. The man was slumped awkwardly in a chair, picking at his teeth. Li saw that he'd been watching him, although he immediately switched his eyes away as if one of the framed maps had caught his attention.

"This is a check stub from the hotel's baggage room," his client went on, handing him the next item. "It's a blue Nike sports bag. Inside it you'll find an M twenty-one with a type five folding stock and a Leatherwood variable-power scope. Are you familiar with that weapon?" Buehl asked, inspecting this famished-looking Chinese who didn't look as if he'd be familiar with a squirt gun, let alone a deadly sniper rifle.

"Yes," Li said, knowing the Army man didn't appreciate anything more than the simplest of affirmatives.

"The weapon's been aligned and sighted in. There are flags on top of the Civic Center which will give you an indication of wind velocity and direction. This is your target." Buehl spread out three eight-by-ten glossies of a bearded man with ugly marks across his forehead. Li assumed he was a rock star who'd incurred somebody's enmity. They made indecent amounts of money, those yowling fools, and great wealth often engendered hatred.

"There's a big function at the Civic Center at six tomorrow evening. There'll be huge crowds, but you'll have a clear shot at him from that hotel window. He'll get out of a limo, walk up the steps, then turn and acknowledge the crowd before going in. That's when you execute. You can't mistake him. He'll be wearing a long white robe, and he'll be the center of attention. You'll need this." Buehl passed across an aluminum Stanley knife. "The window has two small screened sections that slide open. Slash the screen and there'll be plenty of room to work in. Once he's down, drop the rifle, leave the room at normal speed, and go straight to the airport. There's a flight to New York at eight. Here's your ticket. Do you have any questions?"

Li recognized the Delta logo on the ticket jacket. "No," he said.

"Very well, then. Your flight leaves in two hours' time from La Guardia. Better get out there."

Li watched the soldier put the ticket, the photographs, the room key, and the check stub back into the envelope. Got up. Accepted the envelope. Nodded as he was let out.

Going back down the corridor the fishy smell was stronger. Strangely for a Chinese, who see portents in everything, Li thought nothing of it.

In the apartment he'd just left, Cedric Gold, who hadn't said a word during the briefing, remained cocooned in silence. It wasn't hard for Buehl to guess why.

"Look, I don't like him either, but he'll get the job done."

"I just don't think we should use somebody like that. How smart can he be when he can't even read English?"

"He doesn't have to read English. We're not hiring him to work in a library."

"He's just not plugged into things," Gold complained from behind his hand. "If you let Allah and the Koran guide your every waking moment, you're bound to be out of touch. I'll bet he doesn't even know who the target is."

"As long as he recognizes him, that's all that's required," Buehl said.

Gold shifted in his chair, changing the angle of his unfortunate body. "It's just that we can't afford a screwup on this one. I'd be a lot happier if Ronny Patch was handling it."

Buehl was getting tired of explaining things. He let his impatience snap into his reply. "Patch isn't a rifleman, he's a thug. He doesn't know the first thing about fine work. Besides, he's got enough on his plate."

Gold looked puzzled.

"The priest. Then Zaim," Buehl said curtly.

"Oh yes," Gold mumbled. "I'd forgotten."

Not for a moment did Buehl think that his partner was playing games. It was just part of his makeup, these ridiculous memory lapses.

In all his born days, Buehl thought, he'd never met anyone remotely like his partner—so brilliant and, at the same time, such a damn silly fool.

CHAPTER
22

"Drat!" Ronny Patch said from the passenger seat of Vittorio Vargas's big Oldsmobile.

"Drat! Drat! Drat!" Vargas echoed.

They were commenting on the unfortunate presence of a state trooper's car pulled up outside the office of a motel in Mount Kisco. Hennie Van Boder might have added a similar sentiment had he been present, but he was in New York, Colonel Ralph Buehl having insisted that two men were plenty for a job like this. As Buehl hadn't been able to contact them immediately, they'd been late getting started and had only arrived in the area a few hours ago. Still, they'd had ample time to cover the motels where visitors to Hatfield might stay, there being no accommodation in Hatfield itself, and they'd found, quite easily, a Brian Sheridan registered at this motel, in this the nearest town to Hatfield. But what had stopped them from barging into cabin number 2 and hauling out the occupants was the trooper, in his stiff-brimmed Stetson and rigorously pressed shirt, present on some kind of business.

"So what d'you wanna do, Angie?" Patch asked his partner.

"I dunno, Marty," Vargas answered. "What d'you wanna do?"

"I dunno. What d'you wanna do?"

Both knew what was to be done: wait until the cop left, and then go in. Or, if the couple in number 2 departed before the cop did, follow them and grab them later.

They sipped the coffee Patch had got from a machine in the motel office. Watched the cop reading something in his cruiser. Watched a family stow bags in the trunk of a car showing Vermont plates. Watched the door of the bungalow they were staking out stay firmly closed.

"What are they doin' in there?" Vargas was a little hung over, and a rare note of impatience barbed his question.

"Having a quickie for the road, maybe."

"The guy's a priest, for chrissake."

Ronny Patch scratched his untended jaw, a chuckle expanding his cheerfulness. "You ever hear the one about the mother superior and the pretty young novice?"

"Shit," Vargas said, blinking tiredly.

"The kid's describing the cucumber she picked from the convent garden, and she holds her hands up about nine inches apart and the Mother Superior, she's deaf as a post, leans forward, cups her ear, and says, Father who?"

When Ronny Patch cawed at the story, Vargas gave him a look at his dark face and his slightly bloodshot eyes. "You know what you are? You're a goddamn redneck, ya goddamn asshole."

"What?"

"Gimme one good reason why it couldn't be a Protestant nun. Go ahead. One good reason."

"Because, nutsy, the Protestants don't have nuns. Jesus, I'm working with a farmer here."

"They do so have nuns, ya dumb fucking Anglo. You see 'em around all the time. They wear a kind of gray suit."

"Nah, nah, nah. They're IBM executives. And, believe me, the gag don't work with an IBM executive describing a cucumber."

"Hey . . ." Vargas's greased black hair bobbed as he nodded at the cabins.

The door of number 2 was opening.

"How do you think we should play it?" Brian asked as they carried their bags toward their rented Cherokee. He was referring to something they'd started discussing over breakfast: how to handle the actual confrontation. "We're going to need some kind of identity, aren't we?"

Marie didn't sound overly concerned about that part of it. "Buehl and Gold don't know us from a bar of soap, so we can be anybody we say we are. What we need most, though, is an excuse to get in to see them. Something big that'll interest them enough to agree to a meeting."

"How about something financial?" Brian headed the Cherokee out of the parking lot. "We tell them we want to hire them to, let's say, run up the price of a stock. You think they'd go for that?"

"A financial angle's not bad," Marie allowed. "If we could give it a biblical spin, it'd be even better. Gold would jump at something like that."

"Monetary events in the Bible . . ." Brian considered it. "There are quite a few instances in the NT. The parable of the lost coin. The parable of the shrewd manager. The hidden treasure and the pearl."

"Driving the money changers from the temple," Marie contributed. "Thirty pieces of silver . . ."

"The rich young man, the rich ruler, the rich man and Lazarus. The parable of the ten minas . . ."

"How about the OT? Could we do something with one of those rip-roaring disasters, a flood or a famine? Something John Martin might have painted?" When Marie posed this question, she saw something tweak Brian's imagination. His idea appeared in the relaxed line of his mouth before it issued as words.

"A famine . . . now, there's a thought. And a biblical plague." He paused to assemble elements and pat them into shape. "Wheat fields, cornfields . . . no. The coffee crop! How about the coffee crop in Brazil? We want ten percent of it destroyed by a plague of grasshoppers or whatever. Something that will look like a natural disaster."

"Great. Love it. We're agents for some serious money people who are into commodities. They'll take a position in coffee if we can guarantee a price rise, which will happen if part of the crop is destroyed." Marie favored him with a warm look. "You're quite bright for a country boy."

"As long as I remember to take my medication."

They laughed together, feeling good about each other and their prospects for some kind of success in this assignment, although

Brian was more sure of this than Marie. She knew that any advance would be limited, and she suspected that Brian's confidence was basically a first-timer's presumption.

"We're not going to come away with much, you know that, don't you?" she warned him. "We still won't have anything we can take to the police."

"Maybe not. But we'll get a feeling. I want to be able to tell Harry Chifley I know for sure how this thing was done."

"You won't be able to prove it."

"I haven't been asked to prove it. Just find out."

Brian guided the Jeep up onto a north-south highway, two lanes in each direction separated by a double white line. A pleasant dearth of traffic helped persuade him of a satisfactory outcome to the meeting they planned, unencumbered speed becoming a metaphor for unhindered progress.

"Watch it," Marie said quickly, then added, off Brian's questioning glance, "we have company."

Brian saw what she'd spotted: the cruiser they'd noticed at the motel had slotted in behind them. He slowed immediately. A speeding ticket was not the start he was looking for.

Keeping to a sedate 40 mph Vittorio Vargas kept his eyes straight ahead as the cruiser overtook his Oldsmobile and settled in behind the Cherokee they were following. "Will you look at that," he invited, with a disgusted camber to his mouth. "When you want a cop they're never around."

Ronny Patch pushed at his Mets cap. "You think they got protection?"

"Uh-uh. The bogie would've left with 'em if he was watching their ass."

"Speaking of ass, did you get a look at the one on that blonde? Like a coupla wildcats fighting under a sheet."

"Hogs," the Dominican said.

"What hogs?"

"The expression is, a coupla hogs fighting under a sheet."

"Fucking immigrants," Patch said. "They come over here and try to tell us how to talk the language. It's wildcats."

"Hogs," Vargas insisted.

*   *   *

"Good," Marie said as the cruiser pulled out, passed them, and sped off into the distance. "He's decided to go after some bigger fish."

Brian sighed his relief. "I remain unblemished," he told the windshield a moment before it starred into a jagged web as the surge of a souped-up V8 and the roar of a big-caliber handgun folded into the same shattering sound.

They jumped in shock, then registered a series of fast and breath-robbing impressions: a car drawn level and practically scraping against them. A dark-faced man behind the wheel. A man next to him in a baseball cap, his features obscured by his outstretched arms and the double-handed grip he had on the gun he was pointing.

"Pull over, or the next one's in your eye," the driver shouted.

Brian's immediate reactions fought for precedence: the first one, fed by a basic survival instinct, was unthinking obedience. He hit the brakes and swerved blindly toward the shoulder. The second reaction was a quick-reasoned update of that same instinct: to disobey and get as far away from that gun as he could.

He belted his fist into the shattered windshield. Punched out a hole to give himself vision. Mashed the accelerator.

The Cherokee kicked down into passing gear and leaped forward.

It surprised the Oldsmobile—it looked like a trick, and Vargas wasn't expecting anything of that nature; ordinary citizens, like this priest in the Jeep with the Olins rental sticker on the rear bumper, always did what they were told when faced with a bullet. He stamped on the pedal and charged after the insolent bastard.

A constant spray of injected gasoline pulled a prolonged scream from the Jeep's engine. Brian was locked in semipanicked flight, any thought of strategy a nonoccurrence at the moment. He didn't have to wonder the why of what was happening; it was stunningly clear that their snooping had caught up with them.

Marie, her face blanched, her legs braced, and her fingers squinching a hand rest, had a clear understanding of that. She was as rocked as Brian was at the sudden and calamitous turn of events; rocked but not altogether surprised. She knew that certain kinds of knowledge carried the possibility of incipient backlash, and that when they'd discovered the names of the directors of this production it had placed them in a category beyond that of amateur sleuths. They'd become players in the game, whatever it was, subject to the same rewards and penalties as all the other participants.

The Oldsmobile, far more powerful than the Jeep, ballooned in the rearview mirror, howled up on the shoulder of the road. Both vehicles were doing eighty heading for ninety, yet they were so close they might have been lateral extensions of each other. Marie could have reached out a hand and touched the driver, given a tug to that comical goatee like somebody unmasking a pretender.

Vargas jerked the steering wheel, but the big car didn't crunch into the Jeep, it merely nudged it in a cheeky parody of a sideswipe. "Pull over, ya morons," he yelled.

Brian got a grip on his hot lunge of panic, and a tactic presented itself. The goateed man had made a big mistake coming up on the inside, he figured. If that Olds could be moved just five feet to the right, it'd hang up on the guard rail. He shouted through the clammering noise, shouting superfluously to Marie to hold on, then swerved out left and cut hard right.

And got a lesson in aggressive driving.

Completely miscast in the role which had been so suddenly thrust upon him, he'd telegraphed the move with that initial swerve and was beaten to the punch. The other car slammed into the Jeep, drove it left, and held it there half a width over the center line.

Marie cried out. A sixteen-wheeler, cannonballing along in the northbound fast lane, was rocketing toward them. Traveling at too great a speed to brake, and unable to switch lanes because of traffic inside it, the huge rig could only blast its horn and keep coming.

Brian slammed on the brakes.

Vargas, a consummate wheelman, did the same.

Brian floored the gas pedal.

The Dominican was right there with him—the two vehicles could have had dual controls.

The heavy Olds clashed and banged against Marie's door like

an enraged beast trying to get to her, edging the Jeep even farther into the path of the rig. Then, mercifully, the Olds's driver broke off contact, braked hard, and slipped around behind the Jeep, giving it room to escape.

Brian got it back across the double lines a beat before the truck shot by in a buffeting cyclone. "They're bluffing." His voice was a ragged croak. "The bastards are just trying to scare us."

Marie's breathing was torn and out of sync. "They want us alive. They want to know how we knew about Hatfield. They want to know who else knows."

Brian knew she was right, just as he knew that if they were caught, and they delivered this information, they'd become part of the cleaning-up process.

Moisture seeped down through an eyebrow and combined with the fractured windshield to fuzz his vision. He blinked at the sting and tried to still a cerebral swirling long enough to think up a game plan. Grabbed at one that presented itself.

He slowed and drew level with a Trailways bus humming along in the inside lane. With a string of traffic speeding down the oncoming fast lane, the Olds could do nothing for the moment but sit in behind them. Brian figured the stratagem had brought them a minute of reprieve, a minute of essential thinking time, but, once again, he received a vivid demonstration of just how far he was out of his depth. With a move amazing for its impudent recklessness the Olds swung out, zoomed across the center line, cut across the bows of a blaring Audi, straightened in the empty northbound slow lane, then swerved back into the northbound fast lane, which, now that the complaining Audi was past, was free again. Vargas had put his own vehicle in exactly the position he'd put the Jeep in a minute ago, traveling on the wrong side of the double lines against the flow of the oncoming traffic.

From this insane outside position he repeatedly slammed the Olds into Brian's door, barging the Cherokee toward the side of the bus.

Shaken and jounced, banged around in his useless seat belt, Brian still couldn't believe it: at 70 mph the goateed man was casually playing chicken with several cars and vans, forcing their horn-leaning, saucer-eyed drivers to swerve frantically into the inside lane to avoid a calamitous head-on.

Even Marie was stopped by the man's colossal brazenness, his supreme confidence that, as long as there were spaces in that northbound slow lane, he and his partner were safe from oblivion.

She tore her eyes away. Checked to her right. Got a glimpse of a line of open-mouthed bus passengers mesmerized by this piece of highway drama. To her left the Oldsmobile came at them again. Bounced them a foot closer to the hurtling bus.

She could see the method in the driver's apparent madness: knowing they viewed the gun as an empty threat and weren't going to stop—knowing they knew that that gun was not about to shoot out a tire and send them skidding and tumbling into a smoking inferno—he was trying to frighten them into a state where they'd do anything to get out of this maniac situation. He was trying to scare them into swinging in behind the bus and pulling over onto the shoulder.

What they needed was exceedingly obvious: time and space. They had to find a way to separate themselves from this insanity, to get a couple of minutes ahead of that crazy, bullying Oldsmobile and get some help from someone. But all they could see through that punched-out windshield, the wind slamming through it and pounding on their faces, was a mile of highway full of rushing traffic.

Or *was* that all?

Up ahead, an exit sign appeared.

The word spiraled through Brian's flagging intellect. *Exit.* Latin for "he goes out." Plural, *exeunt,* "they go out." He didn't have to wonder why his brain had chosen this particular moment to wander into the coils of etymology; it had decided what to do and was letting a scholar know.

He dropped back behind the bus. Switched to the inside lane.

The Oldsmobile had seen the exit sign, too. With a seamless, gliding move, brilliant in its one-piece execution, the car crossed back to the southbound lane, went around behind the Jeep, and spurted up on its inside, blocking any possible dash for the exit ramp.

But that wasn't the ramp Brian had chosen. He figured that if the Olds had been able to survive for a few minutes against the traffic flow, the Jeep should be able to do it for just twenty seconds.

He called out a warning to Marie, slid left into the fast lane, saw a break in the oncoming cars, gunned the Cherokee over the center line, and took it in a roaring diagonal clear across the northbound lanes, heading for the wrong-way entrance ramp on the other side of the highway.

"Jesus, Mary, and Joseph!" Vargas said, peeling away and charging after the Jeep. "Guy's out of his fuckin' mind."

He meant it. Wrong-way driving was the plain and simple disaster it appeared to be unless you knew what you were doing. And Vargas did. With exquisite use of floor pedals, and a genius split-second timing in his steering technique, he took the big car across two lanes of staggered traffic, causing an atonal symphony of shrieking tires and hollered imprecations but not so much as a dink in anybody's paintwork.

"I tell you," Ronny Patch predicted, "if they crash and burn, the colonel's gonna shove our nuts up our nostrils." He watched the Jeep dodge and swerve around three potential catastrophes and, against all expectations, make it unscathed to the entrance ramp and vanish down it.

Zooming the Olds into the ramp ten seconds later, Vargas avoided a pickup truck by the width of a finger, and accelerated down the entryway, scattering a parade of adrenaline-choked drivers.

The ramp ended in a moderately busy suburban street. The Olds slashed into it in a controlled skid. Vargas saw the Jeep brake a hundred yards farther on, careen to its right, then straighten and zip into a side road. When he arrived at the spot in a howl of scorched rubber, and found that the side road belonged to a country club, Vargas was impressed.

"Hey, that priest," he said as he took the car shooting up the rise of the side road. "He ain't exactly stupid."

Ronny Patch squinched his brow. "You joking? He drives like a brain-damaged Viking."

"He's doing fine. He's driving a four-wheel, right? So he's going for some terrain," Vargas explained. "He's got a head on his shoulders."

"What are you doing?" Marie's shouted question had to fight engine whine and a volley of stones thudding up under the floor. She twisted to look behind her. "We've gotta get to the police!"

"I can't shake 'em on the road." Brian tried to keep from gabbling, but the Olds was hanging on, wailing up behind them. "We have to give ourselves an edge." He slapped at the drive selector. Felt the second pair of drive wheels grip grass as he pulled the Jeep off broken asphalt onto the spread of a golf course, a course which, he saw with a flux of burgeoning hope, featured high greens and elevated tees.

They raced for a hundred yards down the center of a deserted fairway left swampy by a recent rain, muddy water fountaining and drumming on the fenders. Marie, wedged into her seat, swiveled around again. The Oldsmobile was making heavy going of it, the skill of its driver negated by the poor traction the spongy grass afforded its rear wheels.

A slug spanged off the Cherokee's rear bumper, the bang of the pistol shooing some crows from a stand of maples. The gunfire surprised Brian but not Marie—she knew that the gunman in the Olds clearly felt free now to shoot out a tire, knowing that, at their reduced speed on a soft and forgiving surface, there was no chance of tumbling them into a fiery wreck. Instead, the sure-footed Jeep would become a crippled thing unable to run, leap, or hide.

Brian swung a hard right, pulled the shift into low, and powered up the shallow incline of a hill. The Jeep survived two more shots before it reached the crest, took to the air for a brief and weightless moment, then jounced down hard on an immense putting green and was lost from the Oldsmobile's view. The Jeep's bulky tread gouged chunks out of the neatly tended lawn as it churned across ninety feet of dead-flat grass, described a digging turn that ruined weeks of a greenkeeper's careful work, then came charging back on its tracks.

Marie could see what Brian was going to try. He didn't have to tell her to brace herself.

Like a storming tank climbing the side of a trench, the Oldsmobile appeared at the high lip of the green, its radiator leering at the sky.

Brian judged it perfectly. Sent the Jeep belting into the Olds, catching it at a sharp and awkward angle on the center door post. The combination of the hard sideways impact and the inclined angle of the car lifted it up on its right side wheels.

Gravity did the rest.

As if it were taking water in a heavy sea, it tipped slowly, almost regally, past the angle of recovery, and toppled.

It didn't thunder down the hill in a series of spectacular roof-crunching smashes—the incline was too shallow for that—it rolled down sedately, each roll lending miserly momentum to the next.

Three times it turned.

Four times.

Four and a half.

It hung on its side for a long, agonizing moment, then, like a fat and clever beetle, flopped back upright. With just a little more speed, or a deeper dip at the bottom of the slope, it would have finished up on its back, its wheels slowly spinning, its vulnerable underside exposed. But it had come to rest little the worse for its acrobatics apart from a concertinaed rear door and some mud and grass stains on its roof.

But, for Brian, the cruelest blow was the laughter he heard, that and the sight of the goateed man who, instead of being draped over the steering wheel concussed and out of it, calmly unsnapped his seat belt, got out, and shook himself like a cat who'd suffered some mild indignity. The laughter was coming from the other man who was staying in the car, laughing at the Hispanic driver who was holding his head.

There was an element of horror in it for Marie—this thug gunman reacting to their potentially neck-breaking plunge not with hysterical relief but with a kind of naughty glee, like a kid who'd snuck onto a thrilling carnival ride.

Brian didn't try to analyze it. He took the small advantage they had, started the Jeep, which the crash had stalled, and drove as hard as he could back down the slope, back down the mushy fairway, back down the busted road, then fishtailed out onto the suburban street, and barreled away.

There was a time when a station house in a small middle-class Westchester town had little more to regulate than traffic offenses, barking dogs, and the occasional burglary. But as the terrors and dangers endemic to urban living had spread to the affluent suburbs, very little malfeasance, no matter to what heated degree it had risen, created much stir amongst the local constabulary these days. Which was why the duty officer behind his sheet of protective glass was nowhere near thunderstruck when a man and a woman, clearly driven by the exigencies of escape, rushed in.

"Help you?" The policeman, his face at once surly and bland, asked this question even though help was what everybody who came before him was seeking. He watched these two establish control of their breathing, waiting with a tired patience for the wall clock's hour hand to advance by one more numeral and end his shift.

Brian deferred to Marie, knowing she'd handle this situation better than he would. Battling the Oldsmobile he'd been the dynamic one because it had been his hands on the wheel, but his fright had still exceeded hers, and it wasn't because she'd had previous experience in precarious situations. It was just part of her personality: she was good under fire, and he'd just found out that he had no special ability in that area.

"There are two men outside. They're trying to snatch us." Marie rattled the words out, trying to keep it simple. "They tried to run us off the road. They're both armed."

"They known to you?"

"No. I'm a reporter. We're investigating something and we got a little too close to somebody."

"Sounds exciting," the cop said, with no change of expression.

"Look," Brian said, assuming that the cop might pay a little more attention to a masculine voice. "This isn't a game. We've got a real problem and we need some protection."

"Where do you live?"

"New York."

"That where you headed?"

"That's right."

"Okay. Give me five minutes and I'll have an officer escort you to your vehicle."

"I already told you," Marie said, putting some sting into her delivery, "they tried to run us off the road. We get back into that car, they'll try it again."

"Okay, you don't want to do that, my advice is check into a motel. There's one about a mile down the road. Lock yourselves in until it's safe to continue your trip."

"It's not going to be safe. These guys mean it."

A man had come through the door, clearly nursing a grievance. The cop behind the glass flicked his eyes to him in a way that said there were other customers waiting. "Hey," the officer said, fatigue peeking through his flat officialdom, "we're not a security service. We don't have the manpower or the budget to ride shotgun for you all the way to New York. If you can point these alleged kidnappers out to us, we'll have a word with them. If you can't do that, we'll escort you to a local motel. That's the best we can do for you."

"Alleged?" Brian had some color rising up his neck. His voice followed in the same direction. "You want to come and take a look at our car? They shot out the windshield. It has bullet holes all over it, for God's sake."

The man behind stepped around them. "Some son of a bitch stole my wallet," he whined to the duty officer.

Marie took Brian's arm. Walked him away from the window. He was fuming. "No wonder they put 'em behind protective glass."

"I didn't expect much more," Marie confessed. "We have sanctuary, and that's the main thing."

"For how long? They're not going to let us sleep here." Brian looked around him, noting that hospitality of that kind would have been impossible anyway. The architects of the station house had designed an ungenerous lobby; there was little more to it than the enclosed desk, a bench, a wall pay phone, and a notice board showing overexposed photographs of free-roaming criminals.

"We'll be out of here in an hour," Marie predicted.

"How so?"

"I'll get Jack Morrisey to come and fetch us." Marie was talking about the investigator she'd called from the motel, the one who'd dug up the information on Buehl.

"Time to call in the hard guys, huh?" Brian dropped his eyes. "That'll make a welcome change."

"Hey . . ." Marie reached for his hand. "You were magnificent behind that wheel."

"C'mon. I was driving a 1995 blue funk. Another couple of minutes and you would've heard a grown man screaming."

Marie brought her lips to his ear in a quick kiss. "Bullshit," she whispered, then, at normal volume, "You got a quarter?"

Brian searched for change but found only a couple of dimes. He pulled a five-dollar bill from his wallet and didn't even consider asking the cop to break it. He turned to the man who'd come in about a theft; he was sitting on the bench thoughtfully rubbing the shoulder of his sweatshirt and struggling with a crime information form.

"Did they leave you any change?" Brian proffered the five dollar bill. "We have to make a call."

"I'm lucky they left me my sneakers," the man said. He produced a quarter from his jeans, turning aside Brian's offer to trade it for the five.

Marie got Jack Morrisey's office number from information, then called collect but Morrisey wasn't there. She gave her secretary the pay-phone number, asked for an urgent callback, then joined Brian on the bench.

"Contents," the man in the sweatshirt said. He accepted the return of his coin, and continued filling out his form. "Thirty-five bucks . . . one Visa card . . . one snapshot of the kids . . . one brand-new . . ." He looked around at Brian. "How do you spell Trojan?"

Brian helped him with that one, and a couple of other questions, and then the phone rang.

Marie jumped for it.

"Jack . . . thanks for calling back. I'm in deep trouble. Me and a pal . . . a couple of goons are trying to take our heads off. They're armed and nasty . . . No, we're okay . . . Beechwood. Just outside White Plains . . . We're in the police precinct house . . . Bless you."

She hung up. Came back to Brian with a lighter step. "He'll be here in an hour. With some backup."

"Jeez, I thought I had problems," the form filler said, looking at Marie and his tutor with something like sympathetic respect. "It's a jungle out there, ain't it?"

They agreed on that, then the man took his completed form to the duty officer and seemed disappointed not to immediately get his wallet back in exchange.

Over the next forty minutes Brian and Marie shared the bench with several other people, all of them with misdemeanors to report and a corresponding form to complete, which was accomplished with a firmer grasp of correct spelling than the man in the sweatshirt had displayed.

"Traffic must be tight," Marie said, checking the wall clock. "His office is way downtown."

"He said an hour," Brian reminded her. But another ten minutes passed without Marie's friend appearing. Not long after that the duty officer called Brian over and told him that they could wait there for another fifteen minutes, then they'd have to make other arrangements. Brian was starting to argue with him when a man in a khaki fisherman's vest came through the door. A big, wide man, he seemed impregnated with endless strength, his vest open on a red golf shirt pushed out by a gut that was mainly compressed muscle. He took a quick look at the handful of people, then moved with an ursine bulkiness toward Marie.

"Hi," he said. "Jack not here yet?"

Marie got up. Brian came over. "Not yet," Marie answered. "You work with him?"

"That guy . . ." The big man made a face. "Drives like the mailman. Yeah, he calls me when he needs a hand. Coupla mugs bothering you, huh?"

"They're better than that. They're pros. And they're both carrying."

The big man patted at the shoulder of his jumbo-sized vest. "So am I. I got a Heckler in here and a Mac in the car. What do these bozos look like?"

Brian fielded that question; he'd gotten quite a few close-ups of the driver. "One of them's Hispanic. Moon-faced with a goatee. The other one I didn't get a good look at." He checked with Marie, whose head shake indicated that she couldn't help on that score.

"Lemme take a look," the big man offered. He moved to the entrance in a side-to-side gait as if he were carrying one end of a piano. He stood in the doorway as sturdy as a lighthouse and peered out. "I don't see nobody. And here comes Jack. Let's go."

They joined him. "I'll take the curbside," he instructed. "Walk normal but don't dawdle. If they wanna play guns, hit the deck and stay there, got it?"

They started down the steps beside him, wondering if those men would try anything with such a formidable chaperon in attendance.

They made thirty feet without incident.

Fifty feet.

Brian kept Marie close to him, thinking about something: if there was going to be an attack, would it necessarily come from the street side? Maybe the Latino was hiding in a storefront, like the one they were coming up to.

"Almost there," the big man said, his hand in his jacket, his eyes sweeping the street. "The brown Plymouth. That's Jack's car."

They closed on the vehicle parked at the curb, a paint-prepped muscle car with a vented hood and wide-rimmed wheels. The passenger door swung open and a man got out.

He was wearing a sweatshirt and settling a crumpled Mets cap on his head. "They find my wallet yet?" he asked, his eyes ready to splinter into hilarity.

Brian's reaction was identical to Marie's—a half moment of jolting shock, followed by more shock, succeeded by an inflamed sense of overwhelming folly. How could they have been so gullible? So incredibly stupid? What were they, simpletons to be taken in so facilely, to be maneuvered with such trusting faith?

Lashed by dismayed anger, it was a moment before all this was supplanted by the chill of fear.

The sidewalk was reasonably active: people strolling, shopping, deliveries being made; a New York bedroom town going about its daily business. Brian found it hard to believe that the people who passed weren't reacting to the shock on their faces, couldn't smell the tension, couldn't recognize inherent threat and coercion. But, apart from the long looks Marie inevitably drew from both sexes, nobody appeared to find anything exceptional about the group. The man in the fisherman's vest made doubly sure of that.

"We're getting in the car now," he told Brian reasonably, including Marie with a quick eye-shift. "Run, yell, or otherwise perform and I'll kill you. My name's Van Boder. You can call me Hennie," he added, as if he quickly wanted to get off an unpleasant subject. He indicated his grinning partner. "That's Ronny Patch. But, of course, you've already met."

They were bundled into the car and driven half a block to a parking lot belonging to a sleepy little minimarket. Vargas was standing next to his battered Oldsmobile. He leaned into the Plymouth and, nodding at the captives as if they were old friends, said to Patch, "I'm goin' home and lie down. I belted my head in that rollover."

Patch clucked his tongue. "The colonel ain't gonna like that. He just might have the ayatollah freak put a bullet in your brain."

"Fuck the colonel, and fuck the freak. Pardon me, miss," Vargas said.

Van Boder chunked the Plymouth into reverse. "We'll handle it," he said.

He backed and filled. Took the car away.

Out in the street, driving toward the highway, Marie saw a heavy-tired Pathfinder rush by toward town, caught a glimpse of Jack Morrisey's warrior face behind the wheel, and wondered what he'd do when he found them gone. The answer was almost part of the question: he'd ask the duty cop what had happened to them. Maybe the cop had seen them leave with somebody and maybe he hadn't. Either way, it wouldn't make any difference.

Once again she cringed as she thought how easy she'd made it for them. All that the little guy in the sweat had had to do was listen to her conversation with Jack Morrisey, call his buddy, and get him to come in a hurry and be Jack's lieutenant. In her own defense she conceded that Morrisey looked like a hard case himself, so it had been easy to believe that this man Van Boder was his off-sider. Even so, she lamented silently, the bottom line was she'd been faked out by their little shell game like a hayseed on Broadway.

Mad and scared, she watched Ronny Patch going through her handbag—she'd left it in the Jeep when they'd fled into the station house.

"Did you know I was a goon, Vee Bee?" Patch asked with a mischievous wag of his head.

"Who says?"

"Blondie."

"He ain't a goon," Van Boder said to the rearview mirror, as if he were clearing up an understandable mistake. "A goon's a guy beats up on you you don't get square with your bookie. He don't do none of that stuff."

"I can't stand violence," Patch confided to Marie, looking sincere. Then he quizzed his partner again. "Did you know I was nasty?"

"She say that, too?"

"I swear to God."

"That's defamation of character."

Patch pulled out Marie's lip gloss, spread a little on his lower lip, and turned his face to the driver. "How do I look in drag?"

Van Boder thought it was pretty funny. "She got any ID?"

Patch found her press card. "Hey, she's a newspaper lady." He looked up and rayed Marie with his almost permanent grin. "What are you, a sportswriter, sweetie? You go in the Giants' locker room with a tape measure, do you?"

"That's enough," Brian said, putting some quiet steam into it.

Patch looked victimized. "I was talking about their chest measurements, for chrissakes."

Van Boder checked on the rear seat. He was not a handsome man; his head was a pink, bald balloon on which frugal genes had settled a miserly collection of too-small features: a stingy mouth, a penurious nose, economic ears. Nature had compensated for this lack of largesse by awarding him hands and feet of simian proportions and arms of corresponding length. He drove with his seat pushed all the way back. "Let's see your wallet, Father," he said.

When Brian was slow to respond Patch turned, reached back, and expertly slipped the wallet out of Brian's jacket. He winked at Marie, his cheery demeanor restored. "I used to work the subway," he confided.

Brian was disconsolately considering something: nomenclature. He ran through all the people who, like this clownish thug searching his wallet, knew that he was a priest; people with whom he wasn't very well acquainted. It wasn't a list of any great length: Carol Frankel, the receptionist of the late surgeon in Hatfield, was aware of his vocation, as was Father Zaim in Ontario. One of them had made a phone call to interested parties.

Carol Frankel or Father Zaim.

It was no contest.

"Well, lookee here . . ." Patch had unfolded the postoperative report. He passed it to Van Boder, pointing to something near the top. The big man waited till he'd negotiated a ramp to the southbound artery of the Bronx River Parkway before checking the report.

Patch reached for a phone and made a call. Began speaking. "We got 'em, Colonel . . . Nope. He checks out . . . She's a journo . . . You bet we did. A record of the operation . . . That's right . . . Patient K. Your name's down as a referral . . . okay." Patch passed the phone to the rear seat. "Colonel Beuhl wants to speak to you."

Brian couldn't help but be struck by his quick-changing fortunes of late; it was as if he'd been written into some fate-riddled Elizabethan drama, a character whose life becomes a topsy-turvy game of chutes and ladders. Only a couple of hours back he'd been trying to figure a way of getting to talk to the very person who now wanted to talk to him. Except it wasn't supposed to be in quite these circumstances.

"This is Father Sheridan. Your name is Buehl?"

"*Colonel* Buehl. I'd very much like to know why you're involved in this affair, Father. And one or two other things."

An assured voice, Brian thought; a man who prized his stripes of superiority. A no-frills man who got straight to the point. It fit Brian's limited experience of military types, and he came back at him with the same forceful efficiency. "And I'd very much like to

know who you are and by what authority your men have kid-
napped us."

"By my authority, Father. They'll do as I say, so you'd do well
to stay on my good side. But in the interests of avoiding a two-
hour conversation let me make an assumption. I'm going to assume you've been snooping around on behalf of the Church,
which has no doubt been following events with great interest. But
I'm intrigued as to how you traced my creation to Canada. I already know what led you to Hatfield. But how did you know to
go to the seminary?"

Brian tried to flash a message of hope to Marie. She'd been
right: Buehl wanted information, and as long as he went on wanting something from them, they were safe.

"Colonel, if you'll ask your men to release us, I'll be happy to
tell you. I won't tell you with a gun at my head."

"I'm not Catholic, Father, so I can't say I've ever been lied to by
a priest. But I have to admit the possibility exists in this case. Tell
me now, and I'll have them drop you anywhere you want."

"I was never in the army, Colonel, so I can't say I've ever been
lied to by an officer. But, like you, I also have to admit that, in this
case, the possibility exists."

"Put my man on. Now!" Brian heard the quick annoyance and
surmised that Buehl might be a teeny bit sensitive at being verbally
bested. A man like this wouldn't be used to being answered back,
and his natural response would be to pull rank and issue a discus-
sion-ending order.

Brian handed the phone back to the front seat. "He wants to
know how we did it," he said to Marie, not bothering to lower his
volume.

"Good," she replied, but only so loud that Brian could hear.

Twenty-five miles away in Manhattan, in his spick-and-span,
Lemon Pledge–redolent apartment, Ralph Buehl stood straight and
tall, the phone held high as he stared unseeingly through the window at the apartment house opposite. "I want to know how they
found him," he said into the phone in crisp anger. "I don't spend
months on a plan to find out it's a see-through job."

"Maybe there was a leak," Ronny Patch suggested.

"If there was, we'd be dealing with law enforcement, not the

Church. I think that priest must have seen Heloum on television, or maybe in Atlanta, and noticed something I didn't know was there. I want to know what it was."

"Will do, Colonel. I'll get back to you." Patch hung up and saluted the phone. "Ten . . . hunh!"

"Dis . . . missed!" Van Boder snapped out the command before they colluded in a bout of mirth.

Patch, tearing up the surgery report, tossed Brian's wallet back to him and said, "We send up the colonel now and then, but don't get the idea he's a figure of fun. He's one tough cookie. He was a young looey in Nam. Got himself captured. The gooks had him in a rice paddy up to his eyeballs in freezing water for five days, but he didn't crack."

"He got back at them, though," Van Boder assured them, "after he escaped. He came up with a real cute way of interrogating prisoners. He'd shove a gag in their mouth, then stuff a coupla forty-five slugs up their nose. The brass climbed all over him for it, but all unofficial, you understand. No court-martial because they didn't want that kinda thing getting out. But it hung over him and he never got his star. Least that's the way I heard it."

"Which is why," Patch said, sliding into his deep-voiced newscaster impersonation, "he is a bit-ter man today."

"And driven," Van Boder added.

"And driven," Patch mimicked.

The basis of the anecdote wasn't lost on the rear seat occupants. They knew they'd just been informed, in a manner which made it all the more menacing for its cheery delivery, that the man their captors worked for was no stranger to illicit persuasion. And, by extension, his minions were well versed in it, too.

Marie's hand snuck into Brian's. They both derived some comfort from the touch. And not a little strength. That they were facing some kind of ordeal, that these men had something unpleasant in mind for them, was a given. The unknown was how they'd hold up to it, and what would happen if they did.

They knew what would happen if they didn't.

CHAPTER
23

When they switched to the Cross Bronx Expressway, and kept going onto the George Washington Bridge, an eerie thought snuck up on Marie and lodged in her heart: they were taking them to the Pine Barrens. The Barrens had been a Mob burial ground for years, and if Buehl wasn't Mob, maybe the Mafia sold plots like any other cemetery.

But when Van Boder kept going down the turnpike, turned off just before Newark airport, and headed for the Bayonne Bridge, she canceled a New Jersey demise for the same ugly fate in Staten Island.

They crossed more water and drove all the way across the island to the littoral road that links the towns on its northeastern rim.

A mile and a half farther, on Bay Street in Stapleton, Van Boder took the car down a side road that was little more than an alley of puddled mud. The Plymouth bumped and squelched through flooded potholes until it could go no farther, and they got out into a rancid mix of ocean smells, the tart odor of dried tar and the stench of barnacled pilings.

Straight ahead of them, failing to glitter under an occluded sun, the Narrows rolled its mile-wide gray carpet toward Brooklyn, a machine-gun breeze strafing the lower bay. The only vessels in sight were two ferries, a handful of small craft, an anchored Shell tanker waiting to sail up the river to the old Astoria terminal, and a lone freighter wallowing past Sea Gate bound for Europe.

With Patch herding them from behind, Van Boder led the way past a warehouse that was riddled with neglect and tottering. On the right was a stretch of slushy mud ending in an Everest of trash, rusted bed frames, and soggy supermarket boxes full of spoiled food. Seagulls circled the pile in shrieking gluttony, their voracious whirling the only movement in the area. Ahead, an ancient single-story house came into view, its clapboard siding peeled and rotted by the weather.

Ronny Patch put a key into a shiny new mortise lock set high in the door and turned it three times. He grasped the rusted door-knob and pulled the door open. "Okay," he said to his captives, "here's how it is. You played and you lost, so we're gonna have to move you off the board. But you probably already figured that. However, it's your lucky day 'cause we got an errand we gotta run right now, so you're off the hook till the morning. But before we go, we wanna know how you knew about Hatfield. And if you don't tell us," Patch said to Brian, "I'll take blondie inside, pull the elastic out of her panties, and ping her cute little ass till it's all red and puffy."

Brian didn't even think about it. Engulfed by a crimson anger, he jumped at the leering little rat.

Patch saw it coming and spun aside, and then Van Boder had Brian wrapped up in his python arms, spinning and pinning him to his barrel chest, one enormous hand spanning Brian's chin ready to wrench it with a savage tug.

"Talk," he said to Marie, "or I break his neck."

"Let him go!" Marie shouted.

Brian gasped as Van Boder squeezed his jaw.

That was enough for Marie. She started gabbling, rushed out the information, told them everything.

"Cute," the Dutchman said to his helpless victim. "Father, you're a pretty smart guy." He released Brian and pushed him into the darkness of the shack.

Ronny Patch guided Marie in with a chivalrous gesture. "Damn," he said to her. "I was really looking forward to the elastic bit."

He backed out. Slammed the door.

They heard the slick efficiency of the triple-throw lock chunk into place, followed a minute later by the loud rumble of the car starting up and the whine of reversed gears fading away up the alley.

Marie felt for a light switch, and released an audible breath when a dangling bulb sprang on. She went to Brian. "I had to tell him. Van Boder wasn't bluffing."

Brian, embarrassed and mad at being so easily handled, massaged his jaw. "I know it."

They took a look around them, and what they saw offered them little cheer. The place had been some kind of marine workshop once upon a time, an empty tool board told them that, and a greasy workbench against a wall that held a cannibalized diesel engine. The floor was a rough sheet of oily cement. The sole decoration, tacked up on a wall, was a 1993 calendar advertising the outstanding merits of the Hardin Tanker Supply Service. The other walls were featureless apart from an empty closet, some boarded-up windows, and a single doorless opening.

They walked through this opening into a rear section, where they found a remnant of a domestic past—an expanse of torn bedroom wallpaper—and some survivors of its more recent industrial past: a busted vise, a cracked manifold, a section of a rusty driveshaft, several quart-sized oil cans full of a black liquid sludge, and some broken and discarded tools scattered around. Two rooms ran off this one, both of them doorless as well. One featured a cracked toilet with the seat missing, plus a filthy washbasin suffering from what looked like an incurable drip. The other room had once been a kitchen as evidenced by the greasy brown smoke stains on the stamped tin ceiling, but had seen service in later life in a different role, probably as a storeroom. Now it held a variety of things: some old phone books, a plastic milk crate, a beat-up, Made-in-China fan heater, and some long-forgotten builder's leftovers: a roll of tar paper, a burst bag of roofing nails, a couple of sheets of plywood, and some cut boards that had never replaced the weathered ones on the exterior of the house. There was one other item, but it didn't seem to fit with any of the other things: a solid, old-fashioned Chubb safe.

They returned to the main room, Brian carrying the rusty driveshaft. Holding it in both hands like a baseball bat, he slammed it against a window board as hard as he could. It bounced off, leapt from his fingers, and clanged onto the floor. Flapping his hands—the heavy shaft had jarred his wrists—he took a look at the damage. There wasn't any. The board was hardly scratched. "We won't be going out that way," he predicted.

They crossed the floor and checked out the front door. The hinges were on the exterior. Marie knocked on its heavy wood. "Nor that way," she said.

They toured the other two windows and found them identical to the one they'd already examined.

Marie blew out breath. "No wonder they didn't tie us up. This place is like a maximum-security prison."

Brian looked bleakly at their rugged confines. "Thank you, Father Zaim. He must have got to that kid, then tipped us in."

Marie had already surmised this and felt that a confirmation would only make that fact all the more depressing. She took another look at the boards over the nearest window and tried to keep her shoulders from slumping.

Watching her, Brian castigated himself. She wouldn't be here if he hadn't casually invited her to join him in what had become an outstandingly dangerous quest. She was trapped in this festering hole because he'd thought he could use a helping hand. And sometime tomorrow morning a jovial, oversized goon in a fisherman's vest, and a smaller version in a Mets cap, would come through that triple-locked front door and kill her.

Marie was clever. Perceiving the source of his misery, and not wanting to deepen it, she stayed away from any absolving assurances about knowing what she was getting into. Instead, she introduced a surprising topic. "I have a question for you. You ready?" She pressed ahead. "If you could choose any woman in the world to be locked in here with, who would it be?"

"What do you mean? Toward what end?"

"I mean, would you choose Diane Sawyer, Benazir Bhutto, Madonna . . . ?"

Brian recognized her attempt to rescue him from his benthic

plunge, and played along. "Not Madonna. I spent two weeks on a desert island with her once and it didn't work out."

"You know who I'd choose, if I had to choose a guy?"

"Arnold Schwarzenegger?"

"You."

"Schwarzenegger would be a better choice. He could rip away that door."

"No, he couldn't. It's not muscles that's going to get us out of here. It's brains. And you're the brightest guy I've ever met."

Brian went to her, kissed her, and addressed her brave try at morale inflation. "You are slightly sensational, did you know that? You're what women have been working up to all these years."

"I mean it," Marie said, with a sharp and serious attention. "This is not a let's-cheer-up-Brian session. I honestly believe you could get us out of here if you put your mind to it."

"Hell, you'd find a way out before I would."

"Wrong. I'm a vertical thinker. What we need is some lateral thought, and you're good at that."

Brian looked at the boarded windows, the solid door. "My lateral thought tells me we need a large ax."

"My vertical thought tells me we don't have an ax." Marie looked away from him, folded her arms, and said nothing more.

Brian realized that this was her way of telling him that he was now officially at work on the problem. So, as useless as he thought it would be, he took a stab at it.

He began by taking several tours of their jail, checking things in detail. The slats over the windows had been fastened flush to the wall with security screws which even a carpenter's multiheaded screwdriver wouldn't have budged, so he dismissed the windows as an exit. He tried fashioning and inserting scraps of metal into the door lock, but he knew nothing about picking a lock, although he suspected that this one was unpickable anyway.

He went into the back room and took inventory again.

An empty plastic crate, a roll of tar paper, some timber, a portable fan heater, a broom, and assorted junk.

He returned to the main room. Marie was worrying a torn fingernail, purposely not watching him. Brian circled the room employing some tedious, patient logic as he went at the problem from another angle.

"Okay," he said. "It's pretty clear that the only way out is the way we came in, through the door. And if we can't open the door, then we'll have to wait until somebody else opens it. And that somebody will be Ronny Patch in the morning. So maybe the only solution is something that'll work in a couple of fast and violent seconds when he walks in. Maybe you're lying in the middle of the floor looking dead or unconscious. The goons start forward in surprise and—" Brian trailed off. Marie's face told him what she thought of the idea.

"They're pros, Brian. They're not going to just waltz in. They'll stay back and tell us to show ourselves. If we don't, the first place they'll check is behind the door."

"Where I'll be standing with a piece of timber in my hand and egg on my face. You're right. Dumb idea." Brian thought for a moment then shrugged his hands. "So we need to get to them *before* they come in. Which is totally impossible."

He held that thought. Let it go. Then brought it back again.

He looked at Marie, and mentally snapped his fingers. He spun around and hurried into the storeroom and returned carrying the fan heater. He plugged it into a wall socket and sneezed as the machine blew out a warm breeze of accumulated dust. He switched it off. "Make that nearly impossible," he said.

When he shared his idea, Marie went to him and hugged him. "Brian, that's terrific!"

"No, it isn't. It doesn't go far enough. It takes care of Patch, but it still lets Van Boder in. He's huge and he's armed, and once he's in it's all over. The only solution is to be gone by the time they get here, and how do we do that . . ." Brian absently checked his watch. He said, with a far away note in his voice, "We're going to miss lunch."

They missed dinner as well.

Eight, 9:00, 10:00 P.M. came and went and he was still without an idea.

Marie, curled up on the workbench, and lullabyed by the drip of the washbasin tap, drifted in and out of a light doze.

Brian crossed the room to where a waterfront chill snuck in

under the front door, welcoming it as a sharpener for a mind that felt lumpy and blunt. He slid down to a sitting position on the floor intending to keep thinking about the problem until an idea arrived, but that wasn't what happened. Instead, his mind filled with Camille Heloum.

Why was that? he wondered. Because they were both prisoners, trapped in and by their respective roles? His own was laughable enough: investigating priest, but Heloum's was truly hilarious: returned Messiah.

But were they so different? They were both priests who were faking it, weren't they? Brian wondered how you auditioned to play the part of Jesus Christ, and how many actors could have played it as well as Heloum. How would he, for instance, Brian Sheridan, have fared? If Heloum was using the opportunity to grind an ax on behalf of the Eastern Church, which ax would he himself have chosen? Believe in what I say to do, but not in who they say I am? That wouldn't have gone down too well; people don't go bananas over an ideal. It's celebrities they go crazy about. An ordinary man with a remarkable message might have been granted polite interest, but a god with a twisted message was still a god.

Brian pushed himself upright and toured the walls again. If he could find a way to get out of this shack, he knew what he was going to do: he was going to Atlanta.

To talk to Camille Heloum.

Which, if he examined this ambition for more than half a second, was monumentally ludicrous. Was he truly expecting to gain insight from a glorious fraud? Or did he just want to find out what inducement it had taken to get Heloum to accept the role? Whatever the reason, it was going to have to be soon, because he was certain that, like himself, Camille Heloum was on borrowed time. Even the cleverest impersonators slipped up sooner or later, and Buehl would want to get his player off the stage before that happened.

Once again he threw himself at the problem.

And, once again, got nowhere.

Midnight became 2:00 A.M. Became 4:00 A.M.

He looked over at Marie on the bench. Something she'd said

earlier on was haunting him, but it kept dancing out of his memory's reach.

An hour later, for no apparent reason, it decided to present itself, dragging with it a built-in problem.

However, the solution to that problem was what he'd been looking for all this time.

He ran into the storeroom. Kicked through the used and ruined tools, searched the extremities of the room, then, flooded by a fine tide of exhilaration, trotted back into the main room. He leaned over Marie and softly called her name. "Hi, there," he said, as she stirred.

She blinked away sleep, caught him in her emerald focus, then kissed him to let him know his face was a poor actor. "I told you I was in here with the right man."

"The right man would've thought of this hours ago."

She jumped down from the bench. "Go," she said. But instead of an explanation, Marie got a question.

"How well would you say Van Boder knows this shack. I mean, would he be totally familiar with it?"

"I wouldn't think so. I think this is Buehl's piggy bank. His money drop. Van Boder would probably come here in the dead of night, put some cash in that safe, or pull some out, and leave. It's not the kind of place you'd hang around in."

"That's what I'm hoping," Brian told her. Then, forestalling her return query: "Remember I said that what we really need is to be gone by the time they get back? Before Van Boder gets in here? Well, that's what's gonna happen. We're going to vanish."

"We're going to hide somewhere?"

"You got it."

Marie looked around her, then said, carefully, "Brian ... it's a cement floor, so we can't get underneath that. And we can't hide up in the roof because the ceiling is sealed, and we'd never be able to reach it, anyway. So that leaves the closet or the john or the storeroom. And all Van Boder has to do is look in the closet or the john or the storeroom, and he's got us cold."

"Yes and no," Brian said, then laid it out for her. Before he'd got halfway through, Marie burst out laughing.

Brian might have joined her if the hour hadn't been so advanced. He had no idea how close the goons might be to them. All Patch had said was that they'd be back in the morning.

He checked his watch.

Coming up to seven.

And that, by anyone's estimation, qualified as the morning.

Heading north.

Albany, Utica, Syracuse, Rochester . . .

Around about the time Brian and Marie had missed dinner, Patch and Van Boder were crossing the border at Niagara Falls, trading New York State's Thruway for Ontario's Queen Elizabeth Way.

Forty minutes later they were on the outskirts of Elton, where Ronny Patch made a call from a pay phone.

Ten minutes after that they were driving an unlit back road, moving past the seminary's entrance.

Van Boder took his eyes off the road to press the trip counter. "Two miles, right?"

Ronny Patch confirmed it on the end of a loud belch. "That last pizza," he said. "It taste okay to you?"

"I've had better."

Patch lowered his window and threw out the box the offending pizza had been packaged in. "How about the coffee?"

"A six on a ten scale."

"This ain't no gourmet trip," Ronny Patch grouchily concluded.

Van Boder checked a sudden flare in the rearview mirror. Slowed to let a car overtake them. Kept his speed down till the car had vanished. He drove another five hundred yards, hit the brights, and leaned forward. Peered at the green Fairmont that was pulled over onto the shoulder up ahead. He checked the trip counter. "Two miles on the button." He squinted at the figure standing beside the car. "Little guy with a bushy beard. Gotta be Zaim, right?"

Patch was looking, too. "It's either him or Felix the Cat."

Van Boder flashed his lights and slowed.

The figure moved away from the car and waved in friendly and expectant greeting.

The waving arm froze. Then signaled frantically.

Zaim's face expanded, his eyes and mouth looping in terror. He got his legs going, his shoes, slipping on the graveled shoulder, converting the movement to a parody of a cossack dance.

The Plymouth's heavy fender slammed into meat and bone. Carried the weight like the horns of a bull for several yards. Then the right front wheel traveled up and over, the right rear wheel trampling in turn. The car, freed of its battered obstruction, leaped away and vanished around a bend, leaving behind a dark night and the quiet road, and the crushed and broken body.

They traded places for the drive back, Ronny Patch adjusting the driver's seat several notches forward.

"So what did you think of Canada?" Van Boder asked when they reached the Peace Bridge.

Ronny Patch sounded disappointed. "Frankly," he said, "I thought Canada would be bigger than that."

Van Boder chortled. "Ronny, we gotta get you on Letterman."

They hit the Thruway again.

Rochester, Syracuse . . .

Traveling south.

What Brian had found, when he'd raked through the pile of old and ruined tools, was an eighteen-inch hacksaw with a wobbly handle and no blade. And if he hadn't found, in a far corner, the discarded blade from that hacksaw, he wouldn't have been able to do what he was doing.

Which was sawing up timber.

He'd started the exercise by taking the door off the closet, belting out the hinge pins with a chisel for a punch and a busted monkey wrench for a hammer. With Marie on the other end, they carried the door into the storeroom, laid it on the floor, and covered it with junk.

They returned to the main room and, using a two-by-four—they marked it with the aid of a roofing nail—measured the height and width of the closet opening. Then they brought in several of the boards, which had been slated to replace the cracked ones on the shack's exterior, and cut a frame: two side pieces, and a top and a bottom. When they'd finished that, Brian cut a backing for the frame out of a plywood sheet—the coarse hacksaw blade made it hard to saw the wood accurately, but Brian didn't think that was going to matter—then they set the frame on the concrete floor and nailed the backing to it.

He cut three more pieces, three shelves which he nailed, evenly spaced, within the frame. Then Marie found a rag, dunked it into a can of sump oil, and washed down the thing they'd fashioned to give it an aged look.

The last thing they did was dress the shelving with two of the old phone books, several of the sludge cans, some nuts and bolts and the broken vise. Then Brian fetched the broom, swept up the shavings, and returned the tools they'd used, and the surplus timber, to the store room.

All they had to do then was wait.

Which they didn't have to do for very long.

Thirty-five minutes later, the distant throb of traffic, and the gluttonous shrieks of the squabbling gulls, sifted in under the front door.

Along with another sound.

One they hadn't heard for almost twenty-two hours: the squish of tires in mud, and the high-octane rumble of a muscle car's engine.

As he eased the deep-throated Plymouth through the minefield of potholes leading to the shack, Hennie Van Boder puzzled something he didn't quite understand.

"This party in the Avenues . . . you crashed it, right?"

"Well, sure," Ronny Patch said. "They're the best kind. Anyway, I walk in, grab a cold brew, and check out the talent. And there is this knockout chick standing by herself. I mean, this is the Playmate of the Year, and you'd think they'd be a dozen guys with their noses in her crotch, but no, she's being ignored. So I ask a guy what's her story. And he says she's a little weird."

"How did he mean, weird?" the big man asked, stopping the car and getting out.

"I'm getting to that." Ronny Patch got out, too. He removed his stained Mets cap, did some quick gardening on the short lawn of his hair, and replaced his scrofulous headgear. "So I got over and start hittin' on her and she comes on to me. And we go back to her place. And her apartment's kind of weird, too. Stars and planets everywhere. And posters of guys with an extra eye in their foreheads. Weird stuff like that."

Van Boder began to chuckle as they walked toward the shack; Ronny Patch sure knew how to tell a story. "So then what happened?"

Patch checked out a milky morning sky and continued. "So we shuck our duds and hit the sack. And I'm just about to help myself to the smorgasbord when I see I've left the light on." He fished out keys as they approached the house and selected one. "Now, I hate doing it with the light on. I like a little mystery, you know? So I tell her, hold up, I'll just switch the light out. And she says, 'Don't bother, I'll do it from here.' Well, it must've been, what, twenty feet to that light switch, but I tell you, when I see what she's doing, I grab my pants, rush out of that place, and don't stop running till I hit Fourteenth Street."

Van Boder, the perfect audience, said, "Why? What did she do?"

"She reaches out and, I swear to God, her arm stretches all the way along one wall, turns the corner, and travels all the way along the adjoining wall until it hits the fuckin' light switch."

Van Boder went into a series of chortling snorts. "Bullshit."

"I swear to God. I tell you, Vee Bee, there are some weird fuckin' broads walking around loose."

Ronny Patch moved up to the door, ignoring the settled pool of water he had to step in—less than twenty minutes ago, Brian and Marie had filled several cans from the washroom tap and poured the water under the door—and inserted a key into the shoulder-level mortise lock. He turned it three times, then grasped the rusted knob to pull the door open.

And instantly earthed a 120-volt short circuit caused by the fusion of two wires—exposed to nakedness by the sharp edge of a chisel—which had previously been enclosed within the power cord of a beat-up Chinese fan heater.

Patch was hurled back, smacking down onto the puddled ground as if an enraged wrestler had flung him aside. Arms and legs stretched out wide, he lay there in the mud, his left hand pulsing with a crimson burn, afloat in fathoms of unconsciousness.

Van Boder was flabbergasted.

There'd been no spark, no noise, no snap, crackle, or pop. Just his jaunty, irrepressible pal suddenly knocked flat on his ass.

It took him a moment to mentally regroup, to realize that the people inside had somehow booby-trapped the place, and that he was lucky it wasn't him lying there.

He trotted to the car. Opened the trunk. Pushed aside the chain lengths they'd bought to weigh down the bodies, and found a tire iron near the spare. He trotted back. Shoved the end of the tool into the edge of the door, corded his exceptional biceps, and pulled.

His enormous strength forced the door partially open snapping the stripped wires that ran from a power point to a twined grip around the inside doorknob. With his gun out, and his gritted teeth slitting his undersized eyes, Van Boder smashed the door all the way open with a mulelike kick and saw, as light spilled into the interior, an empty room.

"All right, you fuckers, I wanna see your faces."

The empty space looked back at him.

"If I have to come get you, I'll tan your backsides."

Not a peep; just the slow swirl of dust motes in the early light.

"O-*kay!*" Van Boder moved cautiously forward and sprang through the door, expertly covering each side of it.

His eyes swept the room. Took in the greasy workbench, the old phone books, and the broken vise in the shelving against the wall, the bits and pieces of junk here and there . . . the room looked the same but different somehow.

He crossed to the doorway that led to the rear section. Could practically see the priest flattened against the other side with a piece of timber in his hands. He called out, "I'm coming through, Father. You try to nail me, I'll break your fuckin' jaw."

He stamped his foot to fake an advance, then darted through in a crouch, gun up and covering.

Nothing.

Van Boder checked the washroom, then moved toward the storeroom, the only other place they could be.

He issued his threat again before bounding into it.

He swiveled left and right in one swift movement, then relaxed and sniggered through his nose. Over in a corner, some lumber had been stacked vertically against the wall like an Indian tepee.

"Ooh! I wonder where they can be," Van Boder said, as if he were playing with children. He stomped across the floor and kicked down the shelter.

And revealed nothing but dust and a bunch of yellowed newspapers.

Van Boder swung around, his mouth dropping an inch. Jesus Christ, they'd *gone*!

Wait a second . . . nobody walks through walls. Somebody must've let 'em out. But the colonel had the only other key. And why would he want to booby-trap the place? He had to call the colonel, quick.

He trotted out into the main room.

And stopped in his tracks.

Like a stage magician's pretty assistant, the blonde had suddenly appeared—standing in the middle of the room looking calmly back at him.

Van Boder stared at her. For the moment he was more interested in answers than dishing out punishment. "Where the hell have you been? Where the fuck *were* you?"

He didn't notice that the shelving against the wall, the rough bookcase that fitted almost exactly into the closet opening, had been moved out slightly.

Marie pointed a finger. "Up in the roof."

Van Boder tipped his head back. The ceiling looked impregnable. "How the hell did you—?" He broke off. The woman had skipped out the door.

"Hey!" He charged after her. Charged out of the door.

And ran straight into a rusty drive shaft that came lashing around and smashed into his right knee.

Van Boder screamed and thwacked down into the mud, his gun flying from his hand.

Brian raised his weapon again, but the big man was out of it, his face contorted, his eyes jammed shut as he clutched his broken kneecap.

Brian left him. Hurried to Marie, who was checking on Patch.

When Brian found that he hadn't killed the guy, he broke out into a sweat of relief.

Marie rolled the unconscious man onto his side and moved his head back to clear his airway. Then she pulled his gun and held on to it.

They went back to Van Boder. The Dutchman was blinking repeatedly, fighting against shock and foggily trying to understand how he could so quickly have become a crumpled wreck.

"I'll make a deal with you," Brian said to him. "Answer some questions and we'll call an ambulance. Don't answer, and you don't even get an aspirin. What's it going to be?"

He was bluffing but Van Boder was in no shape to think straight. Through a haze of pain he nodded his outsized head.

Brian's first question was one he'd stored up for a long time. "What the hell's this all about? Who's pulling the strings?"

Van Boder got out sections of sentences in a chesty rasp. "Willard hired 'em . . . Buehl and Gold."

"Howard Willard?" Brian traded a quick look with Marie. That was a surprise. "What's supposed to happen?"

"They're gonna hit him . . . Heloum."

"When? Where?"

"Tonight . . . that meeting in Atlanta."

Marie spoke evenly. "Go," she said to Brian. "Call the cops."

Brian jumped up, then stopped. "I have to keep going, Marie."

"I know," she said, aware that there was some kind of destiny at work for Brian Sheridan. "I'll catch you up down there."

"You'll be okay here?"

Ignoring that, Marie said, "You'll need some help. I'll call Jack Morrisey and have somebody meet your plane."

Brian gave that a fast nod and splashed through the mud to the Plymouth. Found the keys in the ignition. Sent the big car whining backward down the ruined alley, plunged out onto Bay Street, and sped a hundred yards to a drugstore. Charged in, broke a bill, ran to the phones in the rear, and called the police and an ambulance.

His second call was to information, which gave him a number in a hurry. He called it. Got an answer on the first ring.

"Atlanta Police . . ."

"Give me somebody in charge, quick!"

"What is the nature of your call, sir?" The woman's voice tinkled with the lazy notes of Southern speech.

He tried to keep from gabbling. "My name's Sheridan. Father Brian Sheridan. I have definite knowledge of an imminent attempt on the life of the man who claims he's Jesus Christ."

"Thank you, Father. I'll pass that information on right away."

Brian spoke faster. "Look, this is not a crank call. They're going to kill that man today."

"I wouldn't worry, Father. He has 'round-the-clock protection."

"Not from people like this. Who's in charge of him?"

"Lieutenant Burdette."

"Let me speak with him. Now!"

"I can't do that. But I'll see that he gets your message. Thank you for your call, Father."

In Atlanta, on the first floor of the police precinct on Decatur Street, the woman who'd taken Brian's call relayed the information to the appropriate department, then turned to her associate sitting next to her at the switchboard. "They're out in numbers today, darlin'. That's my third J.C. death threat so far."

"Beat you," the other woman bragged. "I got five."

CHAPTER
24

At around 10:00 A.M., when Brian Sheridan was boarding a flight for Atlanta, Father Franco Santoro was nervously meeting one at Hartsfield, the city's international airport.

He watched a group of people emerge, just about all of them towheads, perhaps from the Midwest, he thought, recalling the nineteenth-century Scandinavian and German immigration. They had that flat, pasty look of American Protestants, the men big and meaty, the women all with the same tight hairstyle, their broad hips bulging with surplus pounds, their fulsome sweatshirts bearing the statement Jesus Has Come Back. Pilgrims here for the prayer meeting, Santoro figured, an assumption that carried with it a sudden juddering fear.

Jesus has come back.

It was a moment before he was able to concentrate on the next group of travelers to emerge. These people were much smaller in stature than the previous group, darker complexioned and cheerfully boisterous or tearfully dramatic as they fell into the loud embraces of equally demonstrative relatives. He didn't need anyone to tell him that the Delta flight from Rome via New York had landed.

He stood off to one side in the noisy terminal, feeling upset and foolishly conspicuous holding a single carnation as he was; he thought he must look like an upright dead body clutching a flower.

But conspicuous was what he was supposed to be, he reminded himself, the single blossom being for purposes of identification even though the contact man in the Palermo *bottega* would have described him to Vizzini: short and dumpy, maybe even fat and jowly, Santoro thought unhappily.

He watched the passengers stream out into the world his countryman had discovered just over five hundred years ago. He tried to spot Vizzini but, not having received a description, he was just guessing. What does a killer look like, he wondered: would he have dead eyes and an expressionless face the way they were popularly portrayed in the cinema? Or would he—"You waiting for me?" somebody coming around behind him asked in Sicilian.

He looked normal, average, a forty-year-old worker from a ceramics factory or an assembly plant. His black hair was slicked back without a part, the eyes not warm, maybe, but not cold either. The skin of his cheeks advertised an outlaw perhaps, being pocked and cratered, but he didn't hulk or glower, and his full-lipped, Mediterranean mouth was not the cruel slash it might have been.

"Vizzini?"

The man nodded.

Moisture chilled the priest's flanks and iced the back of his knees; this was a man who brought down people with a rifle like a hunter does a deer, or waited in dark stairways, his hand warming the cold metal of a revolver, then stepped out and shot someone in the face. He was talking to a multiple murderer whom he'd met, as arranged by phone, holding a red carnation.

Franco Santoro fisted his hands to fight off a shudder, and wondered how steady his voice was sounding. "The taxis are this way." He discarded the flower on the way to the exit, where he saw the Midwestern group boarding a bus.

Jesus has come back.

In the cab Vizzini unwrapped a sugar cube he'd evidently brought with him off the plane. Santoro watched the stumpy fingers, the meticulously clipped nails neatly tear at the paper. He watched the powerful index finger of the man's right hand. Saw it embracing a trigger. Ligaments and muscles tightening their grip, coaxing the little metal tongue backward, gently and insistently se-

ducing oiled metallic tension. In spite of the air-conditioning
Santoro was sweating heavily.

"So how's it look?" Vizzini asked, watching the traffic build up
on the interstate. He'd done work before in the States, traded jobs
with some of the local families. The country didn't impress him
much. As they said back in the Cala, if you go to America, take
sandwiches and a thermos of coffee.

"Everything's ready," Santoro answered, after taking a moment
to gather himself. They could speak openly: the driver had an Ar-
menian name, and even if he'd been Italian he would have had a
hard time understanding Sicilian. It was doubtful he could have
heard them anyway with his radio blaring the way it was.

"The . . . the gentleman in question will be attending a meeting
this evening," Santoro said, the wobble in his voice plain now.
"You have a hotel room that will give you . . . a good view."

Vizzini unwrapped another sugar cube, popped it into his
mouth, and let it melt on the back of his tongue. "What about the
kicker?"

There were many new street expressions that Santoro's ancient
Sicilian didn't encompass; surely he had to be talking about the
police. "There'll be no trouble with the law. They'll have their
hands full with the crowds."

"Not the law. The rifle." Vizzini said it in the same even tone,
but Santoro, blushing, saw that the man now knew he was dealing
with an amateur, if indeed he hadn't realized it from the very first.

"It's a six-point-seven," Santoro said with a sudden surge of
hazy memory.

Vizzini slow blinked him. "There's no such thing as a six-point-
seven. Has it been delivered?"

Santoro shakily confirmed it. When he'd called the *bottega*
owner in Palermo and told him where he was staying, a man had
arrived a few hours later with a heavy golf bag bristling with a
professional set of black graphite clubs. There were little red sock-
like covers on three of the metal woods. The fourth little red sock
cleverly concealed the blued steel barrel of a rifle. The man had
also supplied him with a hotel key.

Vizzini said nothing more and, thirty minutes later, battling
traffic in the swollen downtown section, they pulled up at the rear

entrance of the hotel, where the man who'd brought the golf bag had booked a room using a stolen Italian credit card owned by Aldo H. Cremici. The reservation had been made with the aid of a plain white envelope containing five one-hundred-dollar bills; there wasn't a desk clerk in the city who wasn't cleaning up, according to the man.

They paid off the cab and went straight up in the elevator. Santoro had already been up there that morning to drop off the golf bag.

He used the key again. Let them both into the room.

Vizzini dropped his cloth suitcase, went straight to the window, and pulled the internal drapes. "That it?" he asked.

With a fuzzy gripping sensation in his stomach Santoro joined him. Looked out at the steps of the Civic Center nine stories below and directly opposite. The crowds, already growing, milled around the steps, swaying gently like a turgid sea. Huge red-and-white banners were all over the building as if some avant-garde artist had attempted to wrap the place.

Jesus Has Come Back, the banners screamed.

Something somersaulted in Santoro's gut.

Vizzini examined the small windows on each side of the main window, sections about two feet square that slid back for fresh air for those guests allergic to air-conditioning. He checked the fine wire screening behind them. "Let's see the piece," he said.

Santoro stared at him.

"The rifle," the other man clarified, although it wasn't terminology that had stopped the priest. He shambled like a sick man over to the closet. Came back with the golf bag.

Vizzini pulled the rifle out. Pulled off its red cap. Expertly checked the weapon over. "Six-point-five Remo with a Zeiss Diavary. Good, I like a floating dot. I guess it's been bore-sighted. Sure it has. What's the drop rate, one and a half at seven hundred?" He looked up and saw he'd been talking gibberish to this fat man. A fat, ill-looking man. "You got a problem?"

Santoro made a tethered sound that could have been a yes or a no.

Vizzini picked up a round from a box of shells. Liked what he saw and broadcast his pleasure. "One-fifty grain with an expanding tip. Nice. When it hits him the lead'll flatten and peel the casing back. It'll open up to the size of a stuffed olive and evacuate whatever's in front of it. Bone, muscle, sinew, the works."

It was the use of the word *evacuate* that brought a fresh rush of nausea, a clean, pristine word, academically medical and horribly unsuitable for describing the grievous rending of flesh. Flesh that had already been subjected to the hideous agony of the . . . flesh that had already been subjected to hideous agony.

"I have to go," Santoro said, breathily.

Vizzini returned the bullet to the box. "What time you gonna be back?" When the fat man looked as if this question was too much for his mind to evaluate, Vizzini took it easy on the dope. "I guess I don't need you. I guess I'm not gonna have much trouble recognizing Jesus, right?"

He thought the guy was going to heave. He made a stab at bucking him up. "Does this joker ride around the streets? You seen him while you been here?"

Santoro gave him a slow nod.

"Is he really a ringer for Jesus?"

"Yes."

"No kidding . . ." Vizzini snorted and shook his head at crazy America.

"He looks just like Jesus. He is quite beautiful," Santoro said, his words sounding as if they were strained through muslin. "There is pain in his eyes, although not on his face. You've never seen anybody so tranquil yet so all-knowing."

Vizzini looked at his client for an extended moment wondering if he were on something. "Is that right?"

Santoro was regarding the weapon in the Sicilian's capable hands, the evil darkness of the barrel through which one of those awful bullets would hurtle with shocking power and intent. He gave a gasp like a moan, turned away, and walked in a half stumble toward the door.

For two solid hours he sat in his cheap hotel room dwelling on the astonishing event he'd witnessed in the garden of a suburban house a few days ago.

He'd thought of little else since.

He'd seen it with his own two eyes: the Transfiguration. Jesus had done this during his first ministry to intimate his coming resurrection to his disciples. Was it to happen again—no, that wasn't what he meant to think, that simply couldn't be, he meant to think something else like . . . something else.

He tried to still the projections tumbling inside his skull. Tried to blank the spaces behind his eyes.

Santoro was predisposed to sorcery, enchantment, thaumaturgy. His mother had been from a tiny town in the boot of Italy, a village called Buonabitacolo, a minute gathering of cottages slumbering in ignorance at the foot of mysterious Mount Cervati. In his mother's day they'd still worshiped the Black Virgin of Viggiano in her black robes and her jewelry, back when processions were closer to pagan ritual than Christian veneration, with leaping goats and braying donkeys and weeping peasants throwing fistfuls of wheat at the statue to break the drought, the madonna a subterranean deity thousands of years older than the Mother of God. Santoro's uncles had ventured forth in the dead of night to try to grab hold of an elf's red hood, which was the only way a gnome would tell you where he'd hidden his cache of gold. For many years the local church had contained, in a glass case, the horns of a dragon. The women of the village had special knowledge: at full moon, for example, the wife of a cripple must never let her husband in until the third knock, for to answer the door at the first or second knock would be to let in the fanged beast he'd become. One of the women had been a witch, a dried-up hag who'd make love potions for young virgins from frog spawn and a drop of menstrual blood. Her husband was a warlock who'd been struck dumb for treading on the devil's tail.

The black jewel of superstition glittered deep within Franco Santoro, as much a part of his makeup as the color of his irises or the whorls on the tips of his chubby fingers. It pulled and tugged at him, warping common sense and negating established belief.

Now, at noontime in Atlanta, it dragged him to his feet.

Got him over to the phone.

At 6:00 P.M. the Roman sun was still an oval oven roasting a city whose inhabitants had once viewed it as an unknowable and blinding deity. The heat moved in slow, roiling waves attacking all and respecting nothing, not even the Holy See, where Father Gaetano Cresta sat frowning in his study.

The object of his ire was an article in *Concilium*, the multilanguage review which often carried the views of radical theologians. The writer complained of institutional arthritis in the Church, a lack of imagination and an absence of critical spirit and creativity. Cresta smacked the paper down onto his desk. The fool! The Church didn't have to imagine anything because the Holy Scriptures were its guide and constant referral. And as for creativity— the buzz of the phone interrupted this mental rebuke: Ludovisi, his secretary, informing him of a call from America.

Cresta picked up. "Yes?"

The voice in his ear was shaky and opaque. "Father Cresta, it's Father Santoro."

"Yes . . ."

"The . . . the job you asked me to do for you . . ."

"What about it?"

"I don't think we should do it."

Cresta had been half expecting this phone call, had wondered if the man might exhibit vacillation, cowardice, and lack of resolve when it got close to the actual act. An appeal to duty would not work now; it was time to bear down with something more concrete. In spite of his fears regarding security Cresta spoke out, and with iron in his throat. "Now, listen to me, Father. It would be wholly unacceptable for you to return without carrying out the obligation you were charged with. In fact, I think you'd find it pointless because if you fail me, if you fail the Church on whose behalf you are acting, I will move to have your duties here severely reduced."

On the other side of a blue sea, a baking peninsula, and a mighty ocean, Santoro gasped. Remove him from his job? The dream position of spending all day engrossed in the endless fascination of postage stamps, their history, their provenance, their value? How unfair!

"Father Cresta, if you could just see this person . . . there is . . . there's some doubt in my mind—"

"There's none in mine, Father. Carry out your instructions. Efficiently and with zeal. Fail, and I'll see that you're disciplined to the harshest degree."

Floundering in a miasma of dismay and fear, Santoro heard Cresta's phone drop onto its cradle.

It sounded like a guillotine at the end of its lethal plunge.

CHAPTER
25

At that moment, at the domestic section of Hartsfield airport, Brian Sheridan walked off a Delta 727 and hurried into a crowded terminal.

The first thing he saw was people waiting on each side of the gate to greet the arriving passengers. The second thing he saw was one of those people holding up a piece of cardboard with his name lettered on it.

The man who'd come to meet him might have starred on the football field once, although he clearly hadn't used his retirement as an excuse to blow up. Around forty years old, he looked as though he'd still be good for a few first downs, a neck as solid as a tree trunk rising out of a floral-patterned beach shirt. His face had known contact but, given his height and weight, whoever had been on the receiving end had known contact of a greater kind.

"I'm Sheridan," Brian said, stopping in front of him.

"Larry Bolling." He had a strong man's soft grip; he'd learned to take it easy on mere mortal folk.

"Would you mind if I asked you for some ID?"

The man showed Brian a Georgia driver's license in the name of Lawrence R. Bolling, and a business card: Acclaim Security Consultants with an address on Charles Allen Drive. Brian felt a little foolish asking for verification but not as foolish as he'd felt when Patch and Van Boder had tricked him back in Beechwood.

Bolling filled Brian in on the way into town. "A woman named Marie called the office. She gave me a message for you. The two guys, Bohl and Gold, is it?"

"Buehl and Gold."

"Buehl and Gold. Jack Morrisey can't locate them. He's gonna keep trying. Marie will be getting in around four. She'll call the office so you two can meet up somewhere. You want to tell me what's going on?" He had a steel-town hardness in his tones. Cleveland or Pittsburgh, Brian guessed.

"You know a guy named Howard Willard?"

"Bagley's number two? Sure."

"He hired Buehl and Gold. They run a think-tank operation. They came up with the Jesus fake."

Larry Bolling looked wise. "I figured it had to be Bagley. He's the one that's getting all the gain. His show's bigger than the Sunday-night movie."

"Bagley's out of the loop. It's all Willard."

Bolling took his eyes off the road long enough to glance at his passenger. "He's doing his boss a favor?"

"Could be. I don't know why he's doing it. But I do know that the fake is due to be killed at that prayer meeting tonight."

"Pro job?"

"Yep."

Bolling didn't show any surprise; he evidently knew that the life of a snake-oil salesman, even one said to be divinely inspired, is seldom a long one. "You got anything you can take to the cops?"

"Not a damn thing. Buehl sent two goons to put us away, but they had some trouble. However, I doubt they'll cooperate with the police. One of them's probably in intensive care anyway."

Once again Bolling checked with his passenger. Brian's clothes were grubby and sweat-stained. He'd managed a fast cleanup in the washroom at La Guardia, but his sleepless night had left him with the red eyes of a drunk. Bolling wondered if the guy was a black belt or something.

"So you're banking on Jack Morrisey finding Buehl or Gold," the bodyguard said, extrapolating. "If he could persuade them to call off the mechanic, you're in good shape."

"When and where is this prayer meeting?"

"Six o'clock at the Civic Center. They're plugging it like Coca-Cola. The crackers'll go for anything down here."

Brian looked at the clock on the dash. Twenty minutes past noon. Jack Morrisey had less than six hours to find Buehl or his partner. "How can I get in touch with Willard?"

"He's at Bagley's house." Bolling switched lanes for the downtown exit. The traffic was incredible. "They all are. Bagley, Willard, and the Miracle Man."

Brian nodded at the car phone. "Could I reach Willard on that?"

"Nope. Bagley's had all the phones cut off."

"Then we'll have to go there."

Larry Bolling moistened a tiny smile. "You must be new in town. The place is surrounded by fainting worshipers. We'd be lucky to get close enough to mail him a letter."

"What do you say we try?"

"You're the client," Bolling said, his tone signifying the beginning of a futile exercise. But Brian was confident, and buoyed by that confidence. It wasn't a confrontation with Howard Willard that bumped his pulse, it was the fact that Camille Heloum would be at that house. If they could get in, he'd at last meet up with Jesus Christ.

Or at least a pretty good facsimile.

They would never have got anywhere near the house had Bolling not recognized a cop working crowd control.

"Hey, Frank . . ."

"Larry . . . what the hell are you doin' here? You get religion or something?"

They squeezed through solid humanity—the crowds filled the street from one side to the other in an unbroken phalanx—and made it to the police barrier. Bolling indicated Brian. "I gotta get my client up to the gates."

"You'll need a backhoe to get through."

Bolling dropped his voice. "There's a bullet waiting for the Jesus freak. We gotta talk to his handlers."

"Shit," the cop said, impressed by the sudden drama in his day.

He got them through the crowd with a combination of verbal

threats and physical bullying, and left them in front of the gates. Behind the gates, a puffed-cheek security guard looked at them with up-front disinterest.

"Excuse me," Brian began.

The guard ambled up. Said, sourly, "Yeah?"

"I need to get a message to Mr. Willard."

"So send up a smoke signal."

"Please. This is extremely urgent."

"Okay, but it'll cost you a hundred bucks."

Larry Bolling stepped up. He shot a hand through the railings, grabbed the guard's blue shirt, and pulled him into the gates. "You'll do it for ten bucks," he said into the surprised face. "And you'll do it now."

"Okay, okay," the guard said quickly.

Bolling released him. The guard stepped back and tried to dignify his backdown. "The boss don't like us running errands. You know how it is."

"Tell Mr. Willard," Brian said, "that Camille Heloum is here to see him. Camille Heloum."

The guard went into the gatehouse and used an internal line. He was back a minute later to unlock the gates and open them just wide enough for Brian and his bodyguard to squeeze through. He took them up the pebbled drive in an electric golf buggy, and let them off outside the French windows. He got out himself and rubbed a thumb and forefinger together in a gimme gesture.

"Oh, yeah," Bolling said, as if he'd forgotten. "We said ten bucks, right?" He grabbed the guard, spun him, whipped a billfold out of the man's back pocket, pulled two fives from it, shoved the wallet back at the flummoxed guard, and tucked the money into his floral beach shirt. "Nice doing business with you," he said, and accompanied Brian toward the house.

"He was lucky you didn't offer him twenty," Brian said. He'd enjoyed Bolling's performance. The guy was hard and he was tough, and Brian wondered if he wasn't going to be thankful for such a man before too long. He'd already tipped his hand with Willard. It remained to be seen how Willard would react, and what forces he could bring to bear.

When they reached the patio, Brian asked Bolling to wait there for him as he was certain Willard would only talk in private. Bolling indulged him, although he made sure his presence could be noted from the house.

Brian stepped into the room, seven hundred square feet of mainly empty space now that Bagley's show was being shot there.

Howard Willard uncoiled from a director's chair. Even taller and thinner than he appeared on TV, he looked older, too, his heavy sweep of hair beginning to dull from white to pewter, lines the length and shape of arrowheads angling each side of a fine-boned and significant nose. The heavy white eyebrows might have come from a cheap disguise kit.

"Good morning," he said, confident and assured and on home ground in his evangelist's black suit. "I was told a Mr. Heloum had come to call, but you are not he."

He sounded different, too, Brian decided; he'd left behind the good ol' boy drawl in favor of correct grammar and an accent with just a hint of Texas around the edges.

"No, I'm not. My name's Sheridan."

"Then why did you lie to the gate man?"

"Because you wouldn't have agreed to see anyone named Sheridan. But Camille Heloum . . . that's different."

"I knew a Billy Ray Heloum at Bible college, and I thought that was who'd come to call. Alas, I find a stranger in my midst."

"Now you're lying to me, Mr. Willard."

"Reverend Willard." Then, with no change in his pleasant manner, he said, "I find you impertinent, Mr. Sheridan."

"It's Father Sheridan. My bishop finds me impertinent, too."

"You're a priest?"

"Swear to God," Brian said innocently.

"Why do I doubt that?"

"You're right, nuns are easier to tell. Their faces are unlined." Brian was following a strategy: match his opponent's brimming confidence. Keep it light. Play the part of a man with aces in the hole, then, bam! turn over the cards and hit him with those aces. Already he could see a glint of uncertainty in Willard's face; he clearly didn't know what he had here.

"A little test, then," the tall man said. "What was the name of the pope who was recognized for hundreds of years, then banished from the papal list?"

"Oh, you mean Pope Joan in the ninth century. Some say she reigned for three years, but Stephen of Bourbon says she gave birth during the procession to the Lateran, whereupon she was immediately dragged out of Rome and stoned to death, thus proving that you can only fool some of the people some of the time. And speaking of fooling some of the people, Reverend, your Jesus is a priest of the Syrian Church, an instructor at a seminary in Elton, Ontario. His stigmata were surgically gained, courtesy of a Dr. Wassenaer in Hatfield, New York, on the orders of Colonel Buehl, whose partner is Cedric Gold. You're their client. Would you care to comment on any of that, or would you rather talk about Pope Joan?"

Willard took it well. He was staggered but he did a good job of keeping his shock a secret. When his eyes flicked to the man out on the patio, Brian was way ahead of him.

"I think he has a gun under that beach shirt. And even if you did bring that chandelier down on my head, I have a partner who knows as much as I do."

Willard nodded as if grateful for the information. It appeared to Brian that the man thought his best defense would be a light smile and some plain talk.

"Did you discover all this?"

"With my partner, yes."

"Well, Father, it would appear that you and your partner have been busy little beavers." He was silent for a few moments, then his smile graduated to a small laugh. "Damn," he said, almost thoughtfully. "Undone by the Catholic Church. Heloum never should have mouthed off against you guys."

"The monster always destroys its creator, Reverend. That's classic."

"You're not wearing a wire, are you? No, I don't think so. It's inadmissable anyway in this state." For a brief moment Willard appeared to be somewhere between concern and irritation, then reverted back to his role of thinking man. "You don't have any proof of this. If you did, you would've brought the police."

"They'll be here, just as soon as one of my confederates can locate Buehl or Gold and offer them a deal."

"You obviously haven't met the colonel."

"I've spoken with him."

"How did he sound to you?"

"As if he'd been sipping cement."

"That's the colonel. He wouldn't go for a plea. He'd regard it as caving in to the enemy. As for Gold, he's so eccentric I don't think a shorter jail term would mean much to him as long as he could read his Bible in prison. So I wouldn't count on either of those two. And anybody Buehl hires won't talk. And he's made certain that those he thought might are no longer with us."

"Including Camille Heloum, who, I believe, is due to check out at six o'clock tonight."

Howard Willard shifted his weight on his narrow feet and remained silent.

"Anyway," Brian said, "Father Zaim will talk. We'll offer him a gym to go with his new library."

"I wouldn't count on Father Zaim, either." Willard considered his situation for a moment. "No," he said, "any accusations of my involvement will be flimsy and unprovable allegations brought by a foreign religion whose Holy Roman nose has been put out of joint. The Church isn't too popular in these parts, Father. The Mass is seen as an exercise in mumbo-jumbo, and any institution headquartered in Europe is felt to be un-American."

Without a crushing rejoinder with which to refute any of this, Brian felt a little marooned. So he switched tactics. This was a prideful man standing in front of him, and you could always use sin against a sinner. "It was a great idea, Reverend. And brilliantly executed. I assume Heloum's light show for the clergy was a piece of electronics . . ."

"Buried lightning. I had the power button under my shoe."

"And the Lazarus number? I think that was my favorite."

Previously unable to brag about these stunts, Willard was happy for the chance now. "Doc Wassenaer, late of Hatfield, helped us out on that one. We got the gate man and the kid's riding instructor in on it. They slipped something into her cornflakes just before her morning ride. She got on the pony and fainted. The instructor gave her a shot of Fentanyl, a short-acting narcotic, blanked with Narcane. Wassenaer said the combination would produce a deathly pallor and fixed dilation of the pupils because there's no nerve stimulation from the brain. No pulse, no heartbeat. When it wears off, you revive. And he was right."

"Sensational stuff. Like I say, it was a great idea."

"It still is a great idea," Willard answered, ready to concede nothing.

"But what's the goal? It can't be to hype an already popular television ministry. Why are you doing it?"

For the first time Willard looked at this priest with something akin to amused contempt. It was as if, Brian felt, the man had suddenly been informed about the years he'd spent driving a dogged-out Ford through the frozen Wisconsin tundra, eating TV dinners by himself, and trying for ages to get the church furnace fixed.

"Why is anything done in this country, Father? Money."

"From where? Bagley didn't ask for any."

"Bagley . . ." Willard sneered at the name. "That idiot thinks selling Buicks is how you make money. He grew up dirt-poor, Father. I didn't. My daddy made a potful of money trading oil leases. Our family was rich for years until his luck ran out. So I looked around to see how I could make money because I didn't like being without it. It was kind of like the ghetto kid who decided to become a chef. Why? Because all the cooks he knew were fat. All the people I knew who were coining it were in the Jesus game. So I cracked the Bible, too, then grabbed hold of the shirttails of the most successful thumper of them all. And the dumbest. Trouble was, years later I was still on a goddamn salary. So I went up to New York and hired me some brains. My occupation fit right in with Cedric Gold's obsession, and he came up with the Second Advent."

"Uh-huh," said Brian, seeing it now. "And half the Bible Belt sent in money even though Bagley didn't ask for any. And you skimmed it."

Willard was shaking his head as if in the unrelenting grip of some kind of comical pain. "Drunkenness and molestation, the traditional crimes of the priesthood. It's rarely theft because you people don't understand money like us poor, spiritually incorrect

Protestant folk." Willard paused, a parody of pity in his slim smile. "The skim from those unrequested contributions barely paid for this production. The real gusher hasn't been drilled yet." Again Willard paused. "You still don't get it, do you, Bob?"

Brian waited. The man had explained why he had no fear of arrest, a position Brian couldn't refute. If somebody knew you'd stolen a cheap watch, and couldn't be apprehended for it, what did it matter if they knew you'd also stolen a diamond bracelet?

"When Jesus is gunned down tonight, his body will be whisked away. All they'll find an hour later is his bloodstained robe. A rumor will spring up that he was seen ascending to heaven. Then everybody will claim to have seen it, too. And a new religion is born. The Church of Jesus Come Again. Howard D. Willard, pastor. We'll clear a hundred million the first year. As the playwright said, what is stealing from a bank compared to owning one?"

The explanation caused no stunned intake of breath in Brian, no feeling of shock or horror, but rather a rueful confirmation of priestly naïveté in money matters. No one who seriously admired riches became a Catholic religious.

"Call it off, Willard. Tell your hit man to pack up his gun and go home."

"He's not my hit man, he's Buehl's. I haven't the first idea who he is or where he is."

"Then call Buehl and get him to call it off."

"Why?"

For the first time Brian began to feel a tentacle of anger enclose him. "Because it's all over, why do you think?"

"But it's not all over. It's just beginning."

Out on the patio Larry Bolling sensed the change in the room and took a half step toward it. He heard his charge increase his volume, although the words were still indistinct.

"Of course it's over. There's no way you can stay out of jail forever. And if you let this murder go ahead, they'll throw away the key."

"I'll probably do some time," Willard conceded, "but not a lot. If you're a Jesus man, this is a very forgiving part of the country. Jim Bakker was sentenced to forty-five years, but he only served five."

"Jim Bakker didn't have anybody killed."

"You're behind the times, Father. Killing isn't the heinous legal sin it once was. If you're the right color and you have money, a killer can get away with a slap on the wrist these days. I'll do seven, eight years tops. Get a good man to front for me and run the new religion from my jail cell. When I come out I'll take over. Most of my flock will believe I was railroaded, an opinion I'll make no move to dispel."

Listening to this confident appraisal, feeling heat scatter through his body, Brian was distressed by this cynical truth, and by a venality that was perfectly willing to trample lives and trade long years of incarceration in return for yachts and swimming pools.

"This is America, Father," Willard said, bringing off a mind reader's trick. "Money's what you're measured by."

"I have to talk to Heloum, Willard."

"And tell him what, that he's going to be killed in a few hours? I have news for you, Sheridan. I think he already suspects."

Far more than anything else he'd heard in that empty living room, this rocked Brian. The evangelist saw it and enjoyed his discomfort. He didn't like this priest whose overeducated mind was a lot sharper than his good looks and athletic build would have led anyone to believe. And he didn't like him for piercing the screen Gold had designed which had seemed impenetrable.

Brian brought himself an inch closer to the other man, a threat of physical punishment inherent in the move. "Where is he?"

Willard regained his seat in the director's chair, thus disguising a definite retreat. "There's an admission charge. Tell me how you found him, and I'll tell you where to find him."

"Willard," Brian said, quietly, "you're a tall, skinny piece of ordure. When I think of what you've caused, and why, I'm put in mind of what a gloomy Greek philosopher once said: 'Sleep is good, death is better, but best of all is never to have been born.' When he wrote those words he must've been thinking of someone like you."

Willard's reaction flooded his face. It was a good blow and well delivered, and he hated having to, literally, sit still for it. The best punishment he could devise was to let this meddling priest be tossed on the horns of Heloum's delusion. "He's in the bungalow in the garden."

Brian turned and left the room. Made a wait-for-me gesture to Bolling, swiftly crossed the lawn, passed beneath the big elm, and approached the little white bungalow he'd noticed on the way in.

Its shutters were closed. It looked empty.

Brian knocked on the door and entered, surprised to find a fine trembling at work beneath his skin.

He went into slate blue darkness, a hazy afternoon light filtering through the exterior louvers tinctured with a strange azure glow. He located the source of this artificial luminence: a twenty-gallon fish tank mounted on a sideboard, its occupants examining its perimeters with apparent unconcern. The bubble of the air filter played counterpoint to the hum of the tank's small electric motor. The only other sound was the scrape of a footstep.

Then a second one, heavier than the first.

Camille Heloum came out of the bedroom, and Brian was jolted. A stunning visual memory shot behind his eyes: the Palazzo Comunale in Rimini—della Francesca's painting of the Resurrection in which a dark-faced, heavy-lidded Christ holding a banner of victory stares at the viewer, his expression at once accusatory yet brimming with an immense sadness that a human being could be so poorly treated.

The man standing in the doorway, in a long-sleeved white shift, with his dark hair spilling to his shoulders, the beard untended except for a combed divide in the center, could have been the model for that painting. Or, more likely, Brian thought, slowly recovering from his shock, the other way around.

Even in the half-light he could see the destruction in the hands and feet. Knowing how those wounds had been induced, and imagining the long, lonely months of painful recovery, he winced in sympathy and brought his gaze back to the man's face. He'd never seen such tranquility in a person, such becalmed quietude. And yet it wasn't peace that dwelt behind those eyes; it was something closer to a hurt confusion, almost paralleling the della Francesca Jesus in his dismay at the easy cruelty of the dozing Roman soldiers at his feet.

"I'm Father Sheridan," Brian heard himself say in a voice that sounded tied off and constricted. When he saw a remote beginning of what might have been a protest at the intrusion, he kept speaking. "I know who you are, Father. You're Camille Heloum."

Brian couldn't tell whether this knowledge meant nothing or everything because there was no variance in those calm, Semitic features. Not for a moment, anyway. But then the gouged brow squeezed a ghost of a frown as if recall were being tested.

"I've been trying to find you for about a week now," Brian told him. "If it had taken a few hours longer, I would have missed you."

"Yes," Heloum said, whether a confirmation of simple chronology or a future calamitous event, Brian was unable to decide.

"Can we sit down?"

Heloum didn't seem to be able to fathom the question, so they remained standing. Brian ran down a mental checklist of all the things he'd been planning to ask this man, and tossed most of them out. There were only a couple of questions that mattered. "Why are you doing it, Camille?"

The fish in the blue-hued tank had time for another circuit before the answer arrived. "My Father sent me."

He spoke so quietly, his viscous accent degrading the pronunciation, that Brian thought he was referring to the seminary rector. "Father Zaim?"

Once again the brows knit in a jog of memory, but the bump wasn't powerful enough to drive speech. Brian presented a brutal truth. "They're going to kill you, Camille. At the prayer meeting tonight."

Over in the aquarium the clown loach dodged a territorial gourami while the motor hummed its monotonous tune.

Camille Heloum remained buried in his sarcophagus of repose.

"I've spoken to Willard," Brian told him. "He won't stop it. And I can't stop it because I have no proof to take to the police. You're the only one who can influence things. If you refuse to go, they can't drag you there. Not in front of all those people."

"I must go."

"Must? Why?"

"Because without resurrection, there can be no belief. And without death, there can be no resurrection."

Brian's quick breath sucked oxygen from a room which already seemed short of that commodity. This wasn't brainwashing. This was the Othello complex, an actor so immersed in the role that he goes home and kills his wife for an imagined infidelity. A complex was like a weather vane in a changing wind, Brian knew, presenting two different sides depending on caprice. Anyone in such a grip would have their lucid moments, too. And sometimes, such moments could be forced into being.

Brian went up to the man, because man was all he was: a marvelous double, an ersatz messiah. He grabbed his arms. They were thin under the shift, almost meatless. The arms of Jesus would probably have felt much the same.

"Listen to me, Camille. Resurrection only works if you're a rabbi from Nazareth, and it's doubtful even then. But it definitely won't work for a Syrian priest from Ontario."

Heloum was startled by the action, and perhaps by the words. Those heavy eyes blinked rapidly, and their focus shortened.

"Why did you do it, Camille? What did Willard offer you?"

Heloum seemed to arrive into his body, his original being taking the place of whatever had been there a moment before. "Restitution." The answer was pried from deep within the man's narrow throat.

"For what?" Brian asked, realization occurring the moment the words were vocalized. Camille Heloum: he'd had the name in his head now for forty-eight hours without realizing he'd known it for five years. Father Heloum, of the University of Thessaloníki, was the author of a brilliant series of commentaries on John of Ephesus, the sixth-century Syrian monk who was said to have written a definitive life of Christ, tragically lost in the Byzantine persecution. Heloum had claimed to have discovered the lost manuscript, but the work had been shown to have sprung from his own fertile imagination. He'd vanished from academe. And then, Brian now knew, surfaced quietly as an instructor in a Canadian seminary.

Willard had obviously induced him to take part in this masquerade by offering whatever it was he most wanted. And the scholar in Brian was certain that what Heloum wanted was money enough to spend a lifetime roaming the libraries of the East looking for the real manuscript.

So how about that? Brian thought to himself: Camille Heloum and Brian Sheridan, scholars both. One of them playing Jesus, the other chasing Jesus.

Or running from him.

Brian stepped back. "He was lying to you, Camille. This role you've been playing is only half over. You have to die in full view for Willard's plan to work. And he's not about to drug you like he did Bagley's little girl. He has to make sure you're out of the way. Alive, you're a potential embarrassment to him. Dead, you're worth millions. Dead, you become the foundation of a new church. A new religion."

"And so it was with Jesus. He had to die in full view for it to suit God's purpose. Alive, he was only a teacher, loved by some, hated by most. Dead and risen from that death, he was worshiped by all in his new church."

"The difference is, Camille, once *you're* dead, you're going to stay that way."

Heloum swayed, drew himself up, and looked at this interloper with a gaze that seemed filtered through frosted glass. "Unless a grain of wheat falls to the ground and dies, it remains only a single seed. But if it dies, it produces many seeds. The man who loves his life will lose it, while the man who hates his life in this world will keep it for eternity."

And Heloum hated his life, Brian saw, hated being branded a cheat and a liar. Loathed the forced anonymity of a small seminary in a tiny town in the vastness of Canada.

Brian knew his appeal had failed; the other entity Heloum had become had reasserted itself. The man was Jesus, and Brian had no blandishments with which to argue him out of the glorification he was certain he owed the world.

Brian left him contemplating, with an untroubled understanding, his coming demise.

Outside, beneath a hot pinwheeling sun, the afternoon was lit like a stage set after the blue gloom of the bungalow.

Larry Bolling crossed the grass to meet him. "What did Willard say? Did you get to see the freak?"

"His name's Heloum," Brian answered. "And the only way we can stop him from being killed is to find the guy who's been hired to kill him."

Bolling hefted his linebacker's shoulders, checked his watch, drew air across the white evenness of his teeth, and leveled with his client. "We've got a little under three hours. We need about five times that."

The only way they could get close to the steps of the Civic Center was to drive by them. Fortunately for their reconnaissance, the traffic was so tangled they were able to do this at a stop-and-go pace, which gave Larry Bolling time to check out the immediate area, although time was what they least had to spare.

They lost a little more of it waiting for a car-park jockey, but by then Bolling had found out what he wanted, and he explained what that was as they entered the lobby of the hotel that stood opposite the banner-bedecked building.

"First of all, we can forget about anywhere between the Center and Bagley's house because the limos they've been using all have smoked-glass windows. The shooter will time his shot for when Heloum gets out of the limo and walks up the steps. He'll be using a rifle because he'll want to be remote from the job so he can walk away. And the only place that'll give him the right line on the steps is this hotel right here."

Brian resisted the impulse to immediately start checking out the lobby; with less than three hours to go the assassin would surely be in place. "Could he be on the roof?"

"Nope. He'd be right under a cop chopper. He's in one of the rooms on the front of the house."

"So we have hotel security search the rooms?"

Bolling wagged his head in a negative. "We'd have to show 'em hard evidence that there's a gunman on the premises, and we can't do that."

"We can at least knock on doors . . ."

"How do we recognize him? Hit men don't have shifty eyes and livid scars down their cheeks. They're just folks. No, all we can do is this: I know the security boss here. He'll get me a guest list if I ask him nice. Then we narrow it down from that."

"And if we end up with six or eight likely suspects?"

Larry Bolling synchronized the raising of his big hands and his faint eyebrows. "Then we get a pin, close our eyes, and play pin the tail on the donkey."

CHAPTER
26

At that moment, six stories above the lobby, and a little to the right, Li Xiayong picked up the Stanley knife he'd been given, pushed out the blade, crossed to the window, slid open one of the lower sections, and cut a long X in the wire screening, neatly and cleanly so it would be invisible from more than a few feet away.

He fetched the rifle from where he'd hidden it—it had been waiting for him in the checkroom just as his gruff employer had promised—unhinged the metal stock, locked it off, then sat on the carpet in front of the window and leaned the muzzle of the barrel through the hole he'd cut. He put his shooting eye to the scope and adjusted its focus. The front steps of the Civic Center leaped into his vision, the definition sharp in the refulgent light of the fine afternoon; he could easily make out the earrings on a woman pressed against a police barrier.

He got up and slid the rifle back into its hiding place. There was nothing more to do except load the weapon, but he wouldn't do that till later, a little superstition he liked to indulge. He checked the position of the hands on his wristwatch. Four-thirty. He'd been in the room reading his Koran for about nine hours straight now. Earlier that day, with the sun beginning to assume its fiery identity, Li had watched its slow ascent on his second day in the city. With his face pinked by the rising orb, and facing in the direction of the Holy of Holies, he'd spread his silk Hereke rug, gone through three *rak'ah* units, then, from a prostrate position, said the *shadadah*, the profession of faith, aloud, correctly, and purposefully, with an understanding of its meaning and with an assent from the heart: There is no god but Allah and Muhammad is his Prophet.

He'd risen, placed his prayer rug over the back of a chair—he'd be needing it again in a few hours—gone into the bathroom and returned a minute later, his narrow ribs glistening with olive oil mixed with a drop of patchouli. He'd moved a cloth over his flanks, around his thin neck and through the sparse bush under his unmuscled arms, then, relaxed by the eminence of ritual, watched the sun swoop on the roof of the Atlanta Civic Center below. Even though it was backlit, night shadows lingering around its front facade, he could still make out the banners that festooned the building, harbingers of today's big event, whatever that was. He was glad he couldn't read those banners, they were prettier that way. He'd wondered what it must be like for the big noses who came to China and couldn't read the signs there. Even a sign for a rubbish bin must look magnificent in the Divine Language if done by a learned hand in red brushstroke on a field of gold.

He'd dressed quickly in suit pants, white shirt, nylon socks, and his plain black lace-ups, opened the manila envelope, and taken another long look at the ascetic face in the photographs. It had a quality, that visage, peace and suffering in the darkness of the eyes, and hurt in the ungenerous mouth—strange qualities, he thought, to find in a rock musician.

Li had left the room and taken the elevator down to the lobby, a cleaner vacuuming the carpet his only witness.

Out in the parking lot he found a good clear spot and stood still and relaxed, feet apart and parallel, head held high as if suspended from the roil of cumulus gathering in the north. Slowly he lowered his arms to hip level, palms facing down, knees bending. He rose up again, paused, then, shifting his weight to his left leg and pivoting on his right heel, made a semicircle with his right hand, shifted his weight again, drew his left hand toward his feeble torso, and grasped the bird's tail.

He raised and flexed his left foot, extended his arms forward, elbows slightly bent, rocked gracefully forward, and played the fiddle. Then turning on his left heel, he wheeled his body to the southeast, shaped his hands, pushed the air with his left palm, and carried the tiger to the mountain.

He went through the entire eighty-eight movements, folding each one into the other with seamless ease, concentrated in mind and nimble in body, letting the vital force penetrate from his cranium to the soles of his feet.

He'd performed the concluding movement, the Ho Ta'i Chi, then, with his internal organs exercised, his whole system warmed and facilitating the unobstructed circulation of his blood, he'd recrossed the parking lot to the hotel coffee shop. He sat at the counter and ordered eggs but only for the grits that came with them. He liked grits; they were not unlike the corn *congee* he ate everyday in a basement restaurant on Mott Street.

When he'd finished the dish, and several cups of egregious American tea, he paid cash, returned to his room, moved a chair to the window, and watched the activity gradually unfolding around the building opposite—equipment trucks arriving, catering trucks pulling up, the crowd, much of which had been in place all night, already jockeying for position on each side of the steps. This rock concert looked like a big one. But weren't those kinds of things held at night, with all their flashing, whirling lights? Perhaps, Li posited, they held them in the daytime in this curious part of the country.

He'd moved his chair so that the light fell over his shoulder, opened his Koran, and begun to read the heavenly words. They were so magical, so inspiringly riveting, that the hands of his watch seemed propelled at twice their normal speed, and he'd been surprised, when he'd heard the knock on the door, to find it was already ten o'clock.

"Maid service . . ."

Li got up and let the woman in. Always act normally.

"I hope I ain't disturbing you none, sir." She wore gold rings on her fingers and had dyed her hair the same precious color.

"No."

"Well, you just go on doin' whatever it was you was doin', and I'll be outta here before you can say Jackie Robinson."

Li regained his chair and his sacred book. The woman, humming an optimistic gospel hymn, did the bathroom first, then came back and made the bed, which was a pillow short. She saw that the diminutive guest had propped it up lengthways and was using it as a backrest in the armchair.

"Your back painin' you, sir? I got me a bad back from all the pickin' up I do. I tell you, there are days I'd trade it in for two busted legs. Will it bother you if I vacuum, sir?"

"The carpet's clean," Li said.

"Whatever you say, sir." Wanting to give full value, the woman did a little straightening in the immaculate room, checked an empty wastebasket, then stopped as she moved by the window. She lolled her tongue against her teeth and made a disapproving sucking noise. "Just look at all that fuss down there . . ."

Li, deep in study, let the loquacious woman's chatter pass over his head.

"I swear that man's just scraps. Our pastor, the Reverend Lovejoy, he's on what you might call first-name terms with the Lord. And he asked the Lord if this man was by way of being any kin of his, and the answer was a no so loud the Reverend Lovejoy said he almost lost his hearing." She turned back from the window, saw that the guest wasn't interested—why should he? He was a Chinee gentleman and they worshiped that smiling fat man—gathered up her cleaning things and moved to the door. "You want me to hang out the Do Not Disturb, sir? . . . Sir? You want the Do Not Disturb sign?"

"Please."

"You have a good day, now."

Li gave it ten minutes, then went over, opened the door, and removed the cardboard notice. In a day already advanced such a sign could look a little suspicious, if anybody had anything to be suspicious about. Or if they were just poking around—that was why he'd removed the rifle from the Nike bag. There were light-fingered maids who'd check a guest's luggage. Not many, but some.

He'd settled back and given himself up to his favorite sura, number twelve, the longest one, about Joseph and the Twelve Tribes of Israel, and how he'd gained the favor of the pharaoh of Egypt by his interpretation of the ruler's dream. And, once again, when he checked his watch he found that time had dissolved, vanquished by the true word of God as revealed in ecstasy to the Prophet over a glorious twenty-year period.

Just an hour and a half to go now.

One floor above and two rooms to the right of where Li read an earthly reproduction of an uncreated and eternal heavenly original, Vizzini was also reading avidly.

Imbued with the love of fantastic stories that was inherent in the Ligurian character, he'd brought several comic books with him, comics he'd perused many times over, repeated readings dulling the experience not one whit. The one he was engrossed in now involved a superhero from beyond the stars who comes down to Earth and, using his extraordinary powers, becomes a benefactor to all and sundry. Vizzini ate up the familiar drawings, turning pages with a snap, anxious not to lose a second in the story's telling, a story in which the hero saves a starving town by using an old ship's boiler to scoop up tons of fish from the sea and pour them into the town's impoverished lake.

A hesitant knocking broke his concentration.

He crossed the room and put his eye to the peephole. Took the door off the chain and opened it. "You're early," he said, far from pleased with his visitor. "We got an hour and a half yet." He didn't like this dopey fatso; all he ever did was sweat and look like he was gonna pee himself.

Franco Santoro brought his trembling dilemma into the room. Vizzini relocked the door and returned to his reading material. Santoro silently watched him for a moment, then his eyes were drawn to the closet. Inside that small space, he knew, was a golf bag holding a dozen clubs and a rifle, a rifle with a barrel the color of midnight and a polished stock the same dark shade as a mahogany coffin.

He shuffled to the window. Saw the thin slit the Sicilian had cut in the wire screen. Saw the scene below: police everywhere, their yellow barriers already being tested by an undulating flood of worshipers, the building they lapped gilded like a palace by the sinking sun.

And the banners that waved like pennons on a medieval castle proclaiming a clear and definitive message.

Jesus Has Come Back.

Eight stories below, the revolving doors disgorged a woman whom several men took a second look at, not because of her evident haste, but on account of her long blond loveliness.

They watched her move quickly across the lobby to the desk—an athletically sexy walk, the hippy lilt of it produced unconsciously—and envied the man she was no doubt asking for.

A desk clerk directed Marie to the second floor—she'd called Larry Bolling's office from the 2:00 P.M. flight she'd taken from New York. The office had told her where to locate Bolling, and that Brian would be with him, a prediction that proved correct. He was sitting at a table in the hotel's security office with two other men, and got up as soon as he saw her.

"Excuse me for a minute," he said to the room, and led Marie into an exterior office. He pulled her into him. Kissed her. Held her for a long moment.

Marie clung. Kissed him back. They'd both had ample time to realize how close they'd come to being killed, and yet it wasn't a collective relief they shared but an individual one based on the fact that the other was safe.

Marie pushed away a little the better to observe him. "You don't look so hot. How do you feel?"

"Like a million dollars in sticky pennies. But you look okay. You look brand-new."

"I never got my handbag back, so I had to borrow airfare from a pal. I cleaned up at her place and borrowed a dress."

He enclosed her again, her cool, pale freshness like a healing transfusion entering into him. He forced himself back to the business at hand. "How are those two lovelies?"

"Patch is out of danger. Van Boder's in a cast up to here. They'll be charged with kidnapping and you name it once they're a little healthier."

"And Buehl?"

"No luck so far. And Gold's apparently wandering around the city somewhere. How are you doing here?"

Brian took her through his meeting with Willard and the revelations the evangelist had volunteered. Brian thought he was handing her a bombshell, but Marie wasn't as jolted as he'd expected her to be; she was far wiser in the ways of the world than he and thus less shocked by its extremities. Of his visit with Heloum he told her little, just that he'd been unable to sway the man. Marie, suspecting that the experience had been something of a cathartic one for Brian, didn't press for any more details.

Brian took her back into the main office. Introduced her to Larry Bolling and the other man, John Honeycutt, the hotel's security boss. Bolling waited till they were seated, then, for Marie's enlightenment, pushed several folded pages of computer printout toward her and began an explanation.

"This is where we're at. The rooms that are checked off are all on the front of the hotel. You've got the names of the current occupants plus info re the bookings. I had a buddy at Decatur Street run those names through the NCC, but we crapped out, which is no big surprise. It's kind of unlikely the shooter's a virgin, and even more unlikely that he'd use his real name if he's not."

Marie scanned the first page and the second. "What are these that are crossed out?"

"Overseas visitors. This guy Buehl isn't going to bring in imported talent when there's so much good domestic product around."

"I'm not going to argue with that," Marie said. "But you must've been tempted to break down the door of eight-oh-nine." She tapped the printout. "Aldo Cremici from Palermo . . ."

"It jumped out at us, too," Brian told her. "It's gotta be tough to be a male Sicilian. People automatically think you're a Mafia don."

Marie flipped through the pages; there appeared to be about forty or fifty names. "How many of these rooms can we go into?"

John Honeycutt spoke up. Short and wide and with a flattened nose, he looked like a moody bulldog. And he had a growly voice to match. "Two, and that's it."

"Hey, c'mon, Johnny," Bolling appealed. "We've gotta have more than that."

Marie assumed these two were pals—perhaps, like a lot of security people, they'd been on the force together—but she could plainly see the dissension between them now; the hotel man was most unhappy with the situation, and willing to be vocal about it.

"No way. This ain't the president of the United States out there. I can't go rousting the customers just because you think maybe perhaps there's a rifleman in the house."

"He's gotta be here. No place else for him."

"You get two rooms," Honeycutt reiterated with irritated insistence. "So choose 'em and let me get back to work."

Bolling shrugged at Marie, who checked with Brian, who checked right back at her. "How do we pick them?" he asked.

Left to make the decision, Marie consulted the list. "We go for two New Yorkers, I suppose. But that still leaves"—she quick-counted—"six other guys from New York. And two women. And how do we know the killer isn't a woman?"

"I don't think Buehl would agree with women shouldering arms. Or gays shouldering arms. So you can bet we're looking for a straight male which, I'm sure you'll agree," Brian concluded, embarrassed by his useless deduction, "is a huge advance for us."

Marie checked her wristwatch. "We have a little over an hour and a quarter." She slid the printout toward Brian. "Choose."

Brian offered the job to Bolling, but he rejected it, claiming to be a lousy guesser. Brian pushed the list back to Marie. "You do it." He had more faith in her than he had in himself. It wasn't because of the classic claim that women were the more intuitive of the sexes, it was because Marie brought a different level of creativity to a problem, his own inventiveness having been somewhat blunted on the grindstone of study. At least in his own estimation.

With a blip of fatigue dancing inside her skull Marie went over the list again. "Of the nine New Yorkers four of them are registered with their wives. There's a woman by herself, and we've decided to scrub her, and four guys by themselves."

"That doesn't tell you much," Larry Bolling offered. "I knew a shooter once used to take his girl along on jobs. It's good cover, for one thing."

Marie tilted back, blinked, and restudied the printout. "With just two to choose from, I'd say we have to go with the odds. Two of these four guys. Ramsey, Klein, Wong, Kolymsky. So, for no particular reason, let's go with the first two."

"C'mon, Johnny," Bolling said, leaning around and half punching the bulldog on the arm, "give us the other two rooms, for God's sake."

"Look, why don't you just get a man up on the roof of the Center with binoculars? Spot him that way."

"Because you'd need more than binoculars to see any detail through those semireflective windows you've got in this fleabag. Give us the two rooms, Johnny."

With his jaw locked by intransigence Honeycutt growled out his answer. "I'll give you one more and that's final. Finito."

"Okay," Marie said, certain the man wouldn't budge. "Who's it gonna be, Wong or Kolymsky? The Chinese or the Russian?" She checked with Bolling, who shifted his weight, his chair acknowledging the move with a squeaky complaint.

"The Chechen Mafia moved into New York some time back," he told her. "And the Hong Kong Triads are moving here in droves ahead of the Commie takeover. Pick 'em."

Marie reached for a pen. Poised it over the two names. Brought it down in a darting swoop. "The Chinese," she said.

"Hotel security," John Honeycutt announced, holding up his ID. "I'm sorry to trouble you, Mr. Ramsey, but this is Mr. and Mrs. Sheridan. They occupied this room before you did, and Mrs. Sheridan thinks she may have left her engagement ring in here. Would you mind if they took a quick look around?"

The man who'd come to the door of 515 looked perturbed. "The maid cleaned this morning," he said. He had a sheet of figures in his hand and a laptop set up on a table.

"It would only take a minute," Honeycutt assured him.

"Sure. Okay." The man waved them in impatiently.

"Sorry to bother you," Brian said, going by him, pretty certain that this was no hired killer. The guy had to be what he looked like: a slightly balding, slightly overweight businessman who had a meeting to go to which had nothing to do with the one across the street.

Working fast, but overlooking nothing, they checked everywhere anybody could hide a rifle: the bathroom, the closet, under the bed, behind the drapes. The room's occupant, back at his computer, wasn't interested in their search.

"No luck?" he asked when they'd finished.

"It'll turn up," Marie said. "Thanks for letting us look."

There was no answer to the next door they knocked on, 610. Honeycutt pulled out a passkey as if the movement was the source of severe physical pain. "I could get canned for this," he predicted as he let them in.

It was easier to hunt around an empty room, but it proved just as frutiless as the previous search and, at Honeycutt's repeated urging, they were back in the corridor a few minutes later.

"We'll never do it this way," Brian said. "It's like trying to win the lottery with just three tickets."

Larry Bolling, who'd remained in the corridor, looked hard at his pal. "Give them some more tickets, Johnny."

"Hey," the security man said. "You're working for these people. I'm not. I'm employed by the management, who'll hammer my head in if they find out what I'm doing." He turned to his friend's clients. "You got two strikes against you. Okay, maybe you'll hit a homer this time."

Li Xiayong looked at his wristwatch and throught he might have time for just one more of the spellbinding suras, but the knock on the door cut harshly into his projection.

It couldn't be the talkative maid again, and he certainly hadn't ordered anything. He could ignore it, but the desk would know, from his absent key, that he hadn't gone out.

He moved quickly to his bag. Pulled out the folder he kept for just such an unexpected occurrence. Scattered papers around the coffee table, business documents pertaining to the restaurant-supply business; Li had found that Americans thought that anything to do with cooking or eating was normal for a Chinese. The documents were in English, but nobody was going to ask him to read them. He picked up a pocket calculator to lend the sham some verisimilitude, and went over and opened the door. The man who said he was hotel security—and he certainly looked the part—told him that the handsome couple behind him had had some misfortune. A missing ring. Li invited them in and regained his chair. Bent over the papers with his calculator and looked industrious.

From the corner of his eye he watched the couple search high and low, the woman checking the bathroom, the man checking the closet shelves. They were thorough. The woman even looked under the bedspread and the pillow, saying that the ring might have come off in bed. Li wondered what kind of acrobatic sex these two had indulged in to cause the possibility of such a thing. The man was indeed fortunate, Li thought. He would have liked to have enjoyed the same plunging acrobatics with the yellow-headed woman whose long legs would have clutched him like twin pythons. Getting aroused again, he knew. It always happened close to a kill.

When everyone had gone, Li put the papers back into the folder and thought about the visit. A lost engagement ring; something a woman might remove to wash her hands. The bathroom would be a logical place to look. But how could a ring be misplaced in the top shelf of the clothes closet where the extra blanket was kept?

Or could they have been looking for something else?

It was unlikely he was suspected, but it was smart to err on the side of safety.

A slight change of plans might be advisable.

Nobody said anything until the elevator had reached the second floor and they got out. The exercise had been such an outstanding failure that both Brian and Marie felt beaten down by it. Larry Bolling looked morose, but Honeycutt looked relieved. "Okay, gotta go," he said, signaling an end to an overambitious and, for him, potentially embarrassing undertaking. "Talk to you later, Larry." He walked away, his chunky body swaying from side to side like a sailor home from the sea.

Brian didn't want to look at his watch; he knew they had very little time left. "We've got to cover those five other rooms," he said.

Marie had already turned toward the elevator. "Come on, we'll fake it." She stopped and looked at Larry Bolling. "Think you could play Honeycutt's part?"

The big man held back. "I wouldn't even try. It won't work without hotel ID."

"Sure, it will," Marie said.

She was wrong.

The man they tried to bluff wouldn't buy their story and called security.

John Honeycutt came rushing up, a bubbling anger propelling his stout frame. "Goddamn it, I turn my back for a minute . . . What the hell do you think you're doing? Get the hell outta this hotel. You, too, Larry."

Brian broke out of character. Came back at Honeycutt with his face tight and his volume up. "I'll tell you what we're doing, we're trying to save a man from getting murdered. We're trying to stop somebody from being killed in front of ten thousand people. And you're worrying about upsetting guests?"

"You got nothing but a hunch," Honeycutt blazed back at him. "And I'm not gonna turn the place upside down for a hunch. Now, hit the boulevard. Out!"

Marie spoke softly into the charged moment, her reasoned calm dissipating some of the heat. She used the man's first name, tried for some accommodation. "You're right, Johnny. I admit it, it was a silly thing to do."

"It was a friggin' crazy thing to do."

"But listen, let us at least talk to the maids. Maybe one of them saw something in a room. A long box or a package or something. I promise we'll stay away from the guests."

"You bet your buns you'll stay away from the guests." The security boss resettled his squat shoulders, which seemed to have a palliative effect on his temper. He shot his cuffs and offered a concession even though he didn't quite know why he was doing it. "Okay, the maids. But if you say word one to a paying customer, you'll go up for trespassing. You got it?" He glared at Brian to enforce the threat, then shook his head at Bolling. "You I thought I could trust."

He left all three of them checking their watches. "Five-thirty," Brian said. He looked spent and defeated. "I don't know what else to do."

Larry Bolling moved his feet ineffectually. "Look, I'm going out front. See what I can spot from out there. I can't help you any more in here, not that I have. Frankly, I don't think the shot was on the table. We needed to get into fifty or sixty rooms, not just three." He held up crossed fingers. "All we can do is hope your information's wrong. And if it's right, then we have to hope the shooter misses."

"They never miss," Marie said flatly. "Not the pros."

Bolling didn't want to agree with that, so he said nothing as he left them.

They hurried down the corridor, heading for the end of it, where they could see a maid's buggy. "Something keeps pinging in my head," Marie said. "Something those goons said when we were in their car."

"When they were trying to pump us about Heloum?"

"Maybe. They told us about Buehl in Vietnam, too. I just wish I could get it."

So did Brian; he remembered how she'd come up with the Fuji blimp by lassoing an elusive thought. But that had taken several hours, and she had less than half of one now. Suddenly he couldn't be indoors anymore. The corridor ended in a blank wall, and, walking swiftly toward it as he was, he felt he'd run into it if he kept moving, an apt analogy of their situation.

He stopped Marie. "I'm going outside. You check with the maids. If you come up with anything, grab Honeycutt and drag him wherever you have to go."

"Where are you going? What are you going to do?" Alarm danced in her eyes, and she moved closer and half reached for him as if she were stopping someone from jumping from a cliff.

"I'm not helping here, Marie. My mind's like a piece of wet cardboard. I'm going down."

"Brian!" She clutched his arm as he turned. "Stay away from him. Don't get close."

"With those crowds? I couldn't, even if I wanted to."

She stood very still watching him go. She knew him now; his little transparencies, tiny white falsehoods he'd employ to baby people's feelings. Her blood seemed to suspend in its course, the pump that moved it rising into her throat. She knew beyond a doubt that he'd be in the vicinity of the bullet. All she could do was what they'd been trying to do: find the man who was due to fire that bullet and stop him.

The maid had nothing for her.

Nothing she'd seen had been out of the ordinary: no long packages, no long boxes in the closets. No huge suitcases anywhere.

The woman on the next floor, six, had a similar bleak tale to tell. However, one floor up Marie got a break. The seventh-floor maid was with the maid from the floor above, who'd come down for a chat. They made a Laurel-and-Hardy pair these two: one large, one small.

"Hi. My name's Marie. I'm helping out Mr. Honeycutt. He's looking for a guest who brought a long package with him. Or a really long sports bag, that kind of thing. That's really all he gave me to go on. Have you seen anything like that?"

"Just how long is long, honey?" the seventh-floor maid asked. She was the large one: a smiling black woman with gold rings on most of her fingers and a matching rinse glowing in her hair.

"A bag that could take, oh, say a golf club."

"The Italian man in eight-oh-nine has some golf clubs," the small maid offered.

"I'm really talking about something the size of a golf club but a lot fatter."

"Uh-uh. I ain't seen nothing like that on eight."

"How about you?" Marie asked.

A treasure flashed when the large woman moved her hands. "Seven-oh-one's got a suitcase that'd break a camel's back."

Marie checked her printout; 701 was registered to a Mr. and Mrs. Wilton from Snowmass, Colorado. "Anything else?"

"A big long package? I had one last week. Man brought his own towel-drying rack with him. Now, you may think that's a little strange, darlin', but folks'll bring anything in. They like the familiar, you know."

"I had me a couple," her friend began, "brought in their own sheets."

"I got me one now," the other woman said, with a wave of

gold, "brought his own little rug with him. Chinese gentleman in seven-fifteen."

Marie could see there was nothing for her here. She thanked the women and went up to nine, but there was no maid in sight. Nor was there on ten. She went back down to the lobby. It was practically deserted, everybody out on the sidewalk to catch the excitement of the crowds. She saw the chunky form of John Honeycutt at the registration desk, talking to a clerk. Above the desk a clock showed five minutes to six.

Marie felt mired in a bog of exhausted helplessness, the computer printout in her hand of no more use than pages from a storybook. The feeling of defeat, and the tremulous fear for Brian's safety, jangled through her as a rising swell of noise rolled in from the street.

The motorcade bringing Camille Heloum to the prayer meeting had been sighted.

While Marie had been on her way down to the lobby Li had pulled the folded rifle out of the floral slip of the pillow he'd used as a backrest, unfolded the stock, locked it off, and shoved a clip into the weapon. He'd then made good on his alternate plan, and now he was sitting looking down at the scene with one leg crossed over the other to give himself a good solid platform.

He eased off the safety but kept the rifle out of sight of anybody on the roof of the Center. When the approaching limo stopped, the rock star would be exposed for several seconds, and that would be plenty of time to sight, suck in a breath, then squeeze the trigger twice.

Li marveled at the crowd, the way it compressed and surged and resonated with a tingling shiver.

He wondered idly if the management would give a refund to those lucky enough to have purchased a ticket to the show.

One floor above, a golf bag lay on a bed, the decapitation of warm summer grass unknown to its matte black irons.

Across the carpet Vizzini was also sitting in the shooter's position and, like his Oriental counterpart, keeping his rifle below the level of the window.

Father Franco Santoro was standing to the gunman's right, his breath coming in uneven chunks, a desert at the back of his throat, his legs feeling constructed of cotton waste. He stared through a drop of saline moisture at the immense gathering, thousands wedged together, and every head turned in the same direction, endeavoring to catch a glimpse of the long black limousine and its motorcycle escort.

He looked at the Sicilian sitting the way the old tailors used to sit in their little cubbyholes near the Piazza Stabile; the man was encased in patient confidence.

Waiting.

Santoro looked back at the excited throng. Raised his eyes to the steps and above the steps to the banners softly billowing in a gentle breeze.

Red lettering on white backgrounds.

Red on white.

His arteries felt blocked.

His brain stumbled.

CHAPTER
27

Riding in the back of the limousine, the tinted windows rolled up and the air ducts pushing a quiet chill against the suede seats, the corpulent Don Bagley on his right, tall, thin Howard Willard on his left, and a bodyguard sitting next to the driver, he watched the crowds dropping to their knees as the stretched vehicle glided by the barricades.

He no longer thought such veneration extraordinary or even undeserved. Memory of a recent life in a Canadian seminary had fused with imagined knowledge of a Judean odyssey much further in the past. The recalled events of yesteryear had shifted, geographically, from those within an hour's drive of Lake Ontario to those within a day's walk of the Sea of Galilee. His memory of pain was not of months of postsurgical recovery in a village not far from New York City, but of iron spikes smashed through his extremities on a skull-shaped hill not far from Jerusalem. The parables learned from years of Bible study had become extempore illustrations of his thinking, and his classroom instruction of student priests in Elton was really a ghost of his outdoor teaching of the Jews in Bethany. The personage of Father Camille Heloum had become like somebody met but dimly recalled.

It had been an easy identity to leave behind; he'd always felt a particular affinity with Christ, had always felt that he would have reacted to Jesus' trials and tribulations exactly as Jesus had, with soft, wise words and a doleful understanding of the inevitability of his arboreous fate. So anything he knew that indemnified his new and correct identity he remembered, and anything he knew that detracted from it he forgot.

And there were quite a few things that deserved forgetfulness, like the many indignities he'd had to suffer: being lowered from an airship, injecting a drug into a horse, pretending to fix a washing machine that had been repaired the night before, curing a lame man who was perfectly healthy, reviving a young girl from a simulated death . . . these and many other impostures and prevarications he'd expunged from his mental scrapbook.

"Lord . . ." As the limo approached the Civic Center, Howard Willard stirred his long body. "We're here, Lord," he said.

There was no reply.

Don Bagley turned his head, his broad face softened by servility. "Lord . . ." he inquired, gently. He gazed for a moment at the indecipherable expression in those doelike eyes, and experienced a frisson of intense excitement—starting next week he'd be personally introducing that calm, reconciled visage on a nationwide tour, something they could do now that they'd established a base support in Atlanta. And then Europe. Latin America. Asia. One look at that ravished brow, that long, thin figure extruded by the cross, a few minutes' exposure to his words, even if they couldn't understand the language they were couched in, and there'd be no more Buddhists, no more Hindus or Islamics. No more Catholics or Mormons or Presbyterians. No more squabbling, no more jihads. The world would be one religion. The Christian religion.

"Lord," Don Bagley said, "we've arrived."

Heloum, who'd been remembering his triumphant entry into Jerusalem, hearing again the crunch of the palm fronds beneath the donkey's hooves, swam slowly back to the present.

The limousine was slowing at the curb.

At the barrier Larry Bolling had told a sergeant he knew that his companion was plainsclothes from New York, and that was all it had taken for Brian to establish himself on the street near the steps.

He had his back to them now, shading his eyes and trying to defeat the images reflecting from the hotel windows. It was impossible to see, impossible to concentrate. The crowd had set up an ecstatic chanting, their girdled numbers like a flooding river about to breach a levee.

When the noise soared yet again Brian dragged his gaze away. Saw, getting close now, the police motorcyclists leading the black car.

Seized by a fit of desperation, he wondered for a wild moment if he couldn't rush up to the limo driver and scream, "Gun! Gun! Get outta here! Go!" But who would he be? Just an unshaven, shabbily dressed nut having his moment in the sun.

With light spearing down from the hotel windows, penetrating his flesh like narcotic needles, he watched the limo pull into the curb.

Paralysis had invaded her body, a refusal of brain or muscle to respond to the simplest stimulation.

Marie stood near the baggage desk, a fixture like the rug on the granite floor, a person on hold, a receiver waiting to react to an imminent event she was powerless to influence.

She watched the sparse activity in the lobby: a baggage man tearing off checks, the concierge on the phone, a bellman pinching his nose as if he were fighting off a headache.

The thinking process began; synapses linking up and connecting at the mind's mysterious speed.

A headache was what the Latino had suffered when the Oldsmobile had rolled over on the golf course. And when he'd told Patch that he was going home to lie down, Patch had said that the colonel wouldn't like that, and jokingly suggested that his boss might have the ayatollah nut put a bullet in his brain.

The ayatollah nut—clearly a hit man that Buehl had used before.

And might just be using again.

Marie fumbled for the guest list. Flicked pages, ripping them in her haste to find an Iranian name among the New Yorkers. But there wasn't one. There weren't any ethnic New Yorkers except Kolymsky in 512 and Wong in 715.

Her feet got it before her head did.

She started running, the words of the gold-fingered maid spinning in her ear: "I got me one now. Brought his own little rug with him. Chinese gentleman in seven-fifteen." Marie had seen that rug on the back of a chair when they'd searched his room. She recognized it now as a prayer rug. Patch hadn't been referring to an Iranian, but to a Muslim, and there were a million Chinese Muslims.

Honeycutt turned at the running feet. Marie didn't wait till she'd reached him before shouting her news. "Johnny, I got him! Let's go!"

Honeycutt's surprise slowed him for a moment. "Whoa. Wait up. What?"

Marie tugged at the security man's arm. Gabbled at him. "It's the Chinese in seven-fifteen. *Come on!*"

He let himself be pulled across the floor. It wasn't what he wanted to do but, even on the edge of panic, he found that the blonde had a way about her.

They jumped into an elevator. Marie hit 7 and mashed the door close button.

"If you're wrong, kid," Honeycutt growled, "you're in deep crap."

A black-suited bodyguard opened the rear door of the limo.

Heloum got out into the coppery glow of a fine Georgian evening. A gasp like a roar exploded from the crowd. People moaned. Some burst into tears. Many called out in stretched and plaintive voices: "Jesus! Over here, Jesus!" . . . "Lord! Look on me, Lord!" . . . "Heal me, Jesus, heal me!"

They swayed, swooned, fell to their knees, sobbed as Jesus Christ in a shiny white robe, trailed by his entourage, and surrounded by his personal security, moved slowly over the red carpet of the Civic Center and began to climb the steps.

"Not a bad job," Vizzini said, admiration enforcing his opinion. "He looks just like he does in the painting my mother has in her front room."

He had the rifle into his shoulder, the muzzle just breaking the slit in the screen, and was viewing Heloum through the scope. He could see him in excellent close-up detail. "What is that, makeup and a wig, or what?" He was talking out loud to himself, or might as well have been, he knew. He didn't expect an answer from the beach ball who was breathing like a drowning man and had probably lost his voice anyway. Some people couldn't stand to see things killed: deer, bulls, whales, people—bleeding hearts, the lot of 'em.

It seemed to Franco Santoro that every sense save that of sight had ruptured. He heard nothing in his ears except a wavering buzz. Felt nothing on his skin. He had a taste in his mouth, but it was sickening, a flavor of metal, as if he'd been sucking on the bullets the Sicilian had just loaded. It seemed that the senses he'd lost had been poured into the one he'd retained, his sight, and that he was seeing the white-robed man mounting the steps as close and as clearly as the Sicilian was through his telescopic scope.

"C'mon, a couple more," Vizzini muttered as the figure paused in its limping ascension. The little black dot that appeared to be floating at the end of the scope pinned itself momentarily to the man's back, but Vizzini wanted a chest shot, so he just rested his stumpy finger on the trigger, certain the fraud would turn once he made the top.

Which he did.

Santoro watched him turn. The figure seemed to rush at him, the lifted eyes seeming to plumb the depths of the priest's mortal soul.

Santoro had seen that solemn gaze before: in a sunny garden when Jesus had transfigured in a blinding blaze of heavenly light.

Only one man had ever done that before.

Jesus.

And he'd come back to do it again.

"C'mon, asshole," Vizzini murmured, his right eye jammed to the sight, his curled finger ready to receive a message. "Get a fucking move on."

Santoro was instantly soaked, enveloped, swamped by a screaming red rage. It imploded within him with the velocity of bursting dynamite, and he moved with the speed and agility of the athlete he'd never become.

He spun, jerked a club from the golf bag, rushed across the

room, and threw his two hundred pounds into a thudding, skull-smashing downward swing.

"Christ killer! he yelled, bringing the club down again and again and again.

"Christ killer! Christ killer! Christ killer!"

Ten-power magnification put the target at the end of the barrel.

Li could make out the weave of the robe when the man at last gained the top of the steps, turned and raised his hands halfway as if surrendering to an enemy. No, Li corrected himself, it wasn't surrender; it was acceptance. He seemed to have opened his arms to receive something, although two copper-sheathed pieces of lead would come as a large surprise, Li thought as he quartered the fine crosshairs on the center of the bearded man's chest.

As his finger coaxed the trigger he heard the commotion in the corridor: somebody urgently running down it and colliding with something. But that didn't alter anything for him; it was exactly why he'd taken precautions a few minutes back. He'd knocked on his neighbor's door, 717, and when there'd been no answer he'd gone back into his room and loided the connecting door between the two rooms.

And moved into 717.

And cut a slit in the window screen through which the muzzle of the rifle now slightly protruded.

Yes. It was always better to take the longer, safer way around the mountain.

Six hundred feet away, in an angled line from that muzzle, Camille Heloum finished his climb up the hill of Golgotha outside the walls of the city near the Damascus Gate.

His shoulders felt roughened by the cross, his legs aching from the weight, his back still stinging from the scourge of the lash. He turned and opened his arms to embrace his fate. He was full of sadness but had no fear of suffering.

Something told him it would be a quicker death this time.

Plates and glasses went flying when Honeycutt crashed into the young waiter carrying a tray out of 702.

The stout man righted himself, then, caught up in Marie's desperate mission, charged after her down the corridor.

The twin bangs of the rifle stopped them as if they'd been the targets. Honeycutt whipped a revolver from a hip holster and sprinted. Yelled at Marie to stay back, rammed his passkey into the lock of 715, and barged into an empty room.

Marie was right behind him.

Honeycutt strode into the bathroom and was back in a second, his face squinched in perplexity.

Until he spotted the connecting door.

He ran to it. Jerked it open. Poured into the room, his gun sweeping it.

When he saw the rifle on the carpet near the window, he swore mightily and leaped for the phone.

For Brian the soft summer evening had turned hard and brittle.

The air had an odor of copper and brass, a flimsy piece of degraded oxygen ready to shatter at the first hint of metallic intrusion.

Impossibly he felt it coming. Or sensed that it would soon be on its way: a bullet sent spinning down the rifling of a barrel.

He whirled and dashed for the steps.

Made them.

Shouted as loud as he could. *"Camille! Get down!"*

A uniformed cop stepped out and blocked the intruder with such force that Brian sprawled. He rolled and looked up and saw Heloum sway backward in a double movement as if wasps had lunged at him.

In the seared air, clear to the point of hallucination, Brian saw two dark spots appear in the middle of Heloum's chest like badges pinned there by an invisible man. Heloum collapsed in intervals, his legs going first, and the rest of his body folding and following them down.

Brian got a snapshot of Don Bagley shocked to a standstill, and that evil bastard Howard Willard acting horrified. As for the worshipers, their collective behavior progressed from dumbfounded surprise to mind-blanked stasis to a howling compound of Shakespearean fury and woe.

He scrambled up. Ran toward Heloum, but the cop who'd floored him barred his way. "Let me by. I'm a priest," Brian said into his face, ready to hit the guy if he had to. The cop might have been Catholic, or he might just have seen something different in this man, but he made no move to stop him a second time.

Lying in a pool of dark arterial blood, his white gown a two-toned garment now, Heloum's eyes were glazed, a nibbling death slowly closing him down. But his dulled gaze focused when Brian reached him, recognition lighting a weak flame. He gave a one-word answer to Brian's unvocalized question: "Yes."

Brian wet his finger and touched it to the priest's forehead. "Through this holy annointing, and His most loving mercy, may the Lord assist you through the grace of the Holy Spirit so that, when you have been freed of your sins, He may save you and in His goodness, raise you up."

Heloum's shattered body appeared to sink into the hard gray concrete as if it were a soft bed of sand. He gathered saliva, ignoring the swallowed blood, faint memory keeping one hemisphere functioning. He wanted to say what he'd said before, but had that been as Matthew and Mark claimed: "Eloi, Eloi lama sabachthani?" My God, my God, why have you forsaken me? Or was Luke correct? "Father, into your hands I commit my spirit."

No.

He remembered now. It was as faithful John had reported. And how apt, considering.

Heloum drew a breath and used his last exhalation to waft three quiet words from his crimson mouth. "It is finished," he said.

Brian stared at the conclusion of a life, stared at the residue left by an ebbed tide of vitality. He was reaching out, slowly and painfully, to close the man's eyes when he was rudely pushed away.

Three men, big and dark-suited, shouted at each other as they grabbed the body. "Get him into first aid! The doc's in there!" They hefted the corpse in a single heave and bundled it over the red carpet toward the doors of the Civic Center.

"*No! Stop 'em!*" Brian yelled. "*Stop those guys!*"

He got up and ran, but the crowd, rippling in shock and disbelief at the shooting, spilled through the barriers and blocked him off. He caught a glimpse of the dark suits vanishing, and the doors slamming shut behind them, and then there was only the wailing, sobbing throng falling to their knees and beginning to keen and cry and moan for their dead Jesus.

CHAPTER
28

Li got back to New York in a roundabout way.

After he'd fled the room and dashed down the stairs to the sixth floor, he'd got lucky with a service elevator and had slipped out through the kitchen. He'd walked several blocks to a parking lot where he'd left a car which, using a stolen credit card, he'd rented the day before. He'd driven northwest and dropped off the vehicle in Chattanooga, where he'd bought a ticket on a feeder airline that took him as far as Philadelphia, and from there he'd caught a bus to the Port Authority.

It had taken him five hours, but it had been a sensible precaution, he thought, riding in a cab on a gentrified section of Varick Street. As had the sandpaper he'd used on his fingertips: the tiny particles would obscure the prints on the rifle and any found in those two rooms. The old tricks were the best.

The job had gone well, and now that it was over, there were some physical needs to attend to.

His blood thumped when he thought of Jenny Choy, who had a supple golden body and a slit like an overripe pear. It was true she was a Christian, which made him a little uncomfortable, but he had to admit that having happiness with a woman of another faith added to the thrill.

He dismissed the cab on Doyer Street and went up the stairs of a building that housed an old tea parlor.

On the second floor he stopped outside the door with the lion-head knocker, rapped for entrance, was ignored, rapped again, and was about to leave when the door slowly opened. Jenny Choy regarded him with tragic disinterest, her face creased by grief, tears irrigating her cheeks. At first Li thought a client had abused her but, upon examination in the dim light of the hallway, her sorrowful face appeared free of cuts or bruises.

"What's wrong?" Li asked.

She shook her head, her short black hair, worn in an old-fashioned pageboy cut, swishing in sympathy as she turned, leaving the door open. Li followed her into an apartment that would have been condemned in any other part of the city: layered with age, the plaster peeling, the dirt-colored floorboards without the benefit of even linoleum, the duct-taped windows giving onto the spidery form of an ancient and unworkable fire escape. A wormy dressing table held photographs of numerous relatives, red-and-gold good luck charms pinned on the wall above them like exploding firecrackers. A tiny bathroom lurked behind a paneled door, and next to that was a kind of internal veranda holding a cooking ring connected to a butane bottle.

But perhaps to leave no doubt in a visitor's mind as to the primary function of this apartment, the double bed in the corner was a thing of glory. Sumptuously decked out, it looked like a parade float with its magnificent sandalwood frame flying a hundred red ribbons. Its flowing yellow silk coverlet was embroidered with a Chu Mei lattice design in treble-stitched gold thread while, mounted above the crimson pillows, a snorting purple-and-green papier-mâché dragon's head guarded occupants from harm.

Li knew that bed very well, and the sensual delights he'd many times obtained on it, but that had been when Jenny Choy had been a teasing sexual tumbler, not this swollen-faced, mascara-smudged mess she was now.

"What's wrong?" he asked again.

"They killed him," the woman sniffled, dabbing lace to a ghost of a nose.

"Killed who?"

"Jesus." She looked woefully at a new addition to the room since Li's last visit, a portable TV set. An anchorman was saying something about a killing. Li caught the word Atlanta. Then the picture changed to a still, and he recognized the long-haired man, the rock star. What had Jenny Choy said?

"Who is it?" he asked, his face vacant with uncertainty and dread.

She burst into a fresh bout of tears. "Jesus. They killed him."

Li was a block of stone. "What do you mean, Jesus?"

"Our Lord. He came back. He returned to earth just as he said he would," she wailed. "He healed people. He worked miracles. Somebody killed him."

"Jesus of Nazareth . . . " Li said slowly. "Born in Bethlehem?"

When the woman nodded tragically, a bright icicle of horror plunged deep into Li's soul. His breath jammed in his throat, his heart tripping. He stared at the screen. They were showing scenes shot previously: thousands and thousands of people on their knees, their eyes shining with faith. A man throwing away his crutches. Another getting up out of a wheelchair. Another scene: people strewing the long-haired man with flowers.

Li saw it all through a shaky haze, heard it through a strange muffled breathing in his ears. A staggering and scandalous realization engulfed his flagging senses—he'd killed Jesus! . . . Jesus who the Sacred Book says was a true prophet of Allah the One God . . . the Jesus whose mother had learned of his impending birth from the angel Gabriel, the same angel who gave the Koran to Muhummad.

Li grabbed the dressing table for support, afraid his knees might unlock. He looked away from the television set, away from the scenes of massed veneration, tuned out the newsreader as an understanding of what was required entered him like an arrow of certainty.

He left Jenny Choy moaning in front of the set, went down the stairs, and walked west past the Bowery to where a multitude of stores had sprung up to service the residential high-rises.

He made a purchase in one of these establishments, then stepped into a Third Avenue bus when no cabs appeared.

He rode past the flophouses and the bars, and the groups of men waiting aimlessly on the sidewalk, seeing none of this degradation. The flames of hatred burned inside him; he was launched on a retributive endeavor whose necessity gripped him in a hug of iron.

He was quite clear now on what had happened and why: when Jesus had been sent by Allah the first time he'd been killed by Roman soldiers, and now, when Allah had sent him a second time, he'd been killed by an American soldier.

Because of his message of peace.

Soldiers hated peace, hated anybody who advocated it. The man who'd hired him had killed a messenger of God, an act for which he'd be plunged into the deepest recess of the fiery pit to twist and turn for all eternity. But in the meantime . . . in the meantime the soldier was free to do as he liked, and if—Li almost swooned as the horrific thought shook his heart—if the Mahdi, the Qa'im, the Twelfth Imam came out of hiding—and some said he was due to appear any day now—what was to stop this soldier from killing him the same as he'd killed Jesus? If a man killed one prophet, would he hesitate to kill another?

Li left the bus at Twenty-eighth Street and, carrying his purchase in a plastic shopping bag, walked east to Second.

He went through the street doors of a familiar apartment house and buzzed the intercom.

Buehl switched off the pictures of the chaotic scenes in Atlanta, went into the kitchen, and made himself a cup of coffee. A real cup of coffee. He never begrudged the time it took to fresh-grind a good blend and percolate it properly; instant anything was not part of his makeup because it had never been part of his training.

He performed the chore carefully and methodically pleased at how things had gone down south. Prepare properly, and the rest was mere routine.

He poured the coffee, added the tip of a teaspoon of sugar, drank the beverage, then emptied the aromatic grounds into an almost full garbage bag.

He was beginning to tie off the bag when the intercom buzzed. He looked at the kitchen clock. Eleven-thirty.

Gold in his nightly wanderings again.

Buehl went into the living room and pressed the door button, returned to the kitchen, tied off the bag, picked it up, left the apartment, and walked down the corridor toward the trash chute.

Halfway there he revised his earlier opinion of the plan performing perfectly. That priest and the journalist had found a flaw. If they'd worked on Heloum's accent as well as his body, he would have remained undetected.

As he drew level with the elevators, and the tarnished wall mirrors framing them in a futile attempt at elegance, it occurred to Buehl that Patch should have phoned in again by now.

He put down the pail and used the mirror to straighten his tie, which was an eighth of an inch off dead center. Assured that his appearance would pass parade-ground inspection, he picked up the pail and continued down the slightly odoriferous corridor as the doors of the first elevator opened.

Li stepped out, surprised to see the stiff-backed soldier marching away to his right. How fortunate, he thought; a few seconds earlier and Buehl would have seen him.

Li watched the man vanish at the end of the corridor. Padded silently after him and peeked around the corner in time to see a door closing.

When Buehl entered the garbage room, the odor turned his head as if he'd been slapped. He saw the source, something that offended not only the membranes of his nasal septums but his sense of civic responsibility as well: some slob had left a broken fish tank for the super to clear away without first getting rid of several dead goldfish. They lay inside the busted glass on a pathetic little beach of sand.

Buehl hinged open the chute and tossed his garbage bag in, the noxious fish smell overriding the scent of olive and patchouli oil which had entered the tiny room behind him.

He turned and, like a graceless ballet dancer, rose up clumsily on the balls of his feet as the curved melon knife Li had bought slashed upward into his gut.

In that first surprised instant Buehl felt the slam of the hilt more than he did a slim, razor-sharp intrusion and, getting just a brief look at his attacker, it flashed into his mind that he was being mugged, that a diminutive Puerto Rican or Haitian had punched him in the stomach. But the next moment, when he focused on Li, and when the Chinese ripped the knife up and diagonally across Buehl's firm diaphragm, he recognized his assailant, and the fact that he'd been deeply stabbed.

Body shock blanked nerves, and he fell like an old man, devoid of coordination, cutting his hand badly on the broken fish tank as he collapsed against it.

Even with his senses leaking away, he was still capable of being surprised, which he was when the Chinese reached down with a knife like a short scimitar and sliced off his necktie. He watched the thin little Oriental use it as a cloth, use it to wipe the knife handle—a precaution Li took because, by now, his fingertips would have lost their protective grains of sand—drop the knife into a plastic shopping bag, and drop the bag down the chute. Watched him use the piece of tie to open the door with as he left.

With death assuming command of him, and his mind beginning to float in strange directions, Colonel Ralph Buehl, former U.S. Army and Citadel man, realized with bitter unhappiness that he'd been wrong about something all his life: the mode and geography of his demise. He'd always thought he'd die the warrior's death and simply fade away someplace honorable and historic, like Walter Reed Army Hospital. Instead, he was dying next to some dead fish in the garbage room of a Second Avenue apartment house.

And without an article of dress without which he'd claimed he'd never be seen dead.

He'd been wrong about that, too.

CHAPTER
29

"Thank you, Pammy," Monsignor Harold Chifley said as his housekeeper brought in the tea things, delivered a dazzling smile, then left to answer a distant phone. Her boss picked up a sandwich cut into an oblong shape no bigger than a credit card. "As you can see," he said to his visitor, "I've straightened her out on the size of the collations."

"Glad to hear it," Brian said. "It's the little things in life that count."

Harold Chifley brushed at an errant crumb that had settled on the stock he wore beneath his Roman collar, its little red badge of rank glowing in the sunlight slicing in through the louvered windows. From the depths of floral upholstery he regarded Brian for a long smiling moment, then said: "You did okay, buddy."

"Thanks, but I'm afraid it was a case of too little too late. Nothing I did affected anything."

Chifley had another of the minuscule oblongs halfway to his mouth. He interrupted the action to look at Brian in a semblance of surprise. "How can you say that? If you hadn't got the better of those two heavies, we'd never have known anything about any of it. You would've been too dead to tell us."

Brian moved his teacup in a gesture that rejected the praise. He looked sadly down at the untasted infusion. "I wanted to stop him from being killed, Harry, and I didn't."

"Because you couldn't. It was never in the cards. But, even so, you did a hell of a job in the time you had."

"You mean, Marie did. I was just sitting there in the bleachers. If that motorcade had been just sixty seconds late, Honeycutt would've grabbed that guy."

"If Archduke Ferdinand's motorcade had been sixty seconds late—"

"World War One might never have happened," Brian finished for his host. "I know. Outrageous fortune and the fickle hand of fate and all that, but they were so close, Harry."

"Look. Think of it this way. For a vacationing priest and a freelance journalist, you did pretty damn well."

The sunlight brought the fine afternoon into the room, tiny projectiles of light hurling themselves at the copper fire screen. Brian watched their reckless pyrotechnics, sipped his Earl Grey, and considered what his friend had just told him. He was right, of course; Harry Chifley had a handle on reality, was able to hold up a situation, shade his eyes and see past the bright luminous exterior to the filament glow at its heart. He and Marie had just been plain lucky to get as far as they had, and even more lucky to come out of it with their skins intact. To suppose they could have done anything to influence the result of something they joined so late in the piece was a flawed supposition.

"Who do you think killed him?" Chifley asked. "Buehl."

"Somebody who was plugged into the thing. Maybe Gold knows. Or Willard. Or the two goons and their buddy. One of them will plea-bargain, you can bet on that, so nobody's going to sneak by."

When Chifley removed his glasses and began to polish them, Brian was certain it was just a bit of business his friend was going through before getting to a subject that disturbed him. Brian knew very well what it was; it was the real reason why he'd come to Chicago.

"So," the churchman said, deciding that his spectacles would now afford him unclouded vision, "I have three questions, one small, one medium, one large. Actually, the small one's more of a guess than a question. I'm guessing your relationship with Marie has gone beyond the professional. Am I correct?"

"I was going to tell you, Harry. I wasn't going to try to hide it."

"I know that."

Brian returned his teacup to its saucer. Placed the china on a side table. "Now that I've answered your small question, I think I can guess at your medium-sized one. You want to know how long it's going to last."

"Right."

The look Brian gave his host had an edge of rebellion. "I honestly don't know. But if you're looking for regret, Harry, I can only give you a piece of it. I don't regret Marie. I do regret that it involved breaking a solemn promise. Maybe you're not much of a person if you can't keep your word. But then I was only half a person all the time I kept it."

"The thing is," Chifley began, leaning forward to make his query that much more acute, "can you now keep your promise and be a whole person?"

"That's the large question, isn't it?"

"That's the big one."

Brian's reaction was a short, expressive lift of his hands. He said, with a shy ardor in his tone, "Monsignor, I've battled with that one in the early hours of evening and the small hours of the morning, and I've come to the conclusion that it's not as complicated as I thought. I think a person has to be true to their obligations. True to the job they take on, true to the path they choose. I think that's very important. But there's one thing that's maybe more important, and that is you can't fake it and know you're faking it, and go on faking it. Because if you're not true to yourself, it's impossible to be true to anything."

"Are you in love with Marie?"

"Very much so. But I'll tell you a funny thing, that didn't influence my decision. I could go on being a priest and still keep Marie, discreetly and without scandal, and nobody would ever know except you and my confessor. But it doesn't come down to a choice between a woman and the Church. It comes down to a choice between me and the Church."

Chifley didn't reply immediately, choosing to let a little gap underscore the importance of what he was about to say. His gray eyes, steadily level and slightly magnified behind his circular lenses, rested heavily on Brian. "You know what I was hoping? This may sound a little corny, but I had hoped that this little sleuthing number I put you through . . ." He stopped to reshape his words. "Well, I'd hoped that in searching for the fake Jesus, you might have got a little closer to the real one."

"You're right, that's pretty corny," Brian agreed, smiling. Then, more seriously, he said, "I was always close to the real one. He's my hero. I think he was an extraordinary person, and the world never saw his like again." Into the silence that that brought, Brian went on. "You remember what one of Dickens's characters said about Christmas, Harry? 'I will honor Christmas in my heart and try to keep it all the year.' Well, I honor Jesus in my heart. And I try to keep him there all the year. And I also try, now and then, at least on my better days, to act something like the way he thought people should act. I venerate him as a man and a teacher. But I can no longer worship him at an altar, or pretend to offer a piece of him."

Harold Chifley gently thumped the arm of his chair. Let out a resigned sigh. "So it's good-bye to a good priest . . ."

Brian watched the copper fire screen seize hold of an arrow of sunlight and joyfully incinerate its captive. Winter or summer, fireplaces seemed to lead merry lives. "No, it's good-bye to a poor one."

The clock on the mantel made three musical bongs. Brian got out of his chair. "I'd better get going. Thanks for the sandwiches, Harry. Hard to find but hard to beat."

Harry Chifley got up like a convalescent. Then, accepting what he couldn't change, took Brian's hand in a warm grip. "I'll be in New York next month. Another conference."

"Great. There's an exhibition at the Morgan Library. The 1913 German dig at Shechem."

"It's a date," Chifley promised.

Brian left the house and walked around the corner to a little park. He joined Marie, who was waiting there on a bench.

"How did it go?" she asked.

"Good. I always like seeing Harry. He's a terrific guy."

With a fine hesitancy thinning her voice, Marie said, "What did you talk about?"

"Buehl and Heloum, et cetera. And some Church matters. And the 1913 dig at Shechem. Archaeology's his passion. Shall we stroll?"

They moved out of the park, walking together but not touching. "I booked a table at Provence for dinner," Brian told her. "The Chicago foodies really rate it."

"Great," Marie said, her volume low.

"But, um, would you mind if we passed it up?"

"You want to go someplace else?"

"Yeah."

Marie looked at him.

"The way I see it," Brian explained, "we can't do better than your quiche, anyway. Would you be awfully disappointed if we just went home?"

"A little," Marie said. She took his arm. "But I'll get over it."

• A NOTE ON THE TYPE •

The typeface used in this book is a version of Sabon, originally designed in the 1960s by Jan Tschichold (1902–1974) at
the behest of a consortium of manufacturers of metal type. As
one who began as an outspoken design revolutionary—calling
for the elimination of serifs, scorning revivals of historic
typefaces—Tschichold seemed an odd choice, but he met the
challenge brilliantly: The typeface was to be based on the
fonts of the sixteenth-century French typefounder Claude
Garamond but five percent narrower; it had to be identical for
three different processes, working around the quirks of each,
such as linotype's inability to "kern" (allow one character
into the space of another, the way the top of a lowercase f
overhangs other letters). Aside from Sabon, named for a
sixteenth-century French punch cutter to avoid problems of
attribution to Garamond, Tschichold is best remembered as
the designer of the Penguin paperbacks of the late 1940s.